R0200712487

12/2019

THE WARNING

DIE · WITH · HONOR

EDWARD LAROCHE
CREATOR, WRITER, ARTIST

D1402418

BRAD SIMPSON
COLORS

JAYMES REED
LETTERS

DONALD HODGES
EDITOR

IMAGE COMICS, INC. • Robert Kirkman   e: President • Marc Silvestri: Chief Executive Officer •
Jim Valentino: Vice President • Eric Ste   f Boison: Director of Publishing Planning & Book Trade
Sales • Chris Ross: Director of Digital S   rketing • Drew Gill: Art Director • Heather Doornink:
Production Director • Nicole Lapalme: C

PALM BEACH COUNTY
LIBRARY SYSTEM
3650 Summit Boulevard
West Palm Beach, FL 33406-4198

THE WARNING, VOL. 1. First printing. April   , Suite 780, Portland, OR 97210. Copyright © 2019 Ed
Laroche. All rights reserved. Contains ma   Varning," its logos, and the likenesses of all characters
herein are trademarks of Ed Laroche, un   harks of Image Comics, Inc. No part of this publication
may be reproduced or transmitted, in any form or by any means (except for short excerpts for journalistic or review purposes), without the express written permission of Ed
Laroche, or Image Comics, Inc. All names, characters, events, and locales in this publication are entirely fictional. Any resemblance to actual persons (living or dead), events, or
places, without satirical intent, is coincidental. Printed in the USA. For information regarding the CPSIA on this printed material call: 203-595-3636. For international rights, contact:
foreignlicensing@imagecomics.com. ISBN: 978-1-5343-1142-8.

image

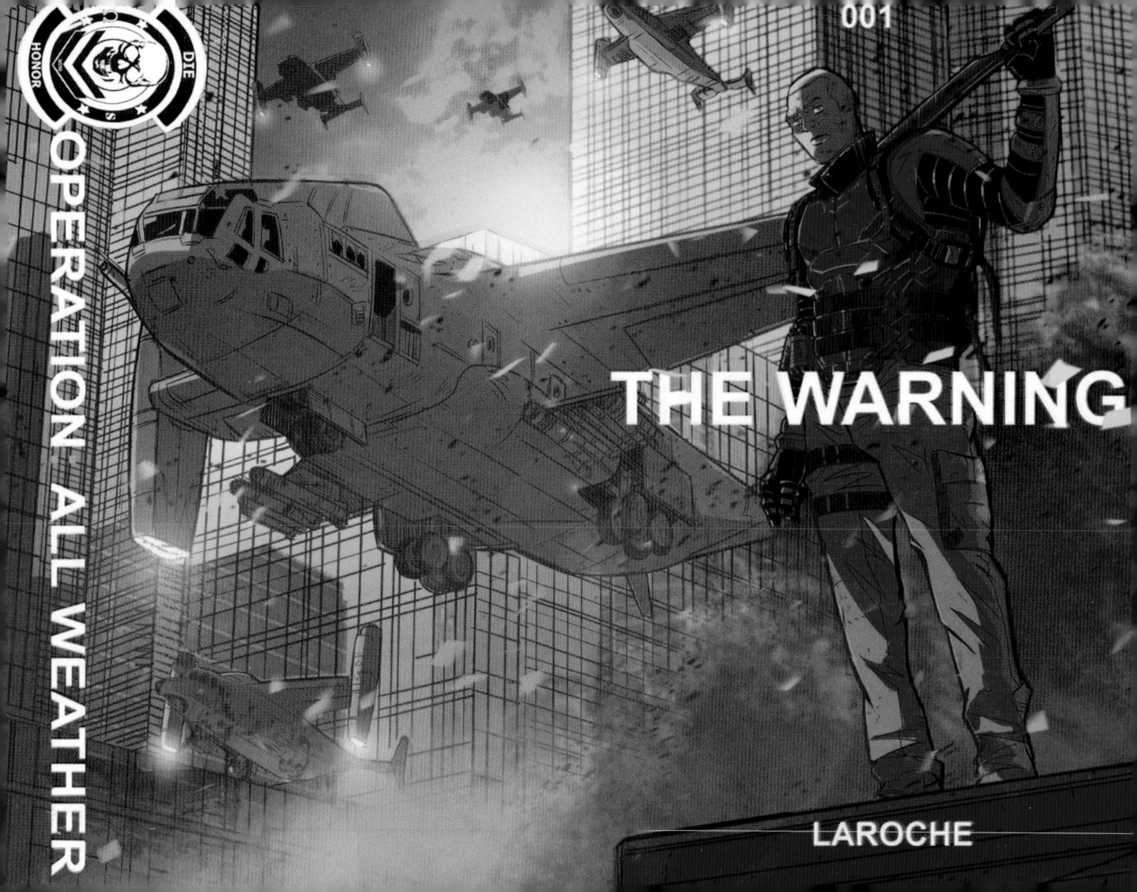
001
OPERATION ALL WEATHER
THE WARNING
LAROCHE

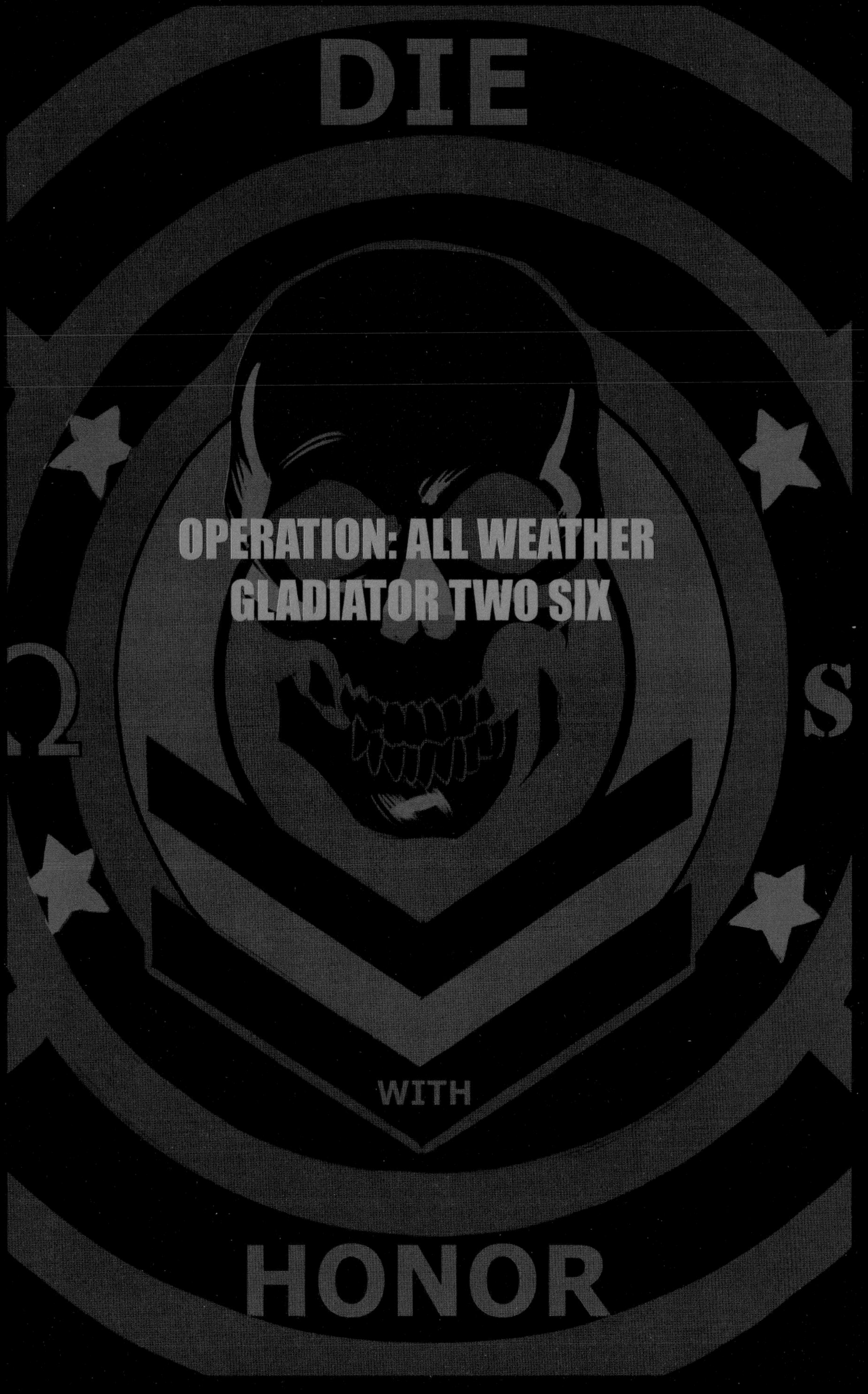
DIE
Ω
S
WITH
HONOR

OPERATION: ALL WEATHER
GLADIATOR TWO SIX

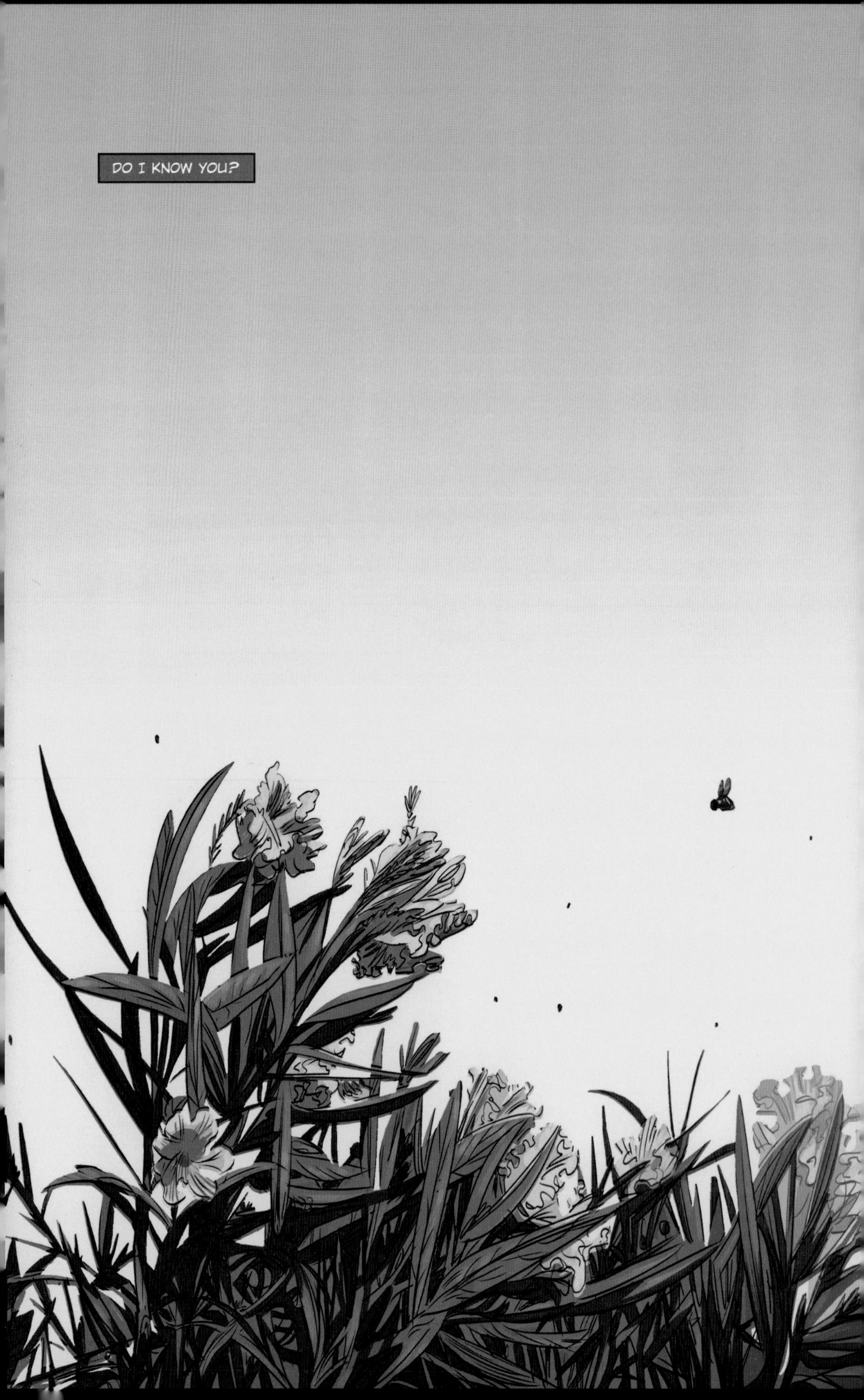

DO I KNOW YOU?

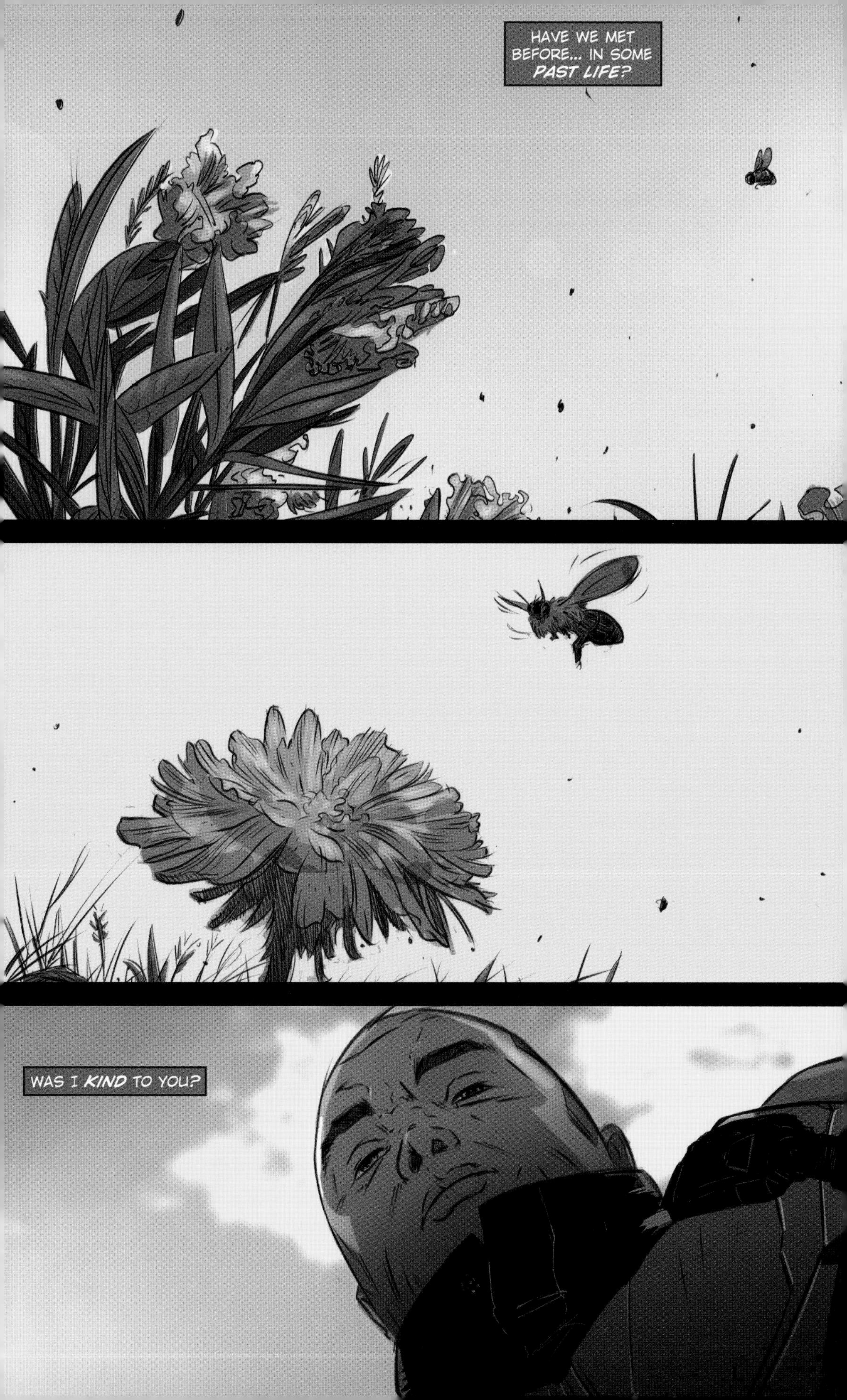
HAVE WE MET BEFORE... IN SOME *PAST LIFE?*
WAS I *KIND* TO YOU?

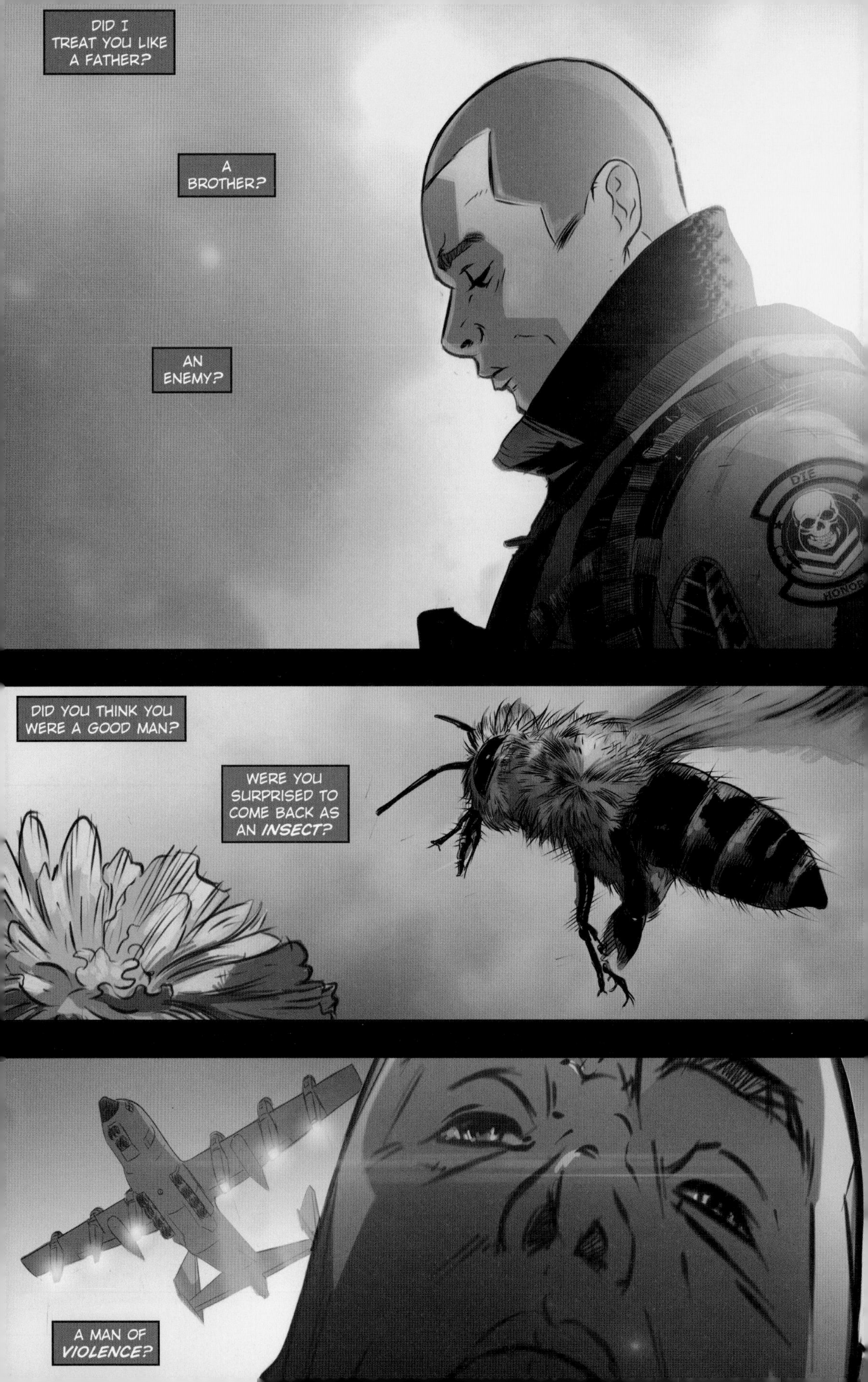
DID I TREAT YOU LIKE A FATHER?
A BROTHER?
AN ENEMY?
DID YOU THINK YOU WERE A GOOD MAN?
WERE YOU SURPRISED TO COME BACK AS AN *INSECT?*
A MAN OF *VIOLENCE?*

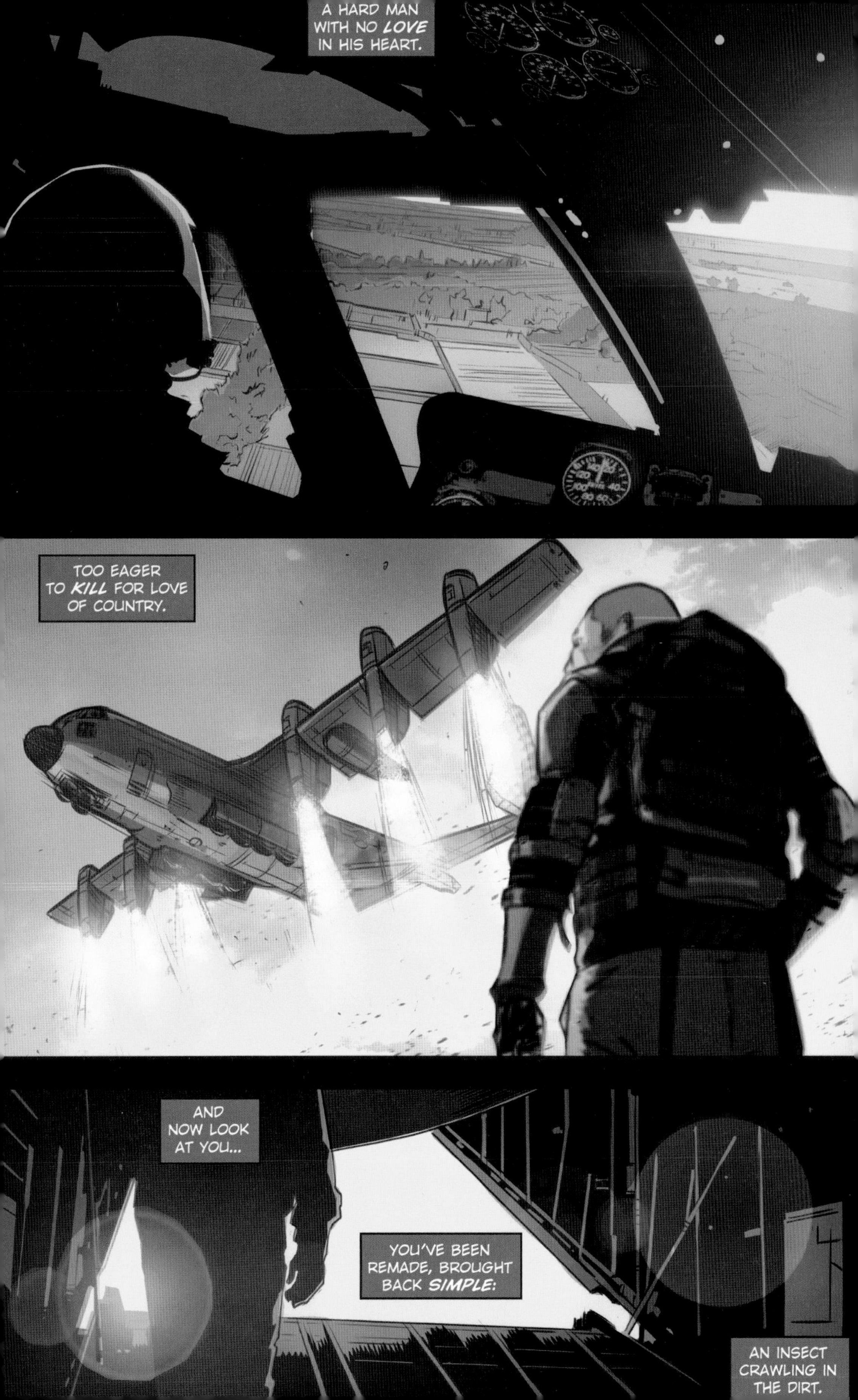
A HARD MAN WITH NO LOVE IN HIS HEART.
TOO EAGER TO KILL FOR LOVE OF COUNTRY.
AND NOW LOOK AT YOU...
YOU'VE BEEN REMADE, BROUGHT BACK SIMPLE:
AN INSECT CRAWLING IN THE DIRT.

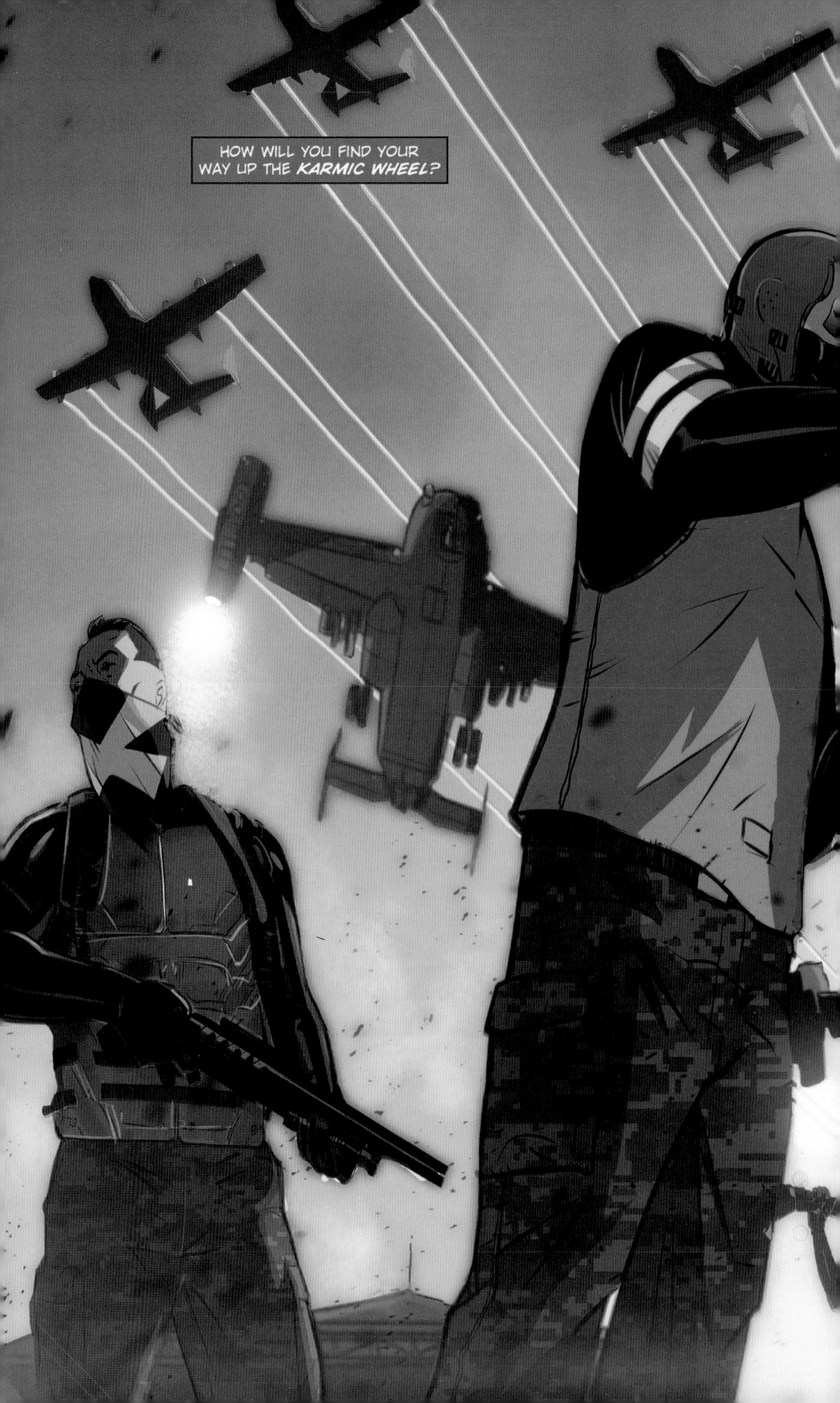
HOW WILL YOU FIND YOUR WAY UP THE *KARMIC WHEEL?*

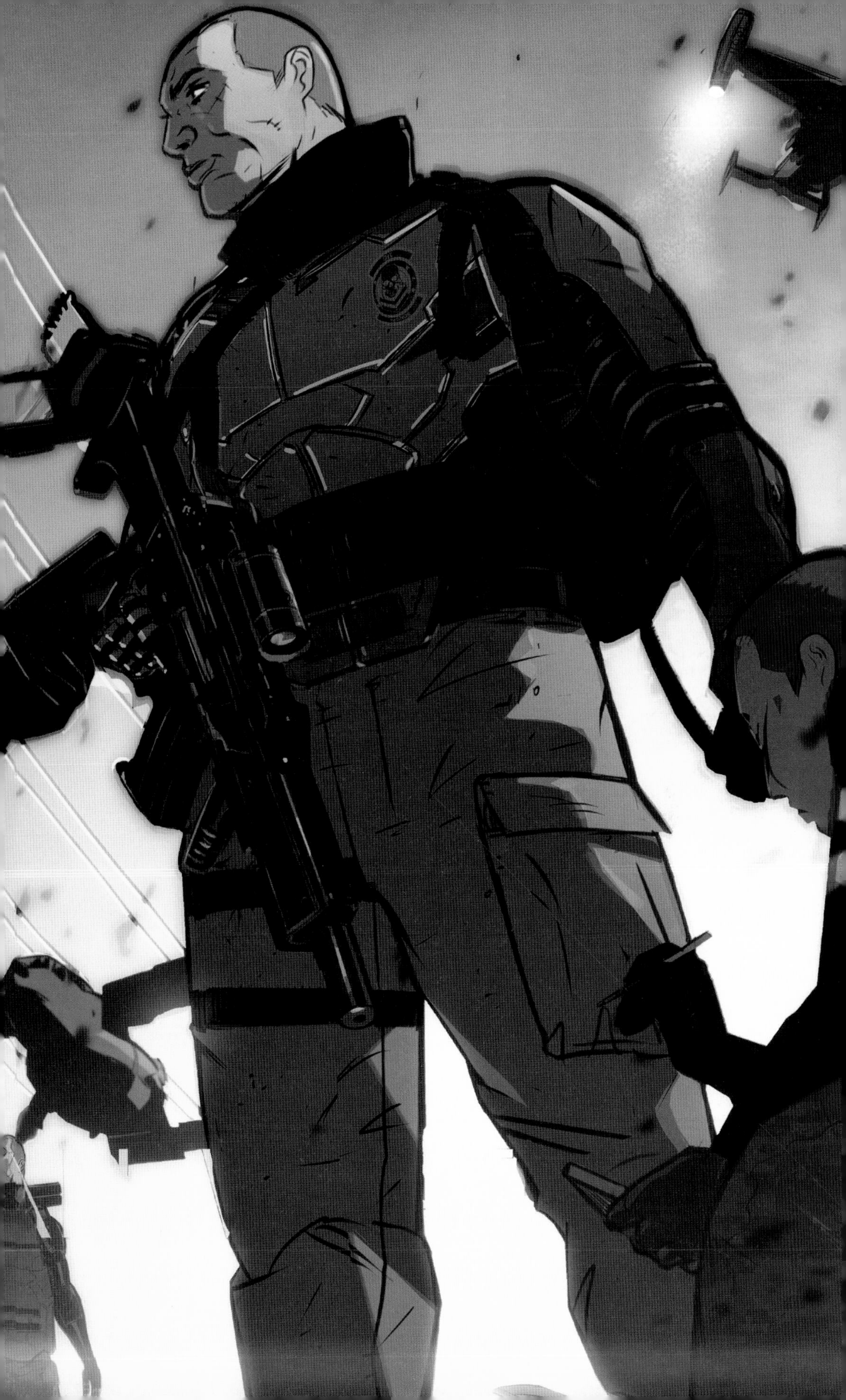

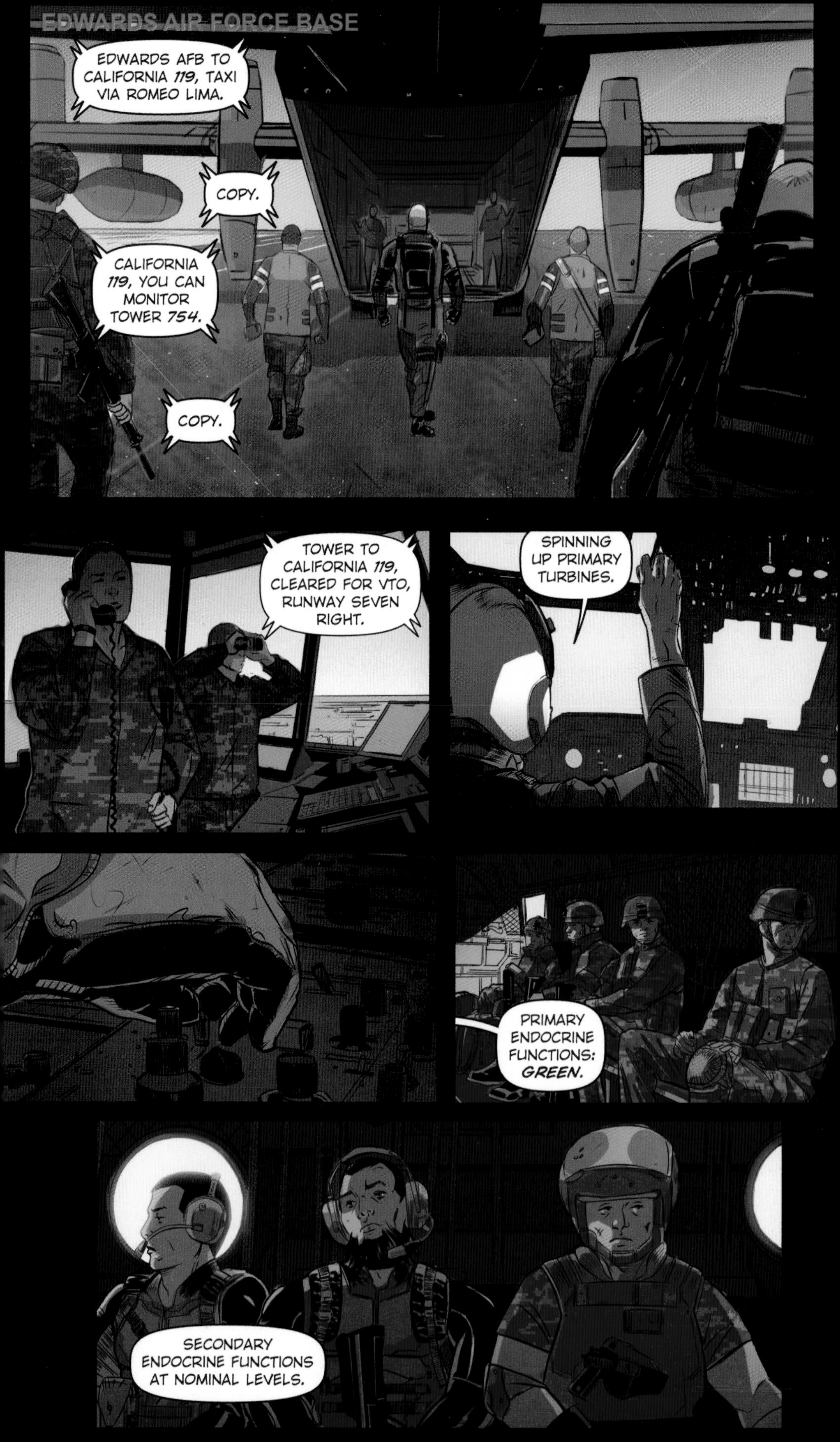
EDWARDS AIR FORCE BASE
EDWARDS AFB TO CALIFORNIA 119, TAXI VIA ROMEO LIMA.
COPY.
CALIFORNIA 119, YOU CAN MONITOR TOWER 754.
COPY.
TOWER TO CALIFORNIA 119, CLEARED FOR VTO, RUNWAY SEVEN RIGHT.
SPINNING UP PRIMARY TURBINES.
PRIMARY ENDOCRINE FUNCTIONS: GREEN.
SECONDARY ENDOCRINE FUNCTIONS AT NOMINAL LEVELS.

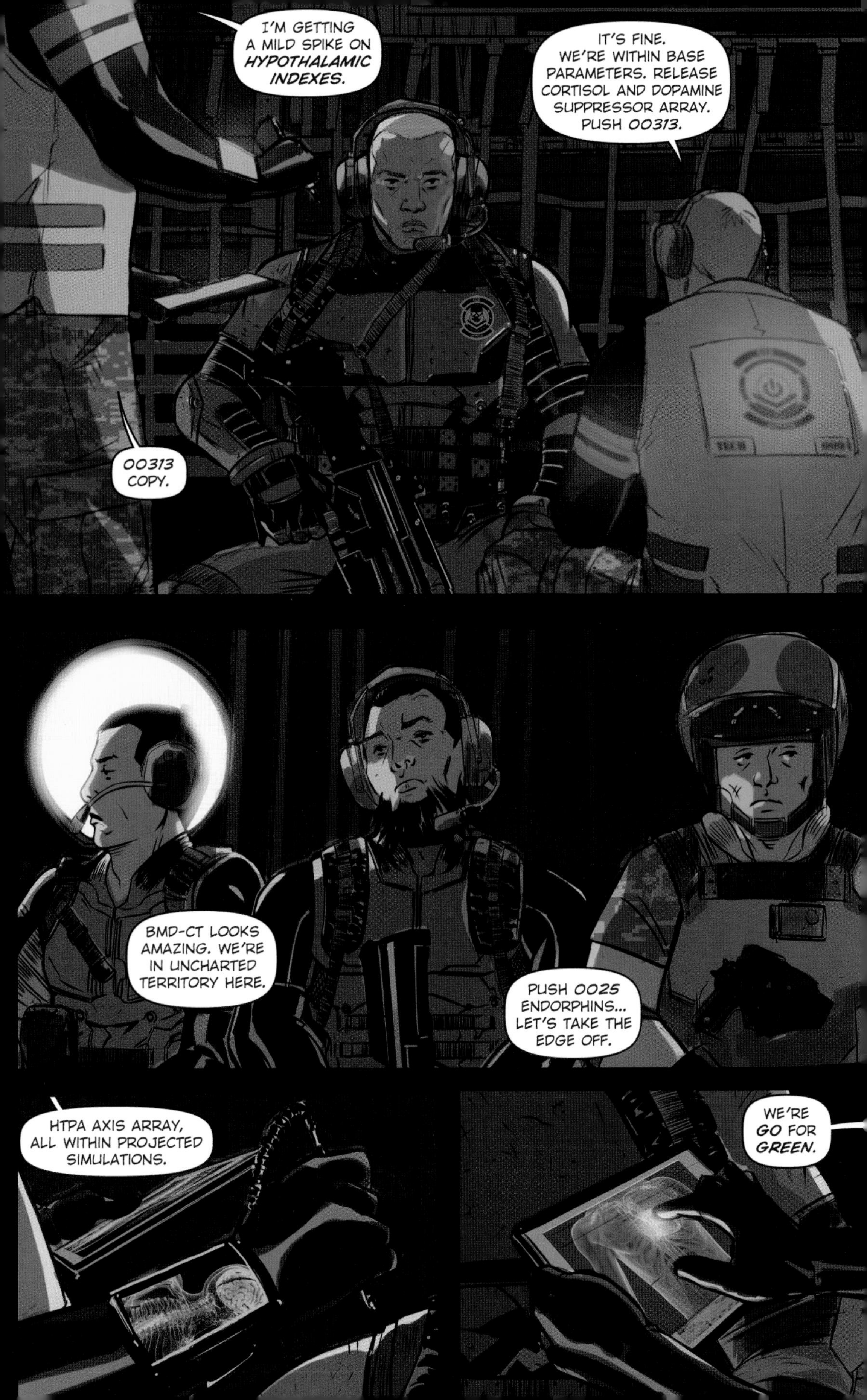
I'M GETTING A MILD SPIKE ON HYPOTHALAMIC INDEXES.
IT'S FINE. WE'RE WITHIN BASE PARAMETERS. RELEASE CORTISOL AND DOPAMINE SUPPRESSOR ARRAY. PUSH 00313.
00313 COPY.
BMD-CT LOOKS AMAZING. WE'RE IN UNCHARTED TERRITORY HERE.
PUSH 0025 ENDORPHINS... LET'S TAKE THE EDGE OFF.
HTPA AXIS ARRAY, ALL WITHIN PROJECTED SIMULATIONS.
WE'RE GO FOR GREEN.

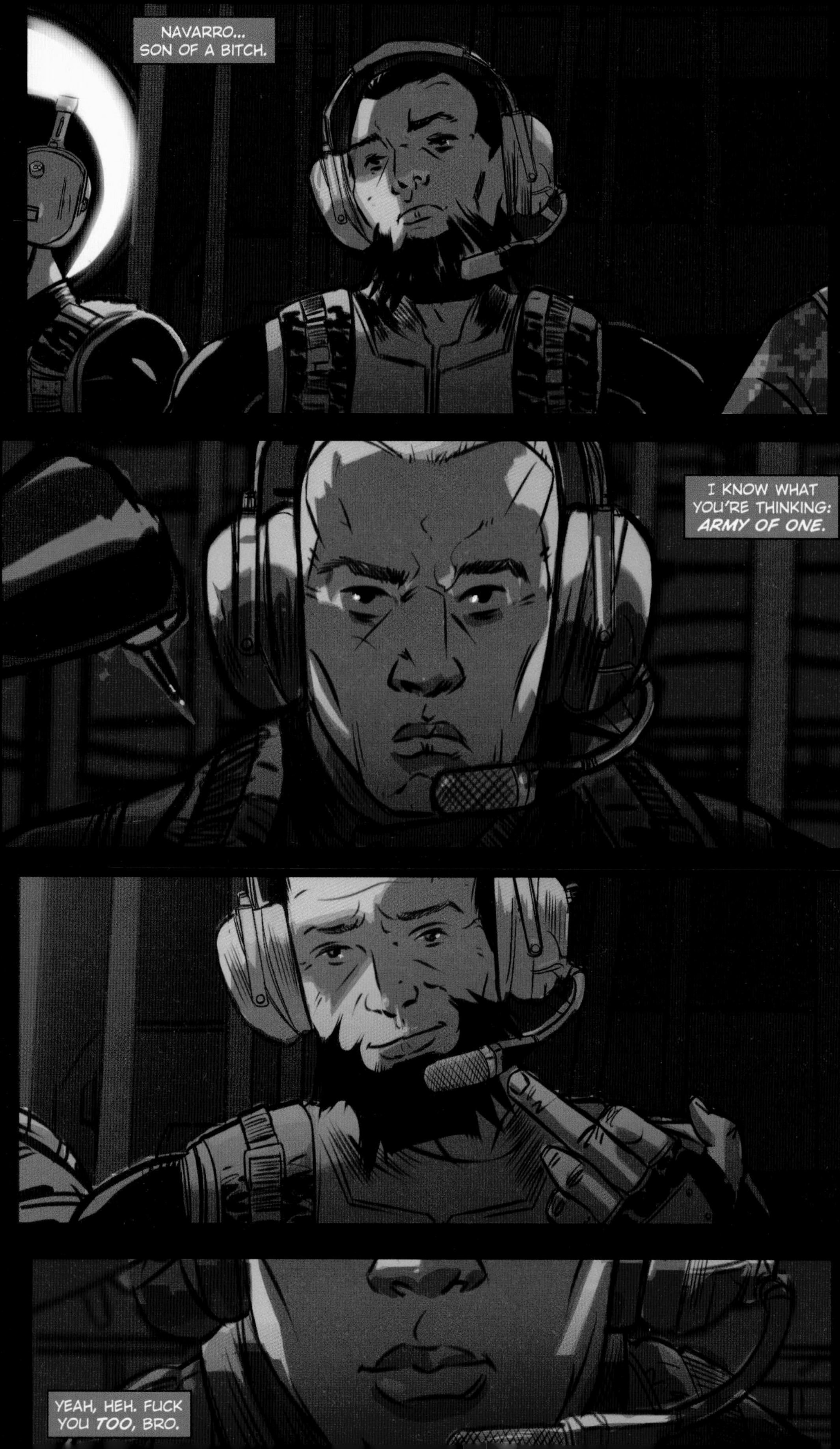
NAVARRO... SON OF A BITCH.
I KNOW WHAT YOU'RE THINKING: *ARMY OF ONE*.
YEAH, HEH. FUCK YOU *TOO*, BRO.

ROGER THAT. 430 17 RIGHT.

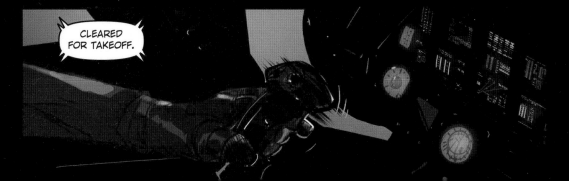

CLEARED FOR TAKEOFF.

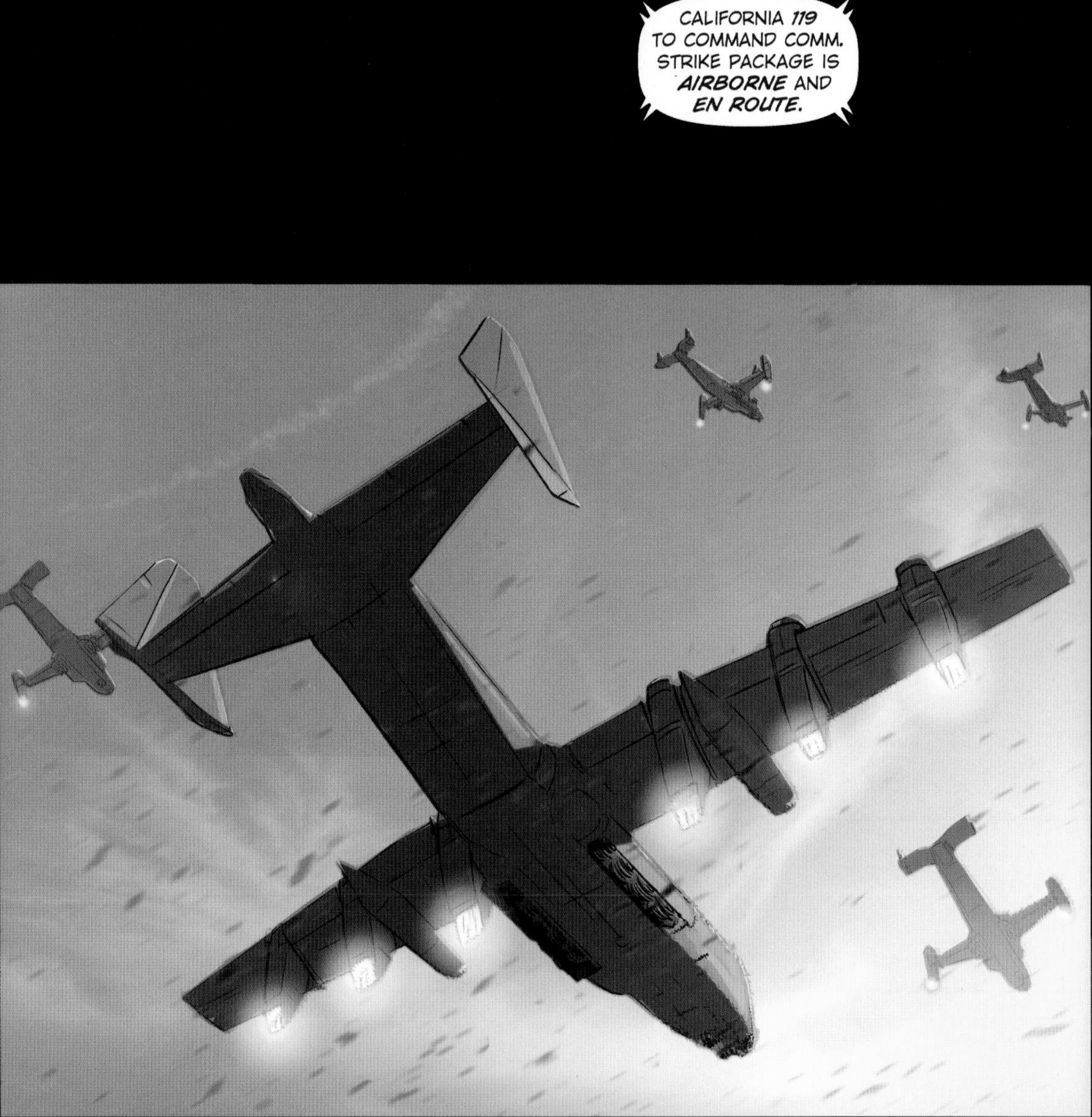
CALIFORNIA 119 TO COMMAND COMM. STRIKE PACKAGE IS AIRBORNE AND EN ROUTE.

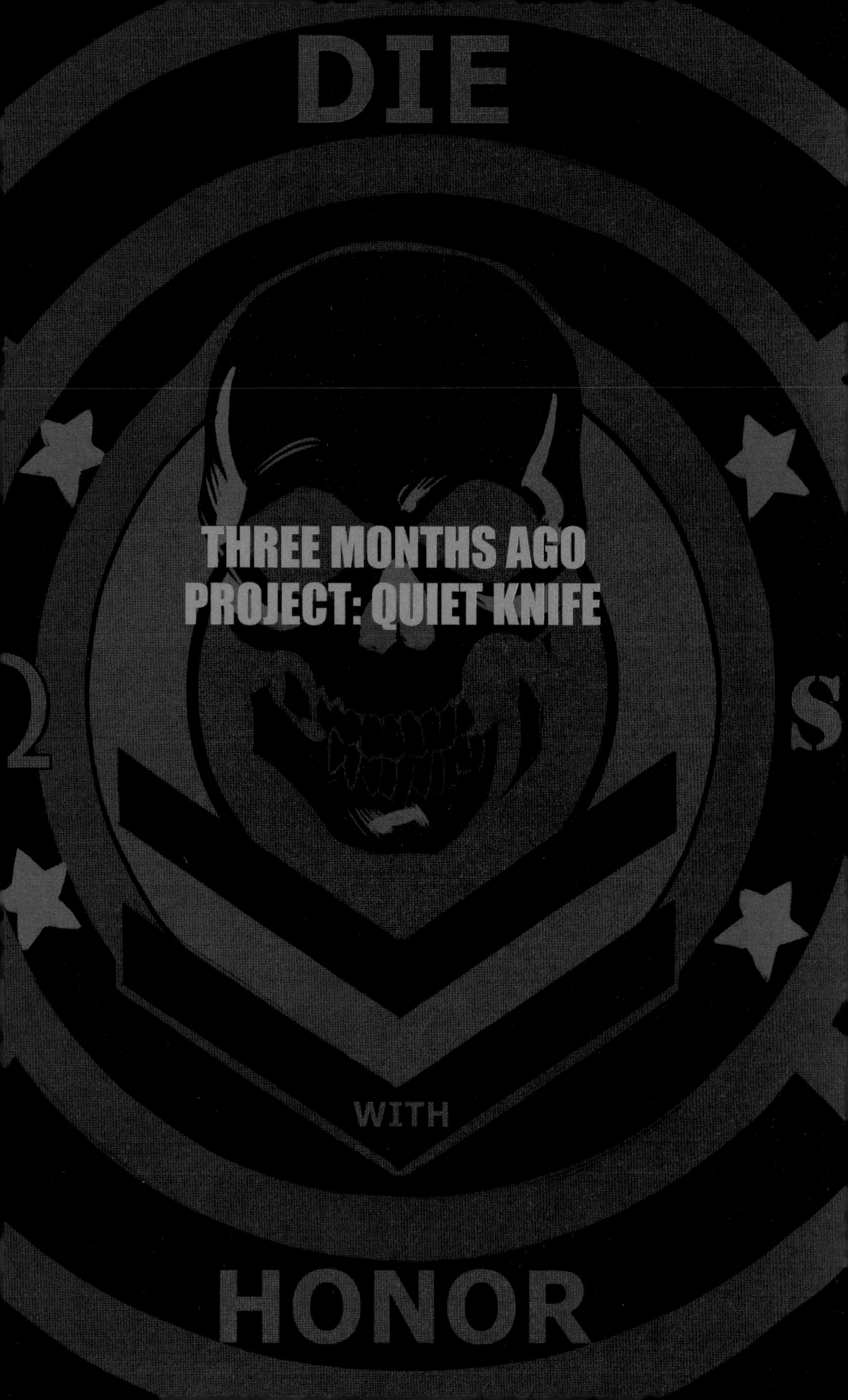
DIE
THREE MONTHS AGO
PROJECT: QUIET KNIFE
WITH
HONOR

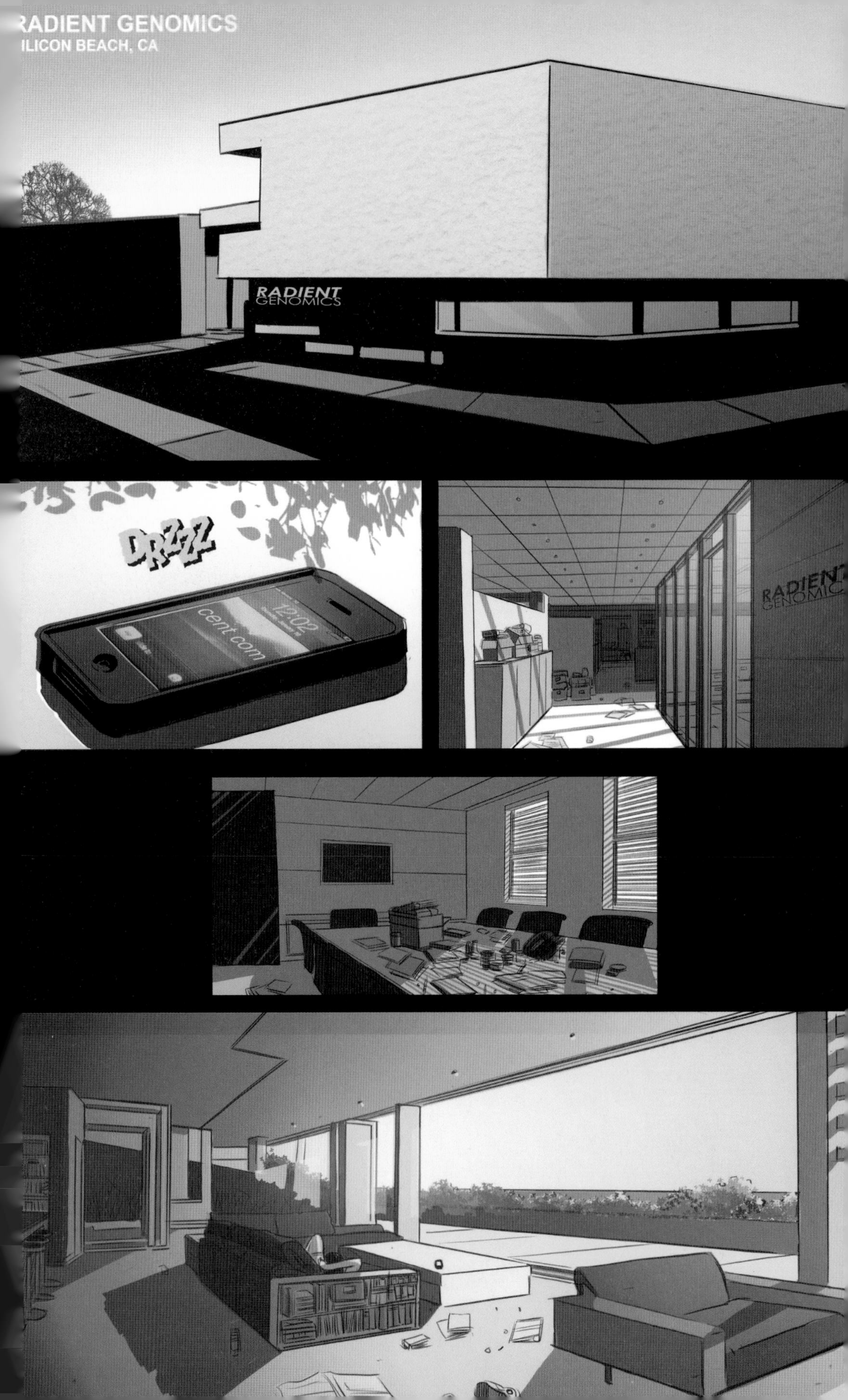
RADIENT GENOMICS
ILICON BEACH, CA
RADIENT GENOMICS
DRZZZ
12:02
cent.com
RADIENT GENOMICS

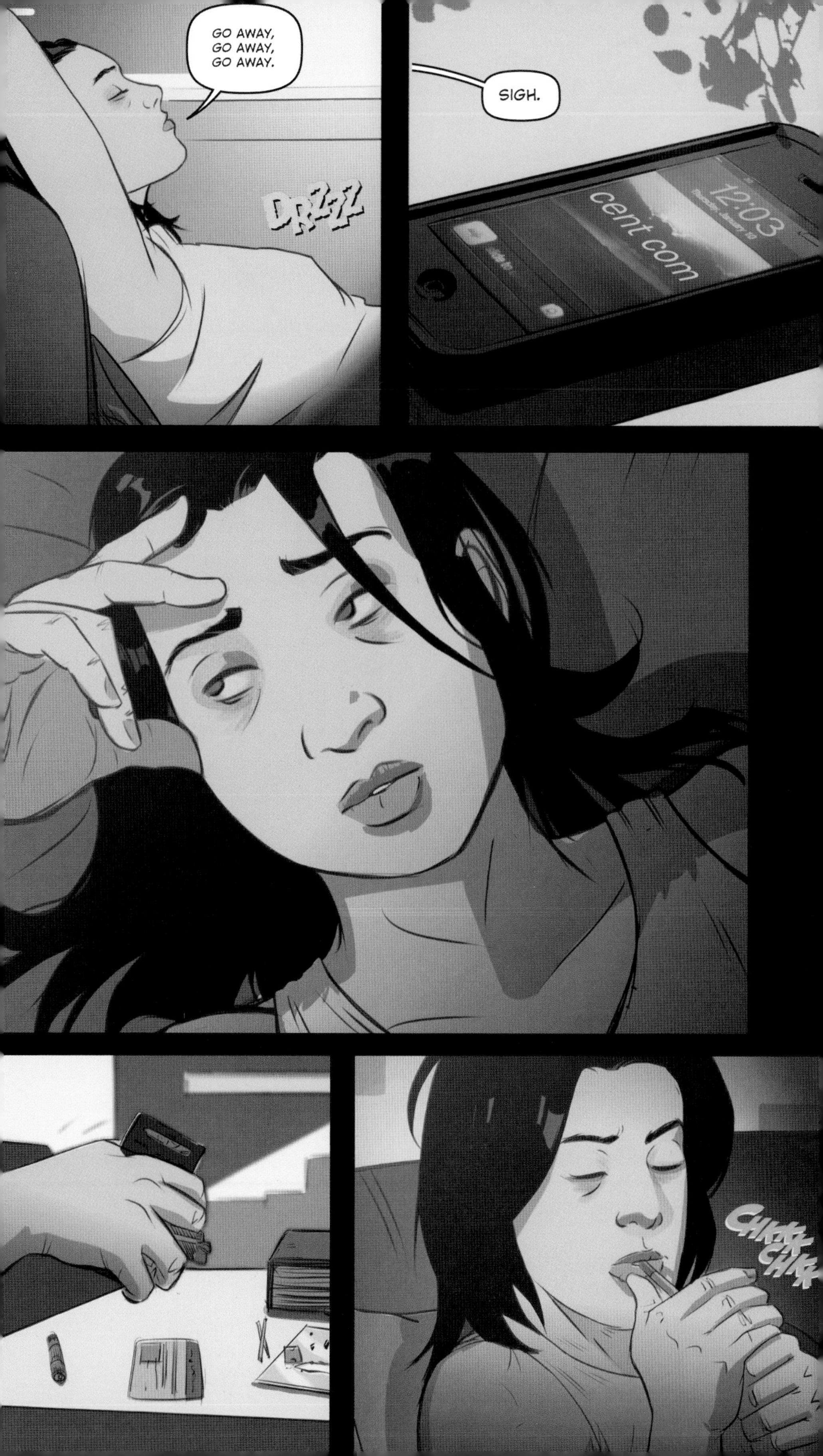
GO AWAY, GO AWAY, GO AWAY.
DRZZZ
SIGH.
12:03
cent com
CHKK CHKK

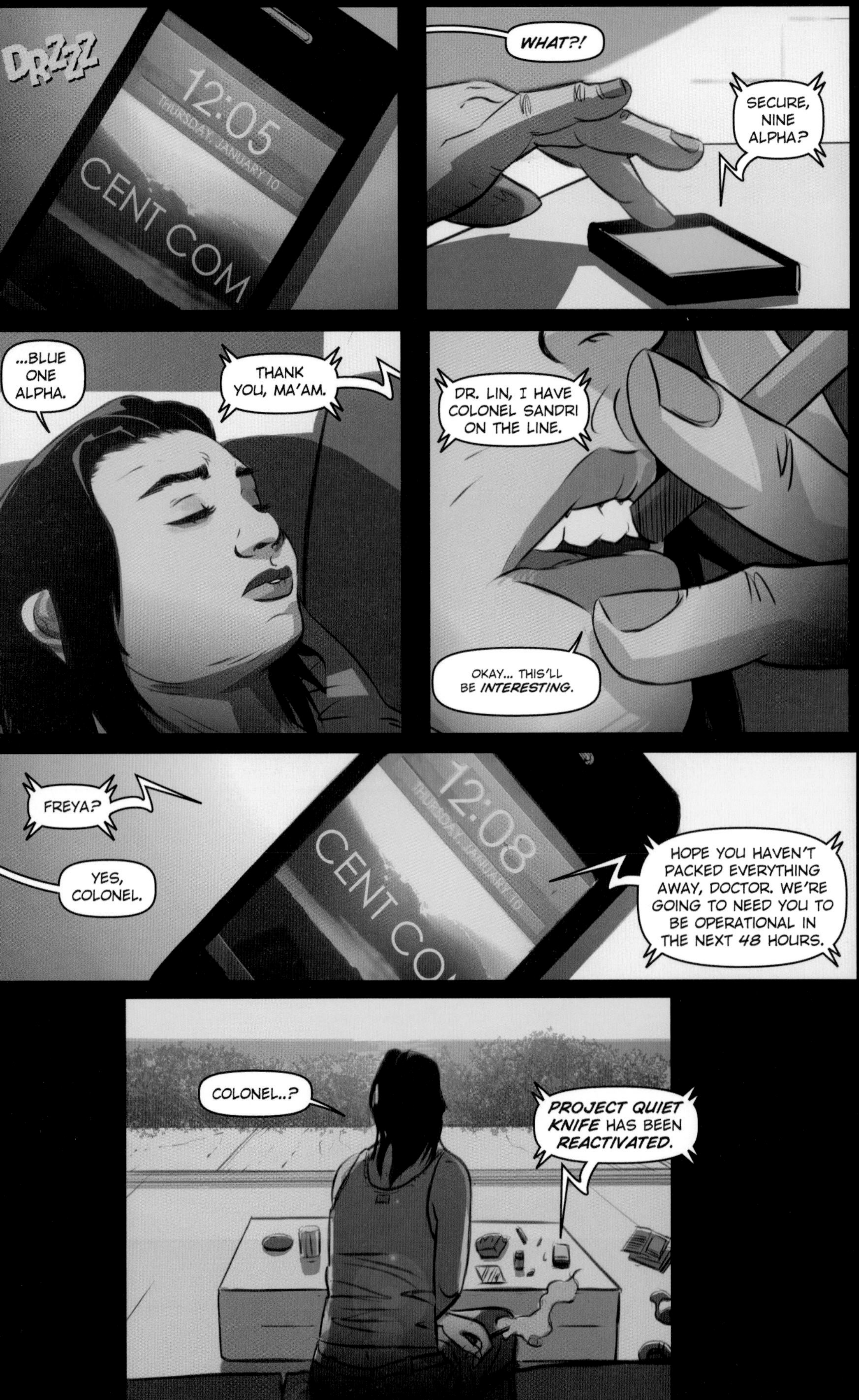
DRZZZ
12:05
THURSDAY, JANUARY 10
CENT COM
WHAT?!
SECURE, NINE ALPHA?
...BLUE ONE ALPHA.
THANK YOU, MA'AM.
DR. LIN, I HAVE COLONEL SANDRI ON THE LINE.
OKAY... THIS'LL BE INTERESTING.
FREYA?
YES, COLONEL.
12:08
THURSDAY, JANUARY 10
CENT CO
HOPE YOU HAVEN'T PACKED EVERYTHING AWAY, DOCTOR. WE'RE GOING TO NEED YOU TO BE OPERATIONAL IN THE NEXT 48 HOURS.
COLONEL...?
PROJECT QUIET KNIFE HAS BEEN REACTIVATED.

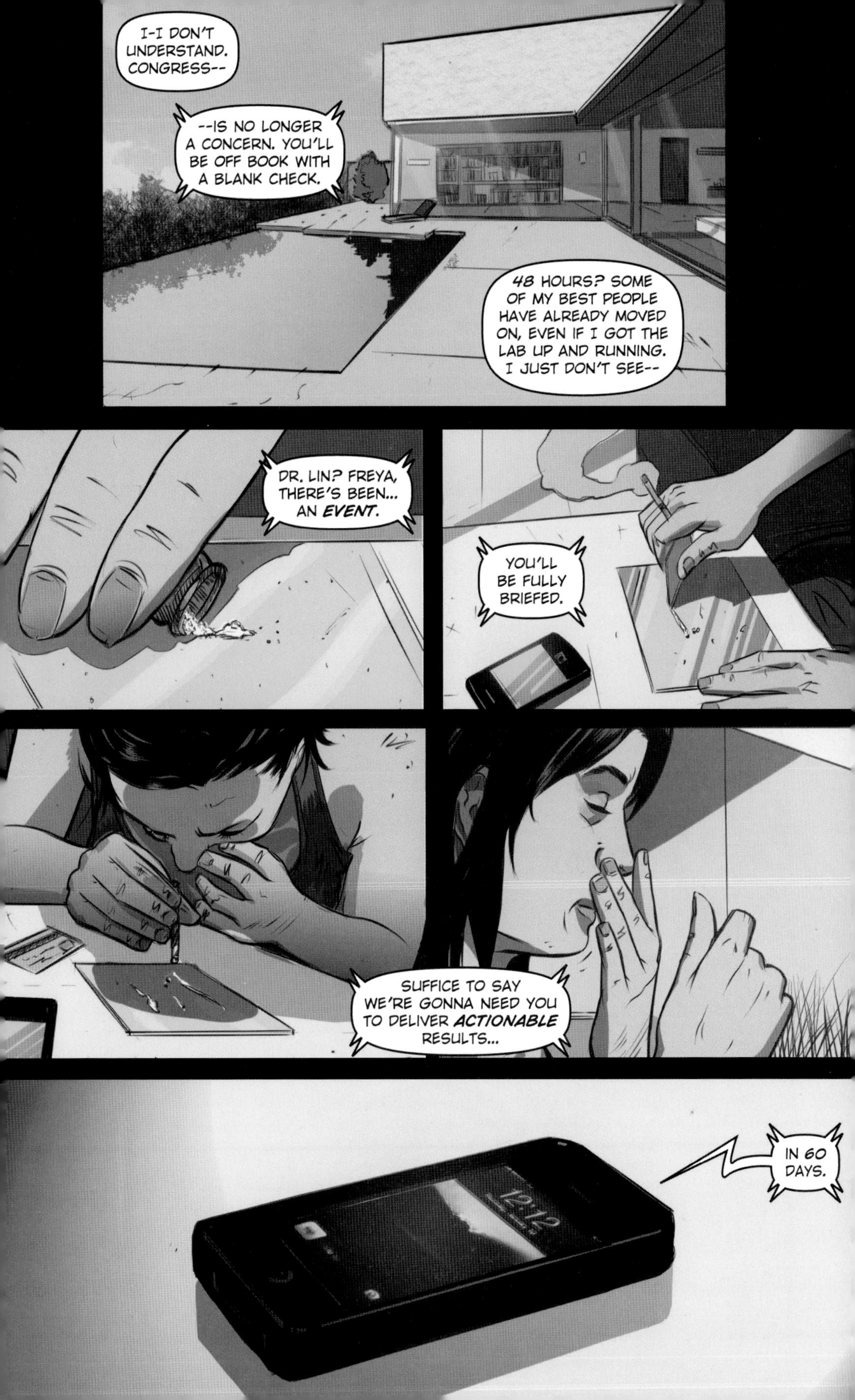
I-I DON'T UNDERSTAND. CONGRESS--
--IS NO LONGER A CONCERN. YOU'LL BE OFF BOOK WITH A BLANK CHECK.
48 HOURS? SOME OF MY BEST PEOPLE HAVE ALREADY MOVED ON, EVEN IF I GOT THE LAB UP AND RUNNING. I JUST DON'T SEE--
DR. LIN? FREYA, THERE'S BEEN... AN *EVENT*.
YOU'LL BE FULLY BRIEFED.
SUFFICE TO SAY WE'RE GONNA NEED YOU TO DELIVER ***ACTIONABLE*** RESULTS...
IN 60 DAYS.

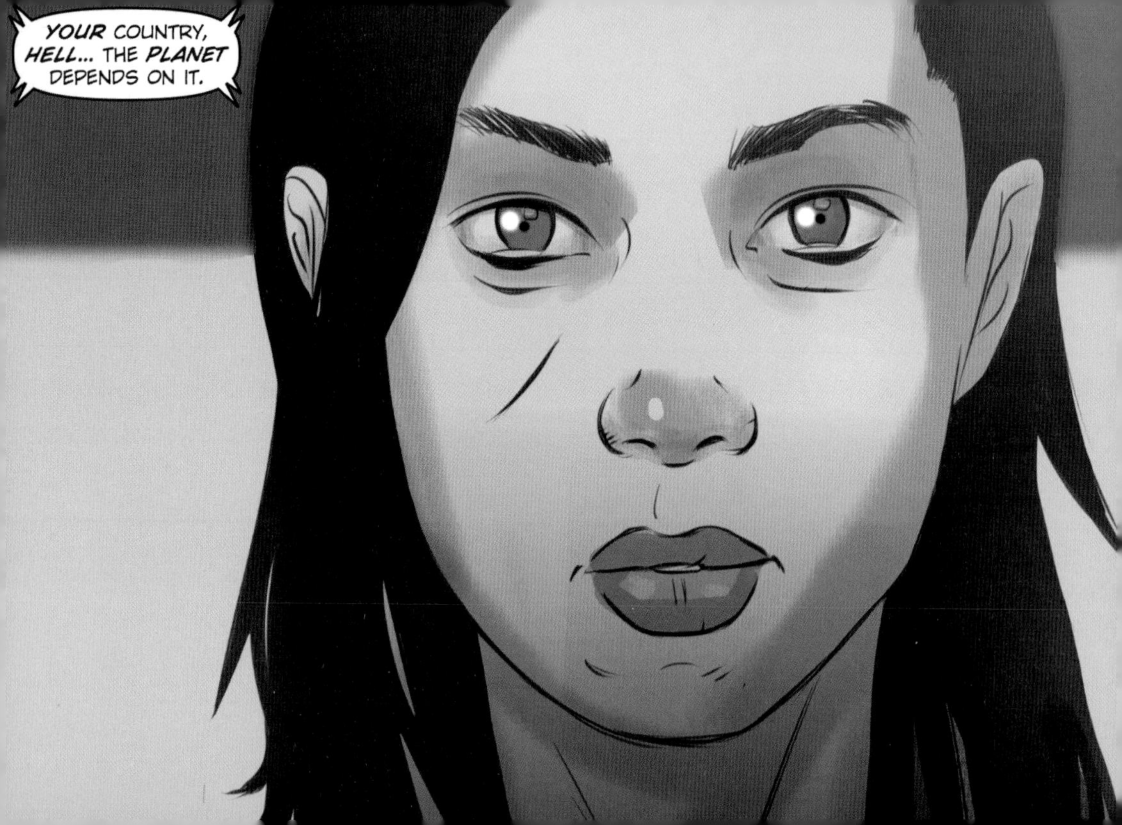
YOUR COUNTRY, HELL... THE PLANET DEPENDS ON IT.

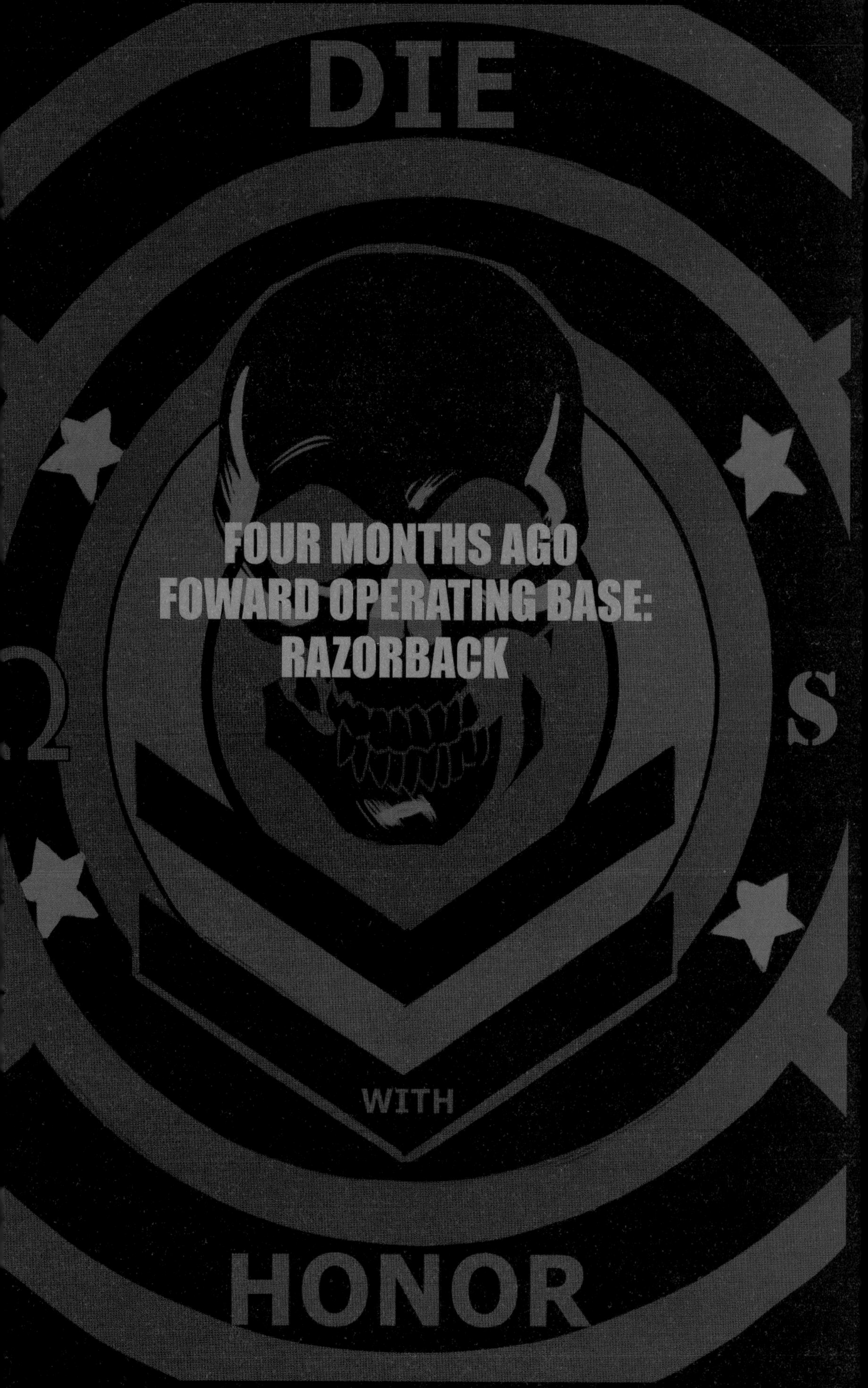
DIE
FOUR MONTHS AGO
FOWARD OPERATING BASE:
RAZORBACK
Ω
S
WITH
HONOR

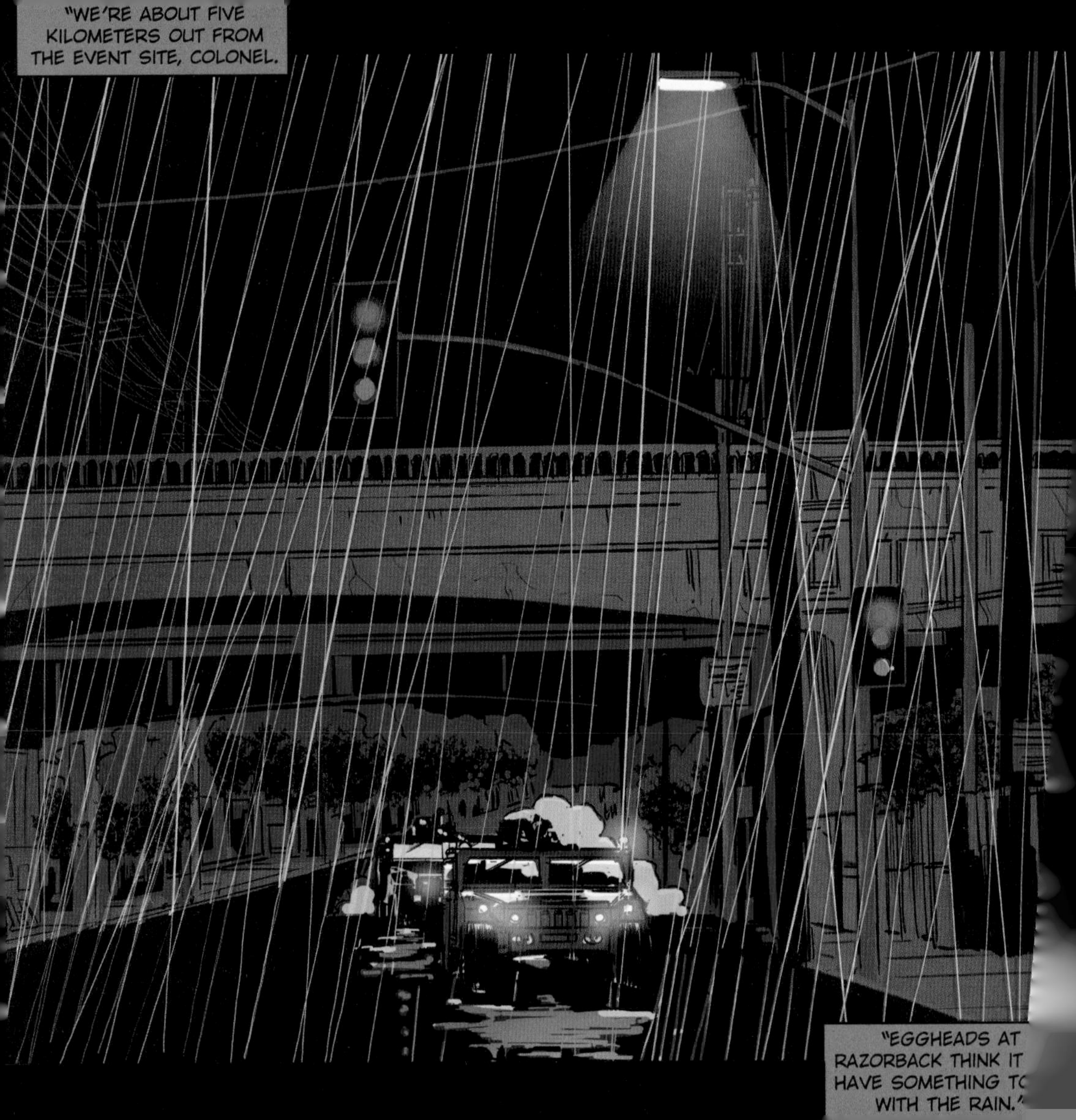
"WE'RE ABOUT FIVE KILOMETERS OUT FROM THE EVENT SITE, COLONEL.
"EGGHEADS AT RAZORBACK THINK IT HAVE SOMETHING TO WITH THE RAIN."

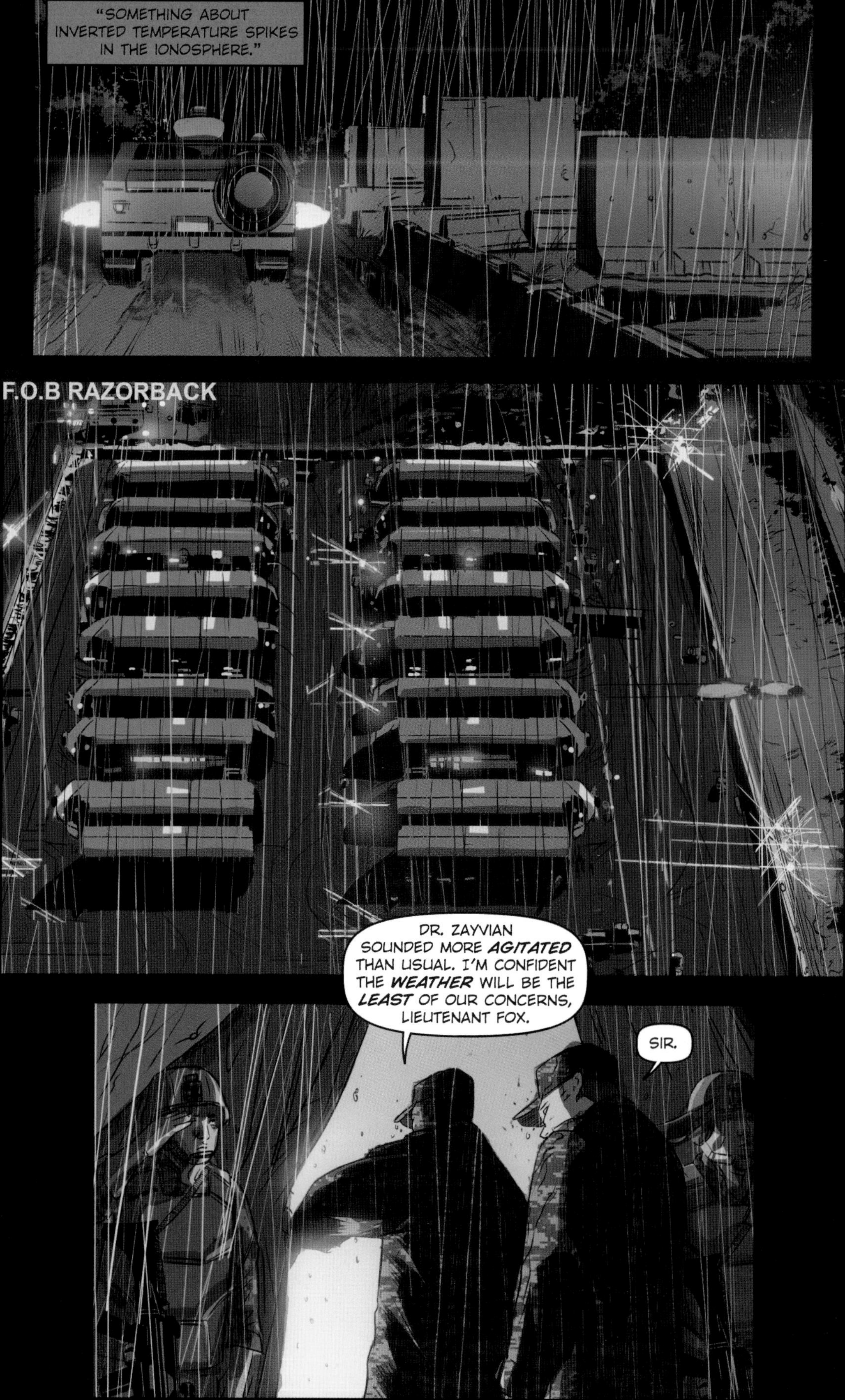
"SOMETHING ABOUT INVERTED TEMPERATURE SPIKES IN THE IONOSPHERE."
F.O.B RAZORBACK
DR. ZAYVIAN SOUNDED MORE *AGITATED* THAN USUAL. I'M CONFIDENT THE *WEATHER* WILL BE THE *LEAST* OF OUR CONCERNS, LIEUTENANT FOX.
SIR.

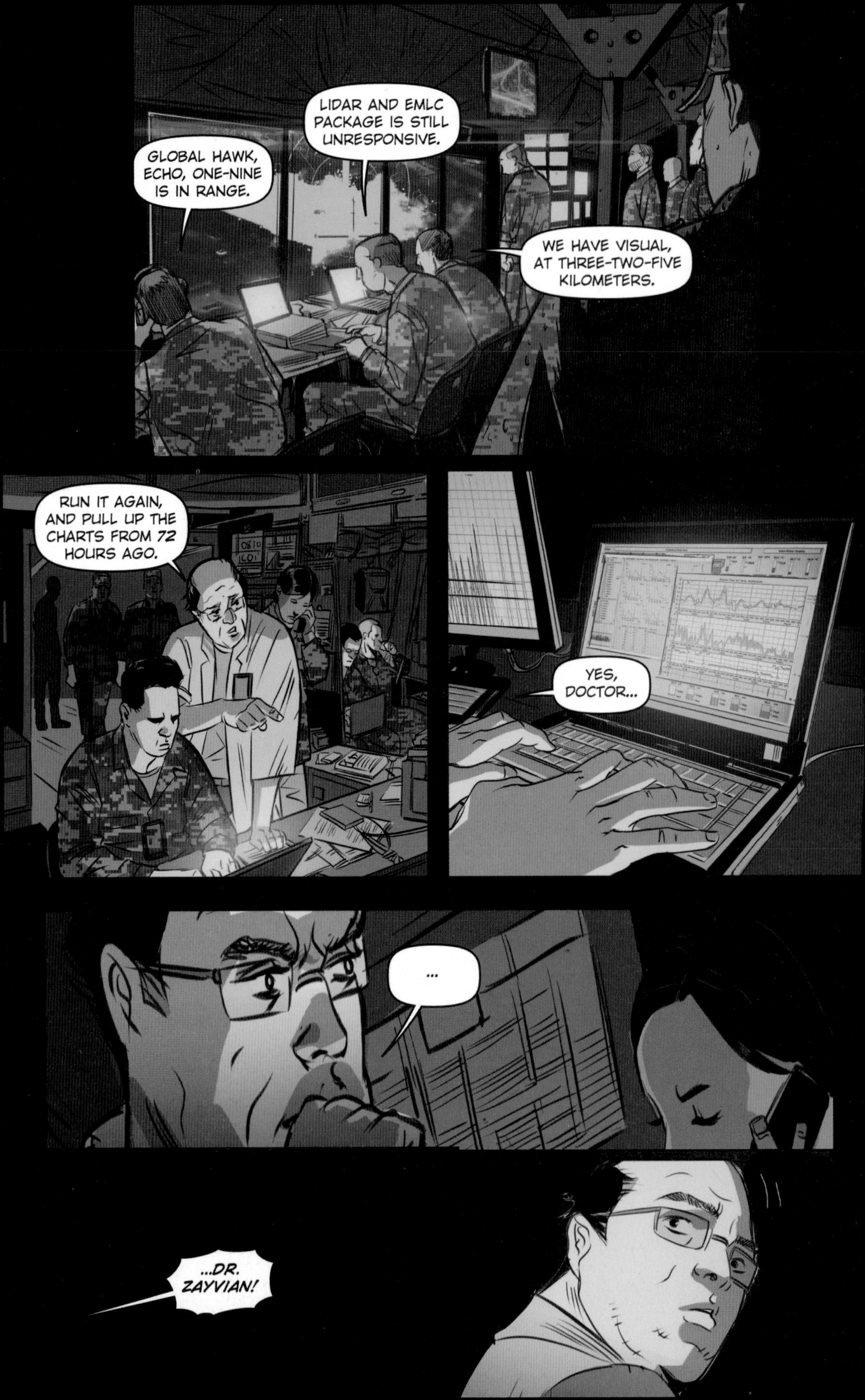
GLOBAL HAWK, ECHO, ONE-NINE IS IN RANGE.
LIDAR AND EMLC PACKAGE IS STILL UNRESPONSIVE.
WE HAVE VISUAL, AT THREE-TWO-FIVE KILOMETERS.
RUN IT AGAIN, AND PULL UP THE CHARTS FROM 72 HOURS AGO.
YES, DOCTOR...
...
...DR. ZAYVIAN!

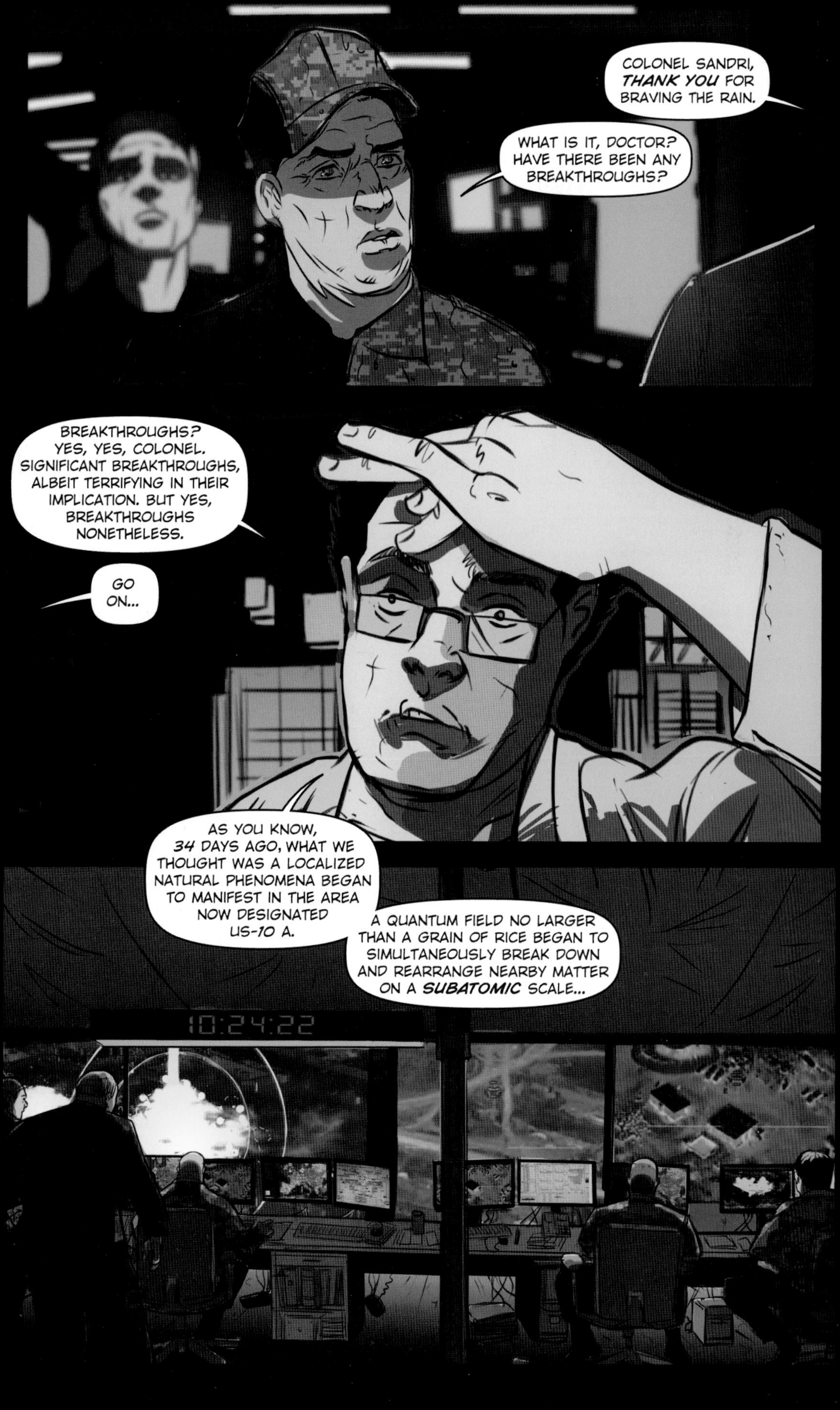
COLONEL SANDRI, THANK YOU FOR BRAVING THE RAIN.
WHAT IS IT, DOCTOR? HAVE THERE BEEN ANY BREAKTHROUGHS?
BREAKTHROUGHS? YES, YES, COLONEL. SIGNIFICANT BREAKTHROUGHS, ALBEIT TERRIFYING IN THEIR IMPLICATION. BUT YES, BREAKTHROUGHS NONETHELESS.
GO ON...
AS YOU KNOW, 34 DAYS AGO, WHAT WE THOUGHT WAS A LOCALIZED NATURAL PHENOMENA BEGAN TO MANIFEST IN THE AREA NOW DESIGNATED US-10 A.
A QUANTUM FIELD NO LARGER THAN A GRAIN OF RICE BEGAN TO SIMULTANEOUSLY BREAK DOWN AND REARRANGE NEARBY MATTER ON A SUBATOMIC SCALE...
10:24:22

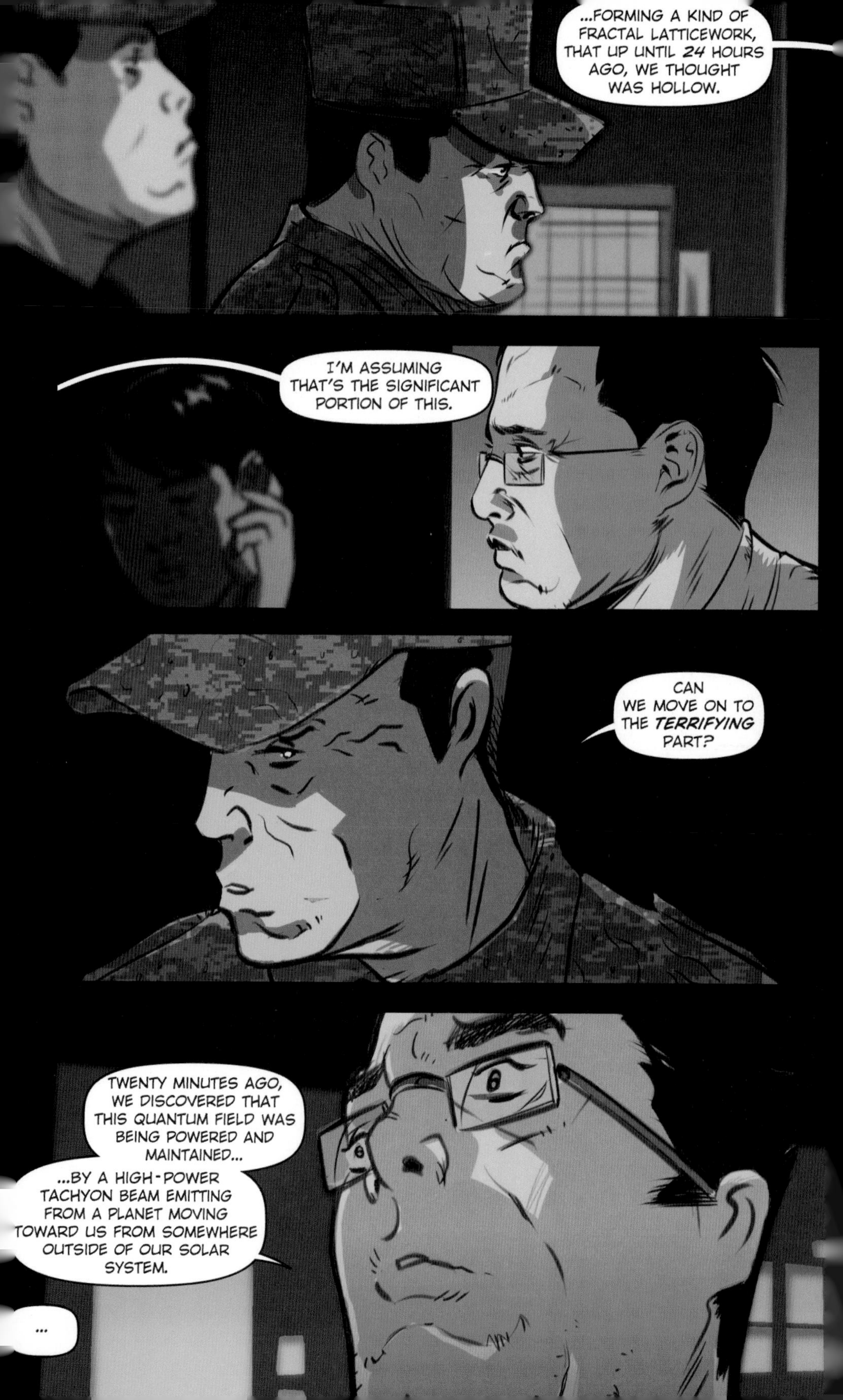
...FORMING A KIND OF FRACTAL LATTICEWORK, THAT UP UNTIL 24 HOURS AGO, WE THOUGHT WAS HOLLOW.
I'M ASSUMING THAT'S THE SIGNIFICANT PORTION OF THIS.
CAN WE MOVE ON TO THE *TERRIFYING* PART?
TWENTY MINUTES AGO, WE DISCOVERED THAT THIS QUANTUM FIELD WAS BEING POWERED AND MAINTAINED...
...BY A HIGH-POWER TACHYON BEAM EMITTING FROM A PLANET MOVING TOWARD US FROM SOMEWHERE OUTSIDE OF OUR SOLAR SYSTEM.
...

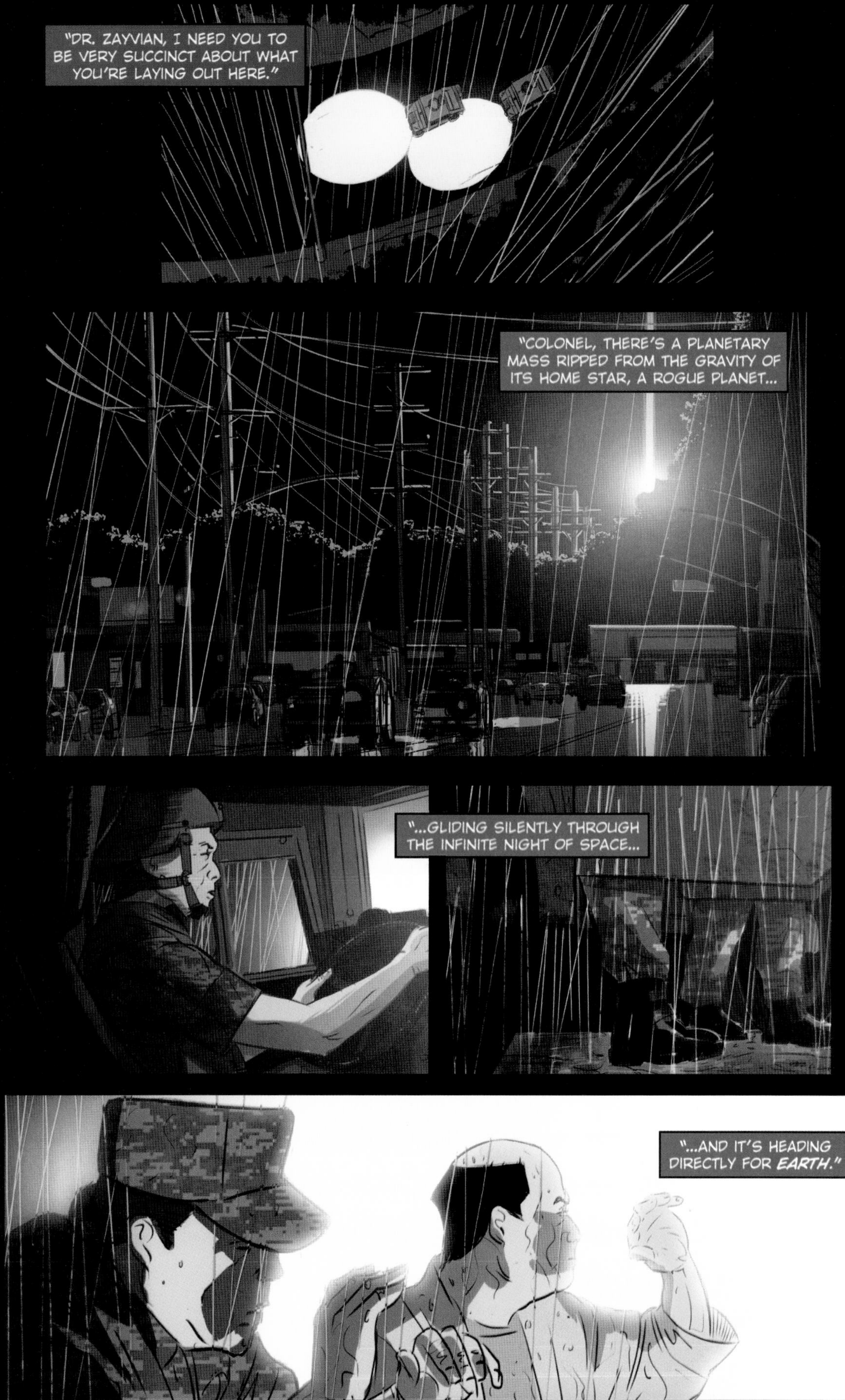
"DR. ZAYVIAN, I NEED YOU TO BE VERY SUCCINCT ABOUT WHAT YOU'RE LAYING OUT HERE."
"COLONEL, THERE'S A PLANETARY MASS RIPPED FROM THE GRAVITY OF ITS HOME STAR, A ROGUE PLANET...
"...GLIDING SILENTLY THROUGH THE INFINITE NIGHT OF SPACE...
"...AND IT'S HEADING DIRECTLY FOR *EARTH*."

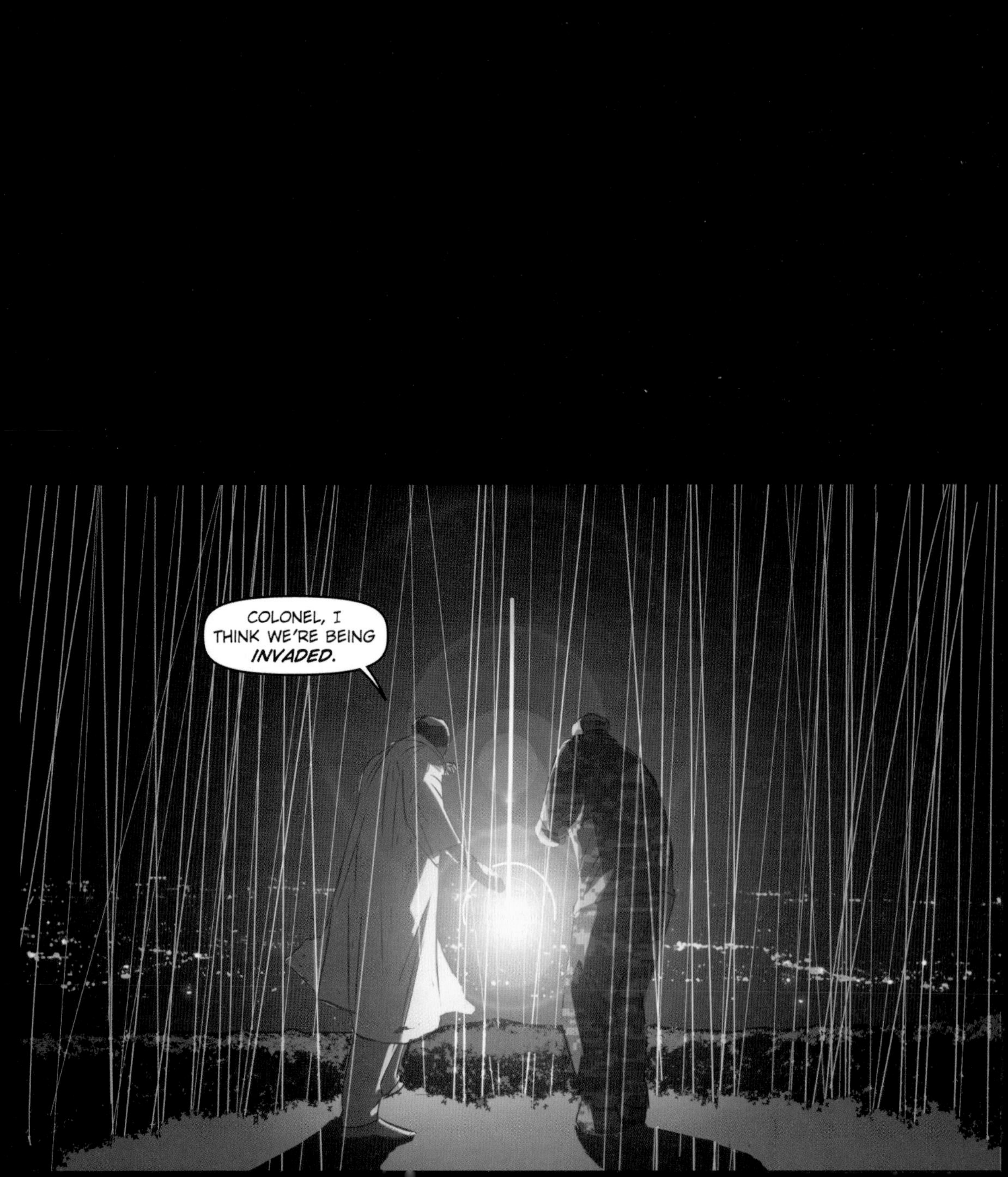
COLONEL, I THINK WE'RE BEING *INVADED.*

OPERATION: ALL WEATHER GLADIATOR TWO SIX

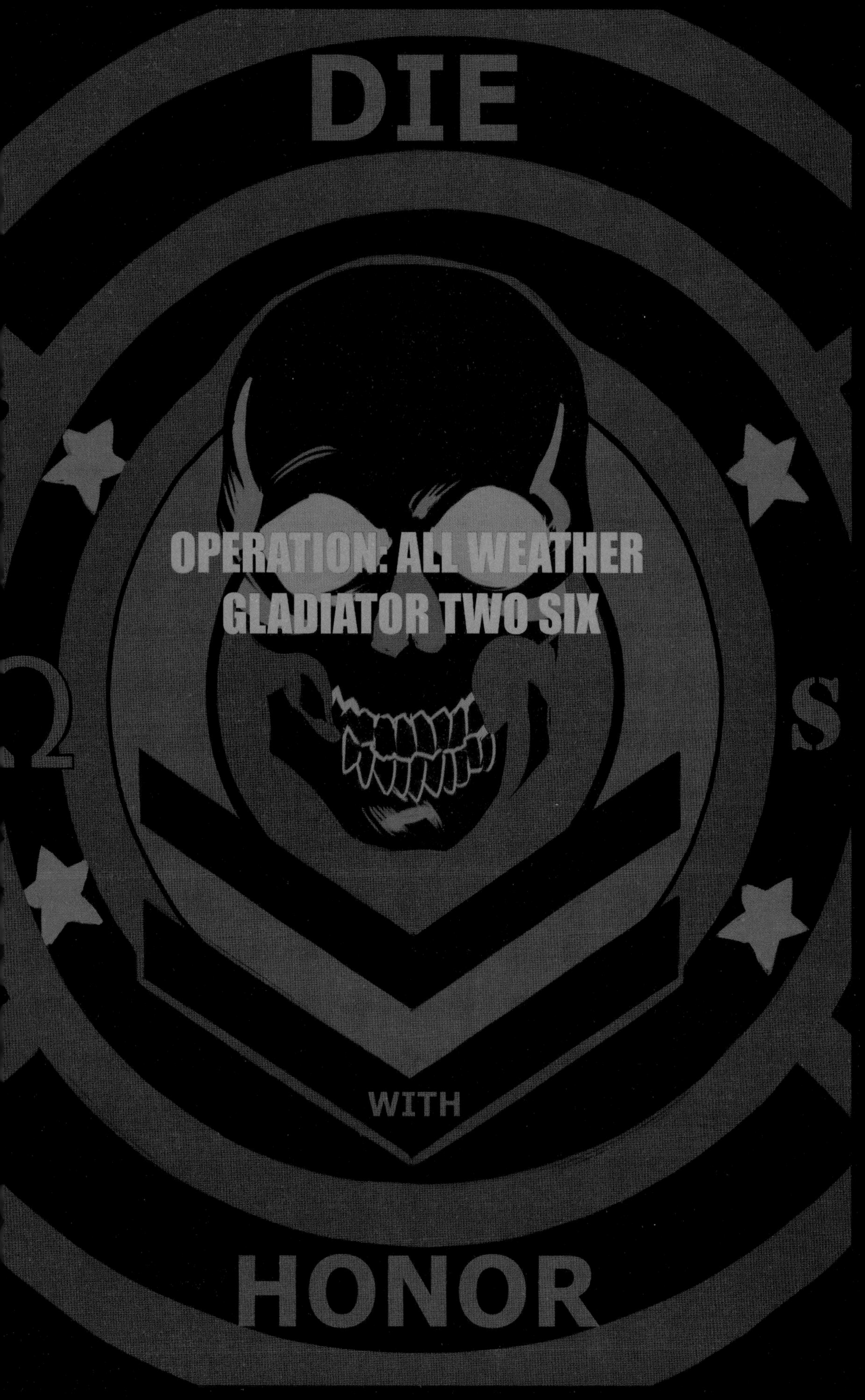
DIE
Ω
S
WITH
HONOR

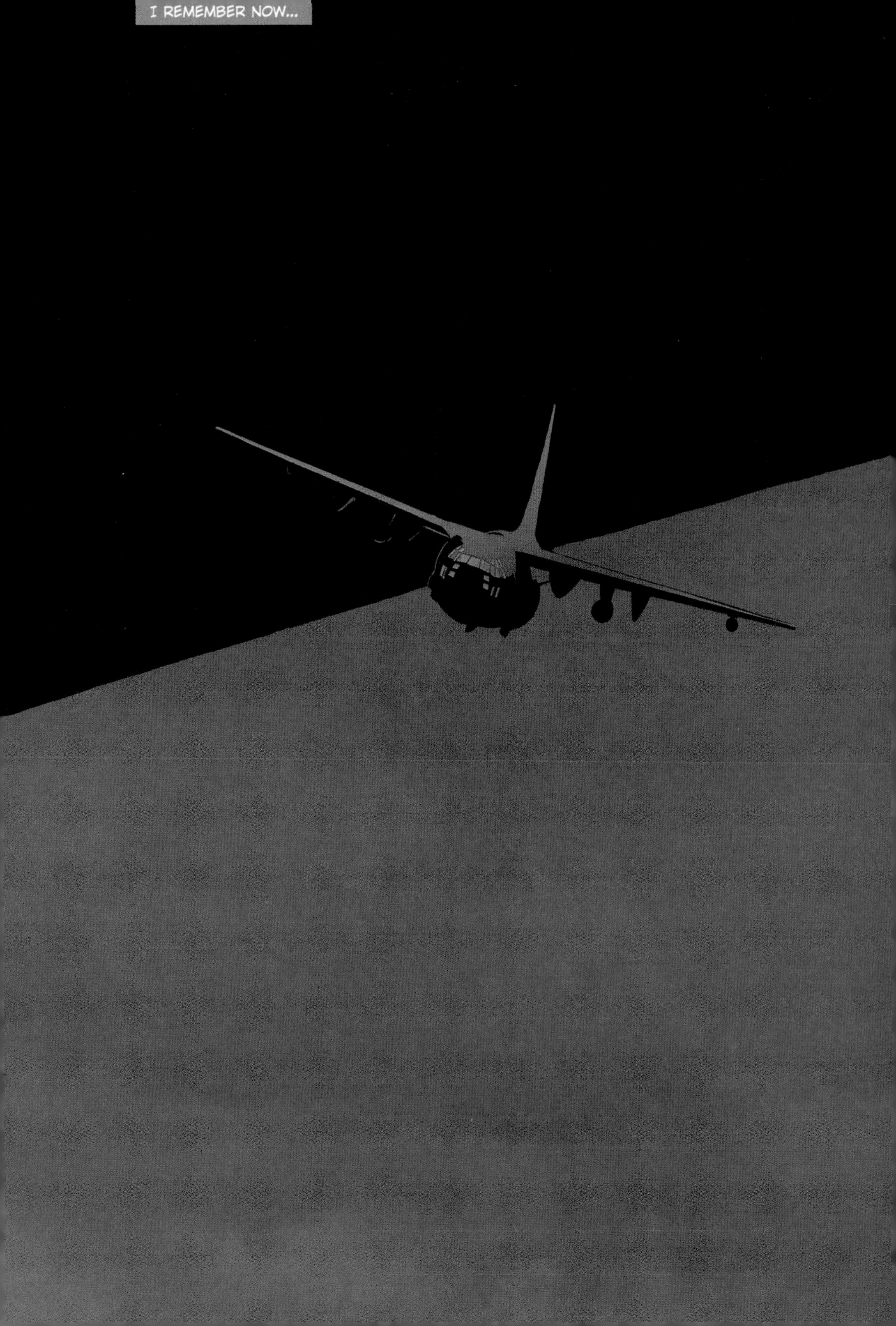
I REMEMBER NOW...

WE MET A LONG *TIME* AGO, ON SOME ANCIENT BATTLEFIELD.

YOU WERE MY BROTHER.

MY FATHER.

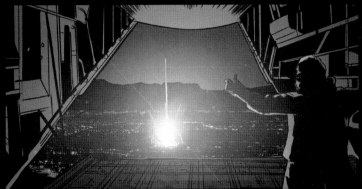

MY *ENEMY.*

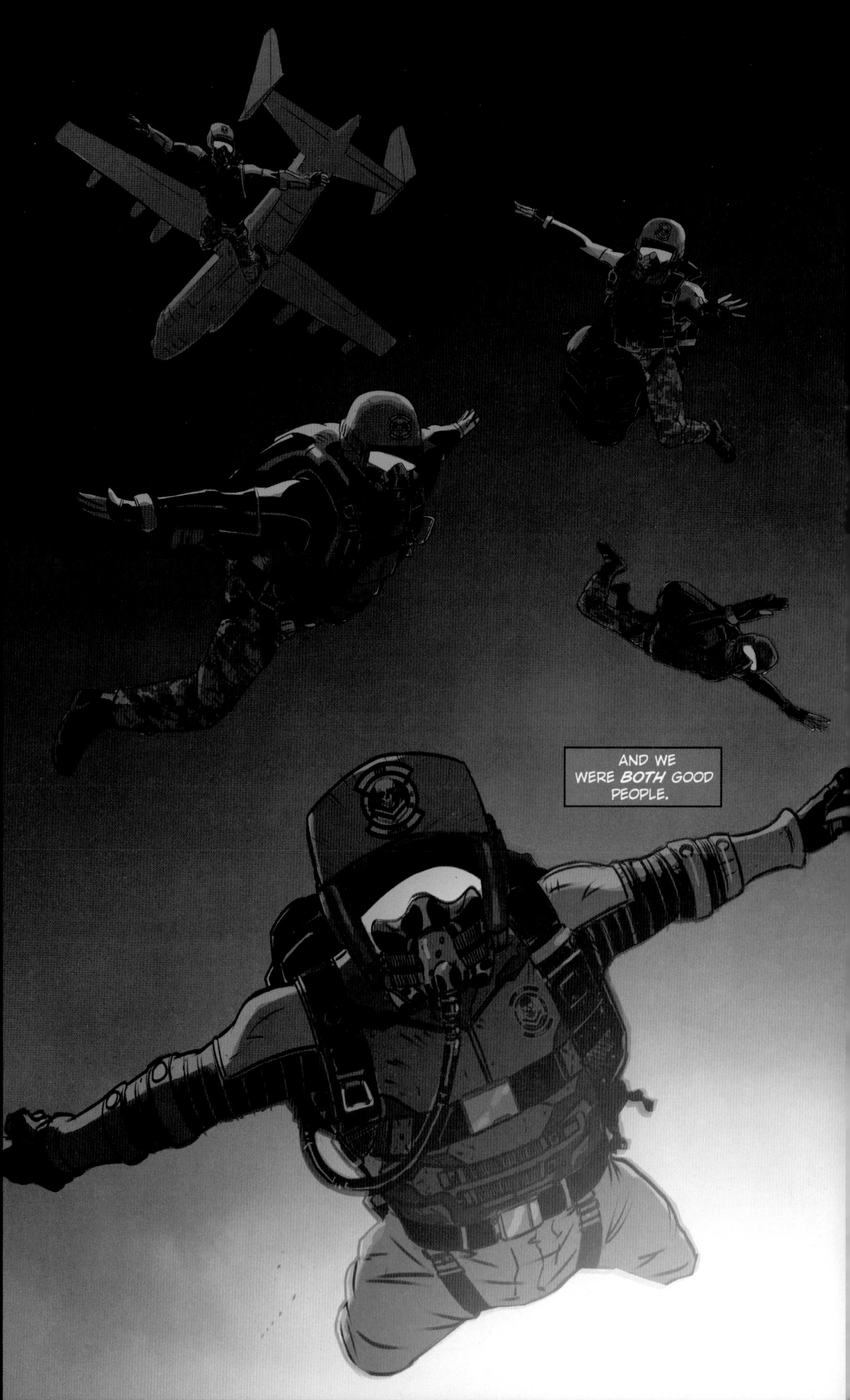
AND WE WERE BOTH GOOD PEOPLE.

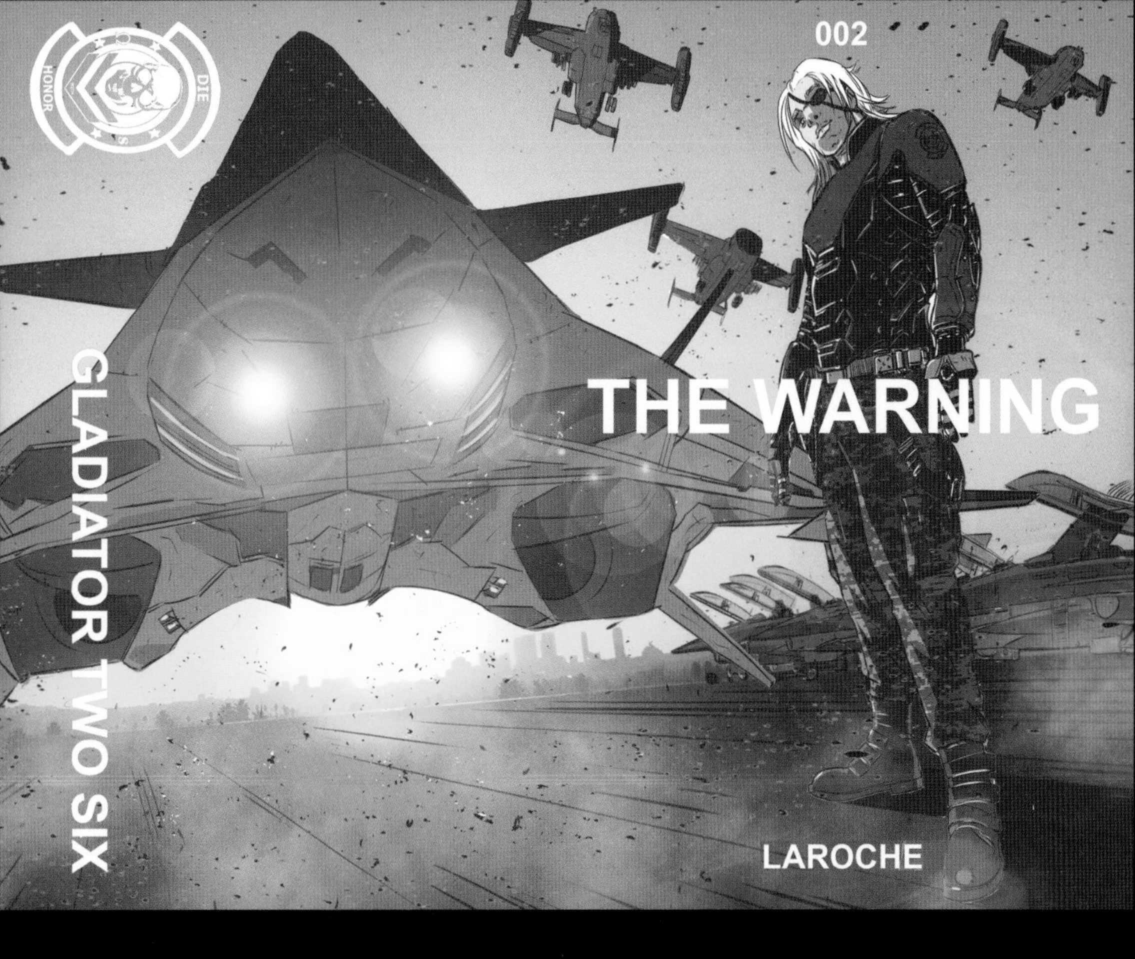
002
HONOR
DIE
GLADIATOR TWO SIX
THE WARNING
LAROCHE

CHAPTER TWO

002

GLADIATOR TWO SIX

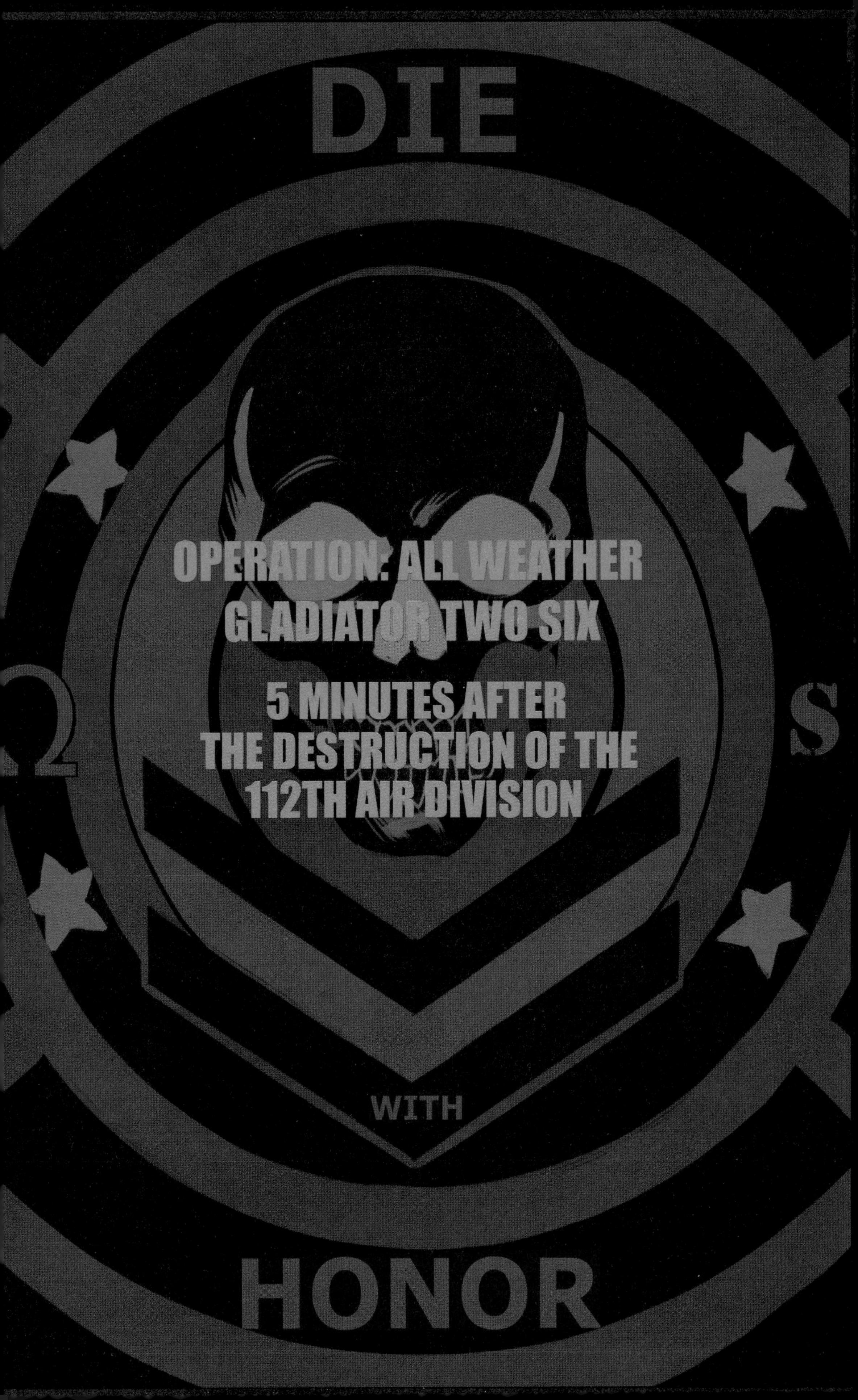
DIE
OPERATION: ALL WEATHER
GLADIATOR TWO SIX
5 MINUTES AFTER
THE DESTRUCTION OF THE
112TH AIR DIVISION
WITH
HONOR

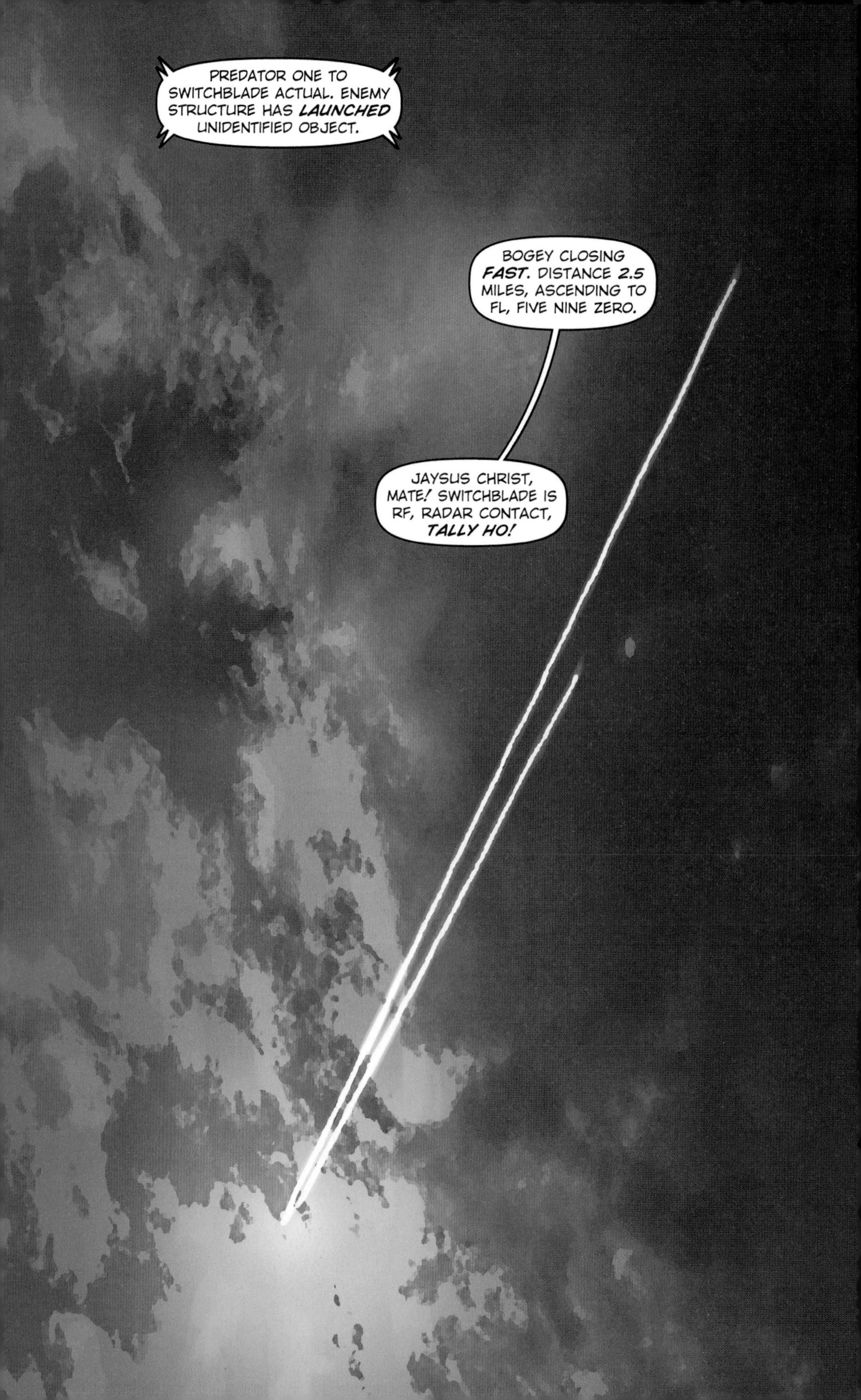
PREDATOR ONE TO SWITCHBLADE ACTUAL. ENEMY STRUCTURE HAS **LAUNCHED** UNIDENTIFIED OBJECT.
BOGEY CLOSING **FAST**. DISTANCE **2.5** MILES, ASCENDING TO FL, FIVE NINE ZERO.
JAYSUS CHRIST, MATE! SWITCHBLADE IS RF, RADAR CONTACT, **TALLY HO!**

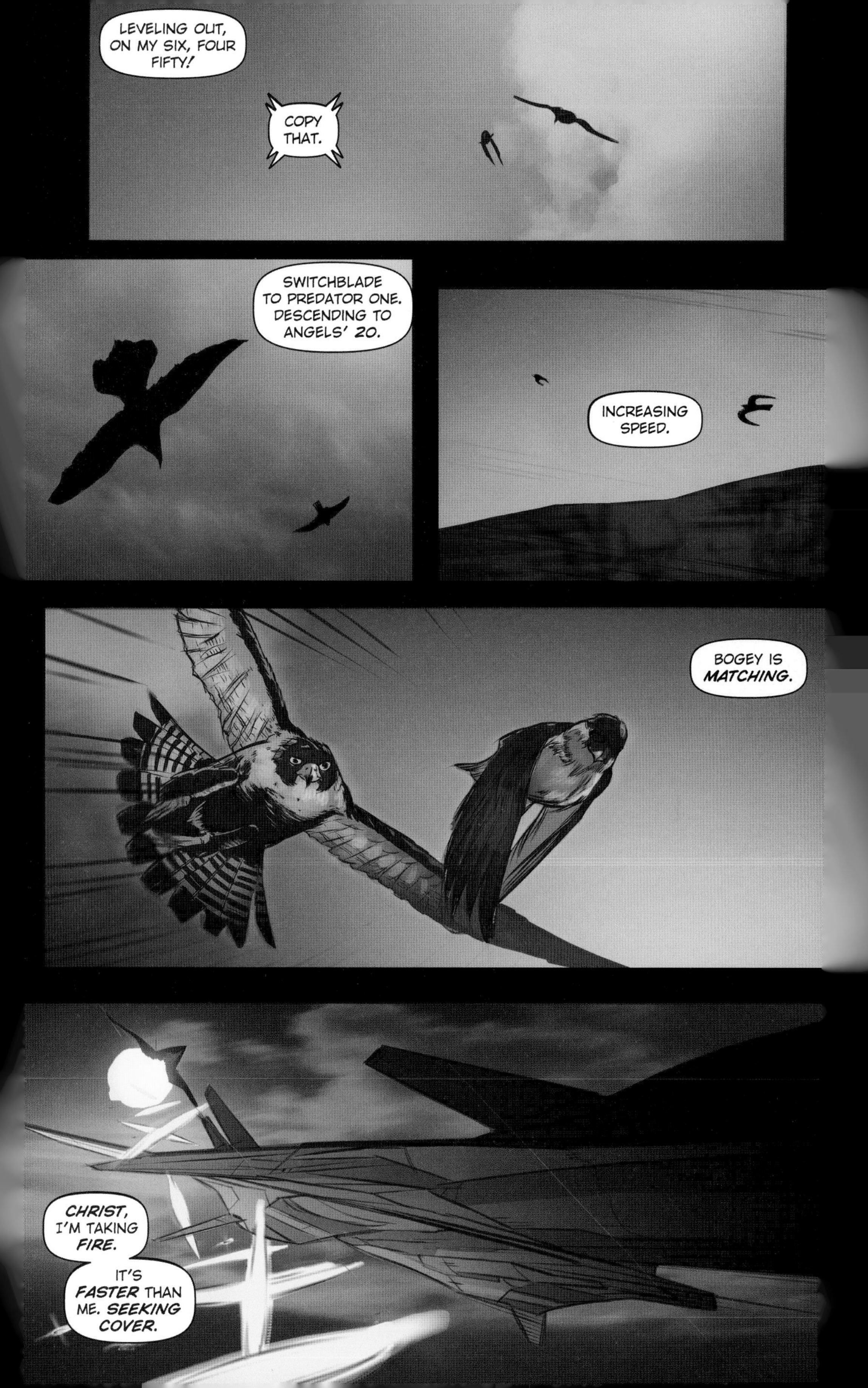
LEVELING OUT, ON MY SIX, FOUR FIFTY!
COPY THAT.
SWITCHBLADE TO PREDATOR ONE. DESCENDING TO ANGELS' 20.
INCREASING SPEED.
BOGEY IS MATCHING.
CHRIST, I'M TAKING FIRE.
IT'S FASTER THAN ME. SEEKING COVER.

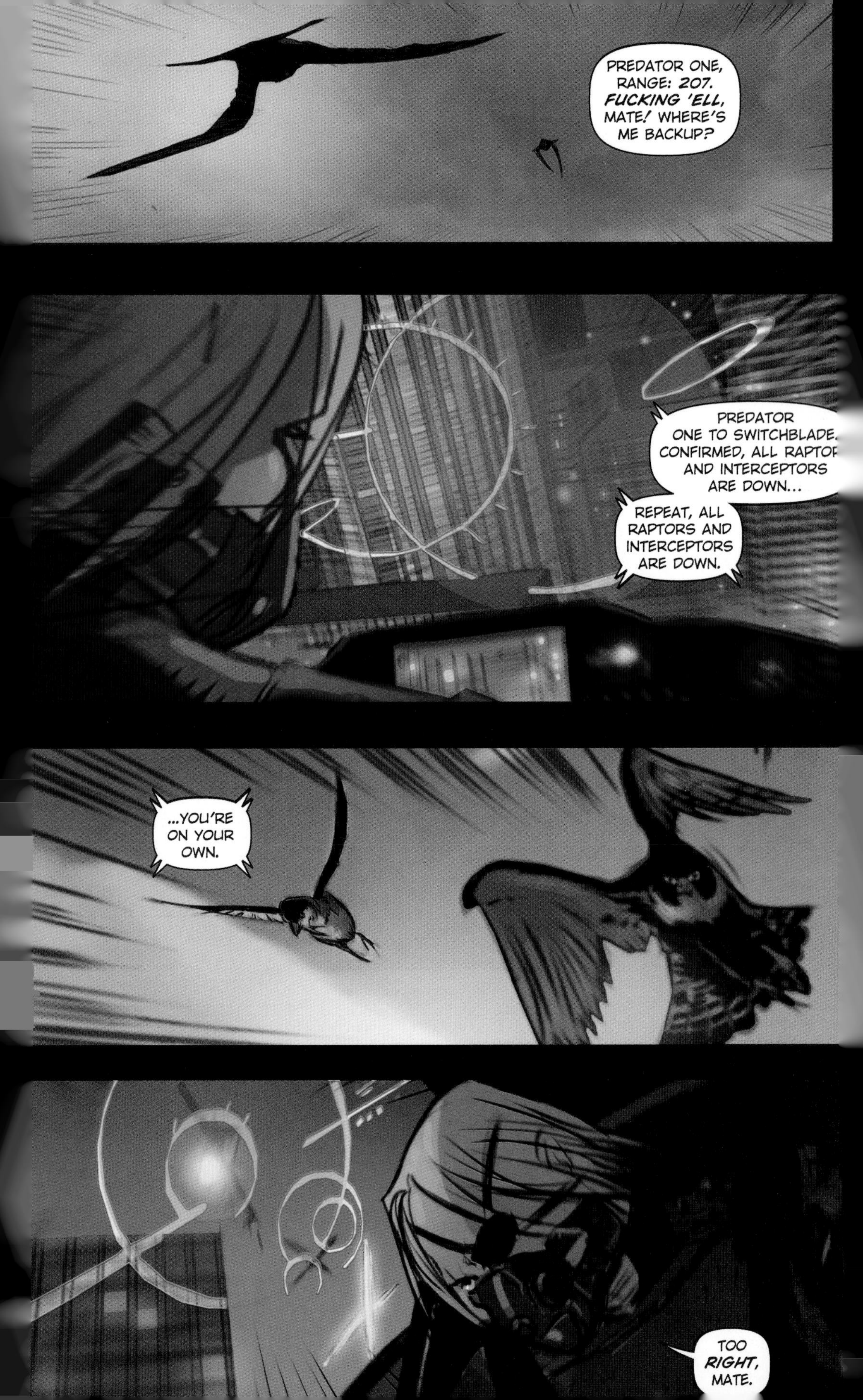
PREDATOR ONE, RANGE: 207. ***FUCKING 'ELL,*** MATE! WHERE'S ME BACKUP?
PREDATOR ONE TO SWITCHBLADE. CONFIRMED, ALL RAPTOR AND INTERCEPTORS ARE DOWN...
REPEAT, ALL RAPTORS AND INTERCEPTORS ARE DOWN.
...YOU'RE ON YOUR OWN.
TOO ***RIGHT,*** MATE.

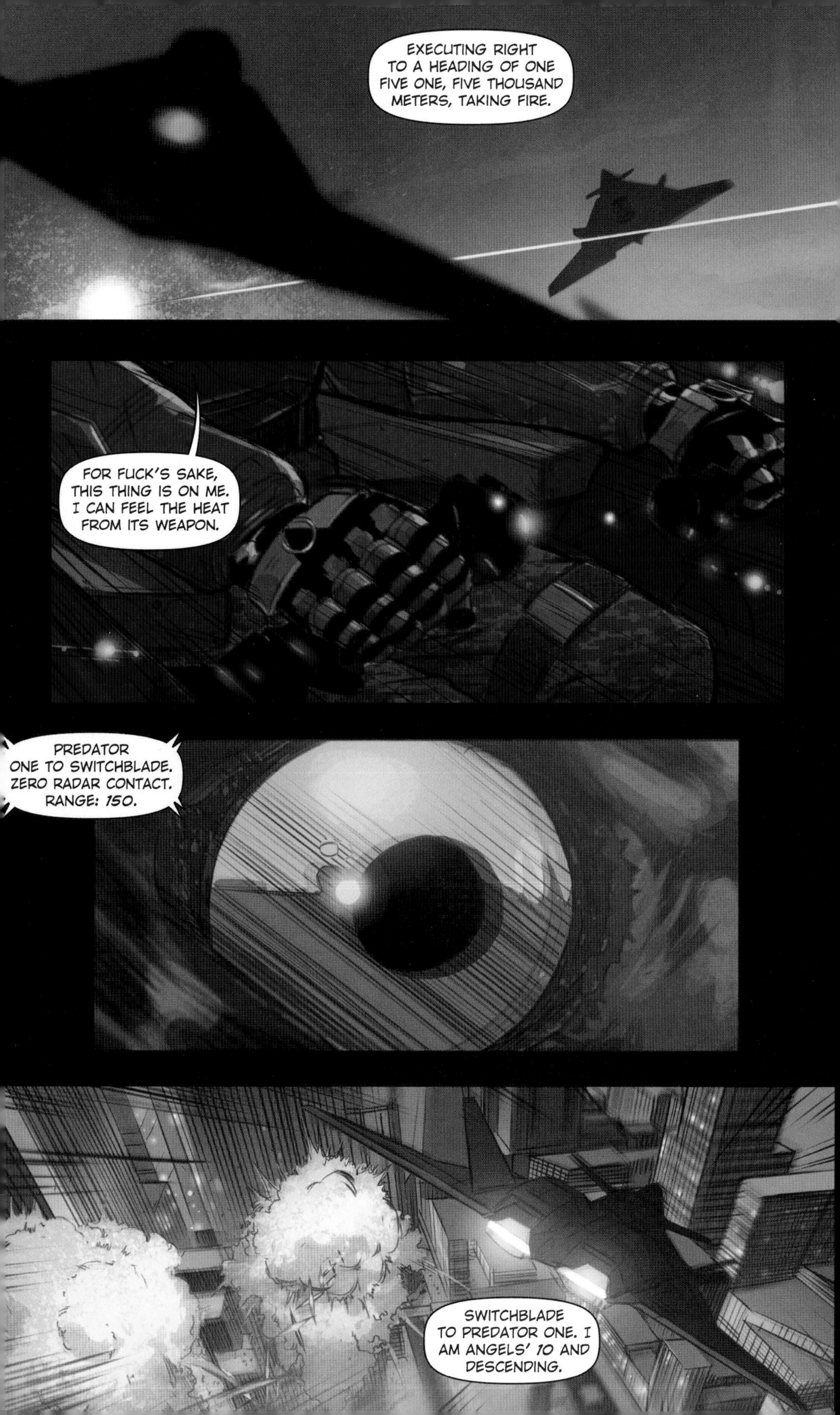
EXECUTING RIGHT TO A HEADING OF ONE FIVE ONE, FIVE THOUSAND METERS, TAKING FIRE.
FOR FUCK'S SAKE, THIS THING IS ON ME. I CAN FEEL THE HEAT FROM ITS WEAPON.
PREDATOR ONE TO SWITCHBLADE. ZERO RADAR CONTACT. RANGE: 150.
SWITCHBLADE TO PREDATOR ONE. I AM ANGELS' 10 AND DESCENDING.

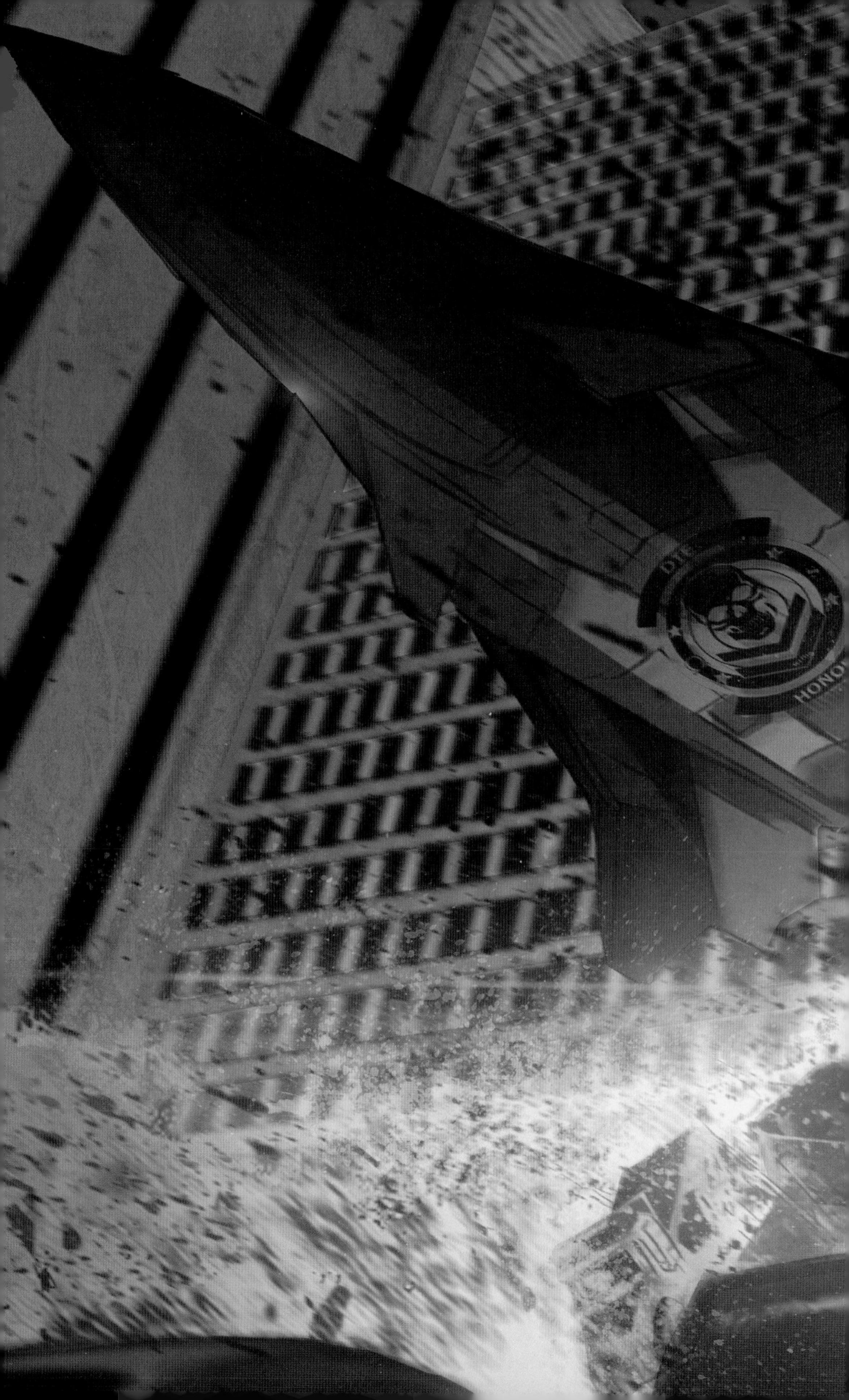

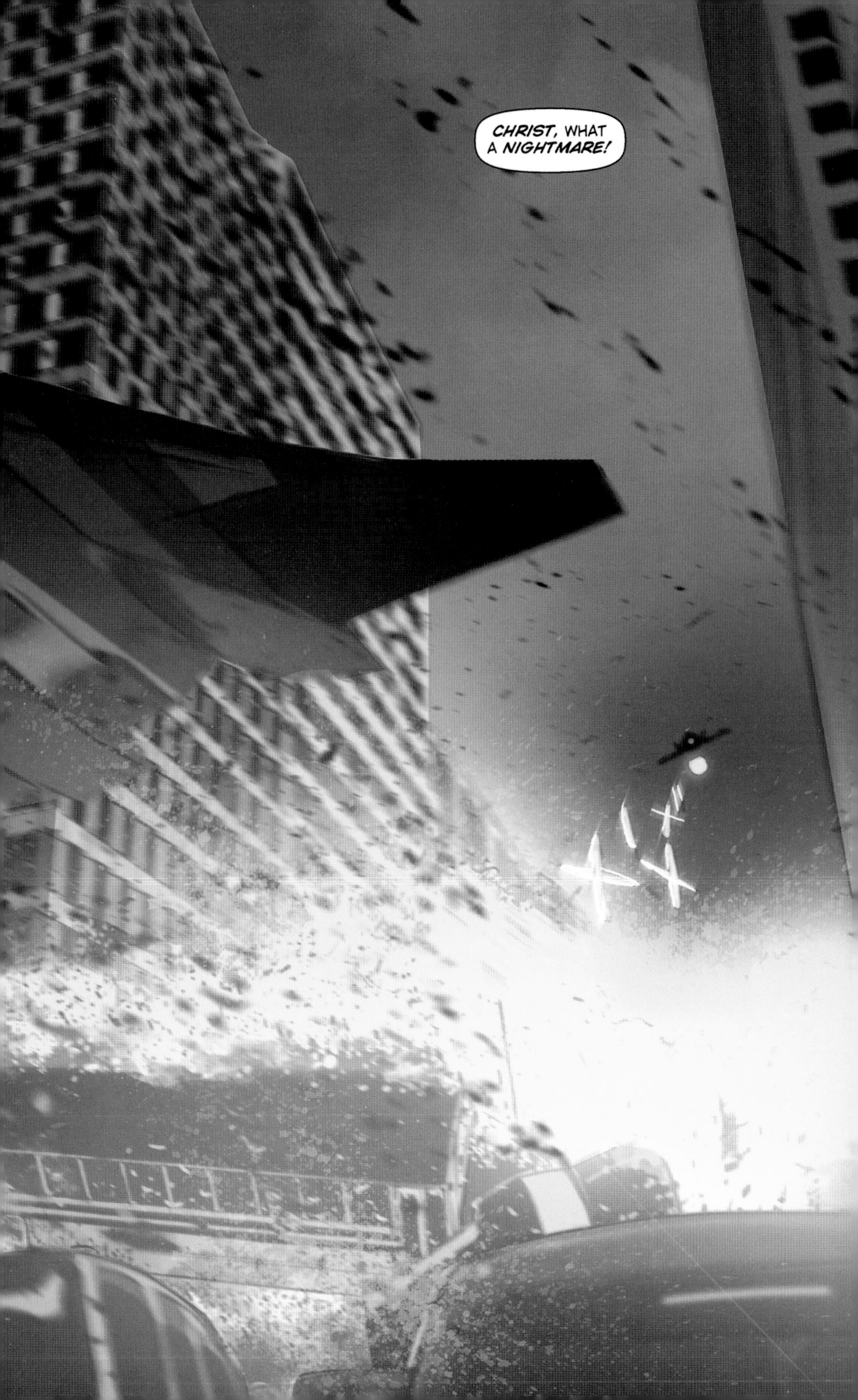
CHRIST, WHAT A NIGHTMARE!

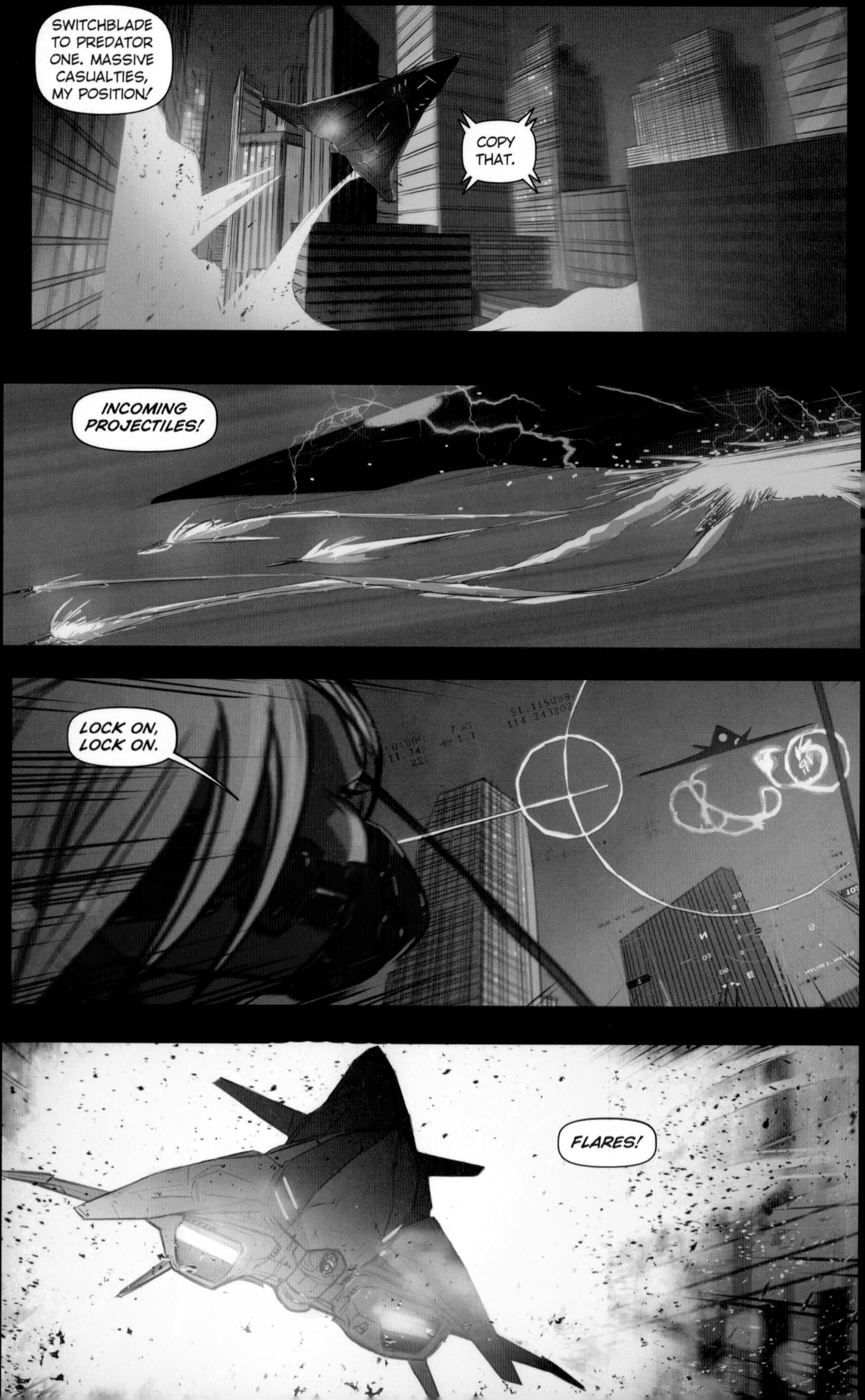
SWITCHBLADE TO PREDATOR ONE. MASSIVE CASUALTIES, MY POSITION!
COPY THAT.
INCOMING PROJECTILES!
LOCK ON, LOCK ON.
FLARES!

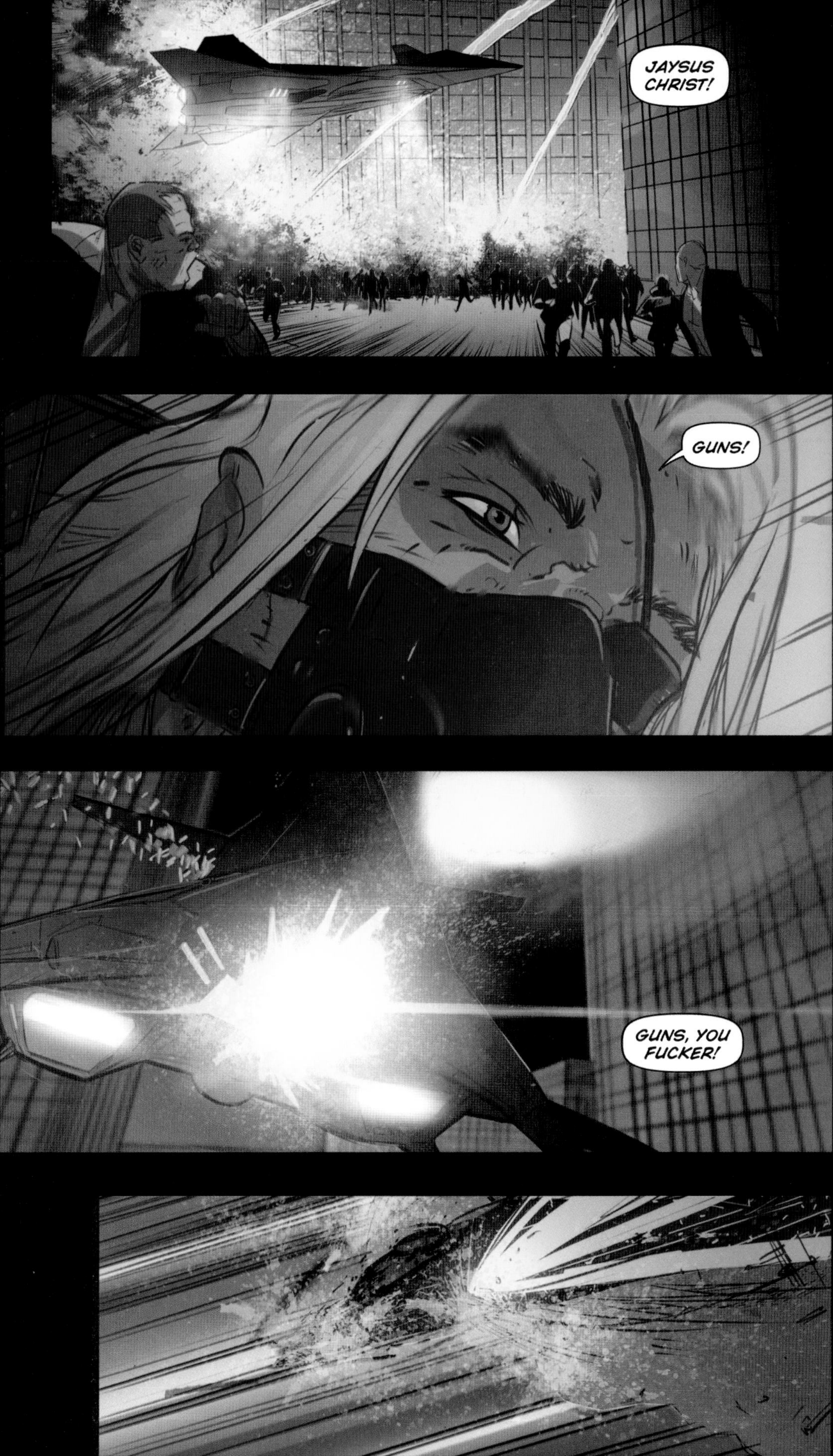
JAYSUS CHRIST!
GUNS!
GUNS, YOU FUCKER!

PREDATOR ONE TO SWITCHBLADE ACTUAL. WHAT IS YOUR FLIGHT LEVEL?
PREDATOR ONE TO SWITCHBLADE. WE HAVE CONFIRMATION ENEMY STRUCTURE HAS LAUNCHED ANOTHER BOGEY. DO YOU COPY?
BURN!

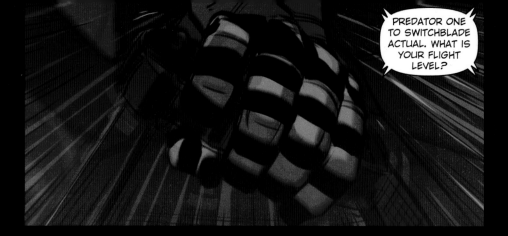

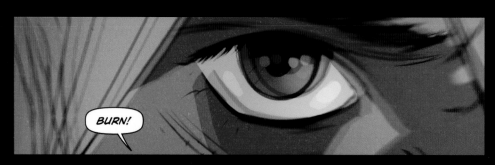

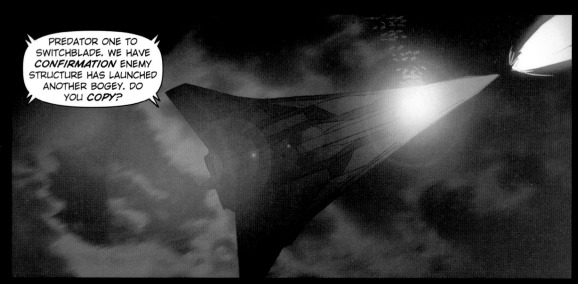

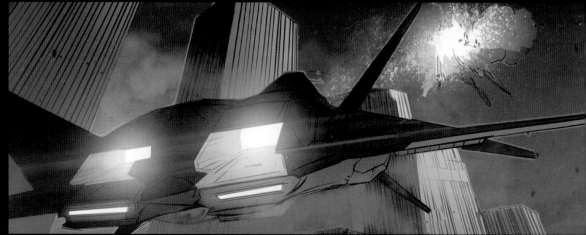

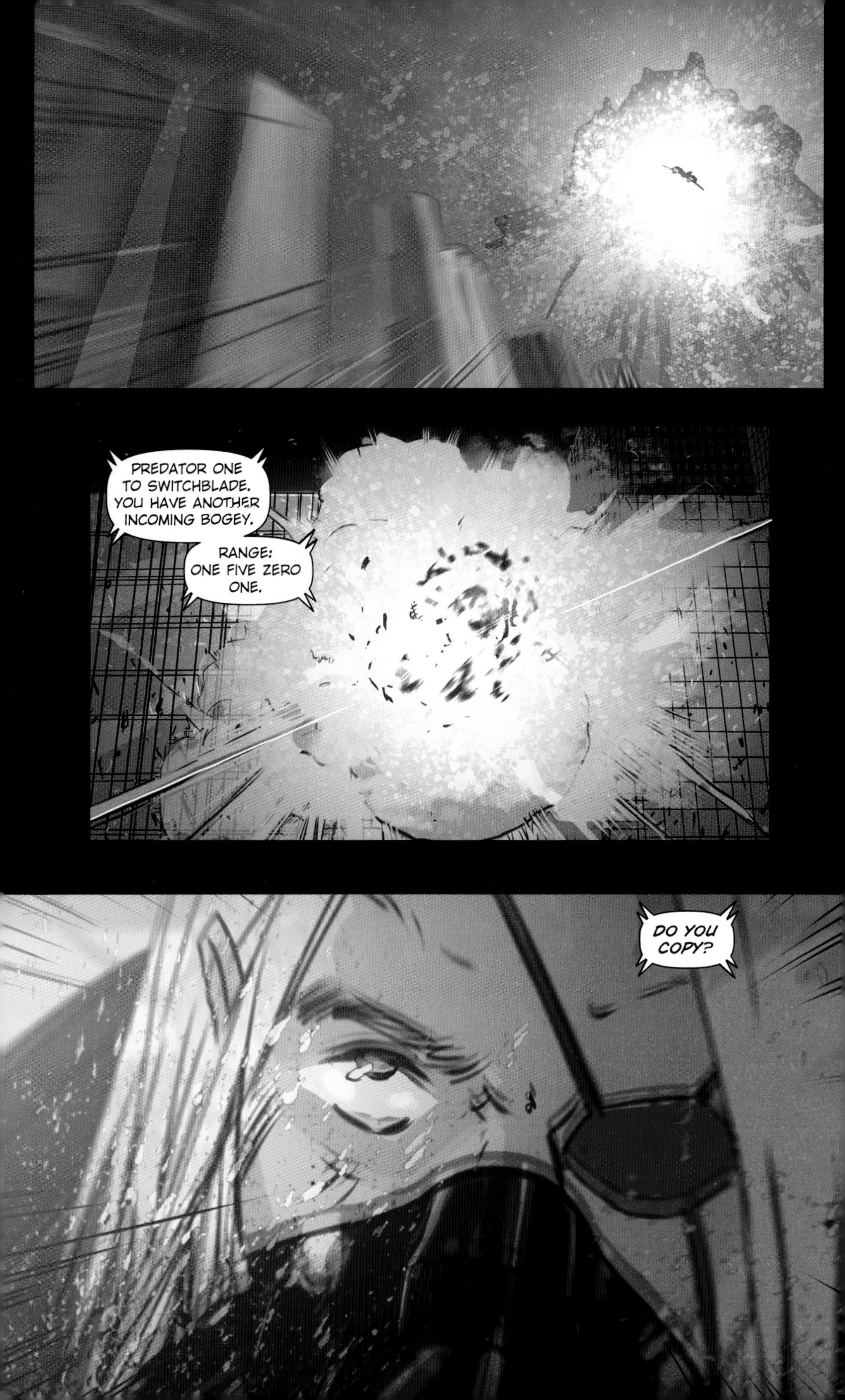
PREDATOR ONE TO SWITCHBLADE. YOU HAVE ANOTHER INCOMING BOGEY.
RANGE: ONE FIVE ZERO ONE.
DO YOU COPY?

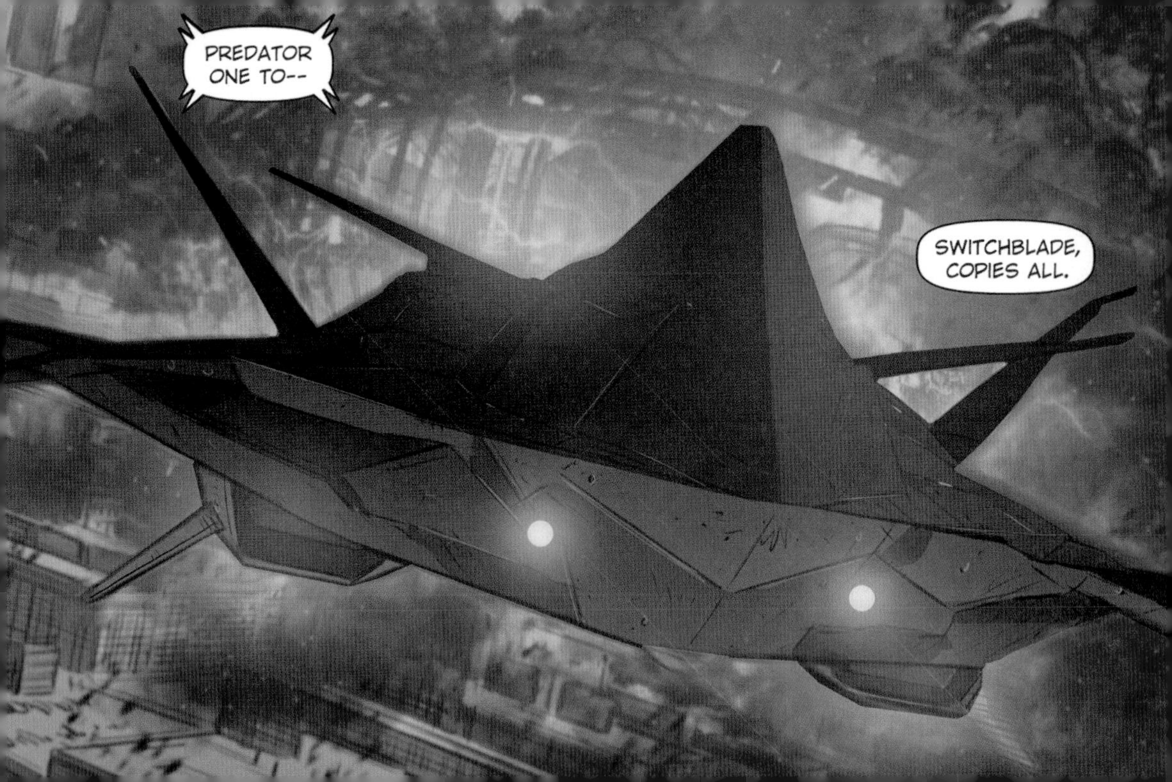
PREDATOR ONE TO--
SWITCHBLADE, COPIES ALL.

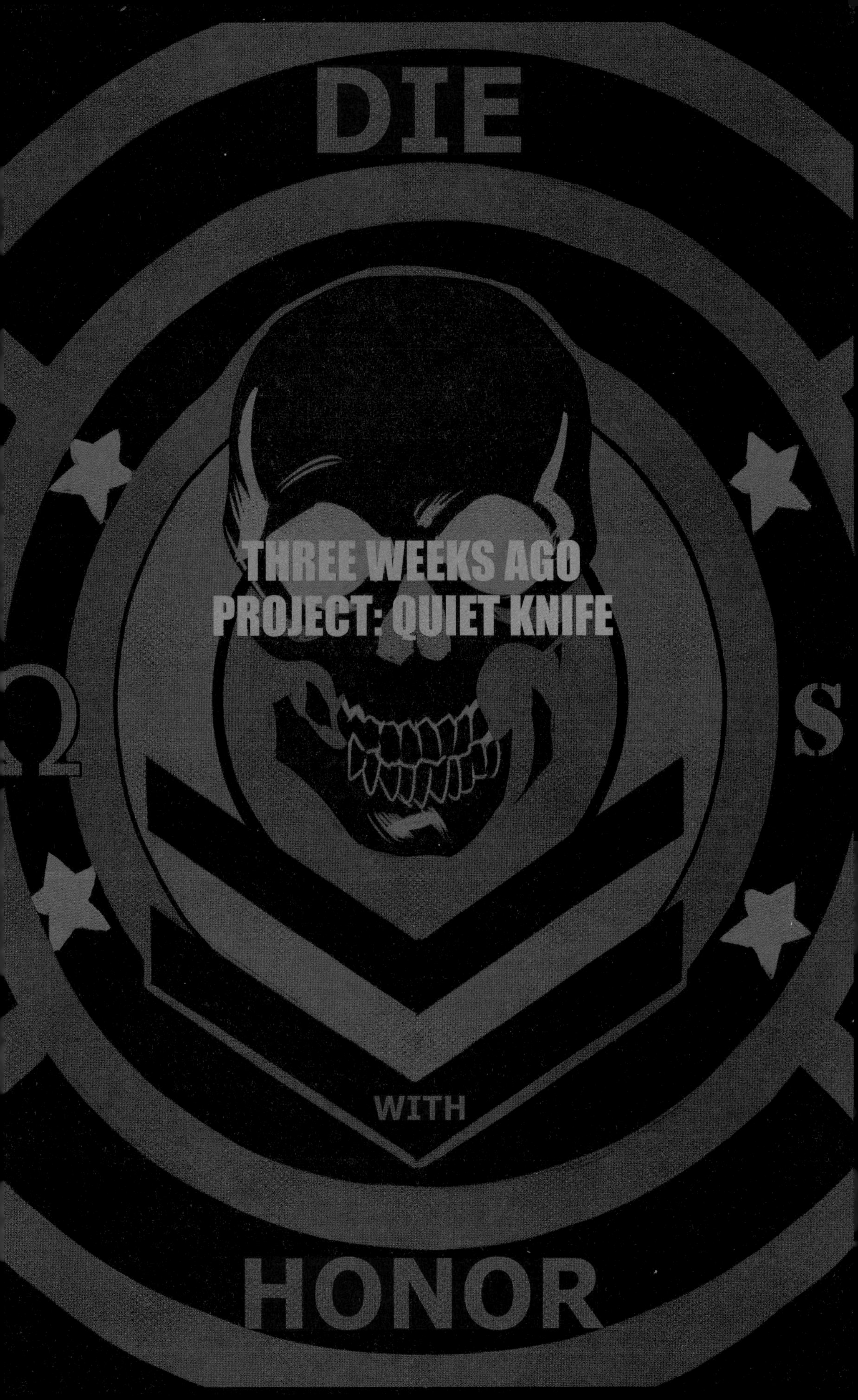
DIE
THREE WEEKS AGO
PROJECT: QUIET KNIFE
Ω
S
WITH
HONOR

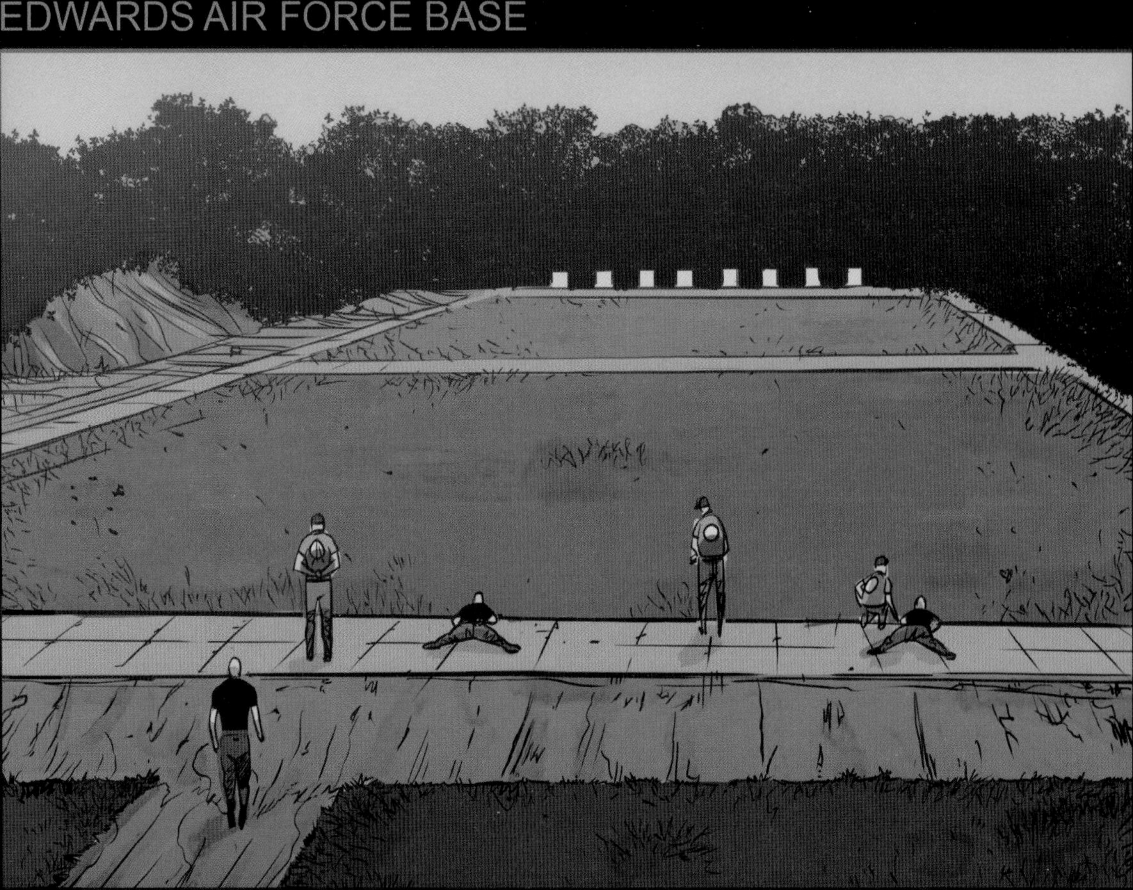
EDWARDS AIR FORCE BASE

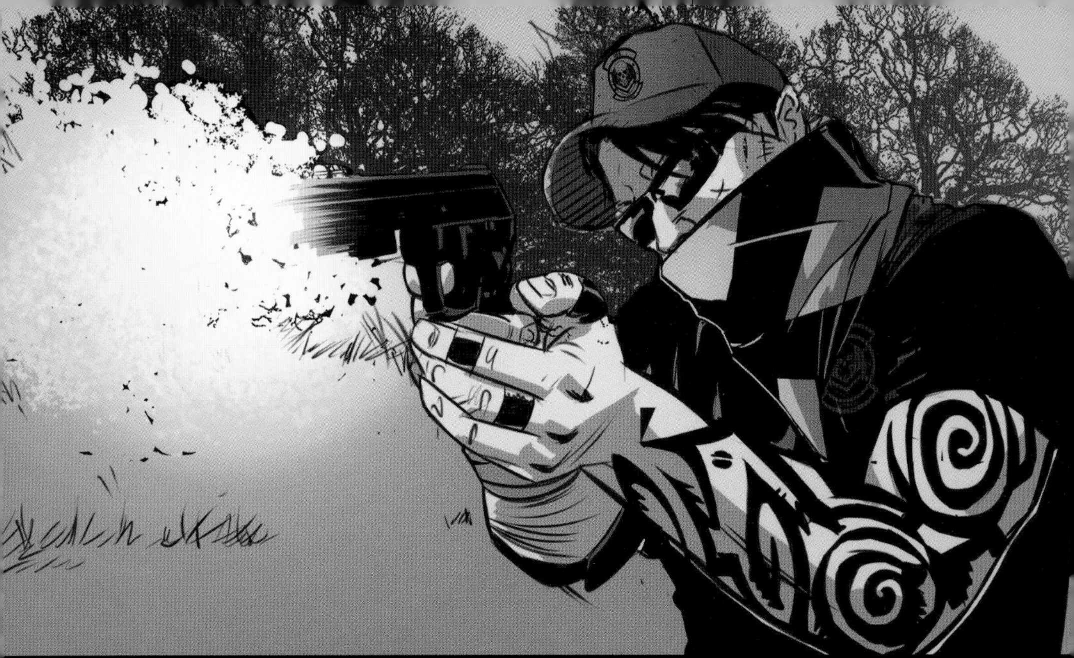

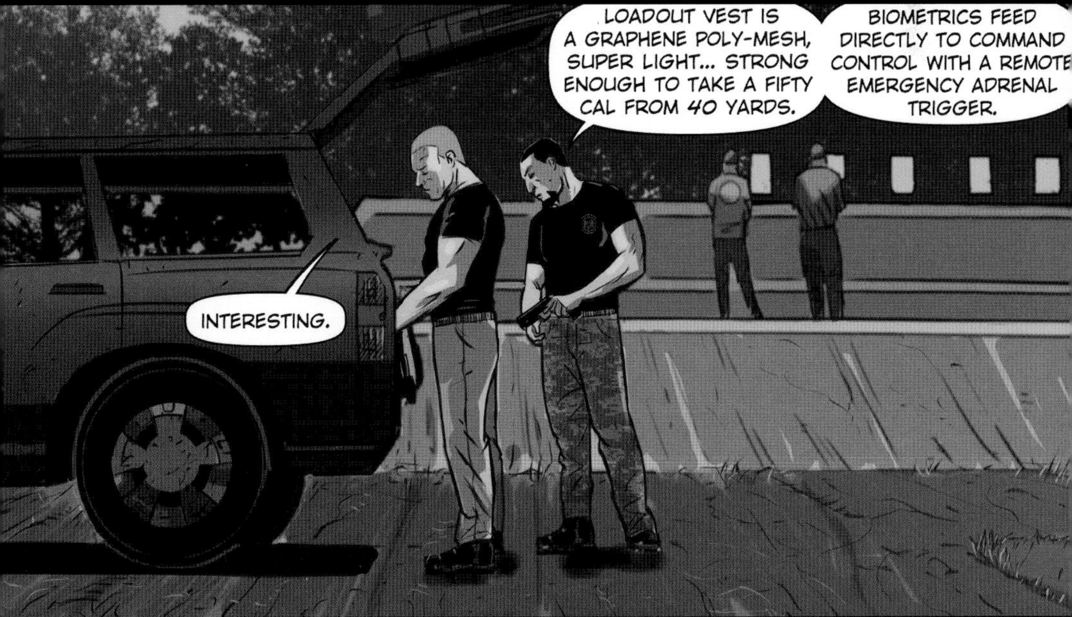
LOADOUT VEST IS A GRAPHENE POLY-MESH, SUPER LIGHT... STRONG ENOUGH TO TAKE A FIFTY CAL FROM 40 YARDS.
BIOMETRICS FEED DIRECTLY TO COMMAND CONTROL WITH A REMOTE EMERGENCY ADRENAL TRIGGER.
INTERESTING.

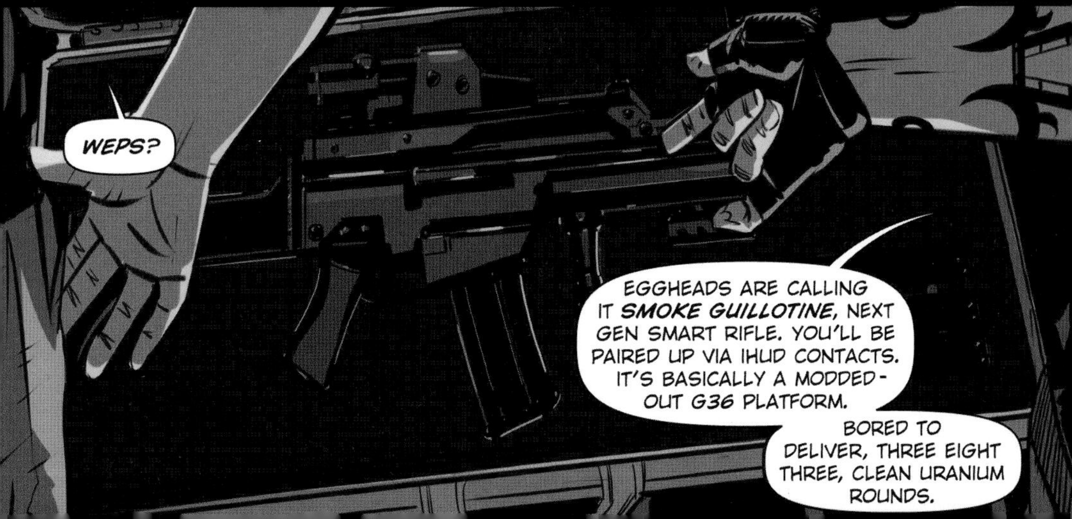
WEPS?
EGGHEADS ARE CALLING IT SMOKE GUILLOTINE, NEXT GEN SMART RIFLE. YOU'LL BE PAIRED UP VIA IHUD CONTACTS. IT'S BASICALLY A MODDED-OUT G36 PLATFORM.
BORED TO DELIVER, THREE EIGHT THREE, CLEAN URANIUM ROUNDS.

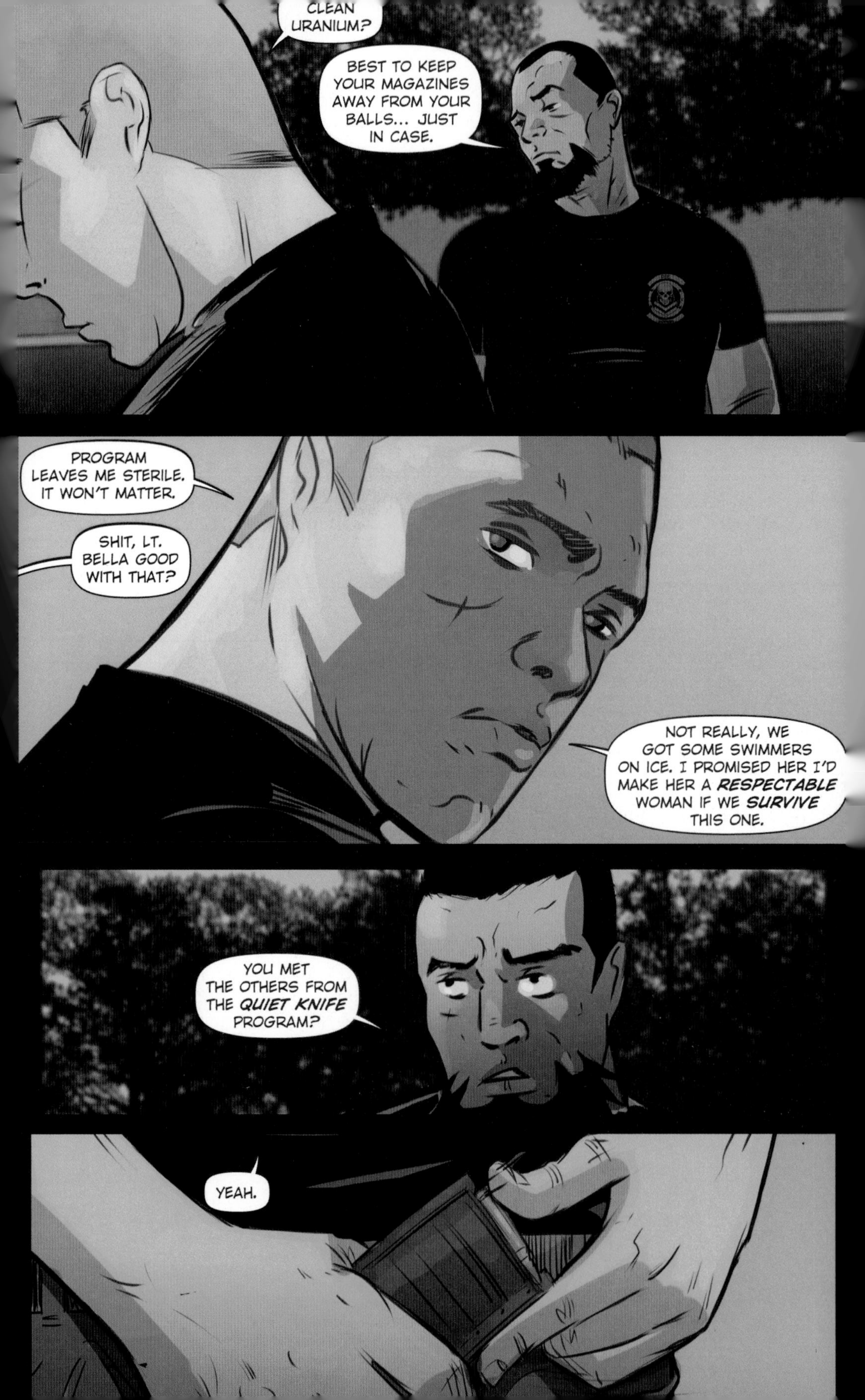
CLEAN URANIUM?
BEST TO KEEP YOUR MAGAZINES AWAY FROM YOUR BALLS... JUST IN CASE.
PROGRAM LEAVES ME STERILE. IT WON'T MATTER.
SHIT, LT. BELLA GOOD WITH THAT?
NOT REALLY, WE GOT SOME SWIMMERS ON ICE. I PROMISED HER I'D MAKE HER A *RESPECTABLE* WOMAN IF WE *SURVIVE* THIS ONE.
YOU MET THE OTHERS FROM THE *QUIET KNIFE* PROGRAM?
YEAH.

ONLY FOUR OF US MADE IT THROUGH. ETHIOPIAN HEAVY WEAPONS FROM THE IDF, PAIRED TO A MOBILE TARGETING PLATFORM CALLED ***JACKKNIFE***.

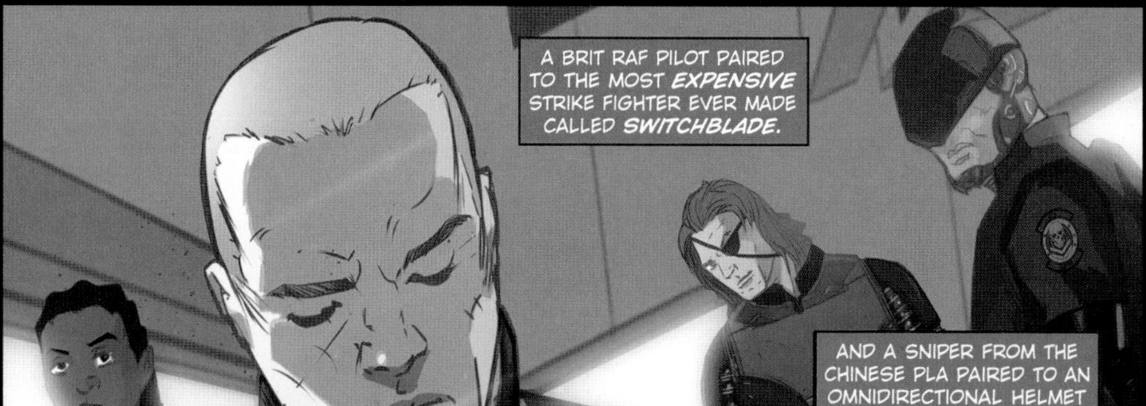
A BRIT RAF PILOT PAIRED TO THE MOST EXPENSIVE STRIKE FIGHTER EVER MADE CALLED SWITCHBLADE.
DIE
HONOR
AND A SNIPER FROM THE CHINESE PLA PAIRED TO AN OMNIDIRECTIONAL HELMET CALLED SILENT SEA.

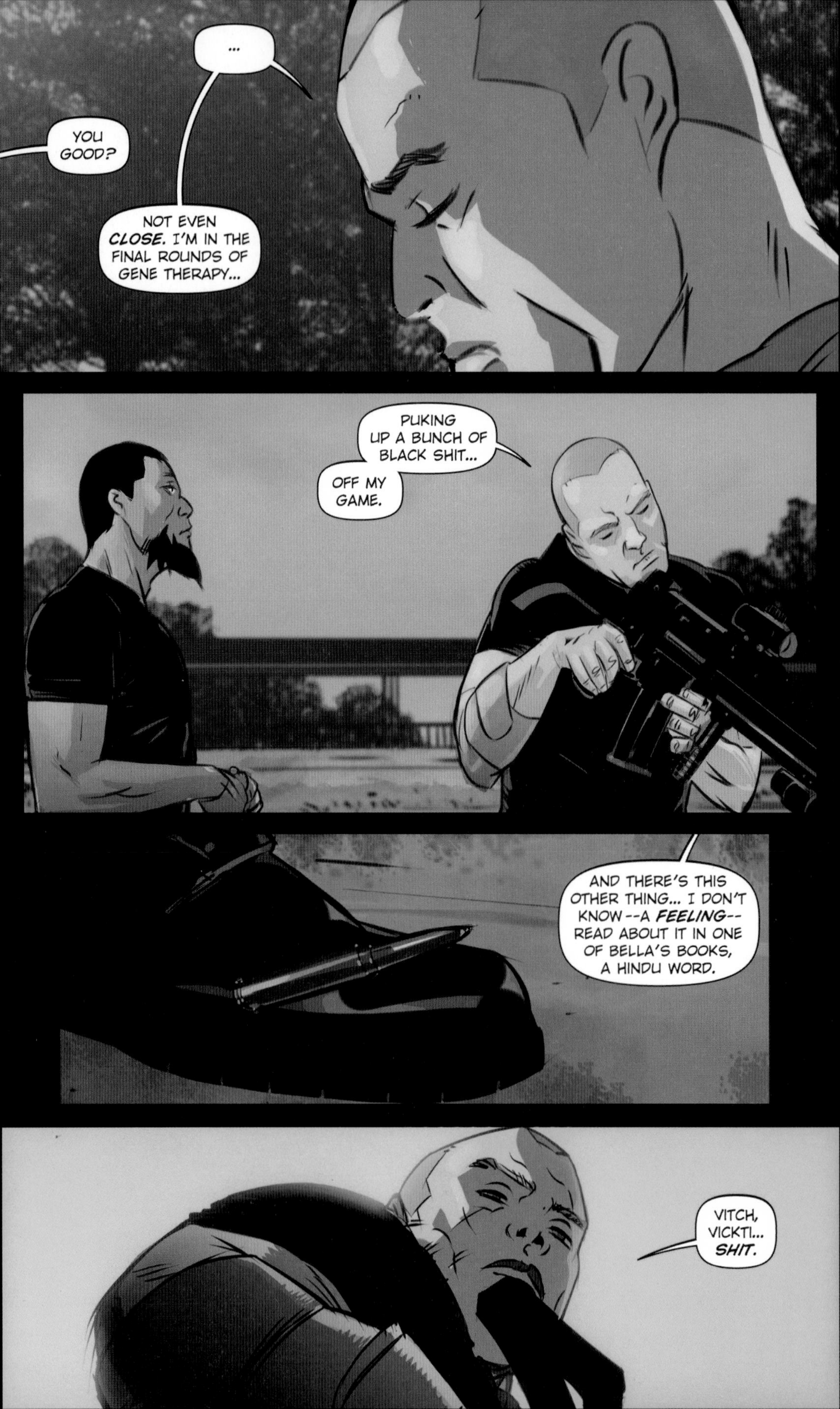
...
YOU GOOD?
NOT EVEN CLOSE. I'M IN THE FINAL ROUNDS OF GENE THERAPY...
PUKING UP A BUNCH OF BLACK SHIT...
OFF MY GAME.
AND THERE'S THIS OTHER THING... I DON'T KNOW--A FEELING--READ ABOUT IT IN ONE OF BELLA'S BOOKS, A HINDU WORD.
VITCH, VICKTI... SHIT.

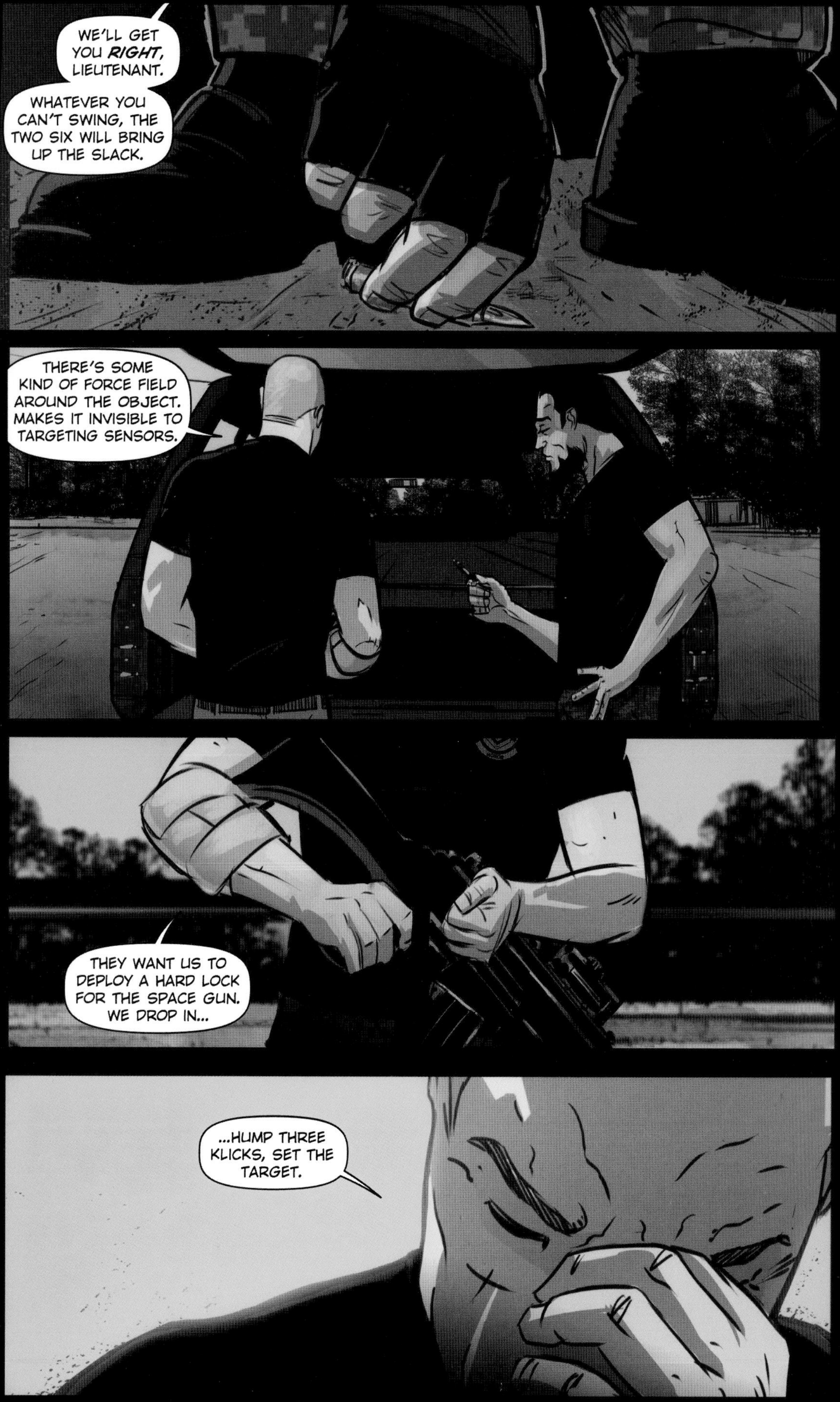
WE'LL GET YOU ***RIGHT***, LIEUTENANT.
WHATEVER YOU CAN'T SWING, THE TWO SIX WILL BRING UP THE SLACK.
THERE'S SOME KIND OF FORCE FIELD AROUND THE OBJECT. MAKES IT INVISIBLE TO TARGETING SENSORS.
THEY WANT US TO DEPLOY A HARD LOCK FOR THE SPACE GUN. WE DROP IN...
...HUMP THREE KLICKS, SET THE TARGET.

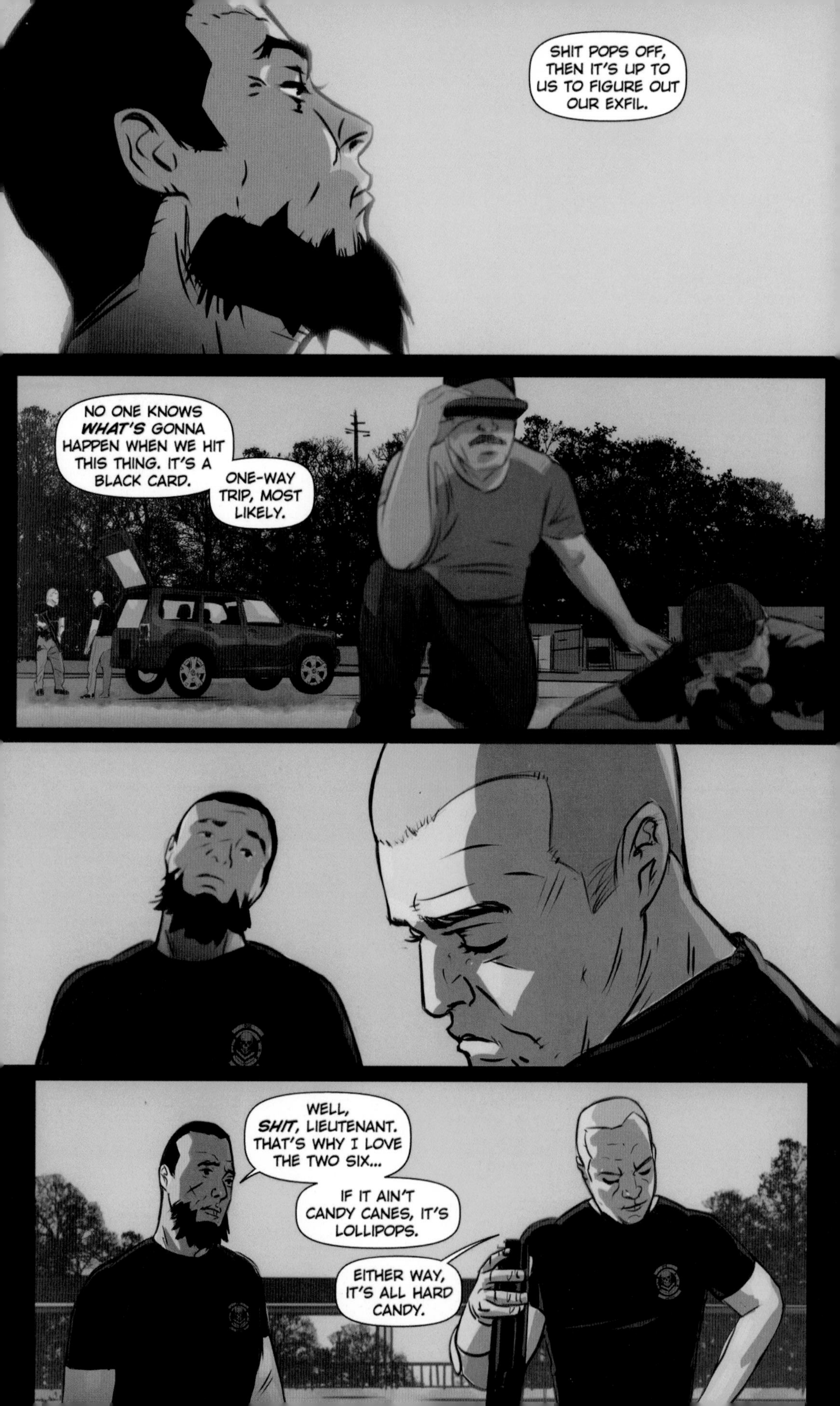
SHIT POPS OFF, THEN IT'S UP TO US TO FIGURE OUT OUR EXFIL.
NO ONE KNOWS *WHAT'S* GONNA HAPPEN WHEN WE HIT THIS THING. IT'S A BLACK CARD.
ONE-WAY TRIP, MOST LIKELY.
WELL, *SHIT*, LIEUTENANT. THAT'S WHY I LOVE THE TWO SIX...
IF IT AIN'T CANDY CANES, IT'S LOLLIPOPS.
EITHER WAY, IT'S ALL HARD CANDY.

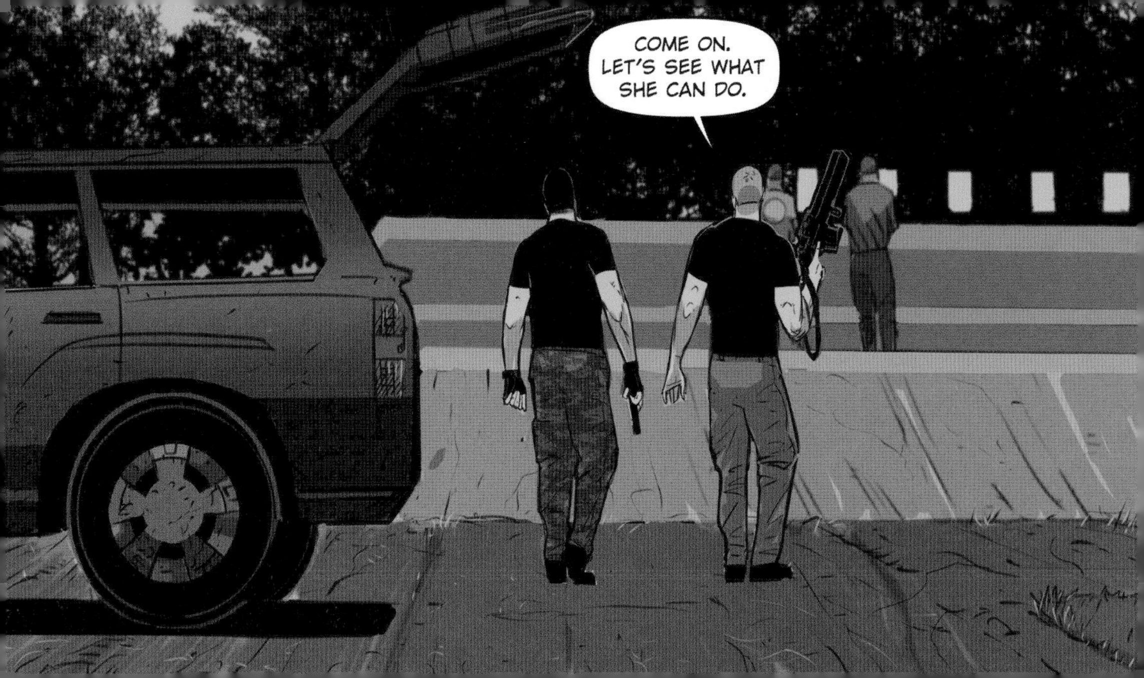
COME ON. LET'S SEE WHAT SHE CAN DO.

OPERATION: ALL WEATHER
GLADIATOR TWO SIX

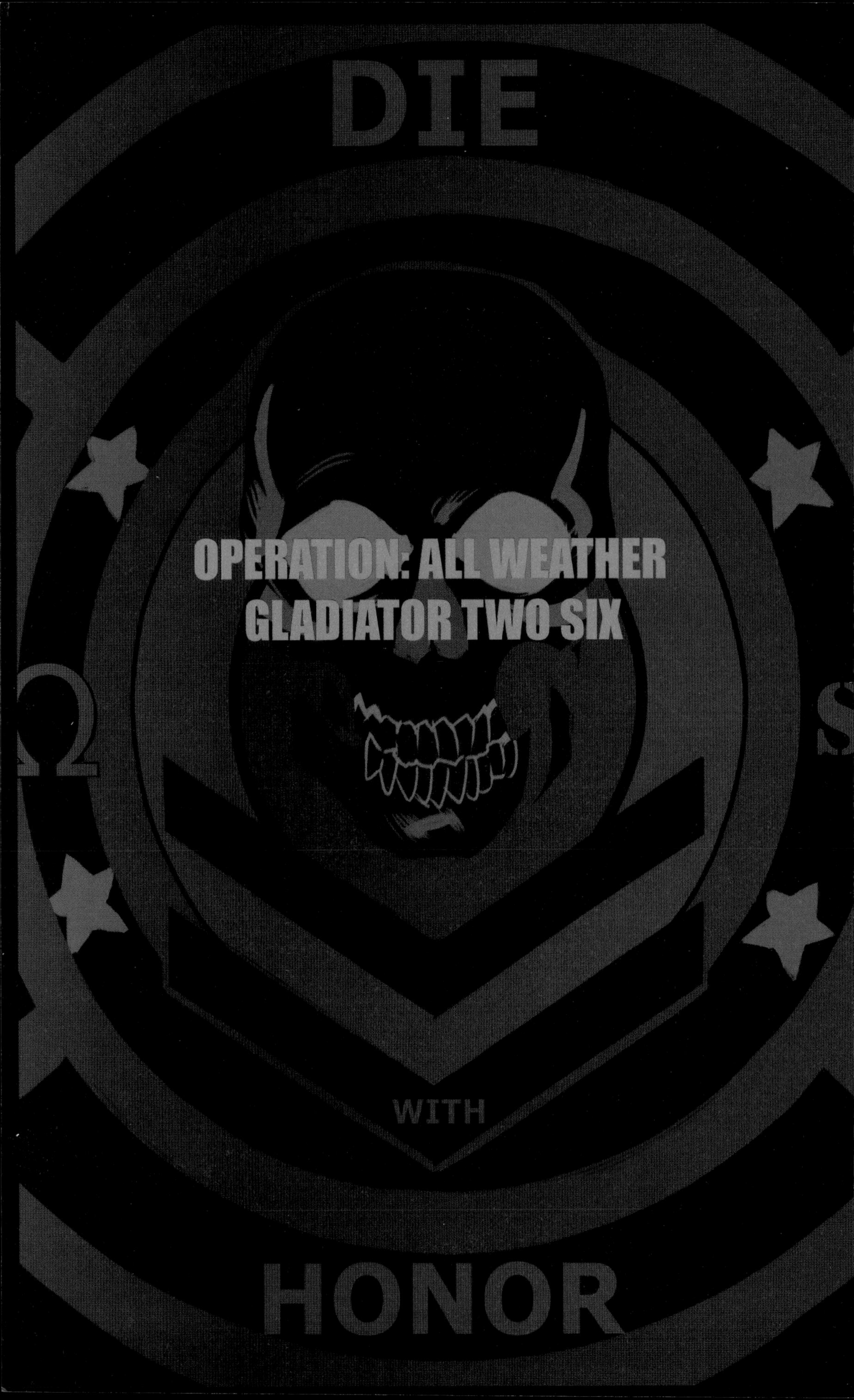
DIE
WITH
HONOR

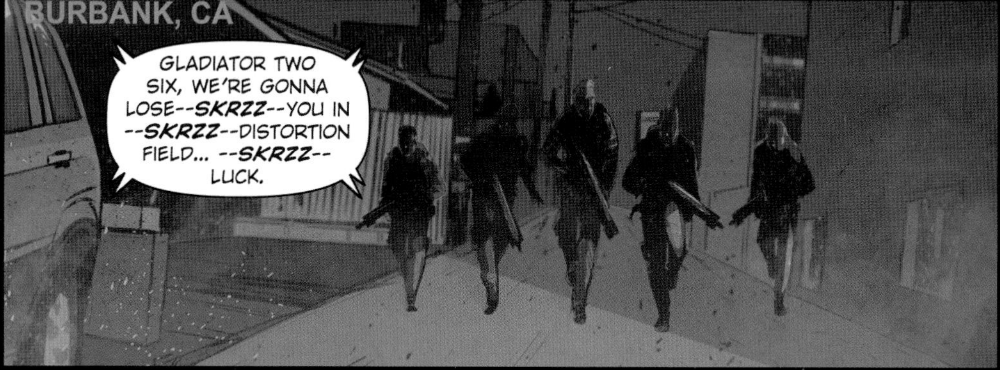
BURBANK, CA
GLADIATOR TWO SIX, WE'RE GONNA LOSE--SKRZZ--YOU IN --SKRZZ--DISTORTION FIELD... --SKRZZ-- LUCK.

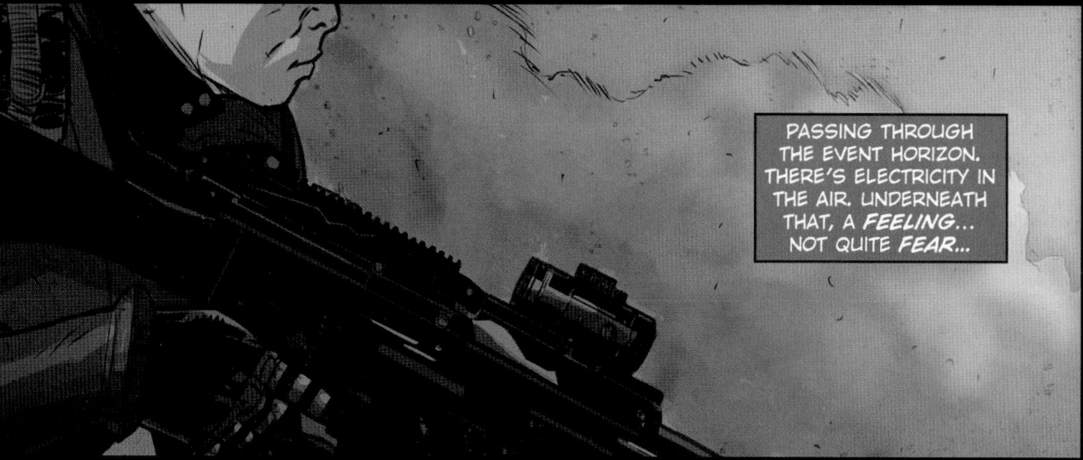
PASSING THROUGH THE EVENT HORIZON. THERE'S ELECTRICITY IN THE AIR. UNDERNEATH THAT, A FEELING... NOT QUITE FEAR...

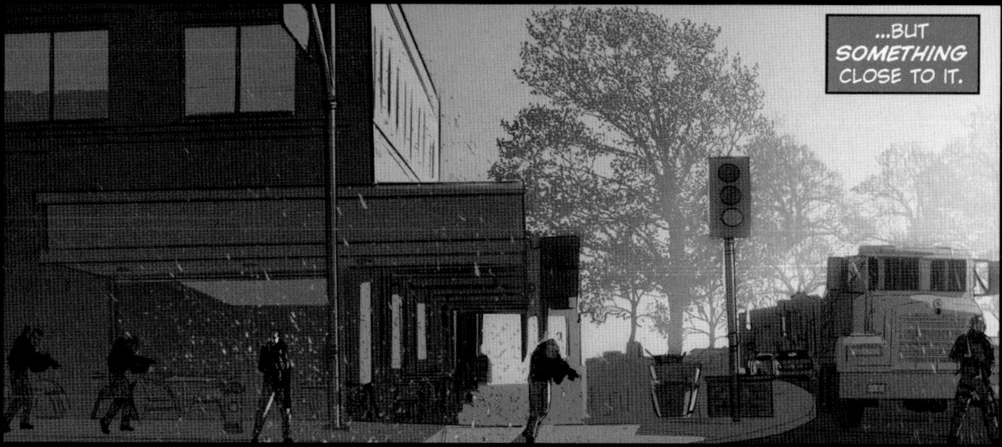
...BUT SOMETHING CLOSE TO IT.

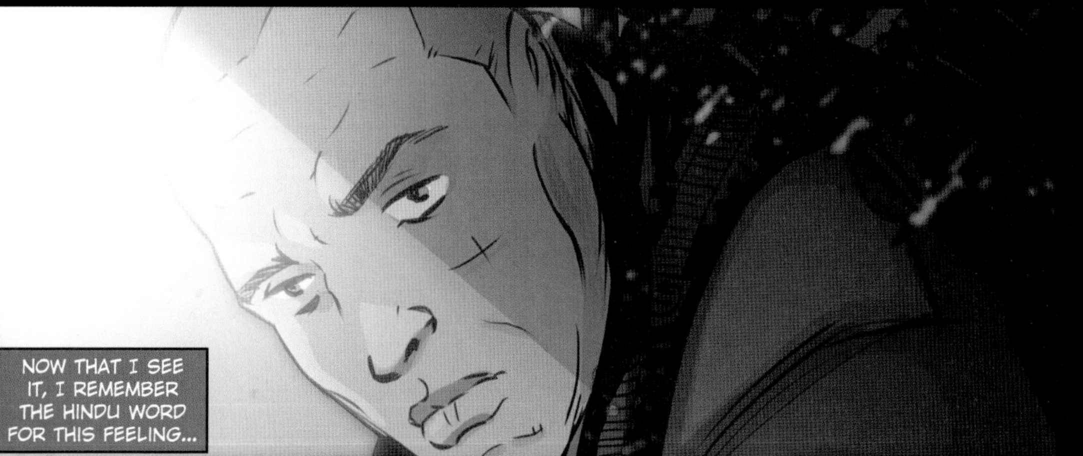
NOW THAT I SEE IT, I REMEMBER THE HINDU WORD FOR THIS FEELING...

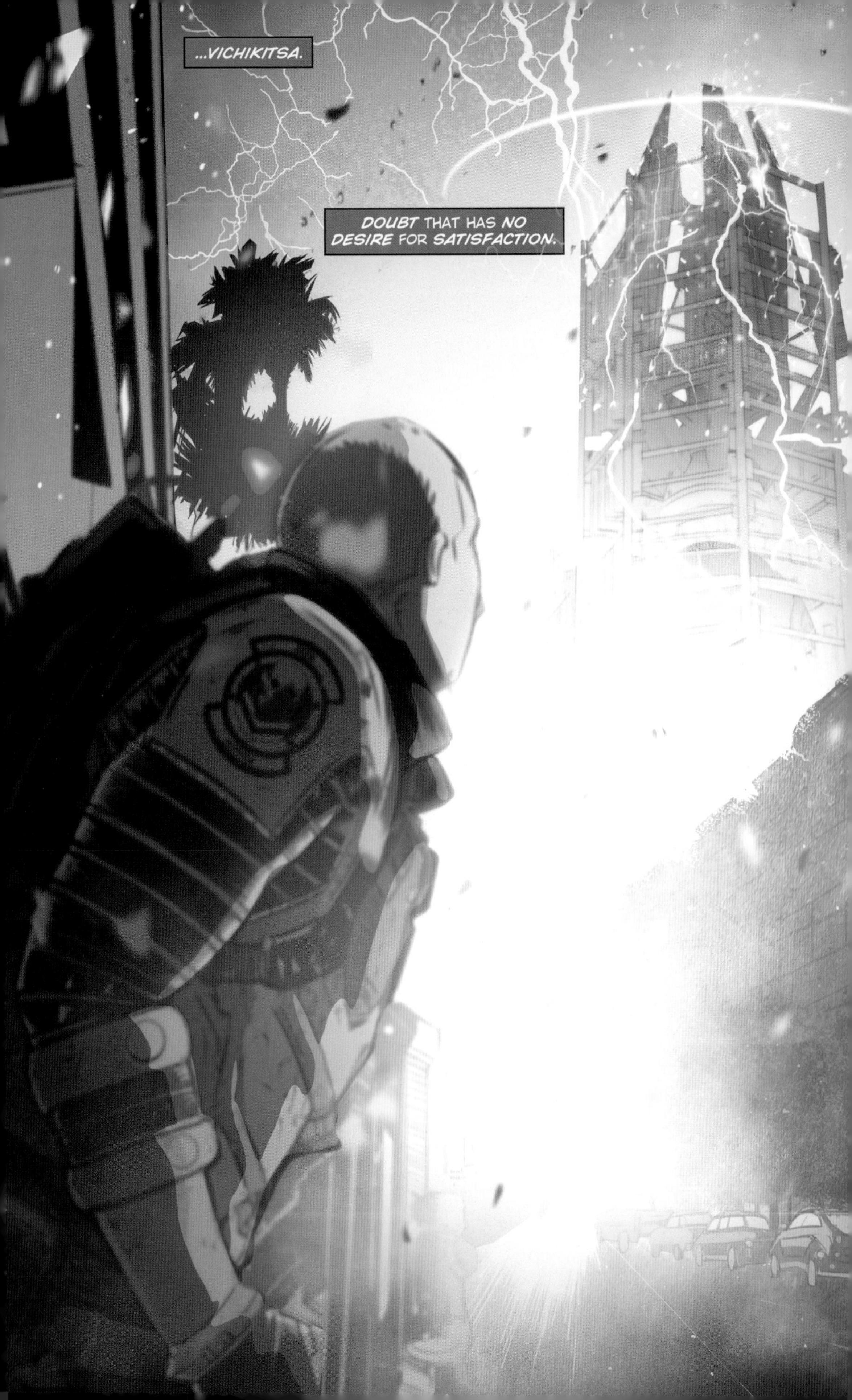
...VICHIKITSA.
DOUBT THAT HAS NO DESIRE FOR SATISFACTION.

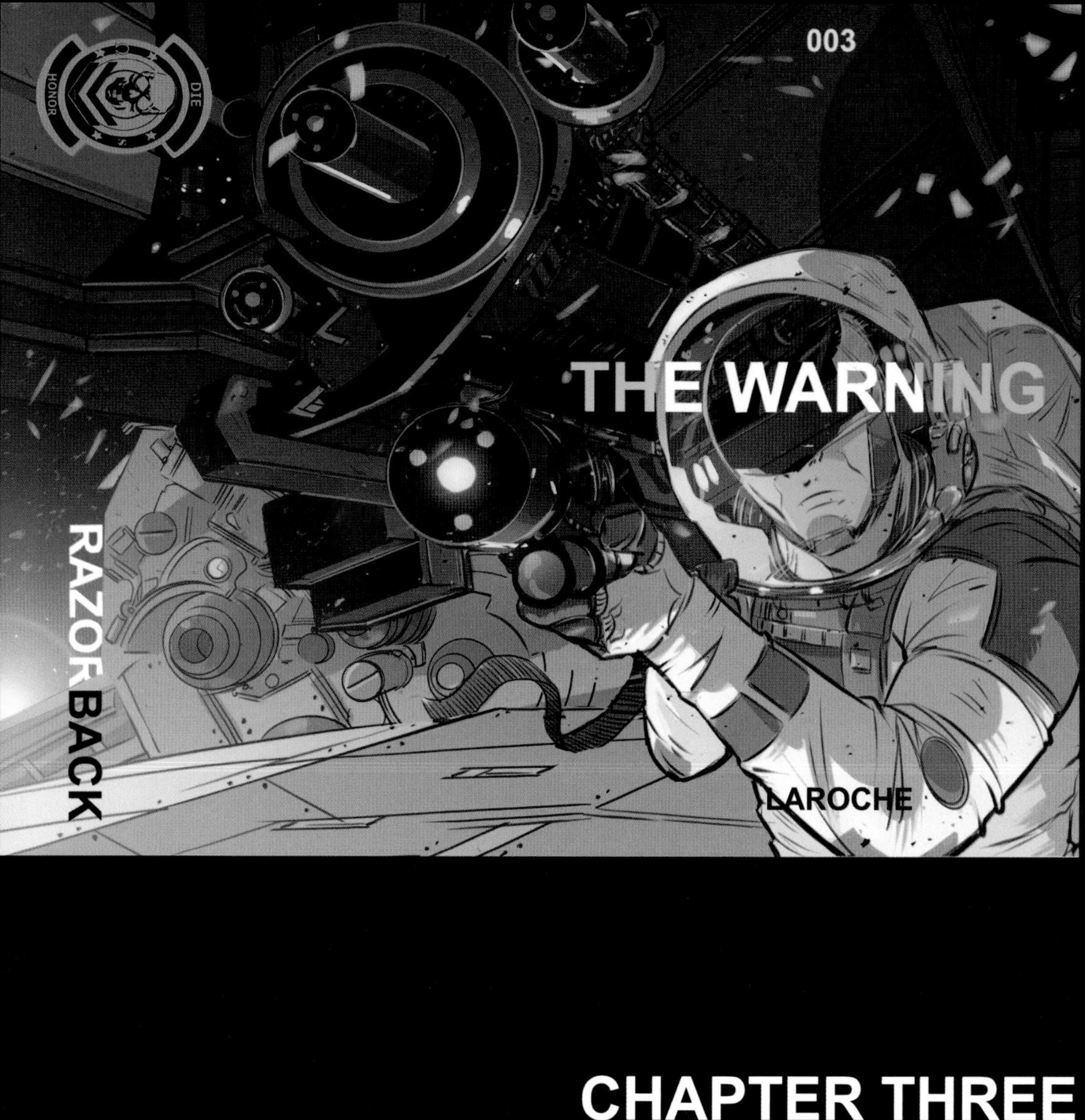
HONOR
DIE
003
THE WARNING
RAZORBACK
LAROCHE

CHAPTER THREE

003

RAZORBACK

OPERATION: ALL WEATHER
GLADIATOR TWO SIX

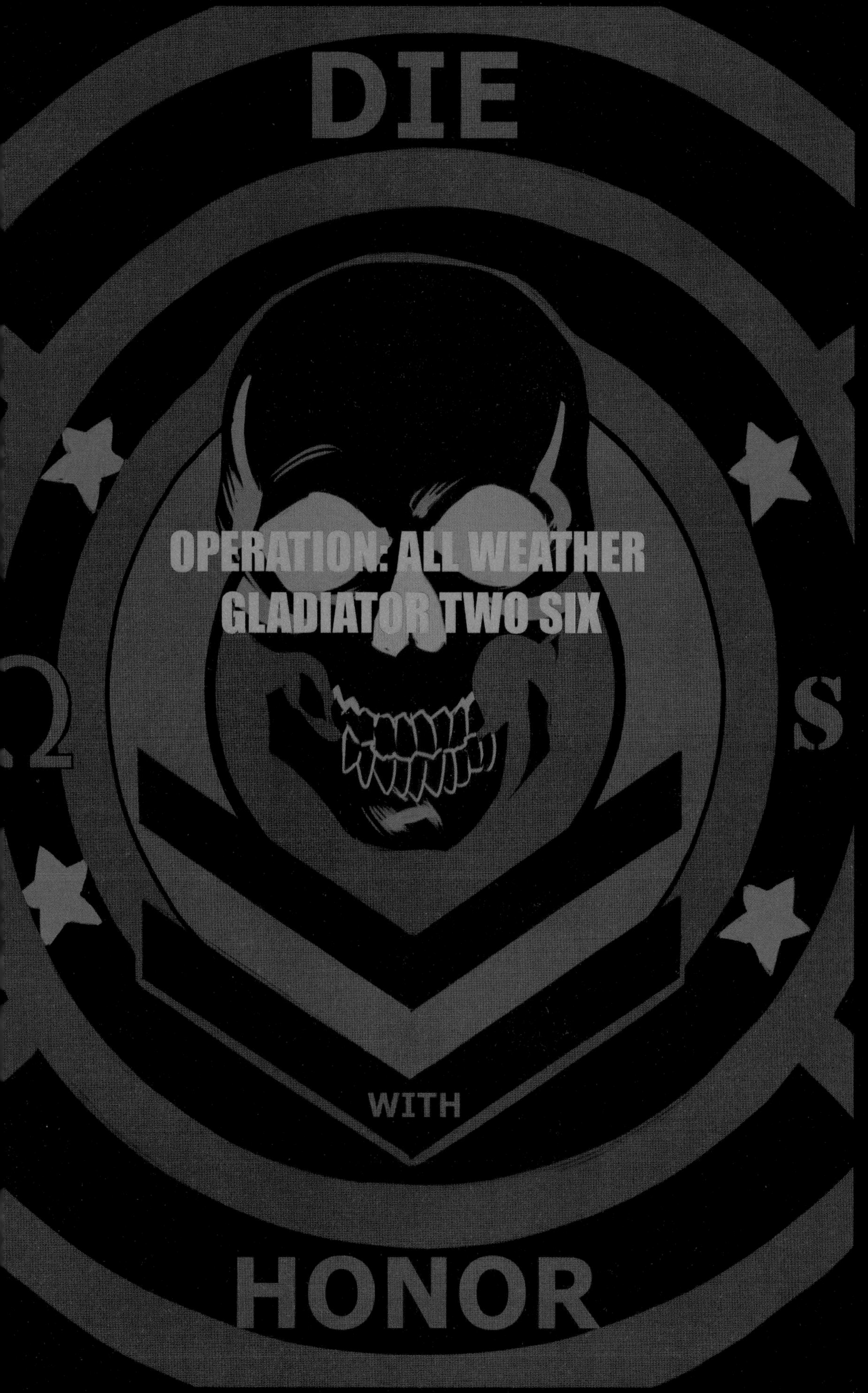
DIE
Ω
S
WITH
HONOR

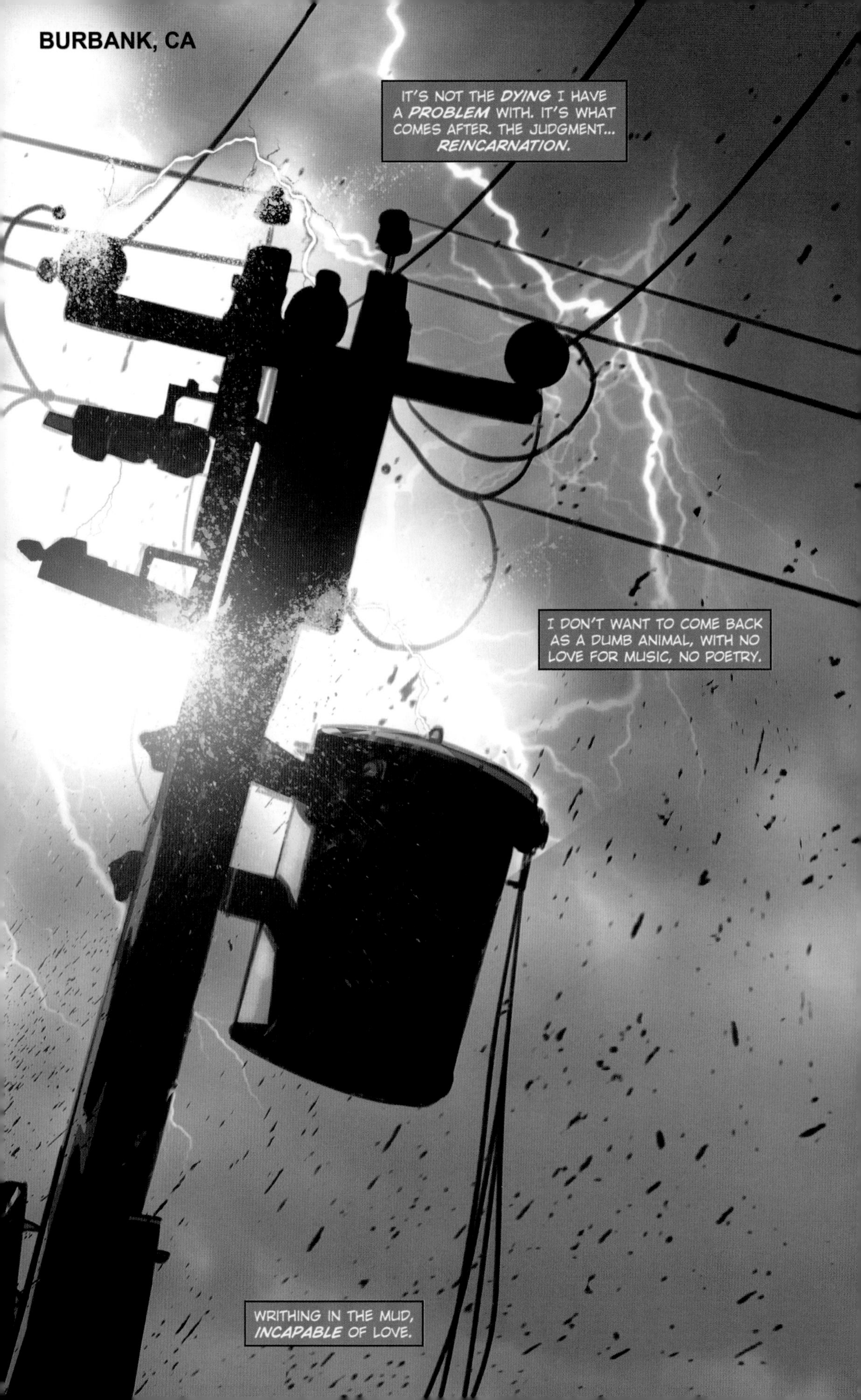
BURBANK, CA
IT'S NOT THE DYING I HAVE A PROBLEM WITH. IT'S WHAT COMES AFTER. THE JUDGMENT... REINCARNATION.
I DON'T WANT TO COME BACK AS A DUMB ANIMAL, WITH NO LOVE FOR MUSIC, NO POETRY.
WRITHING IN THE MUD, INCAPABLE OF LOVE.

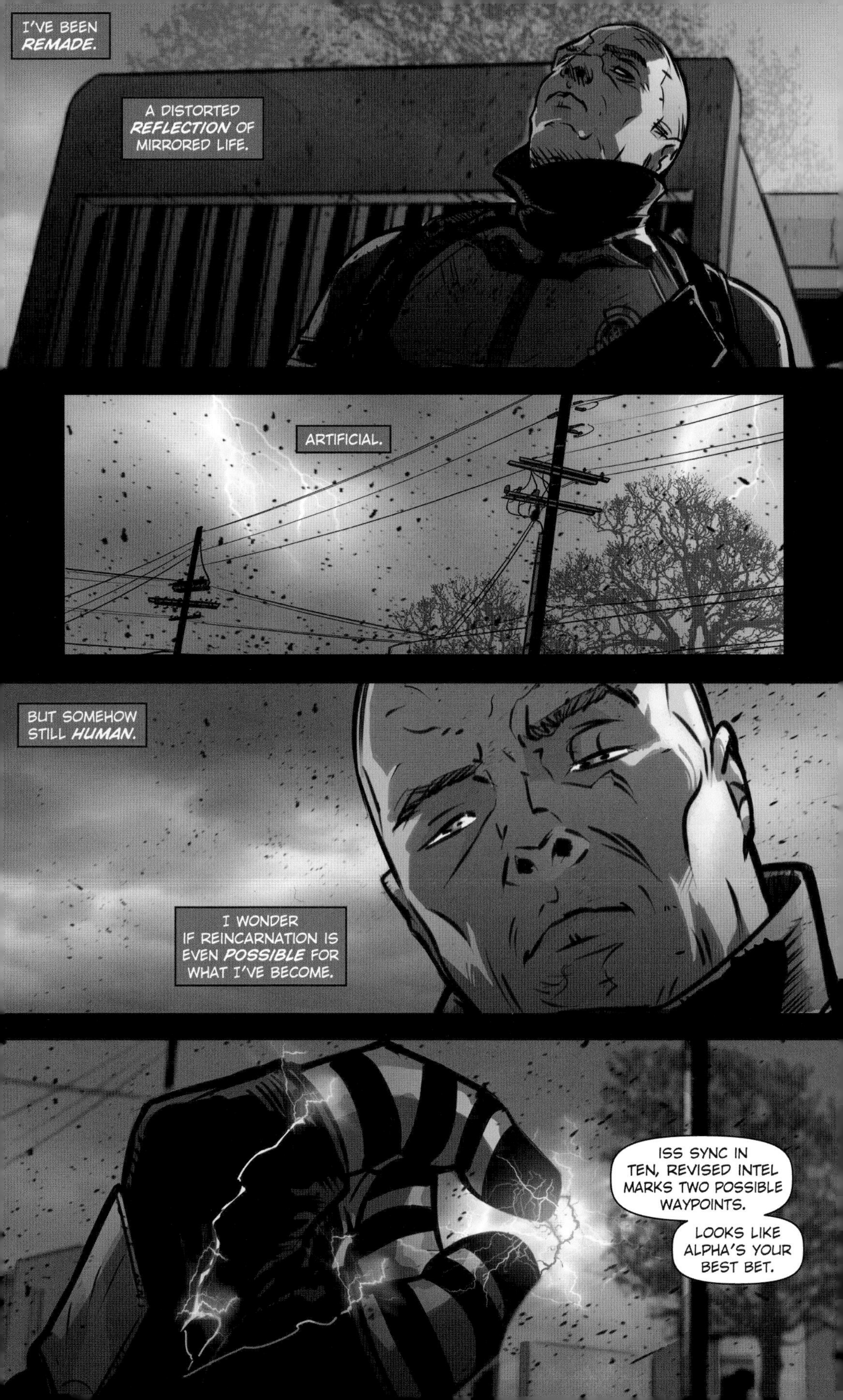
I'VE BEEN REMADE.
A DISTORTED REFLECTION OF MIRRORED LIFE.
ARTIFICIAL.
BUT SOMEHOW STILL HUMAN.
I WONDER IF REINCARNATION IS EVEN POSSIBLE FOR WHAT I'VE BECOME.
ISS SYNC IN TEN, REVISED INTEL MARKS TWO POSSIBLE WAYPOINTS.
LOOKS LIKE ALPHA'S YOUR BEST BET.

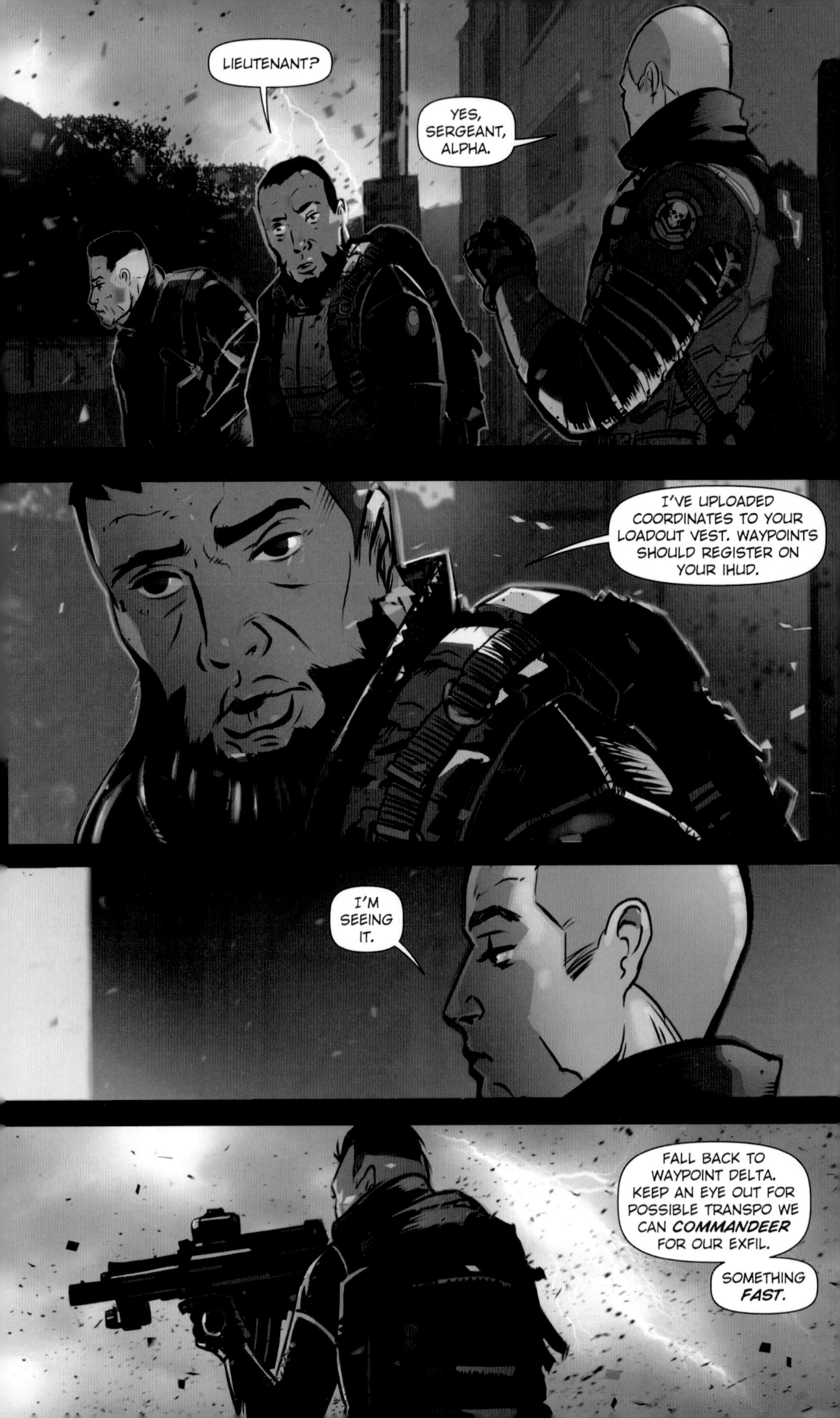
LIEUTENANT?
YES, SERGEANT, ALPHA.
I'VE UPLOADED COORDINATES TO YOUR LOADOUT VEST. WAYPOINTS SHOULD REGISTER ON YOUR IHUD.
I'M SEEING IT.
FALL BACK TO WAYPOINT DELTA. KEEP AN EYE OUT FOR POSSIBLE TRANSPO WE CAN *COMMANDEER* FOR OUR EXFIL.
SOMETHING *FAST*.

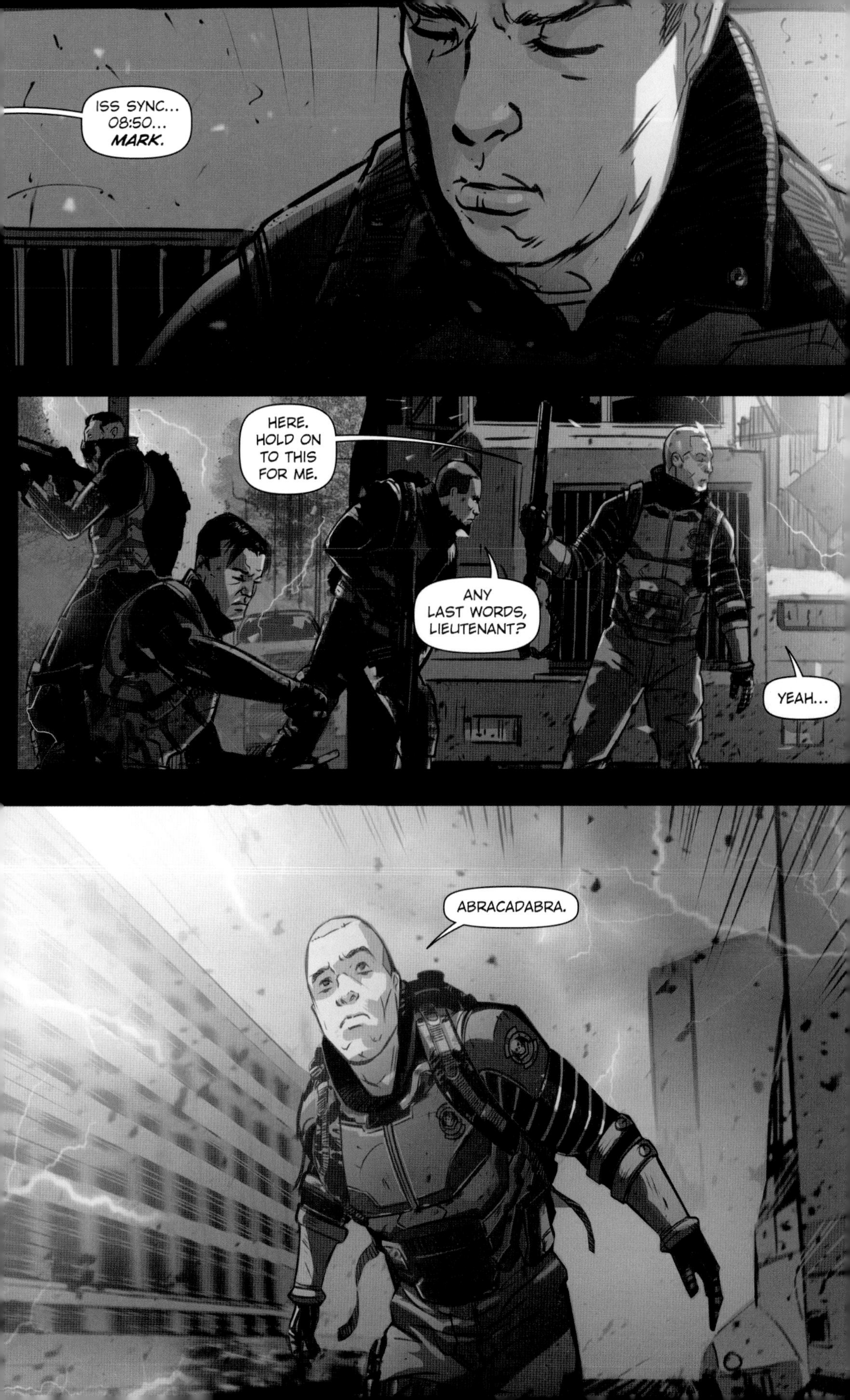
ISS SYNC... 08:50... MARK.
HERE. HOLD ON TO THIS FOR ME.
ANY LAST WORDS, LIEUTENANT?
YEAH...
ABRACADABRA.

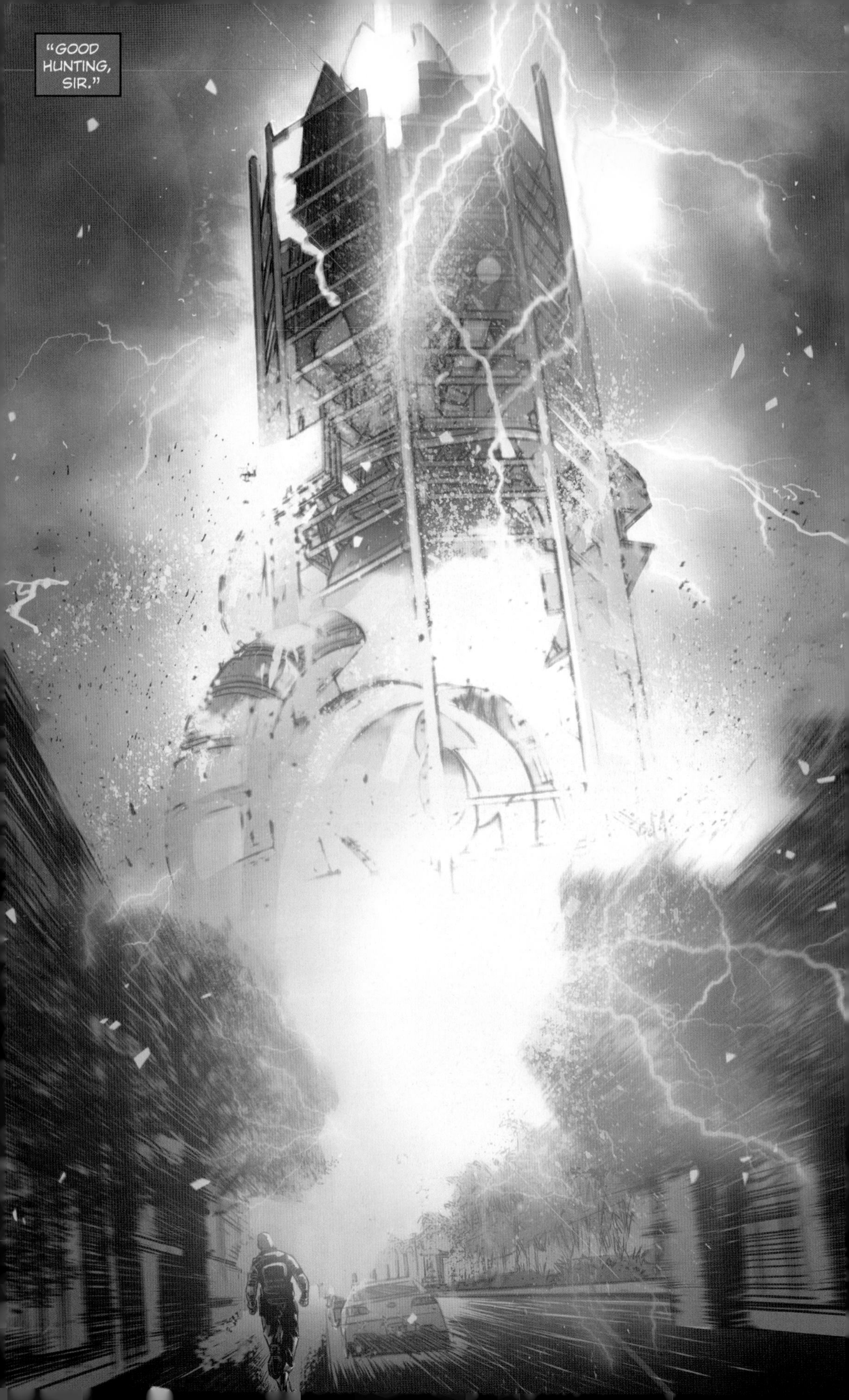
"GOOD HUNTING, SIR."

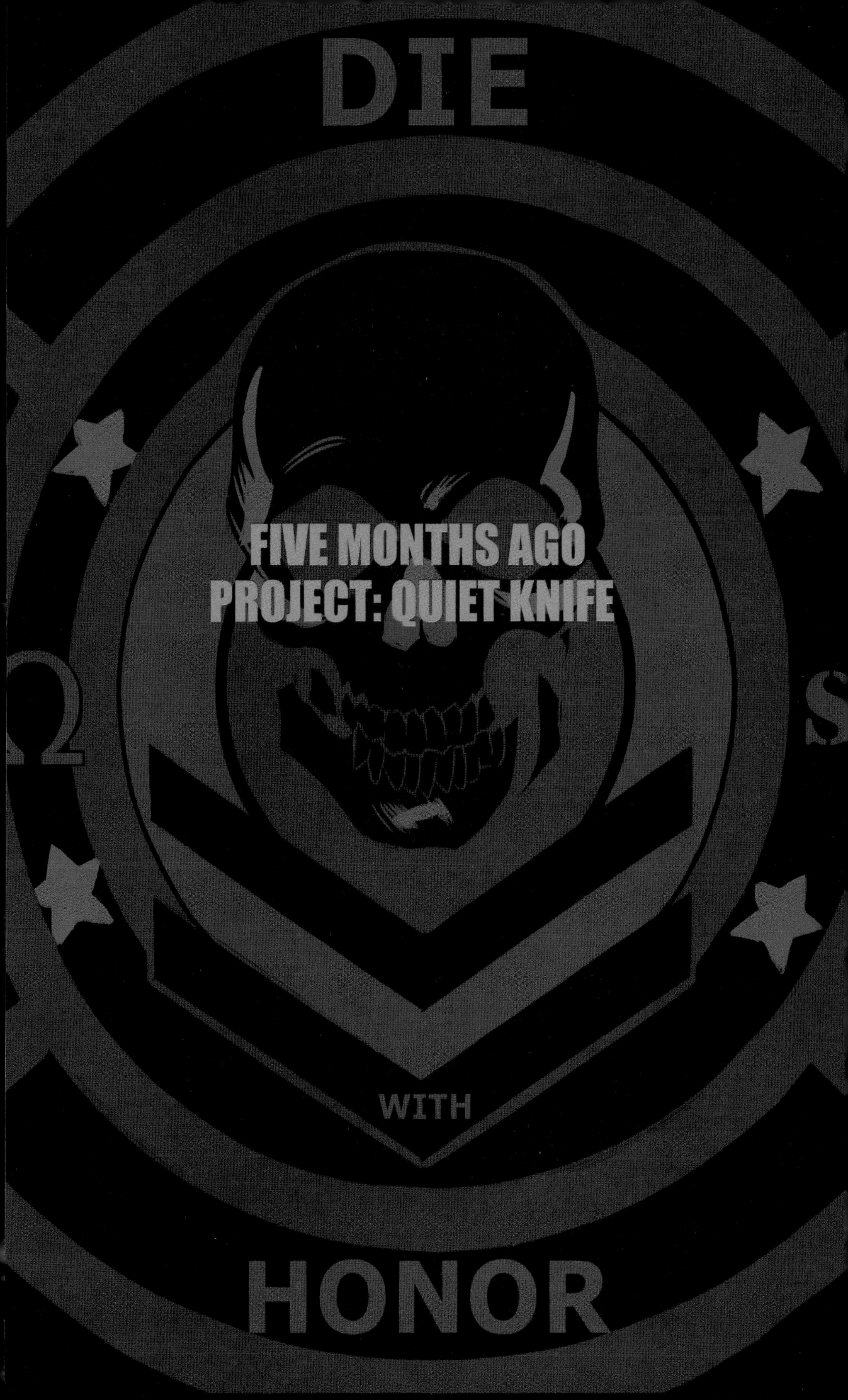
DIE
FIVE MONTHS AGO
PROJECT: QUIET KNIFE
WITH
HONOR

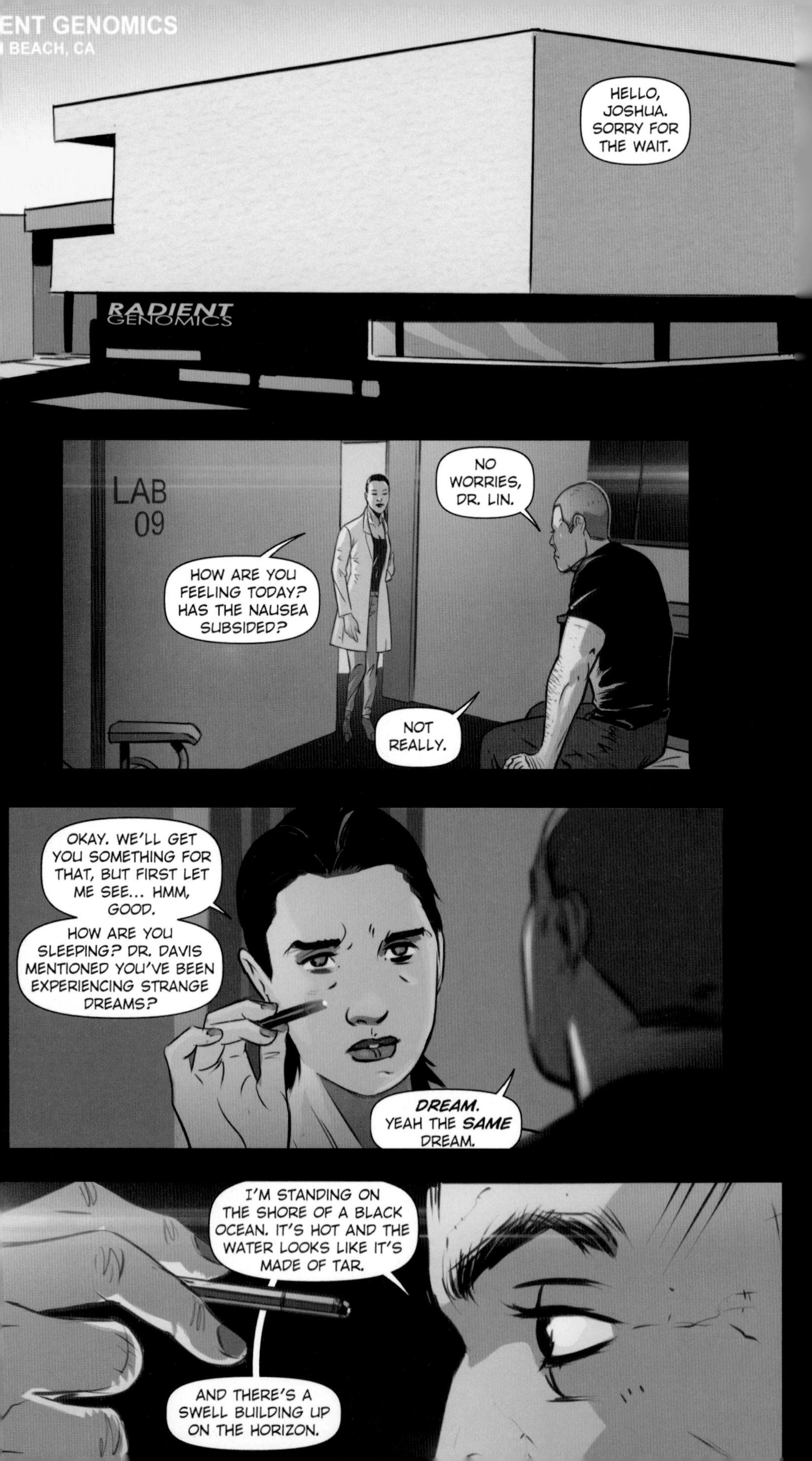
ENT GENOMICS
BEACH, CA
HELLO, JOSHUA. SORRY FOR THE WAIT.
RADIENT GENOMICS
LAB 09
NO WORRIES, DR. LIN.
HOW ARE YOU FEELING TODAY? HAS THE NAUSEA SUBSIDED?
NOT REALLY.
OKAY. WE'LL GET YOU SOMETHING FOR THAT, BUT FIRST LET ME SEE... HMM, GOOD.
HOW ARE YOU SLEEPING? DR. DAVIS MENTIONED YOU'VE BEEN EXPERIENCING STRANGE DREAMS?
DREAM. YEAH THE SAME DREAM.
I'M STANDING ON THE SHORE OF A BLACK OCEAN. IT'S HOT AND THE WATER LOOKS LIKE IT'S MADE OF TAR.
AND THERE'S A SWELL BUILDING UP ON THE HORIZON.

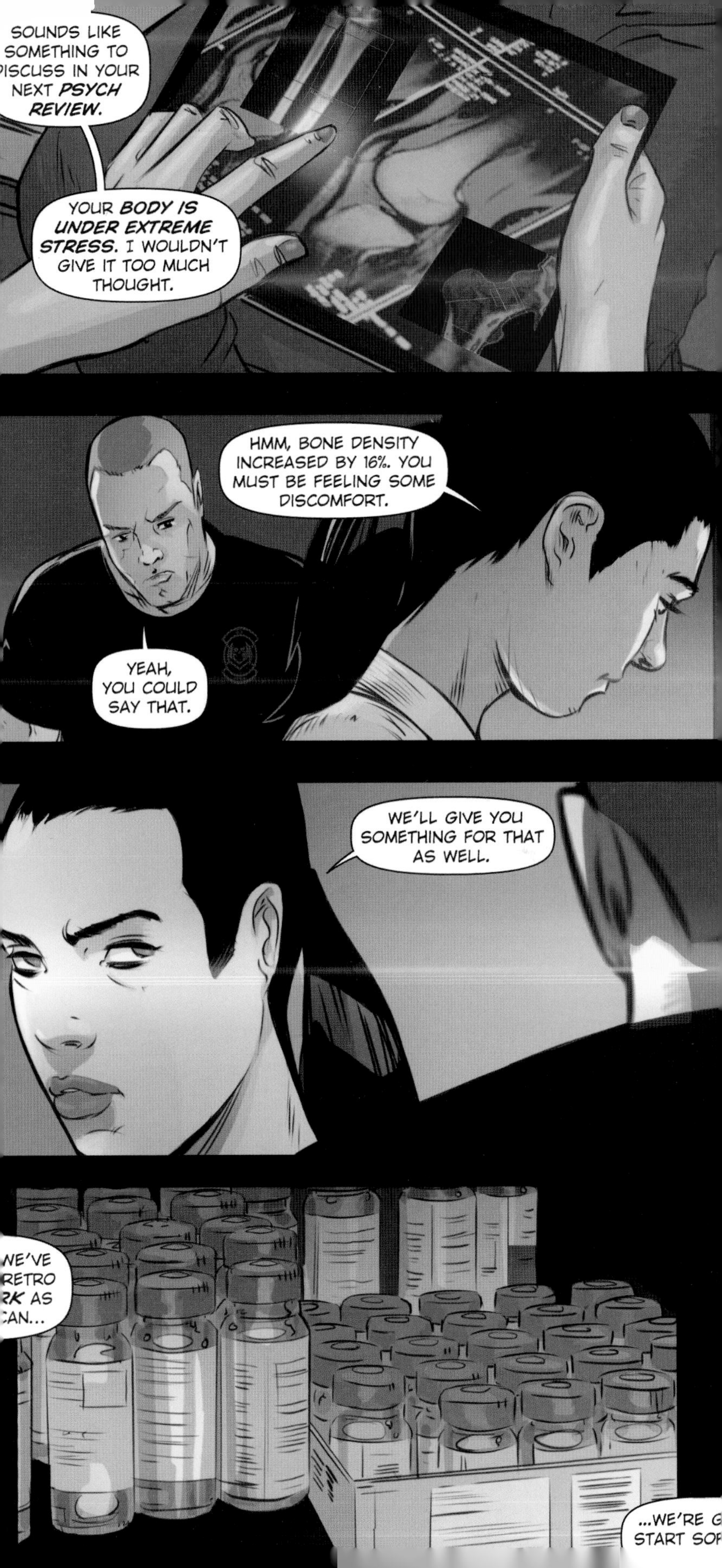
SOUNDS LIKE SOMETHING TO DISCUSS IN YOUR NEXT PSYCH REVIEW.
YOUR BODY IS UNDER EXTREME STRESS. I WOULDN'T GIVE IT TOO MUCH THOUGHT.
HMM, BONE DENSITY INCREASED BY 16%. YOU MUST BE FEELING SOME DISCOMFORT.
YEAH, YOU COULD SAY THAT.
WE'LL GIVE YOU SOMETHING FOR THAT AS WELL.
WE'VE RETRO RK AS CAN...
...WE'RE G START SOF

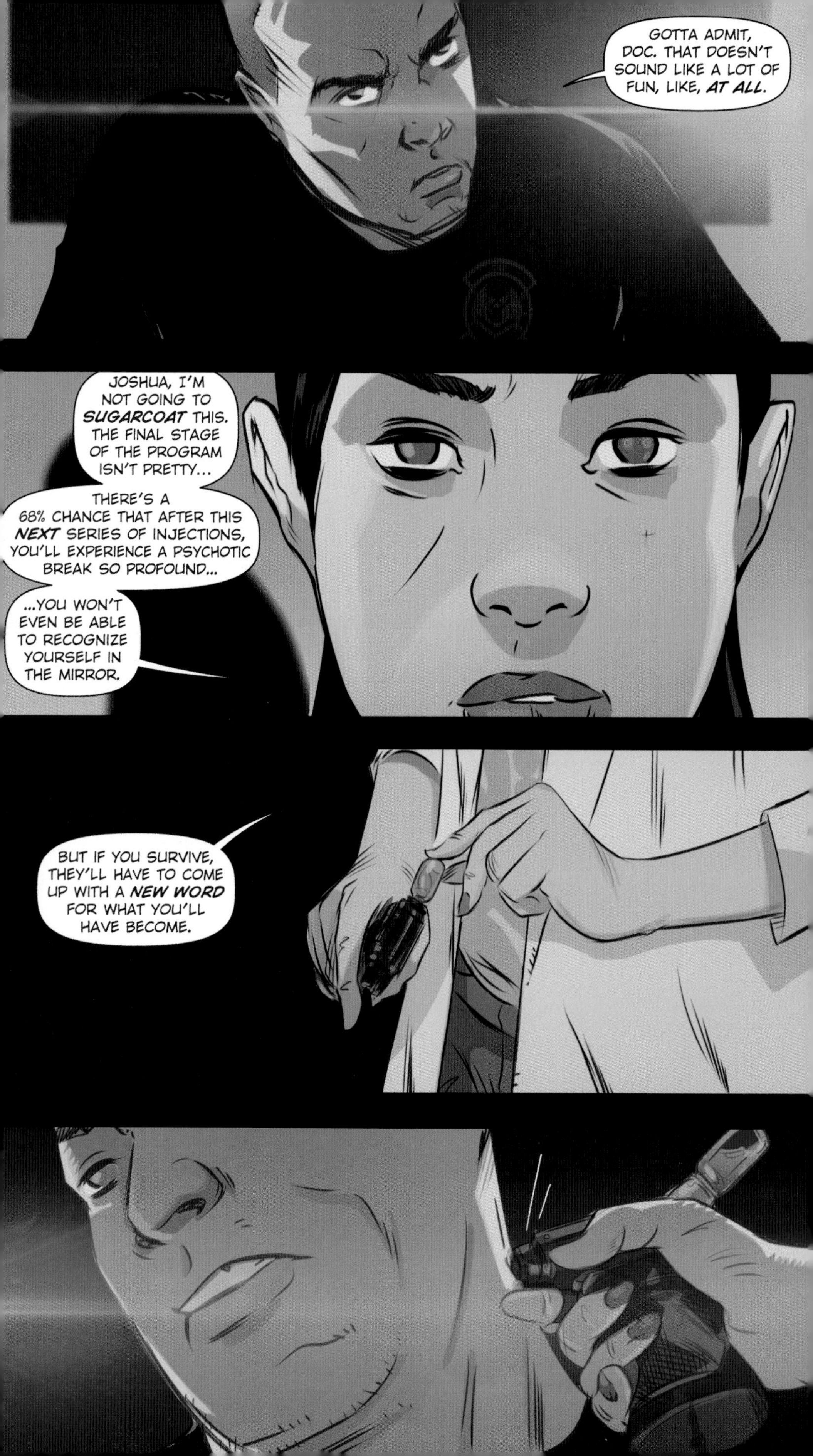
GOTTA ADMIT, DOC. THAT DOESN'T SOUND LIKE A LOT OF FUN, LIKE, AT ALL.
JOSHUA, I'M NOT GOING TO SUGARCOAT THIS. THE FINAL STAGE OF THE PROGRAM ISN'T PRETTY...
THERE'S A 68% CHANCE THAT AFTER THIS NEXT SERIES OF INJECTIONS, YOU'LL EXPERIENCE A PSYCHOTIC BREAK SO PROFOUND...
...YOU WON'T EVEN BE ABLE TO RECOGNIZE YOURSELF IN THE MIRROR.
BUT IF YOU SURVIVE, THEY'LL HAVE TO COME UP WITH A NEW WORD FOR WHAT YOU'LL HAVE BECOME.

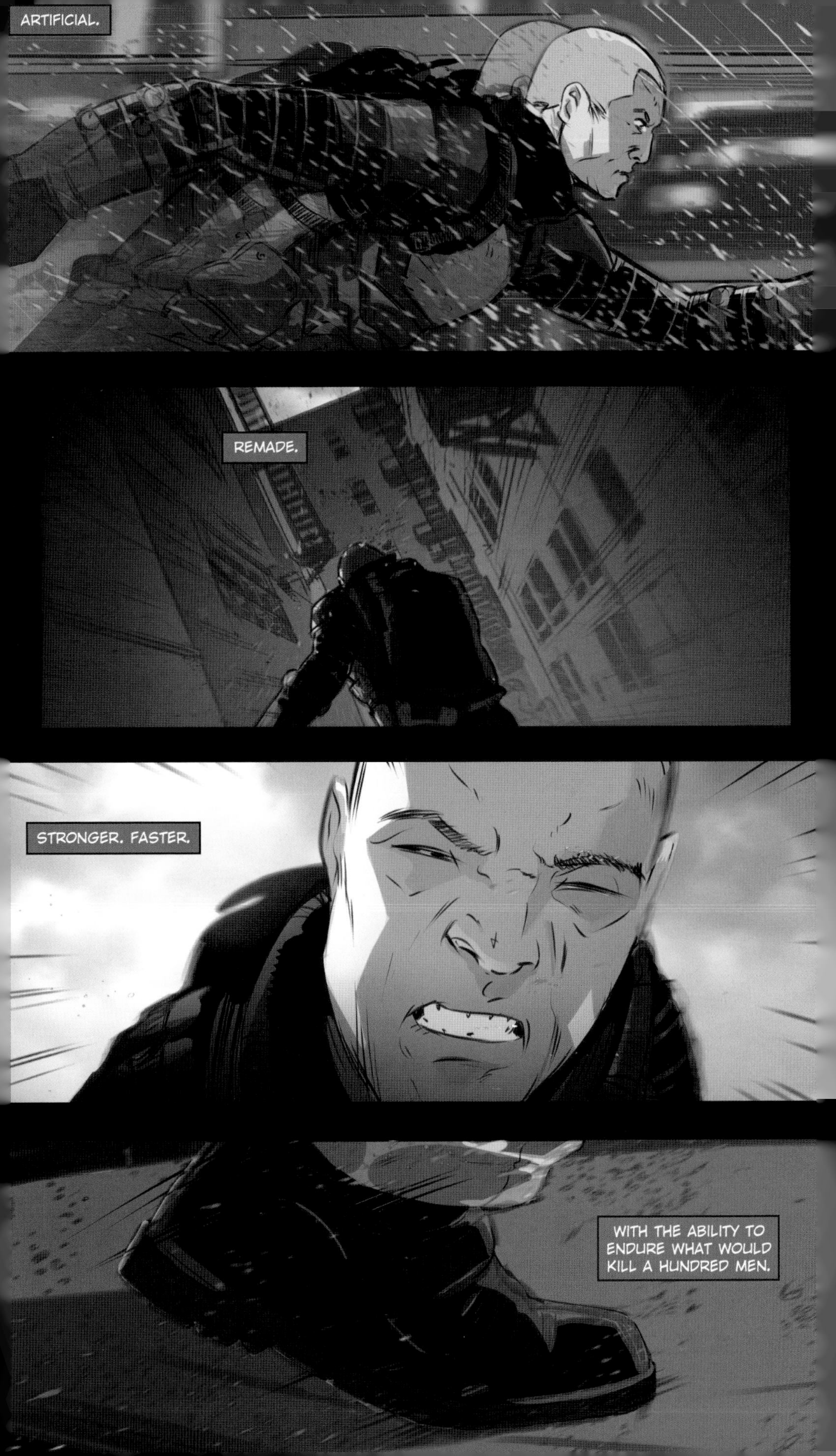
ARTIFICIAL.
REMADE.
STRONGER. FASTER.
WITH THE ABILITY TO ENDURE WHAT WOULD KILL A HUNDRED MEN.

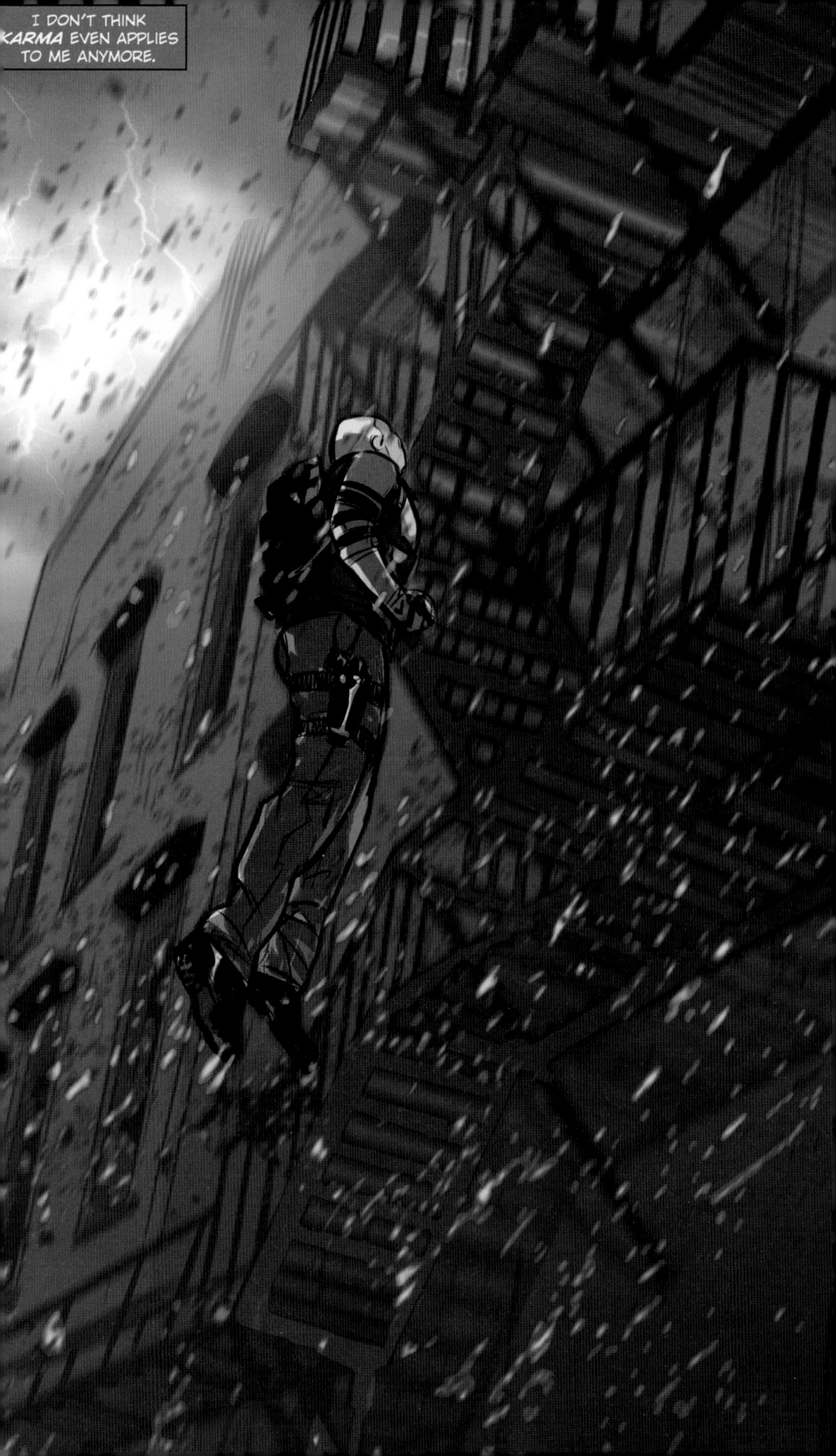
I DON'T THINK *KARMA* EVEN APPLIES TO ME ANYMORE.

DOOT

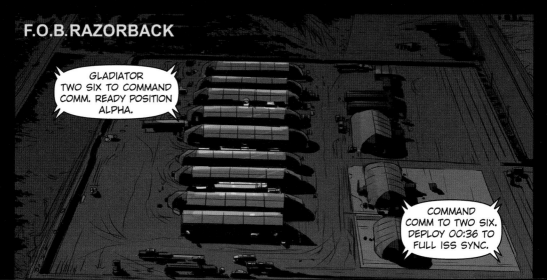

F.O.B. RAZORBACK

GLADIATOR TWO SIX TO COMMAND COMM. READY POSITION ALPHA.

COMMAND COMM TO TWO SIX. DEPLOY 00:36 TO FULL ISS SYNC.

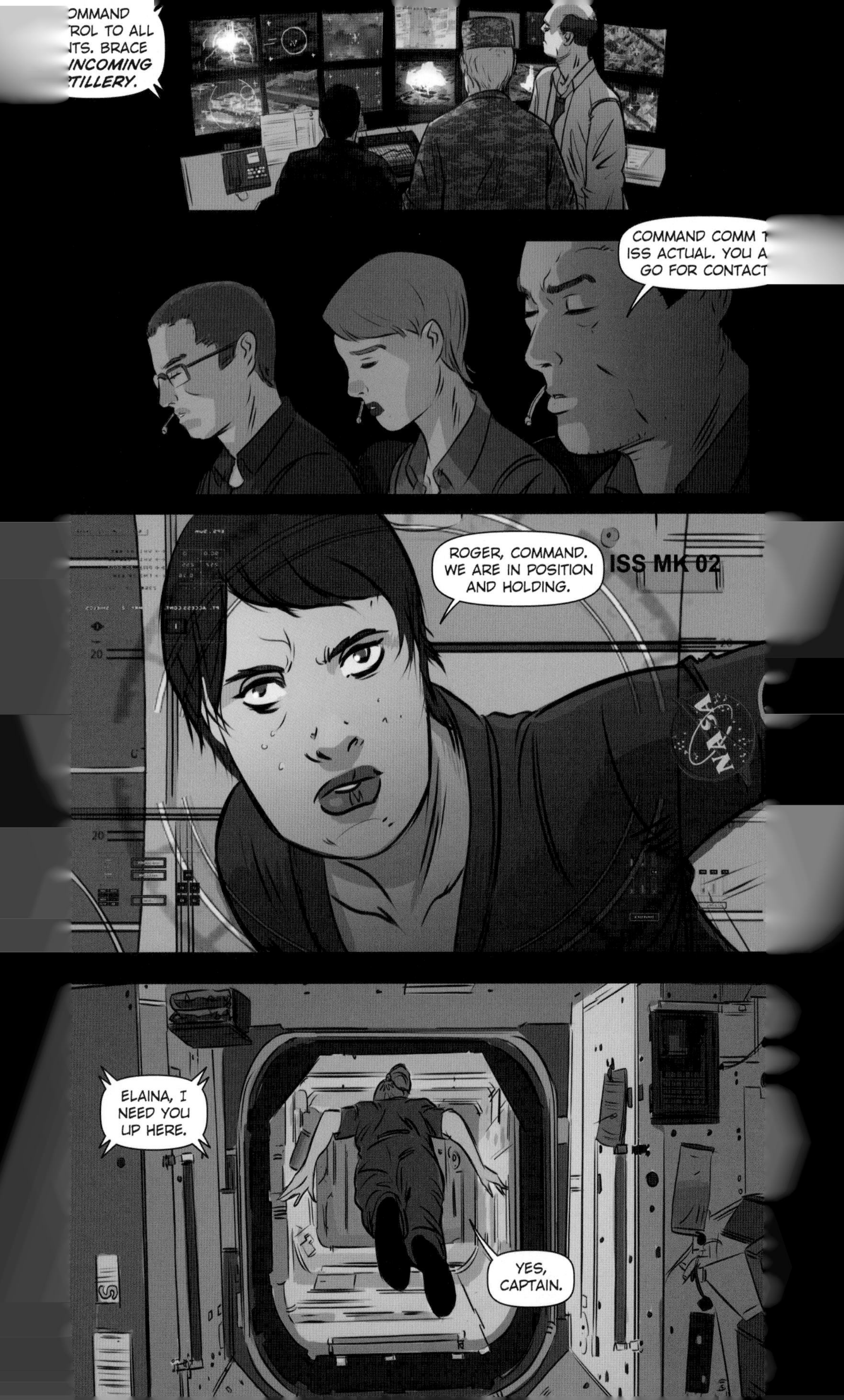

OMMAND TROL TO ALL ITS. BRACE INCOMING TILLERY.
COMMAND COMM T ISS ACTUAL. YOU A GO FOR CONTACT
ROGER, COMMAND. WE ARE IN POSITION AND HOLDING.
ISS MK 02
ELAINA, I NEED YOU UP HERE.
YES, CAPTAIN.

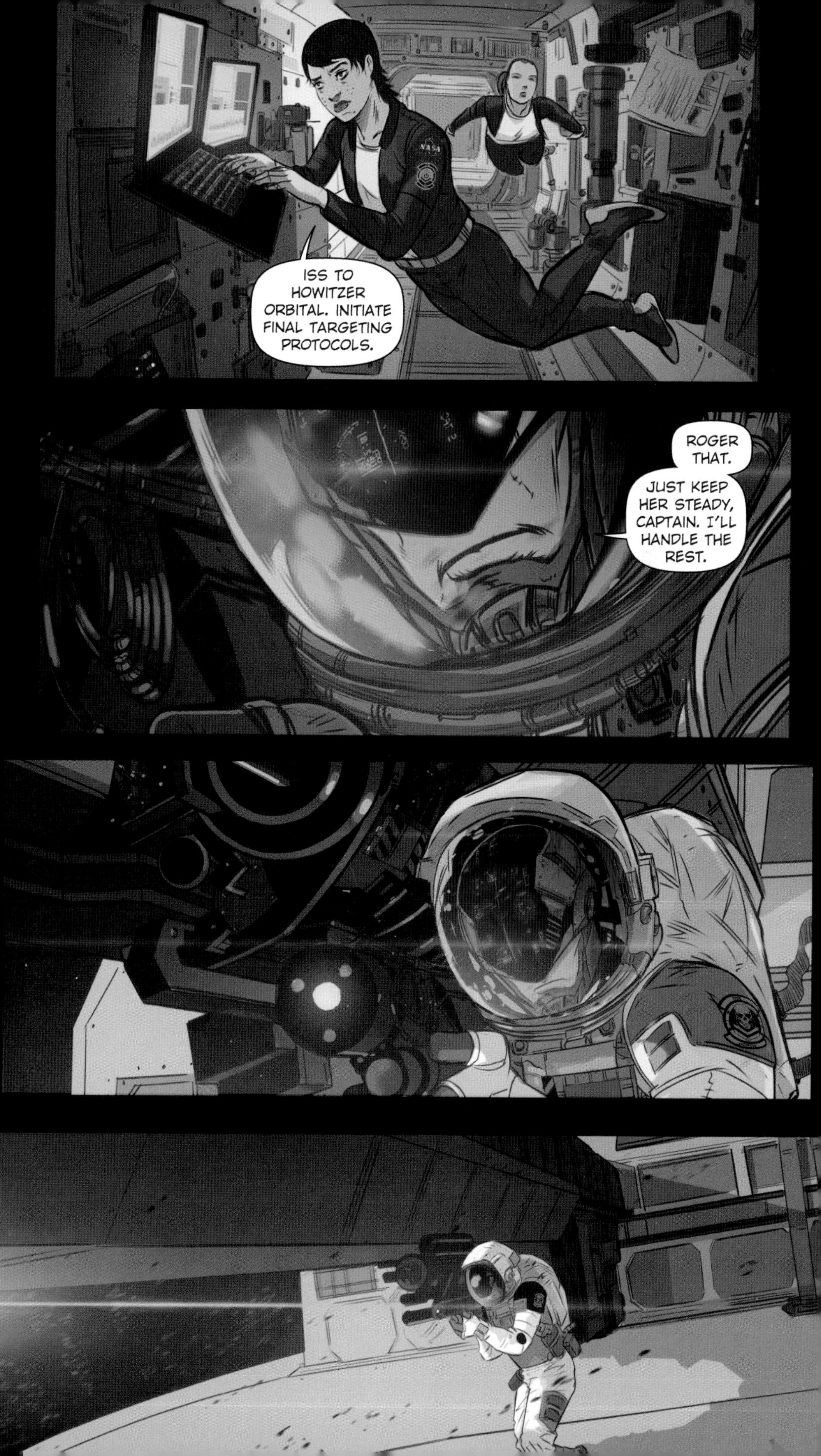
ISS TO HOWITZER ORBITAL. INITIATE FINAL TARGETING PROTOCOLS.
ROGER THAT.
JUST KEEP HER STEADY, CAPTAIN. I'LL HANDLE THE REST.

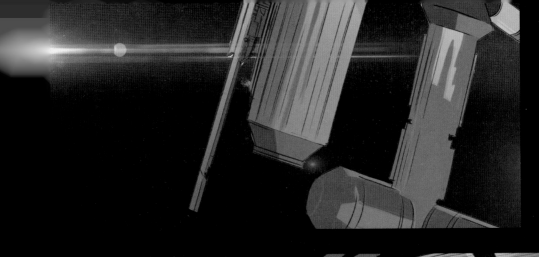

IK 2
ARTH ORBIT

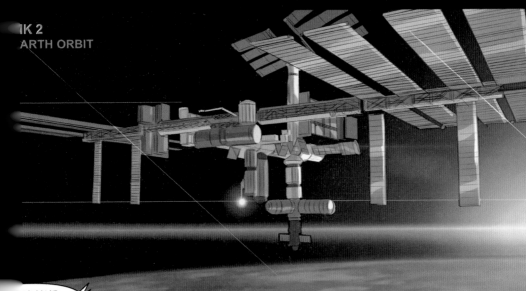

MMAND
ROL TO ALL
. TARGET'S
OMAGNETIC
DEGRADING.
STARTING.

DOOT
DOOT

CVN-71
THEODORE ROOSEVELT
NORTH PACIFIC OCEAN

COMMAND COMM TO ROOSEVELT. YOU ARE GO FOR GREEN.

ROOSEVELT TO SWITCHBLADE ACTUAL. YOU ARE YELLOW...

MOUNT UP, CAPTAIN.

COPY THAT.

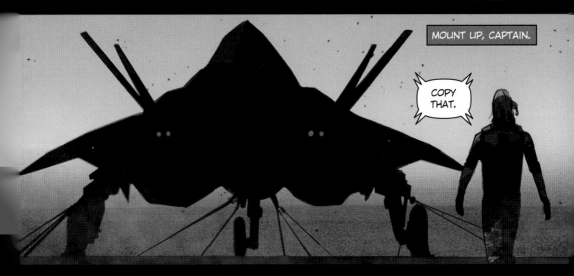

ROOSEVELT TO JACKKNIFE ACTUAL. YOU ARE BLUE. HOLD FOR STANDBY.

AFFIRMATIVE.

COMMAND COMM TO GLADIATOR TWO SIX. READY TO CONFIRM HARD TARGET DEPLOYMENT.

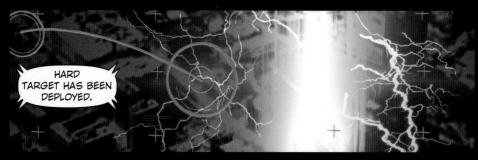

HARD TARGET HAS BEEN DEPLOYED.

GOOD PING. WE'LL BE WITHIN 150 METERS OF THE OBJECT. GRID 257, NORTH 50 DEGREES.

ISS SYNC HOLDING. WAIT FOR GREEN.

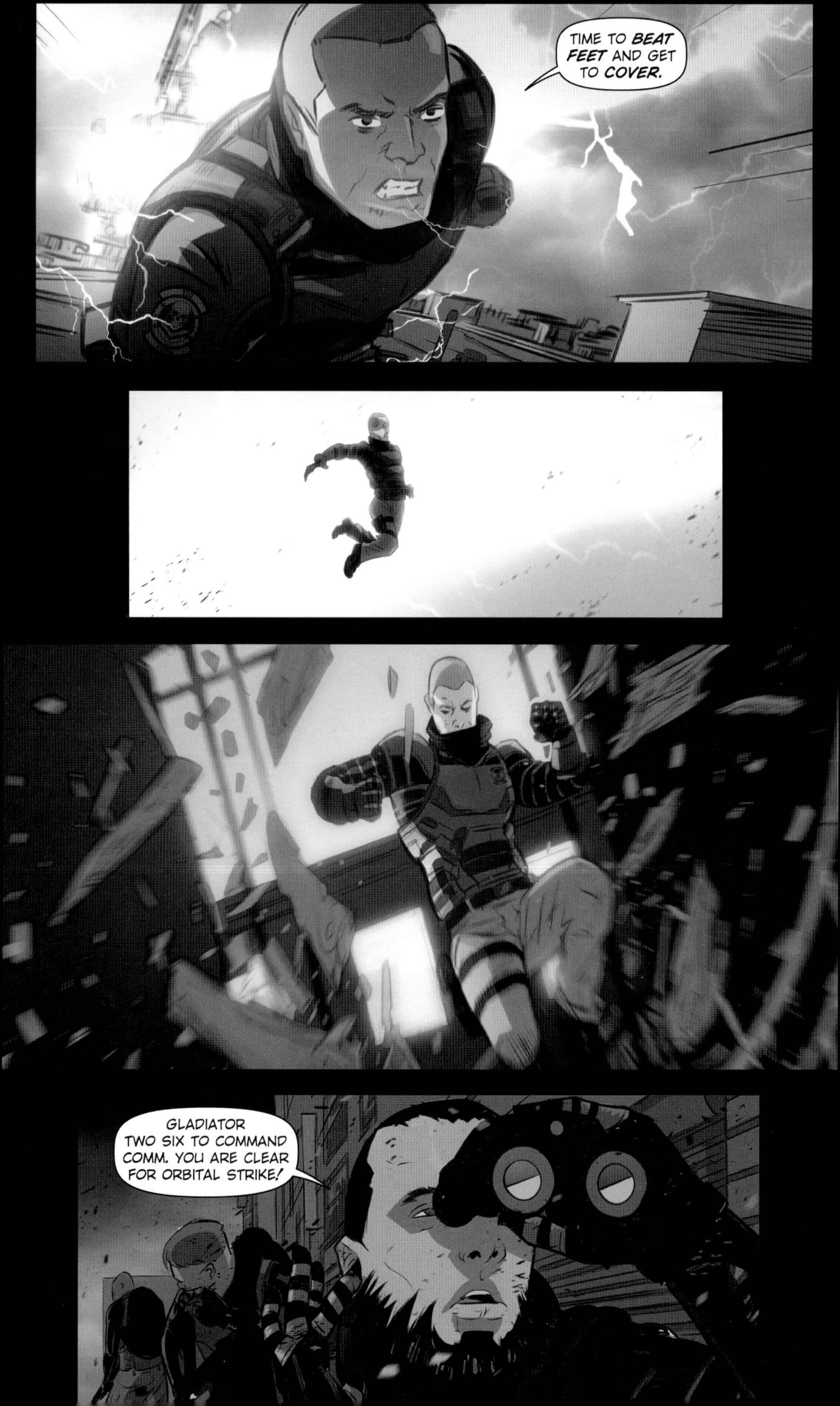
TIME TO BEAT FEET AND GET TO COVER.
GLADIATOR TWO SIX TO COMMAND COMM. YOU ARE CLEAR FOR ORBITAL STRIKE!

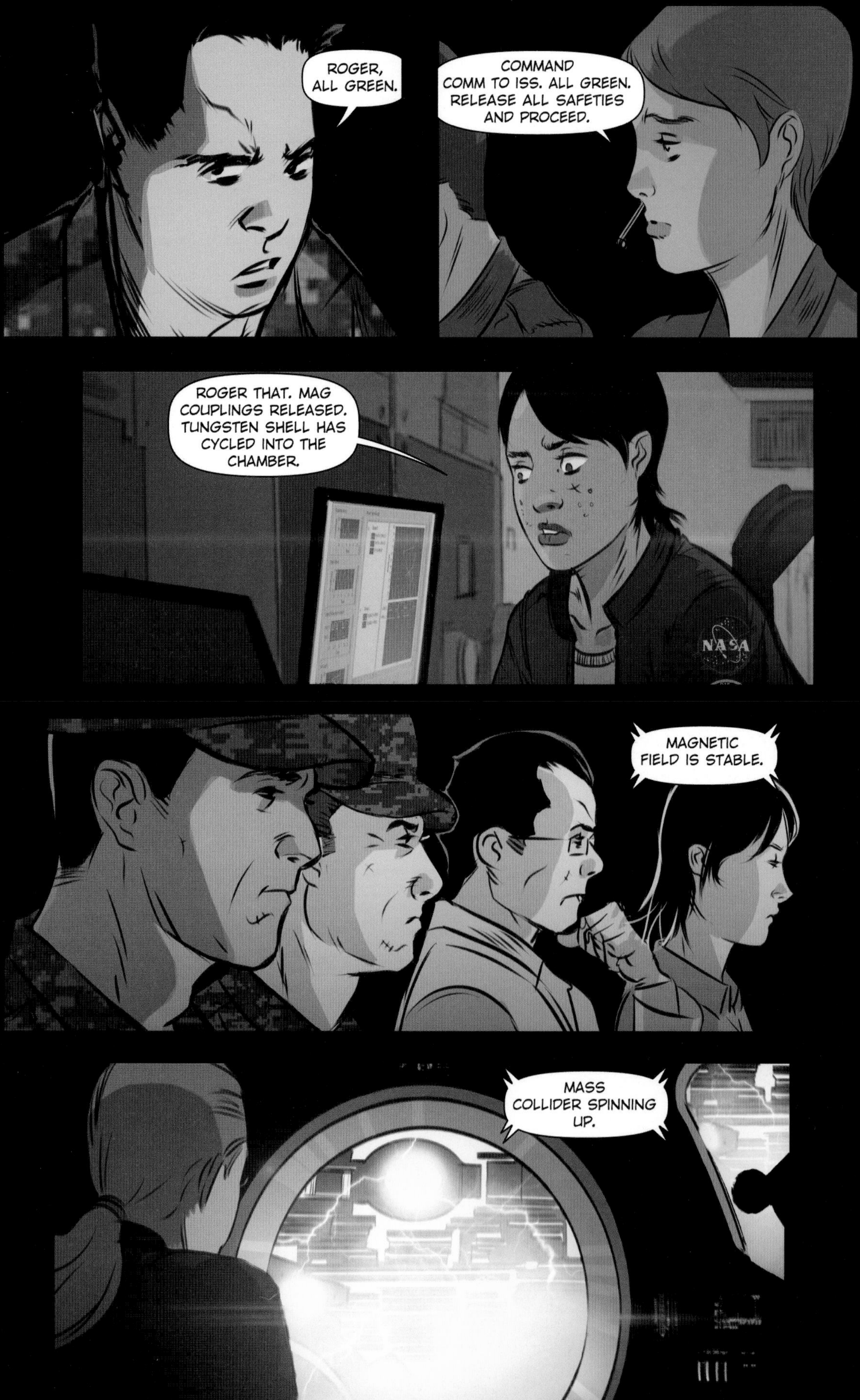
ROGER, ALL GREEN.
COMMAND COMM TO ISS. ALL GREEN. RELEASE ALL SAFETIES AND PROCEED.
ROGER THAT. MAG COUPLINGS RELEASED. TUNGSTEN SHELL HAS CYCLED INTO THE CHAMBER.
NASA
MAGNETIC FIELD IS STABLE.
MASS COLLIDER SPINNING UP.

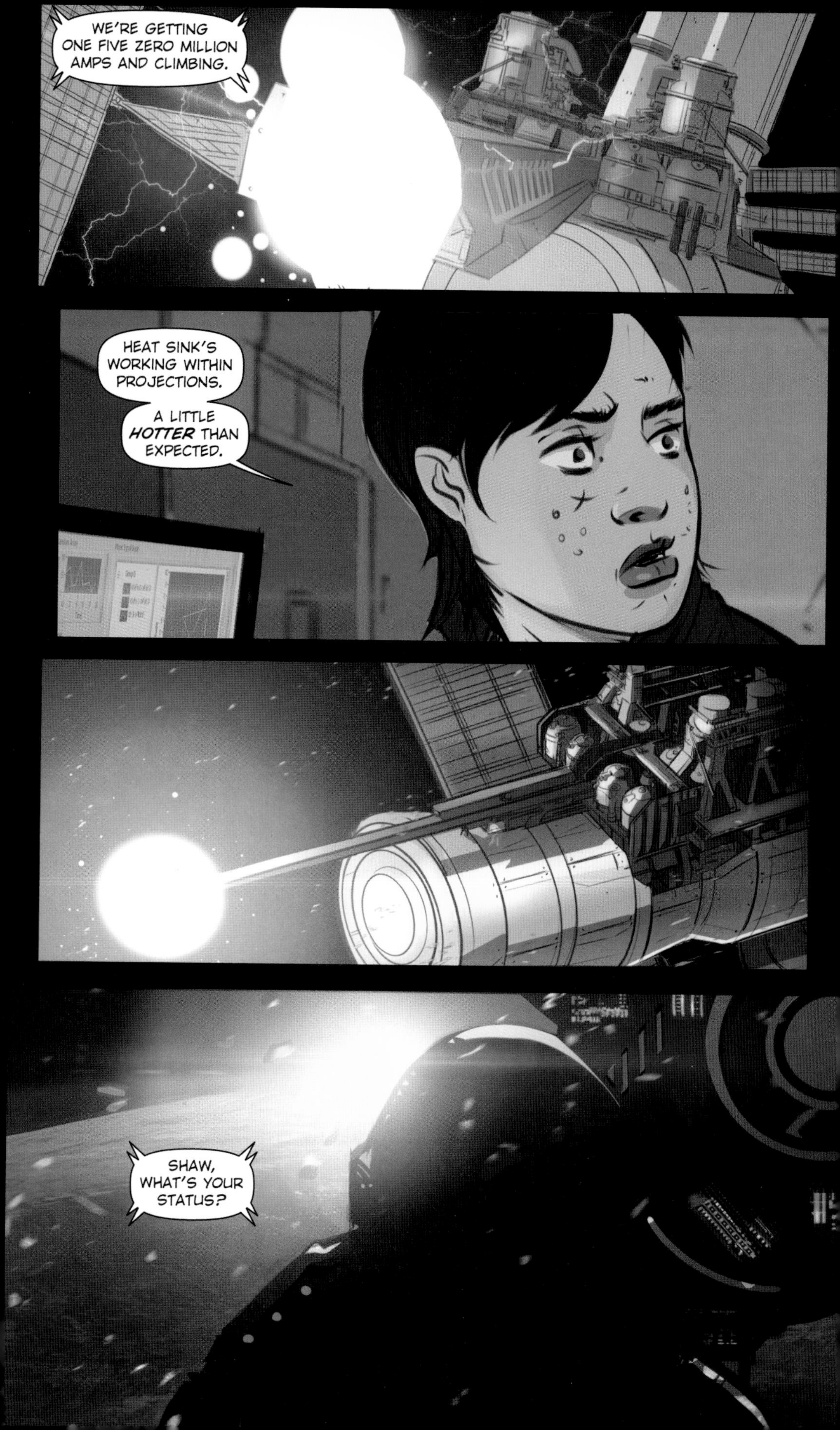
WE'RE GETTING ONE FIVE ZERO MILLION AMPS AND CLIMBING.
HEAT SINK'S WORKING WITHIN PROJECTIONS.
A LITTLE **HOTTER** THAN EXPECTED.
SHAW, WHAT'S YOUR STATUS?

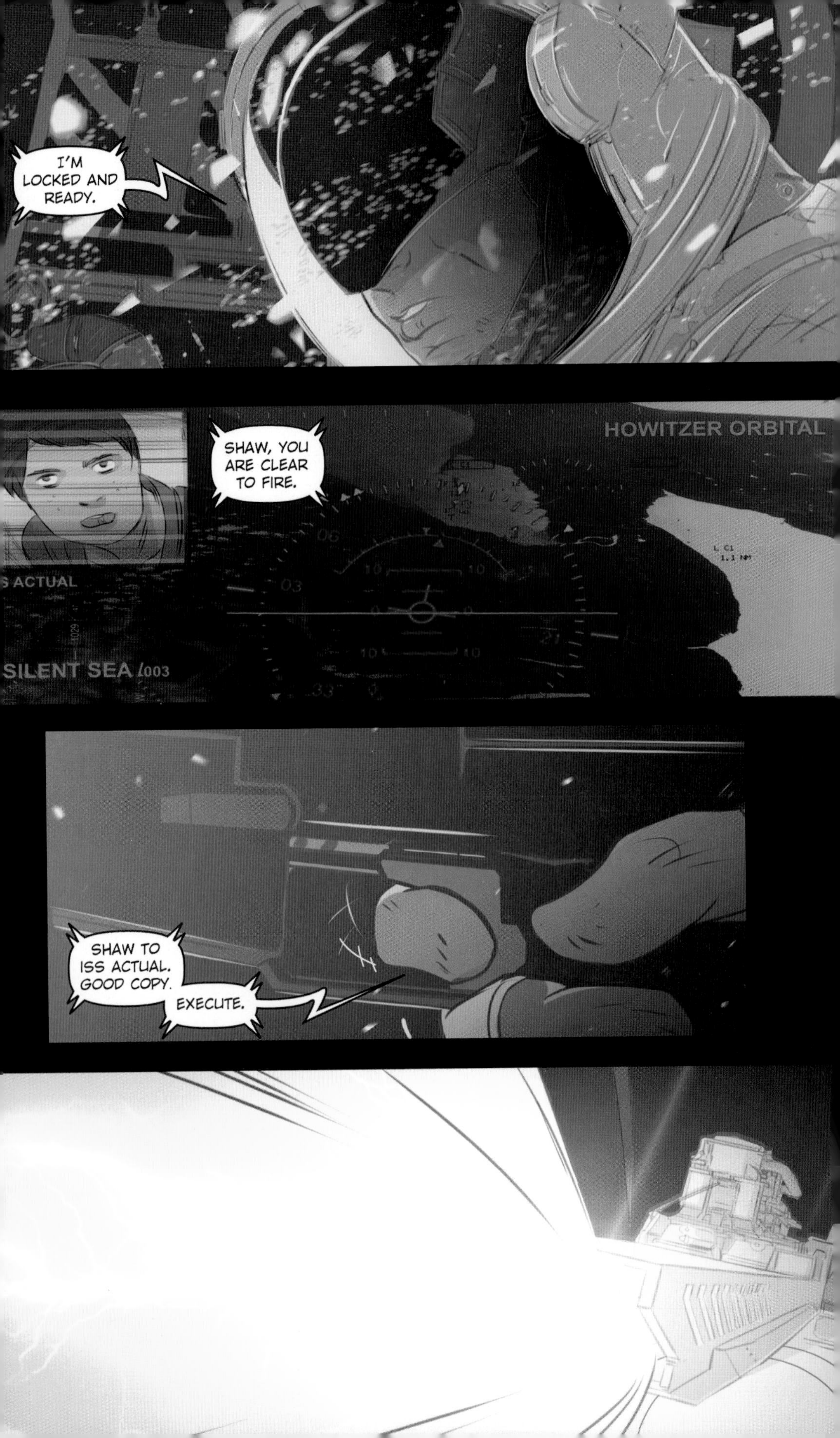
I'M LOCKED AND READY.
HOWITZER ORBITAL
SHAW, YOU ARE CLEAR TO FIRE.
S ACTUAL
SILENT SEA /003
SHAW TO ISS ACTUAL. GOOD COPY.
EXECUTE.

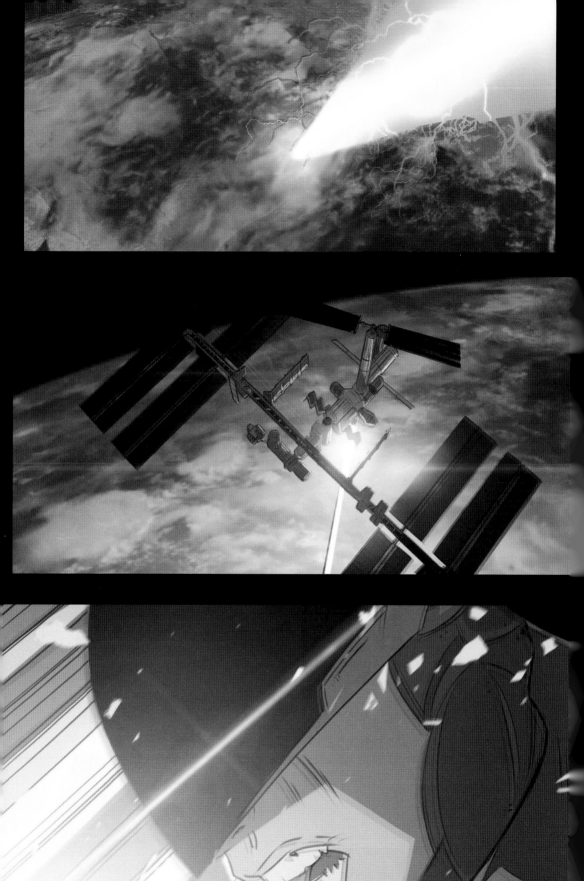

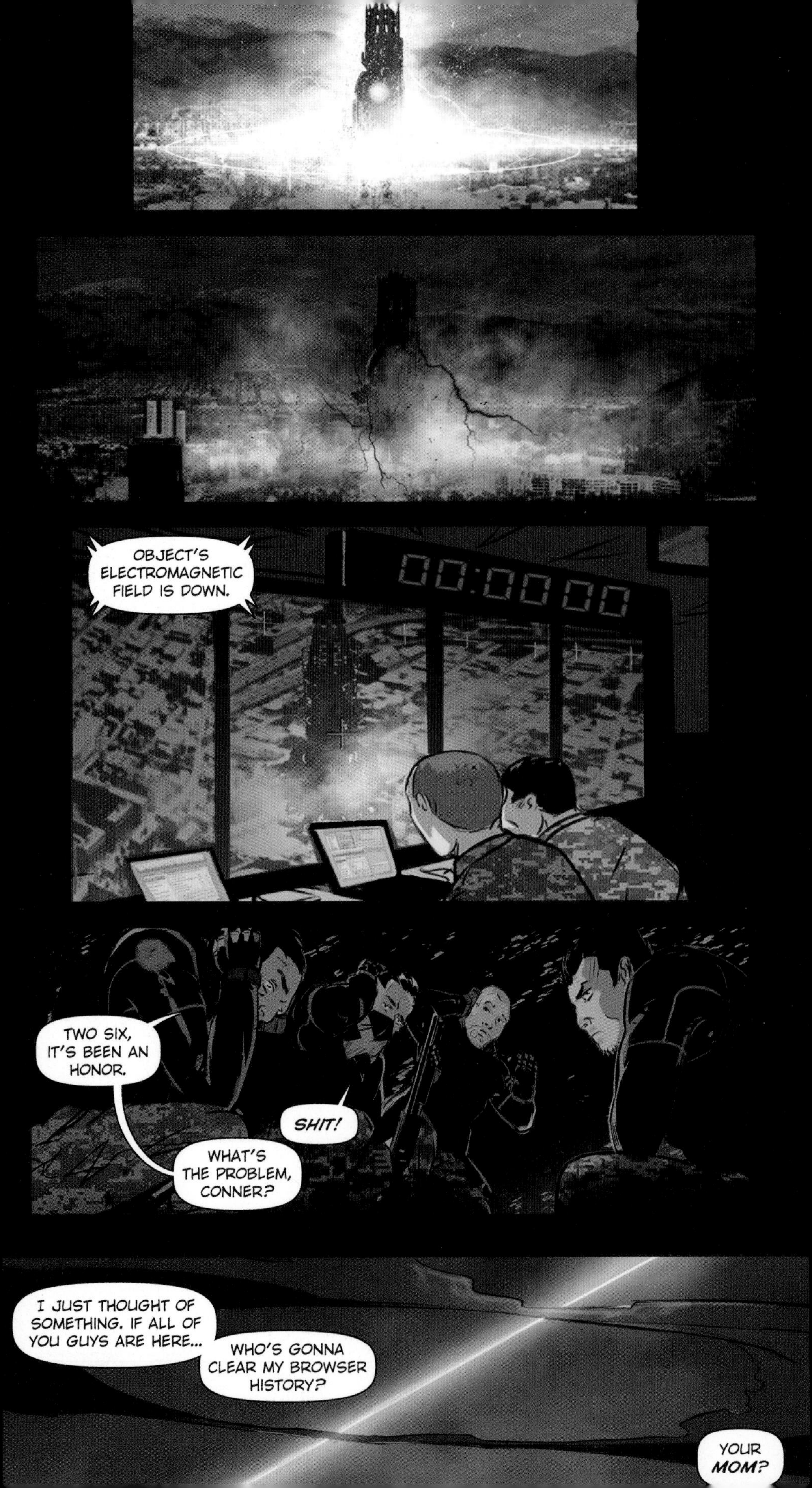
00:00 00
OBJECT'S ELECTROMAGNETIC FIELD IS DOWN.
TWO SIX, IT'S BEEN AN HONOR.
SHIT!
WHAT'S THE PROBLEM, CONNER?
I JUST THOUGHT OF SOMETHING. IF ALL OF YOU GUYS ARE HERE...
WHO'S GONNA CLEAR MY BROWSER HISTORY?
YOUR MOM?

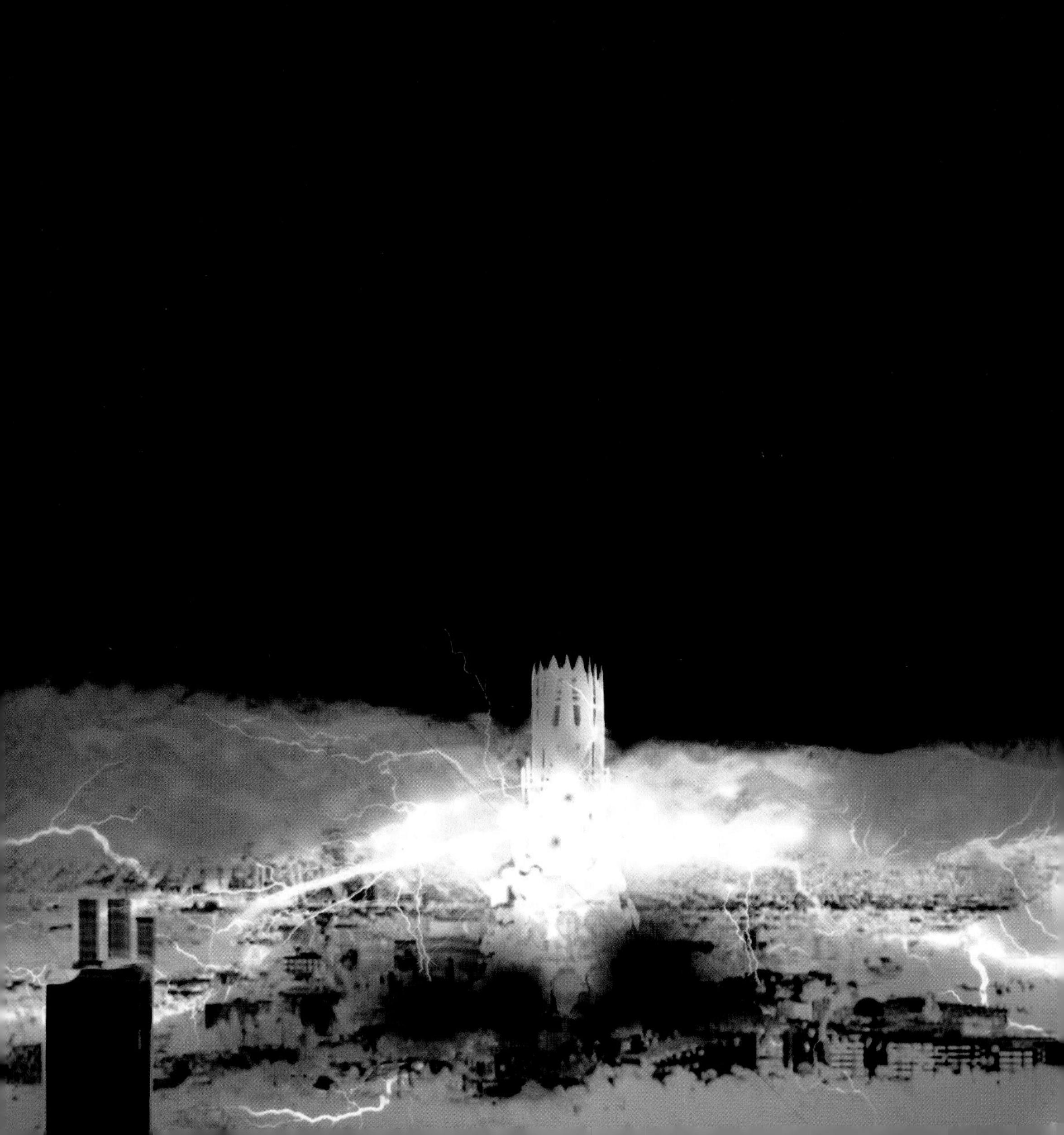

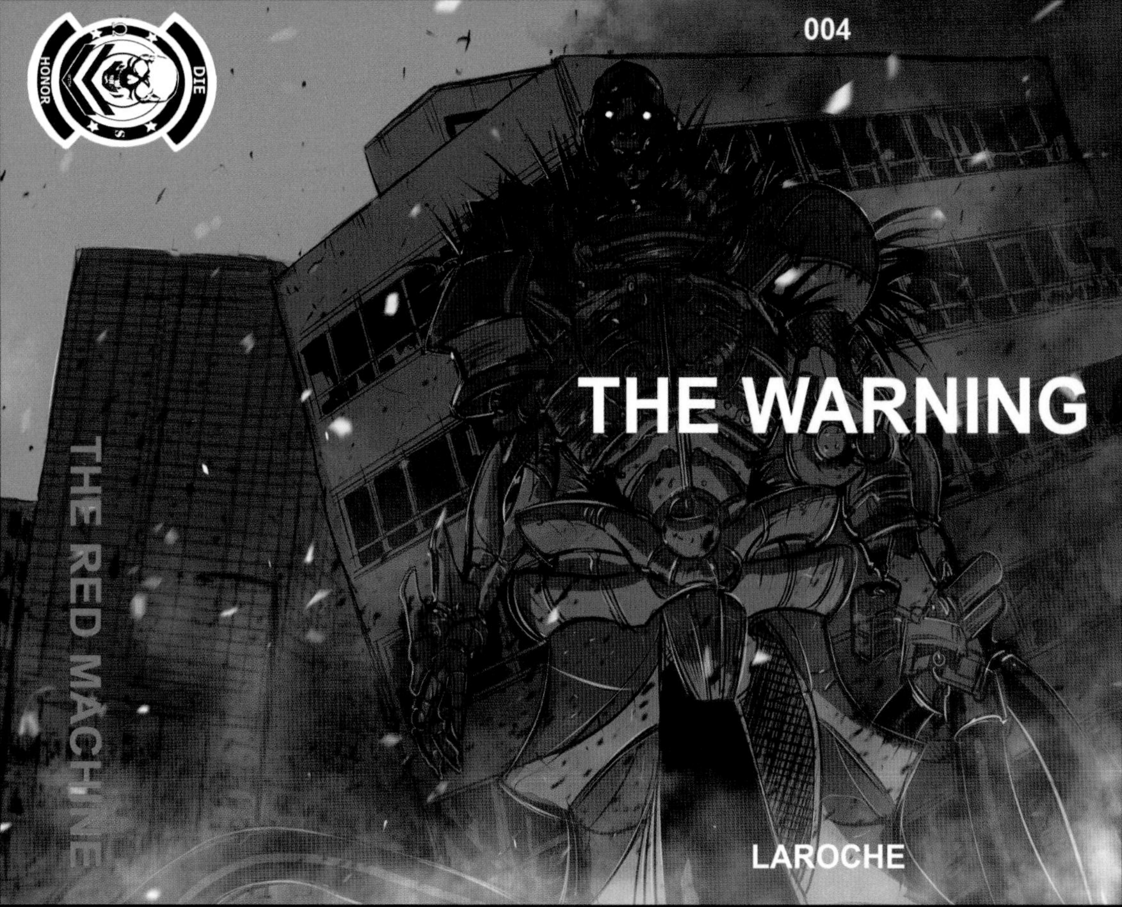
HONOR
DIE
004
THE WARNING
THE RED MACHINE
LAROCHE

CHAPTER FOUR

004

THE RED MACHINE

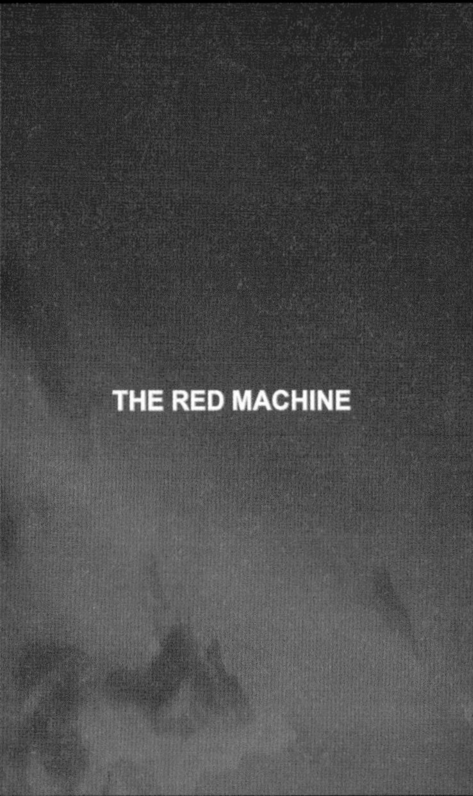

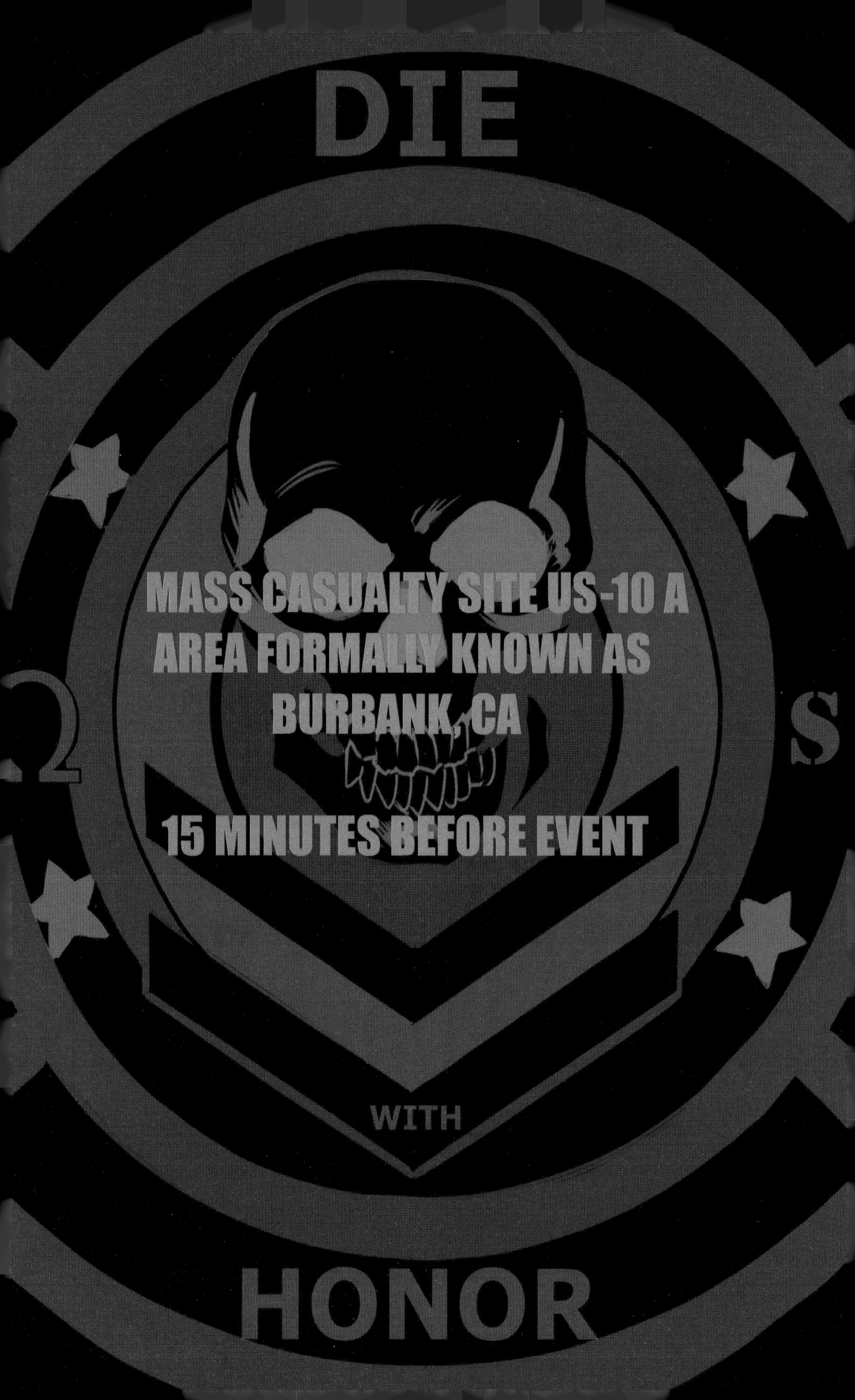
DIE
Ω
S
MASS CASUALTY SITE US-10 A
AREA FORMALLY KNOWN AS
BURBANK, CA
15 MINUTES BEFORE EVENT
WITH
HONOR

WORLDSTAR!

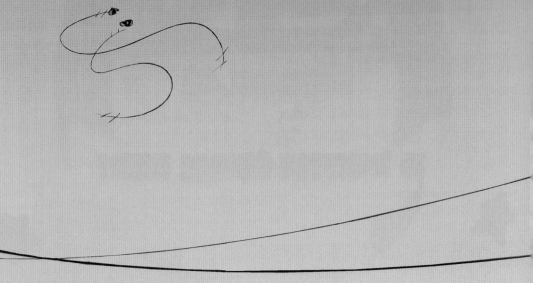

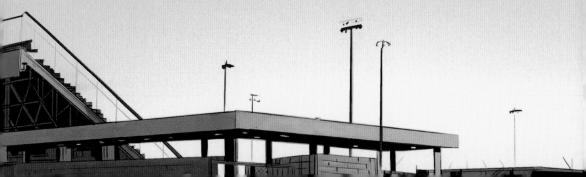

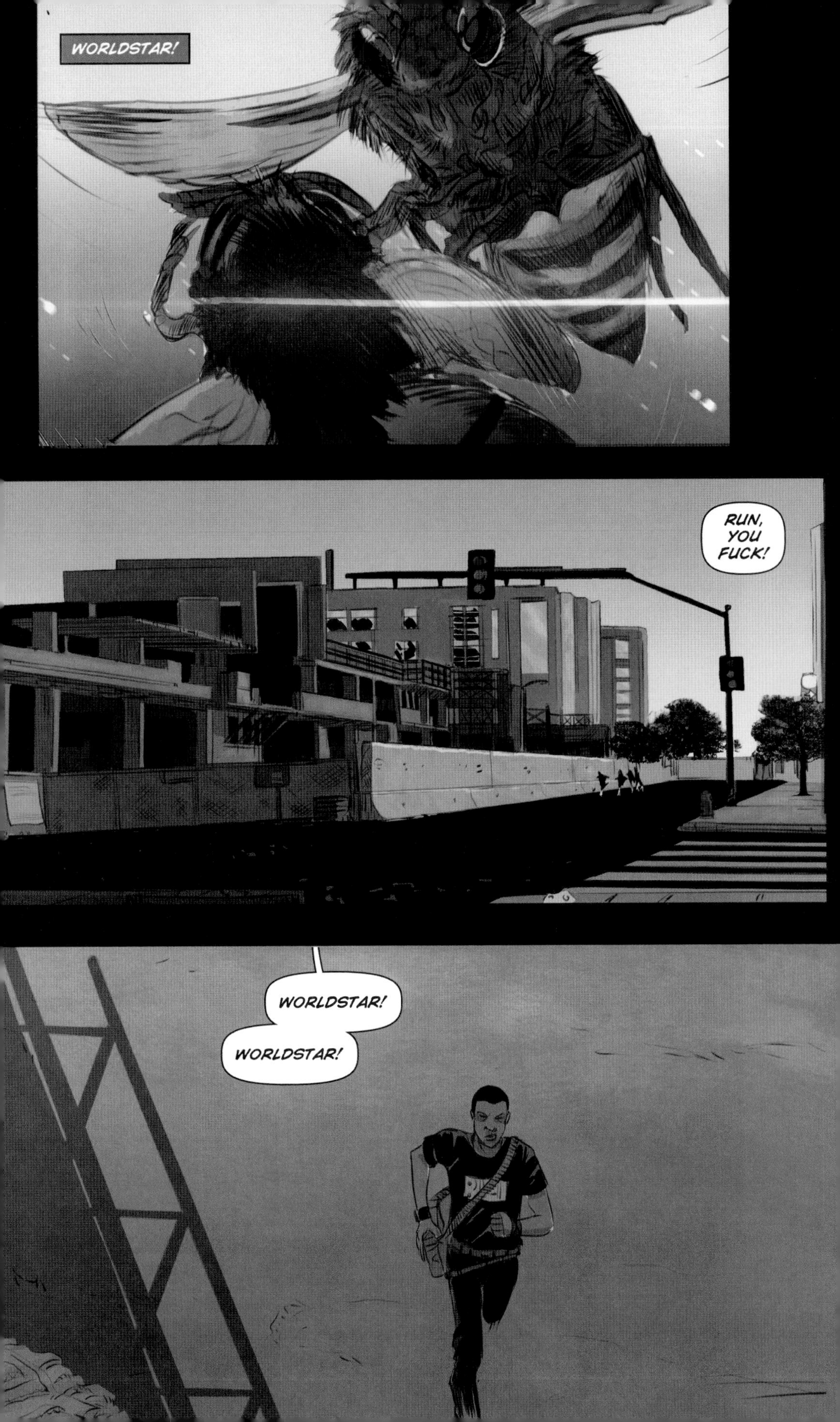
WORLDSTAR!
RUN, YOU FUCK!
WORLDSTAR!
WORLDSTAR!

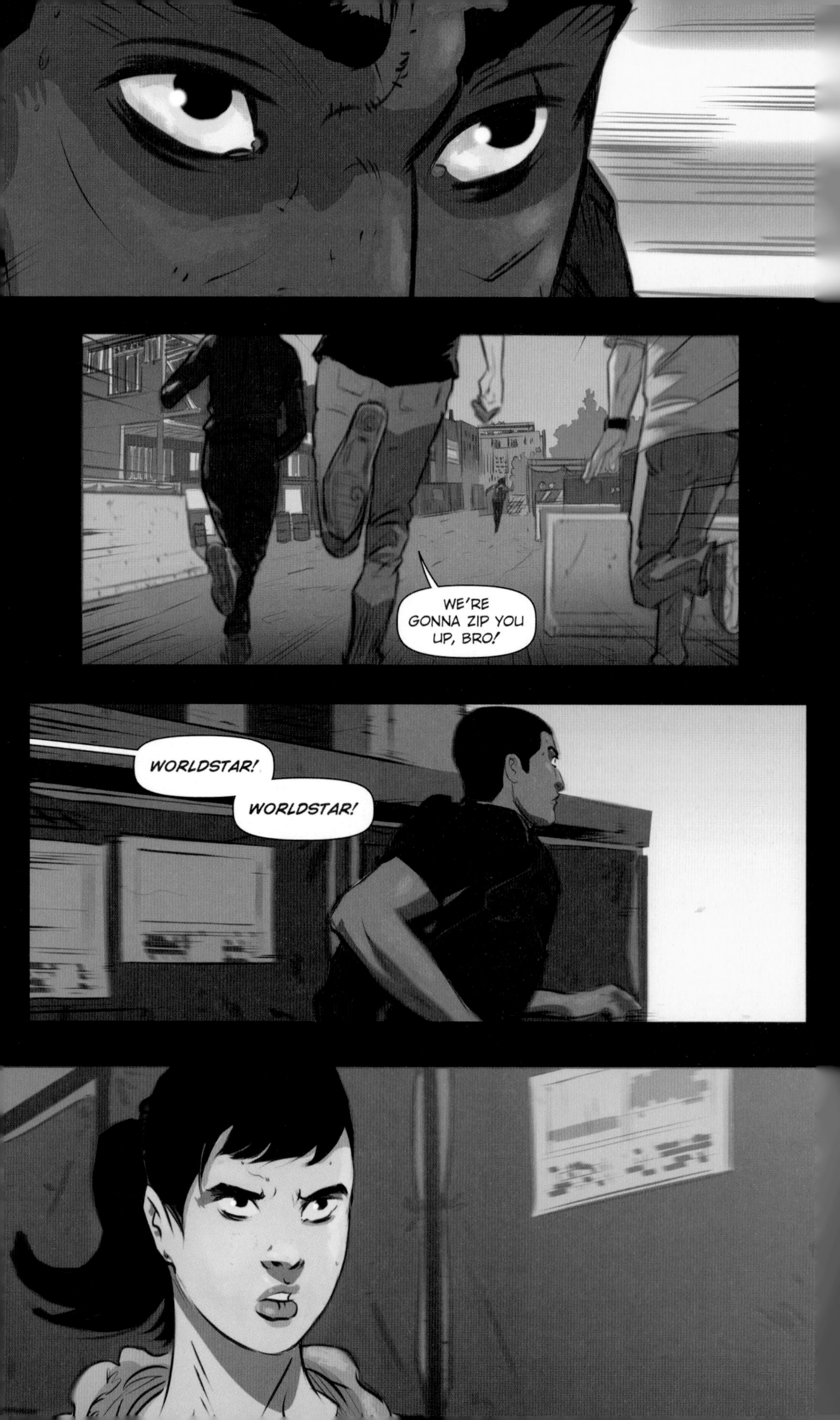
WE'RE GONNA ZIP YOU UP, BRO!
WORLDSTAR!
WORLDSTAR!

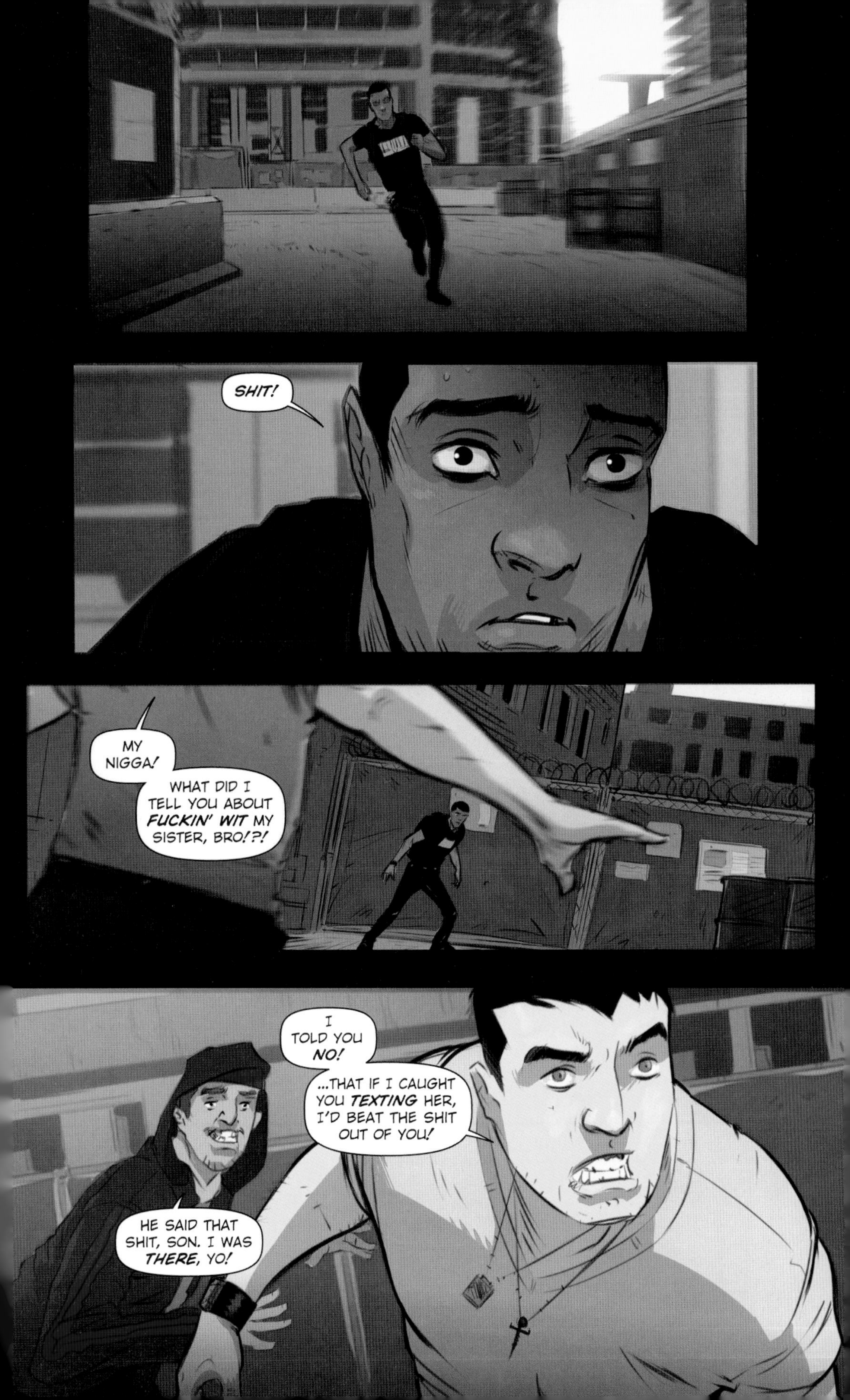
SHIT!
MY NIGGA!
WHAT DID I TELL YOU ABOUT FUCKIN' WIT MY SISTER, BRO!?!
I TOLD YOU NO!
...THAT IF I CAUGHT YOU TEXTING HER, I'D BEAT THE SHIT OUT OF YOU!
HE SAID THAT SHIT, SON. I WAS THERE, YO!

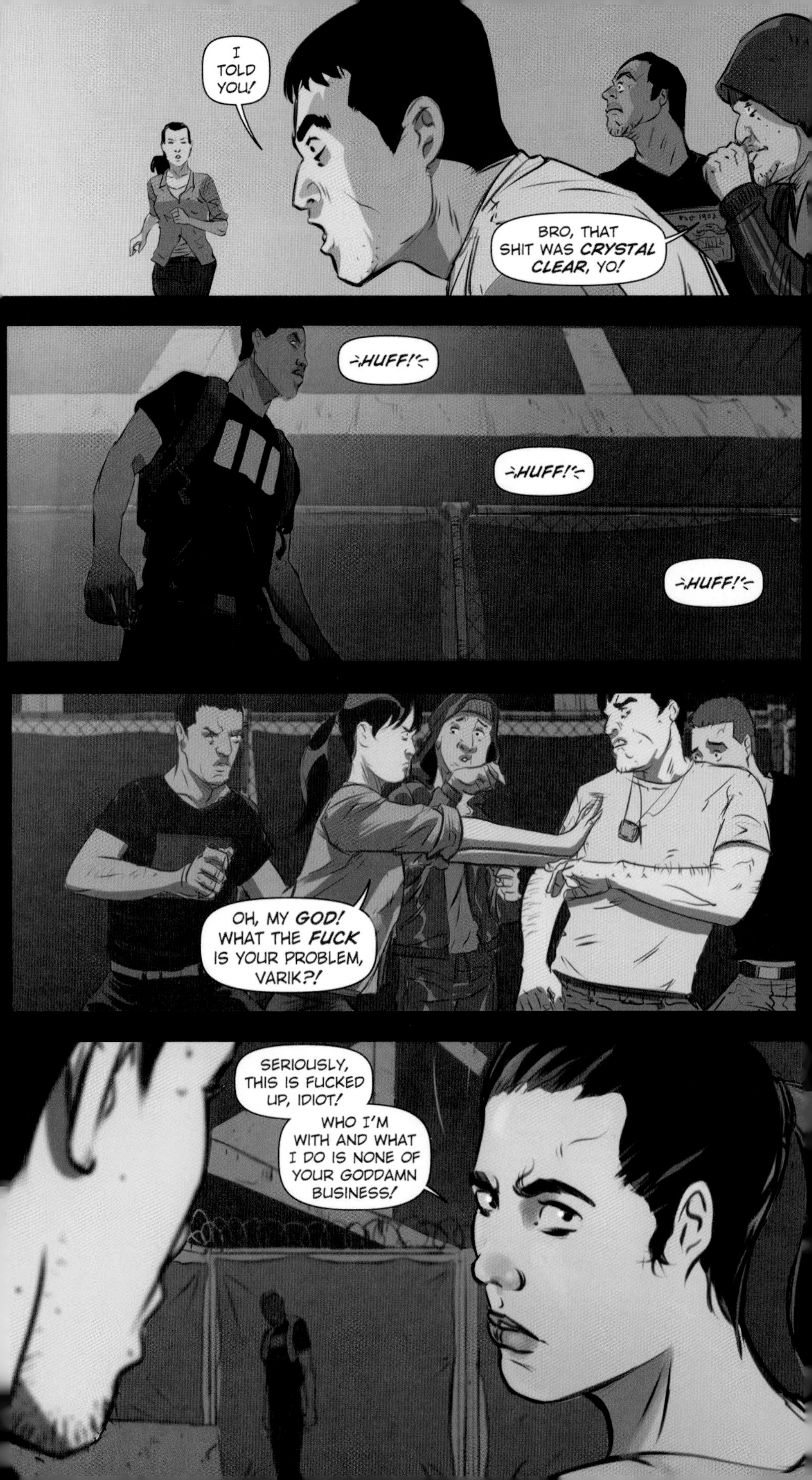
I TOLD YOU!
BRO, THAT SHIT WAS CRYSTAL CLEAR, YO!
HUFF!
HUFF!
HUFF!
OH, MY GOD! WHAT THE FUCK IS YOUR PROBLEM, VARIK?!
SERIOUSLY, THIS IS FUCKED UP, IDIOT!
WHO I'M WITH AND WHAT I DO IS NONE OF YOUR GODDAMN BUSINESS!

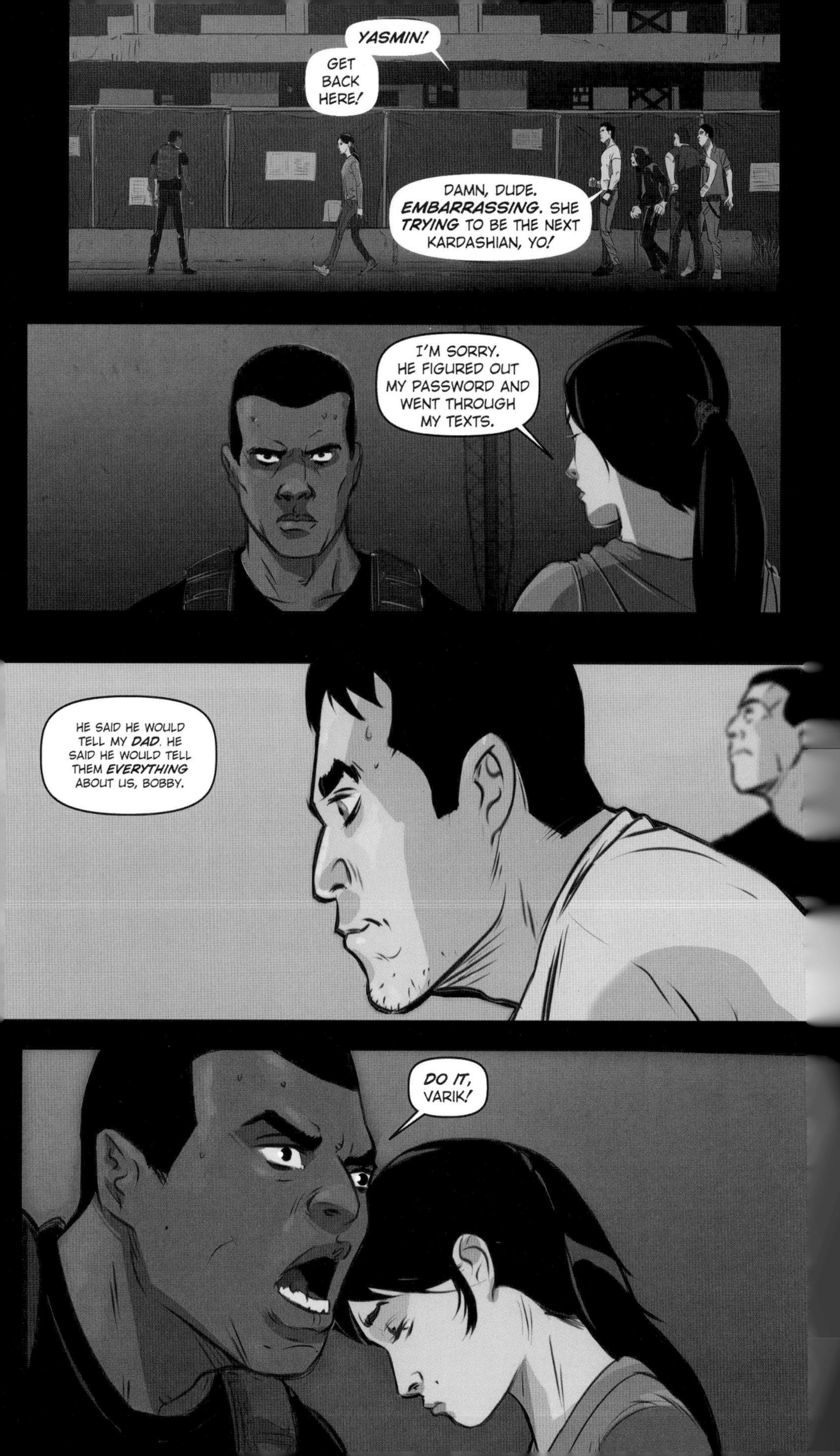
YASMIN!
GET BACK HERE!
DAMN, DUDE. EMBARRASSING. SHE TRYING TO BE THE NEXT KARDASHIAN, YO!
I'M SORRY. HE FIGURED OUT MY PASSWORD AND WENT THROUGH MY TEXTS.
HE SAID HE WOULD TELL MY DAD. HE SAID HE WOULD TELL THEM EVERYTHING ABOUT US, BOBBY.
DO IT, VARIK!

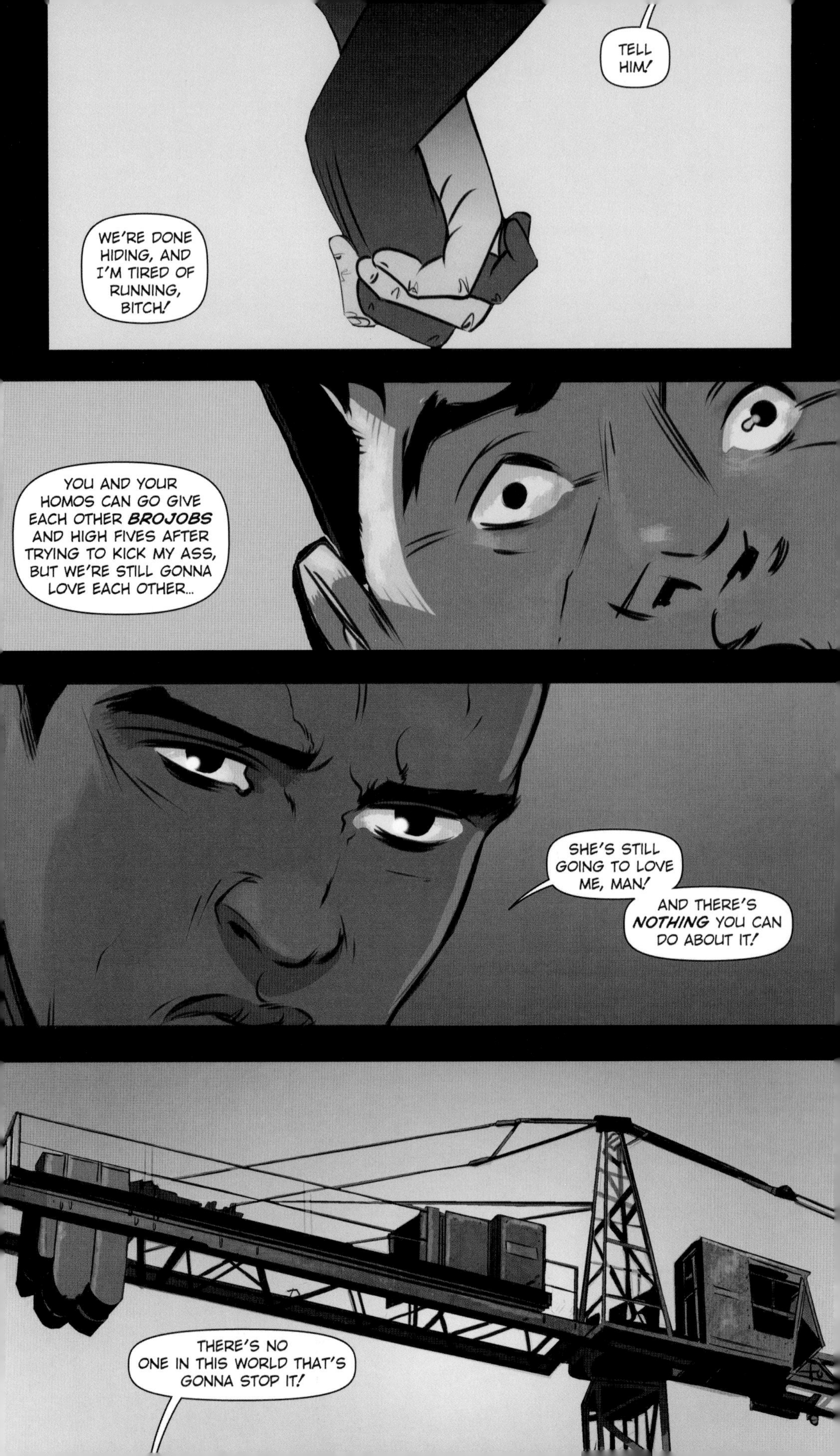
TELL HIM!
WE'RE DONE HIDING, AND I'M TIRED OF RUNNING, BITCH!
YOU AND YOUR HOMOS CAN GO GIVE EACH OTHER *BROJOBS* AND HIGH FIVES AFTER TRYING TO KICK MY ASS, BUT WE'RE STILL GONNA LOVE EACH OTHER...
SHE'S STILL GOING TO LOVE ME, MAN!
AND THERE'S *NOTHING* YOU CAN DO ABOUT IT!
THERE'S NO ONE IN THIS WORLD THAT'S GONNA STOP IT!

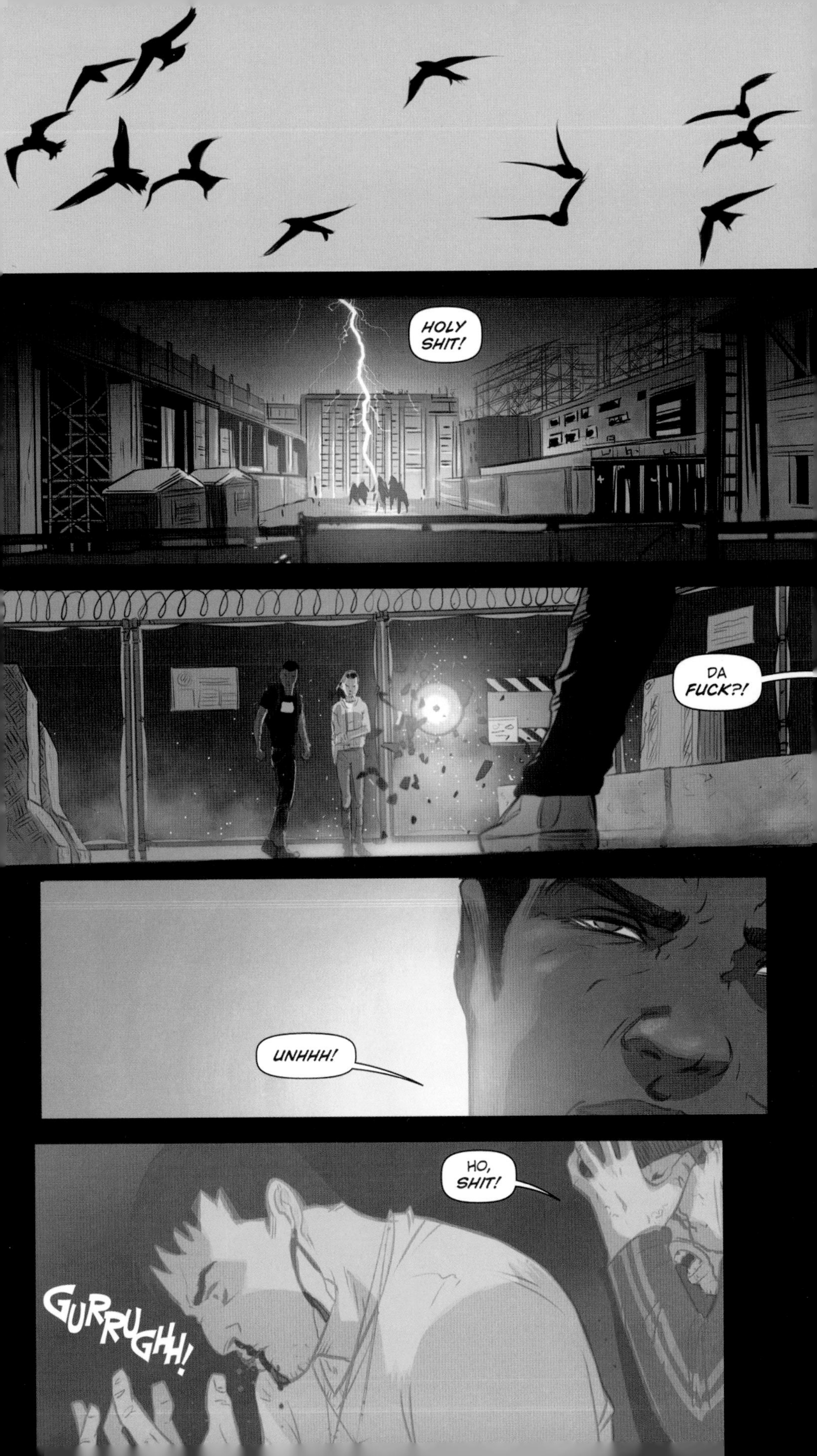

HOLY SHIT!
DA FUCK?!
UNHHH!
HO, SHIT!
GURRUGHH!

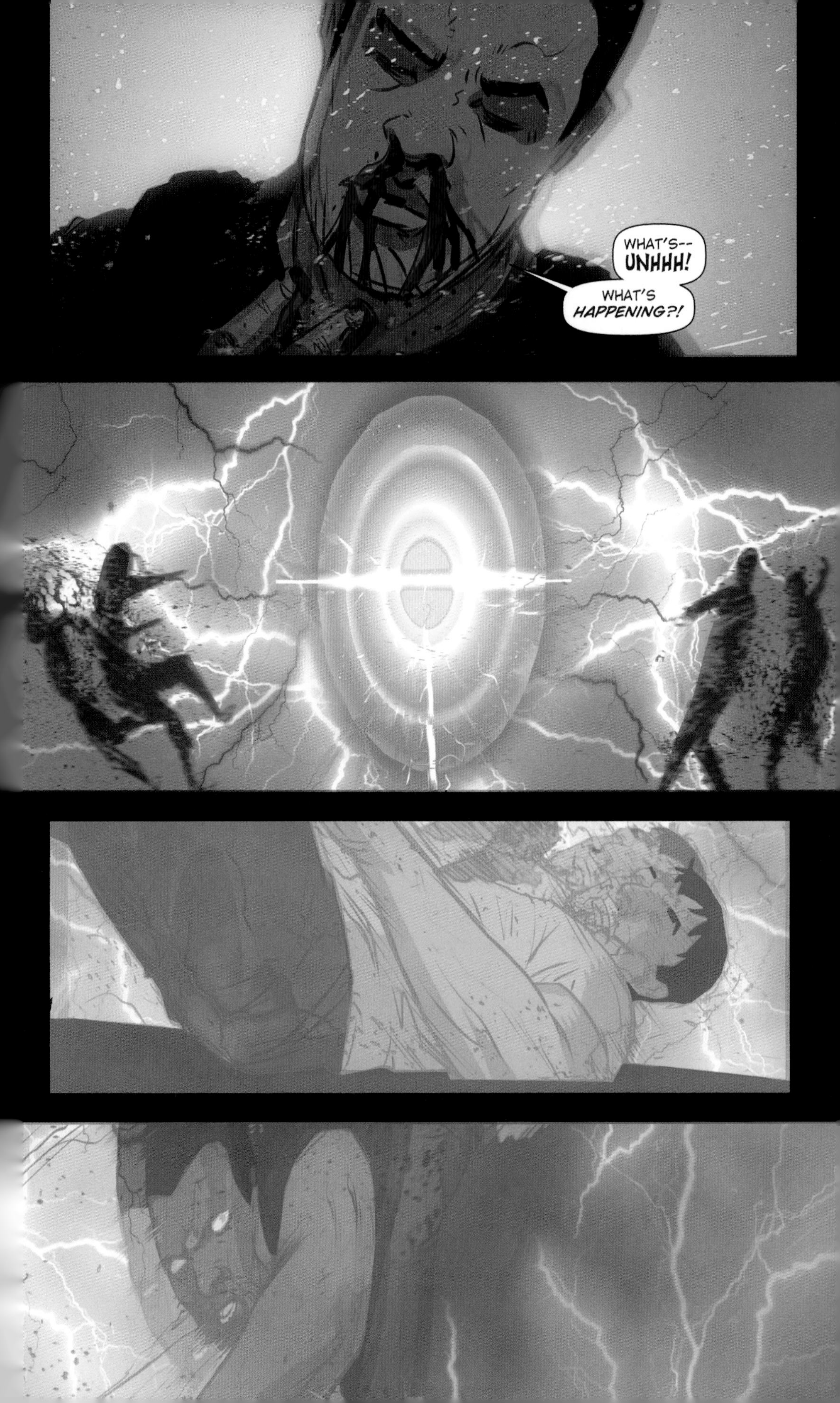
WHAT'S--
UNHHH!
WHAT'S
HAPPENING?!

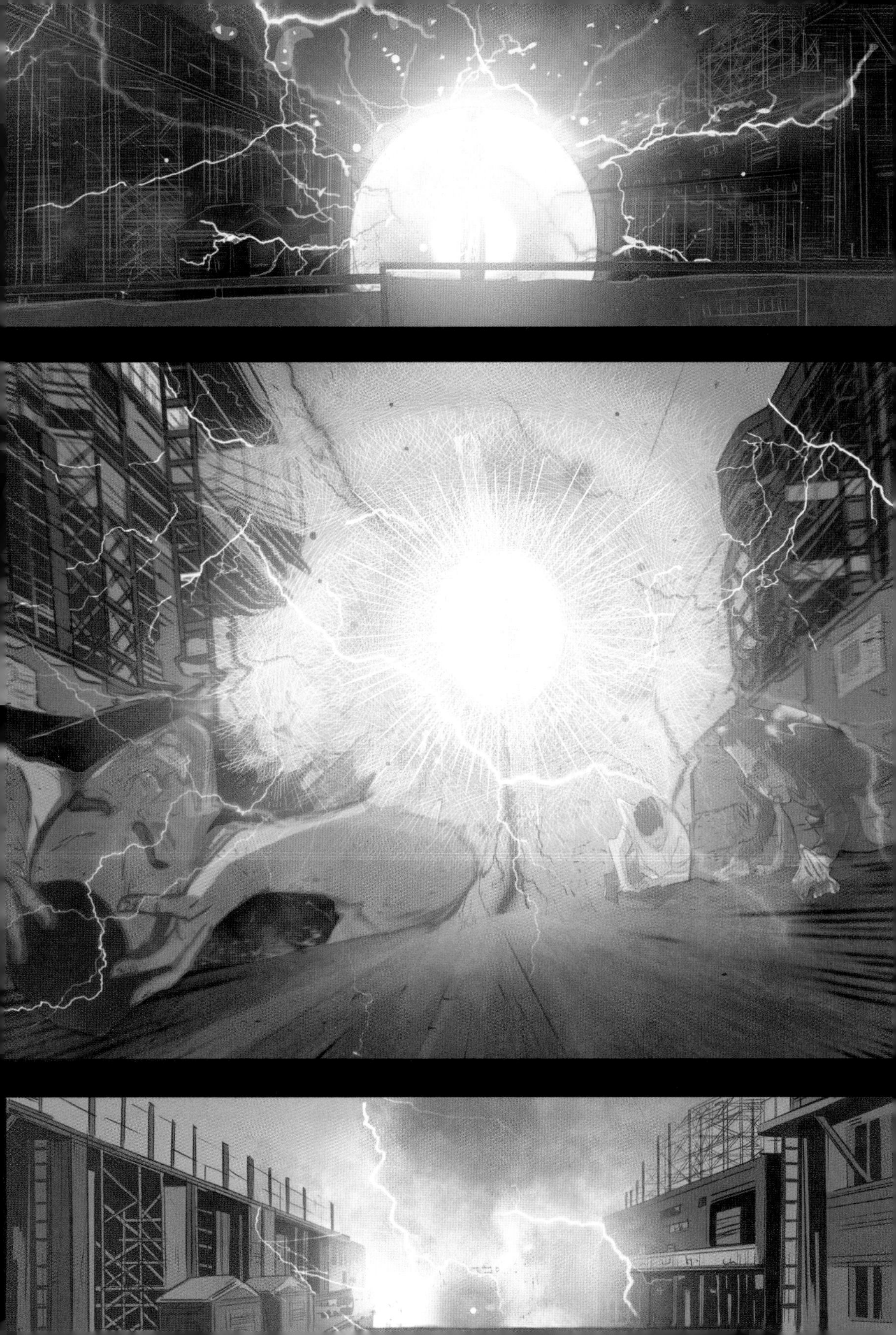

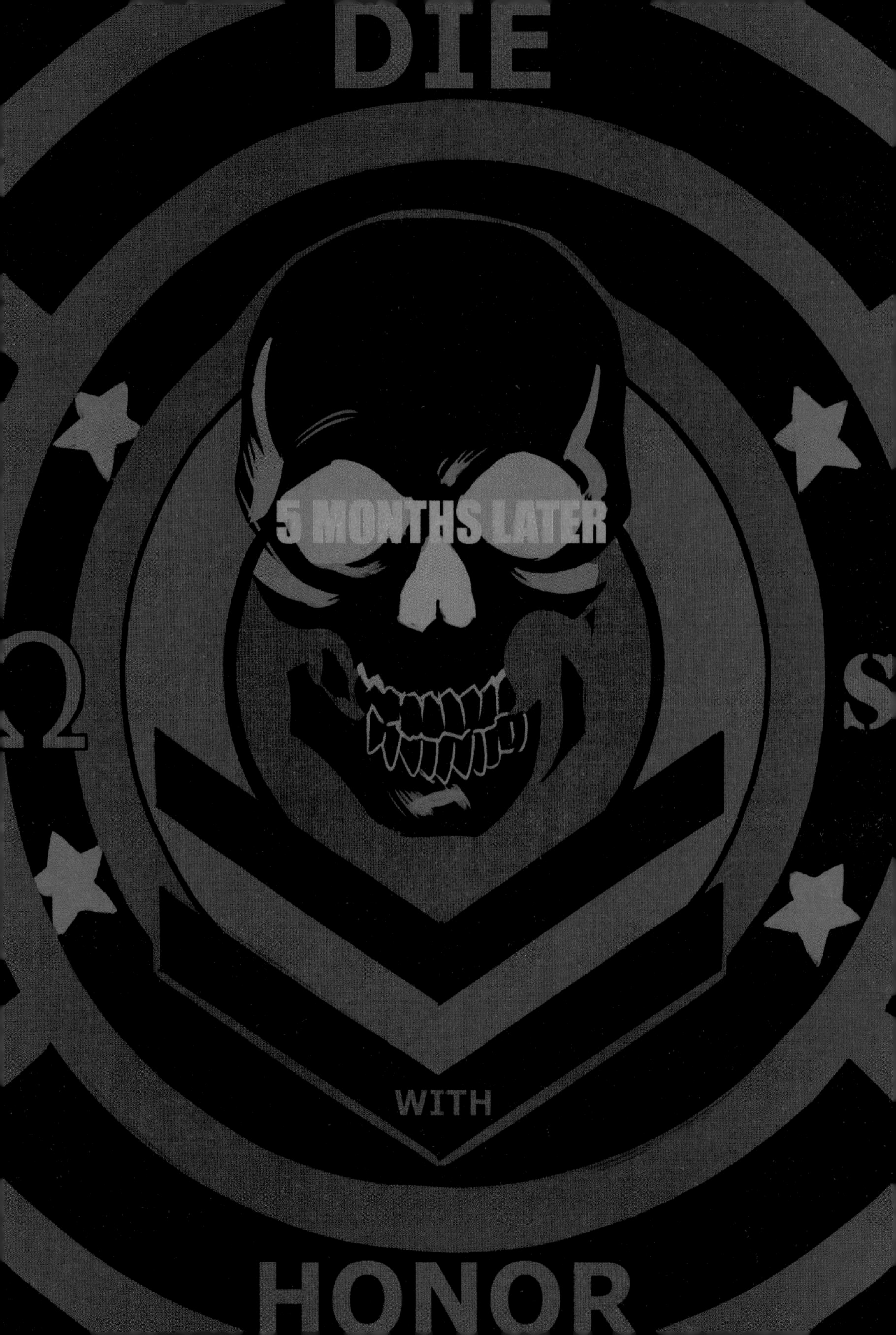
DIE
5 MONTHS LATER
WITH
HONOR

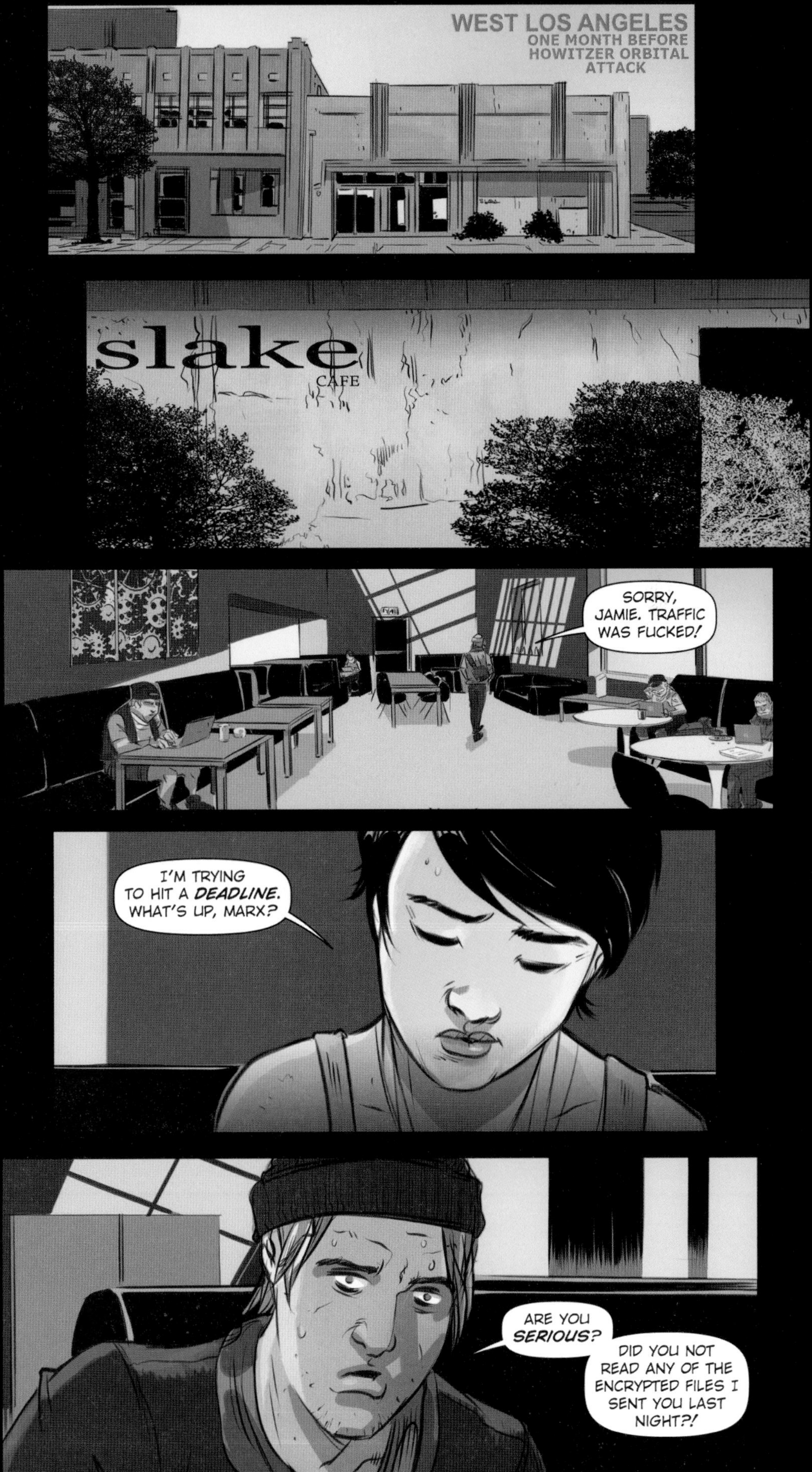
WEST LOS ANGELES
ONE MONTH BEFORE HOWITZER ORBITAL ATTACK
slake
CAFE
SORRY, JAMIE. TRAFFIC WAS FUCKED!
I'M TRYING TO HIT A DEADLINE. WHAT'S UP, MARX?
ARE YOU SERIOUS?
DID YOU NOT READ ANY OF THE ENCRYPTED FILES I SENT YOU LAST NIGHT?!

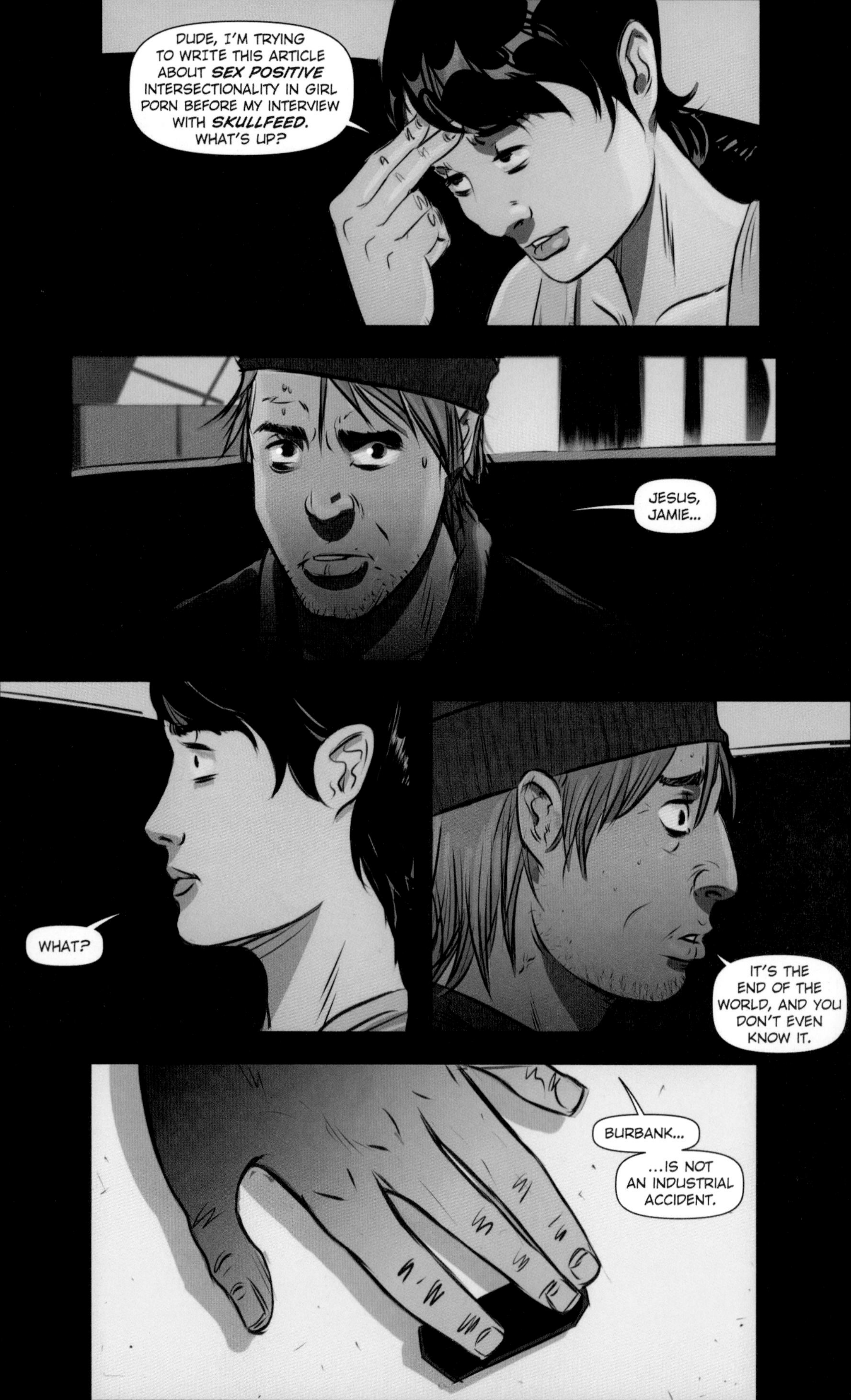
DUDE, I'M TRYING TO WRITE THIS ARTICLE ABOUT ***SEX POSITIVE*** INTERSECTIONALITY IN GIRL PORN BEFORE MY INTERVIEW WITH ***SKULLFEED.*** WHAT'S UP?
JESUS, JAMIE...
WHAT?
IT'S THE END OF THE WORLD, AND YOU DON'T EVEN KNOW IT.
BURBANK...
...IS NOT AN INDUSTRIAL ACCIDENT.

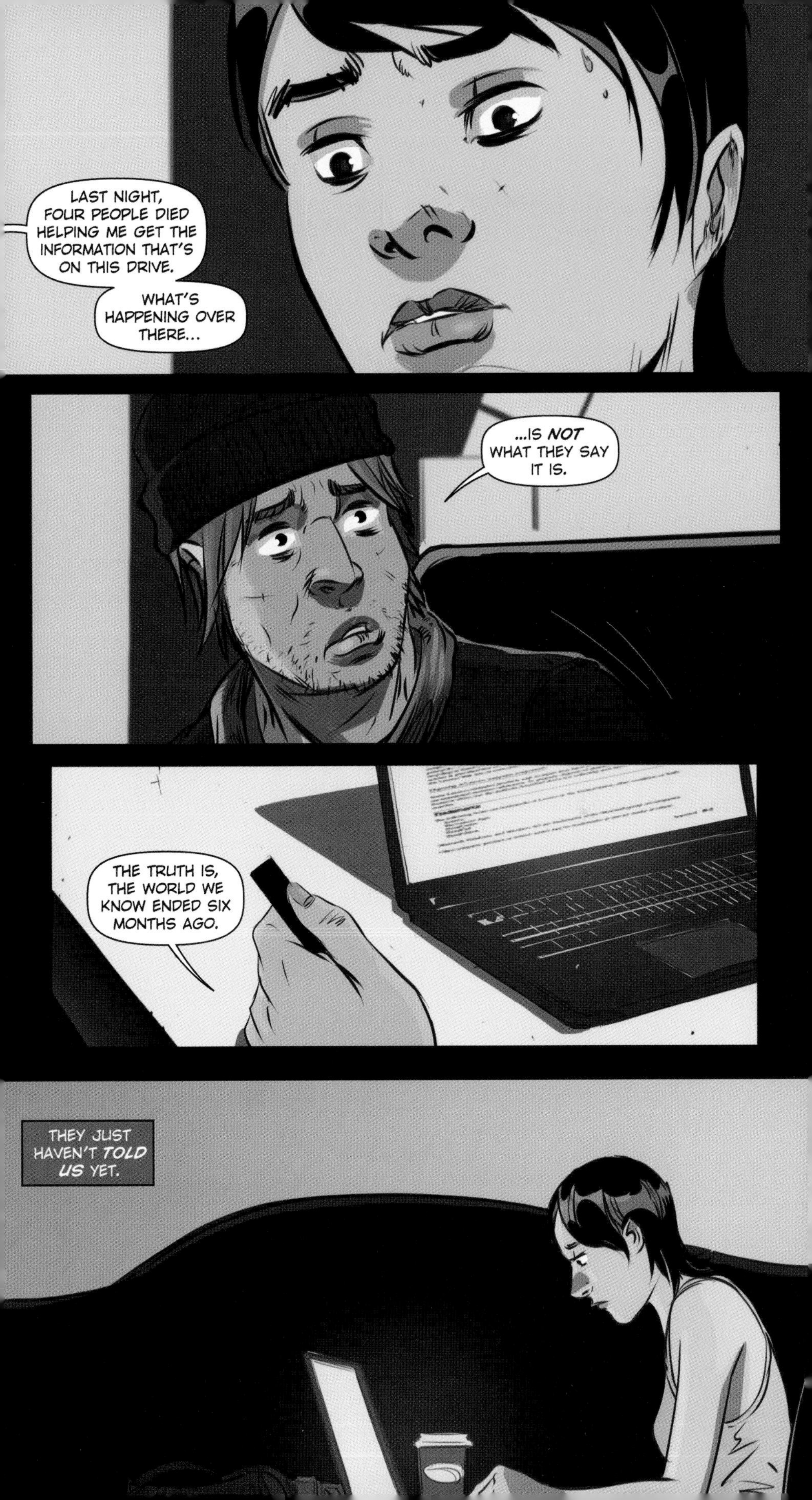
LAST NIGHT, FOUR PEOPLE DIED HELPING ME GET THE INFORMATION THAT'S ON THIS DRIVE.
WHAT'S HAPPENING OVER THERE...
...IS NOT WHAT THEY SAY IT IS.
THE TRUTH IS, THE WORLD WE KNOW ENDED SIX MONTHS AGO.
THEY JUST HAVEN'T TOLD US YET.

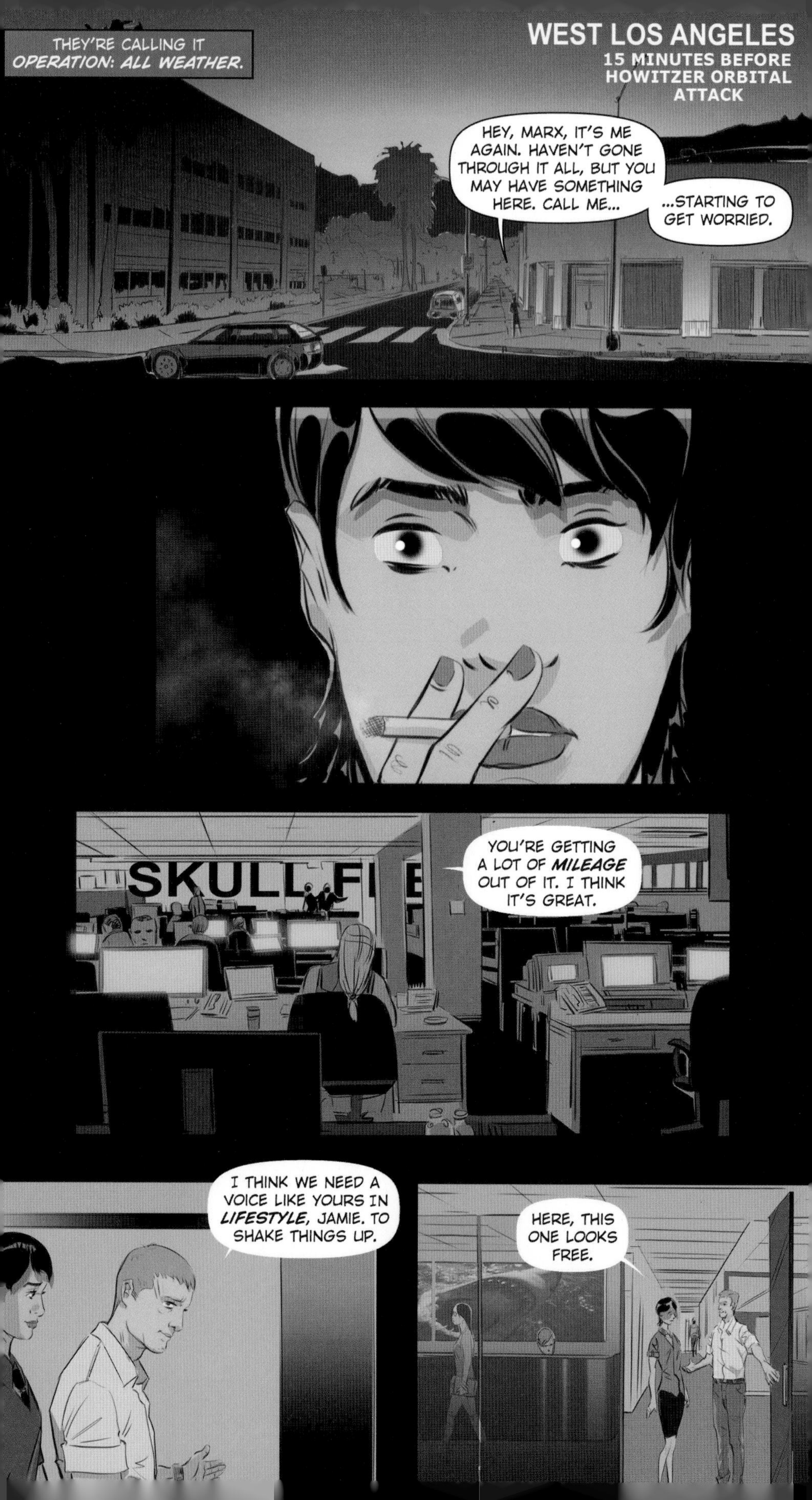
THEY'RE CALLING IT OPERATION: ALL WEATHER.
WEST LOS ANGELES
15 MINUTES BEFORE HOWITZER ORBITAL ATTACK
HEY, MARX, IT'S ME AGAIN. HAVEN'T GONE THROUGH IT ALL, BUT YOU MAY HAVE SOMETHING HERE. CALL ME...
...STARTING TO GET WORRIED.
SKULL FI E
YOU'RE GETTING A LOT OF MILEAGE OUT OF IT. I THINK IT'S GREAT.
I THINK WE NEED A VOICE LIKE YOURS IN LIFESTYLE, JAMIE. TO SHAKE THINGS UP.
HERE, THIS ONE LOOKS FREE.

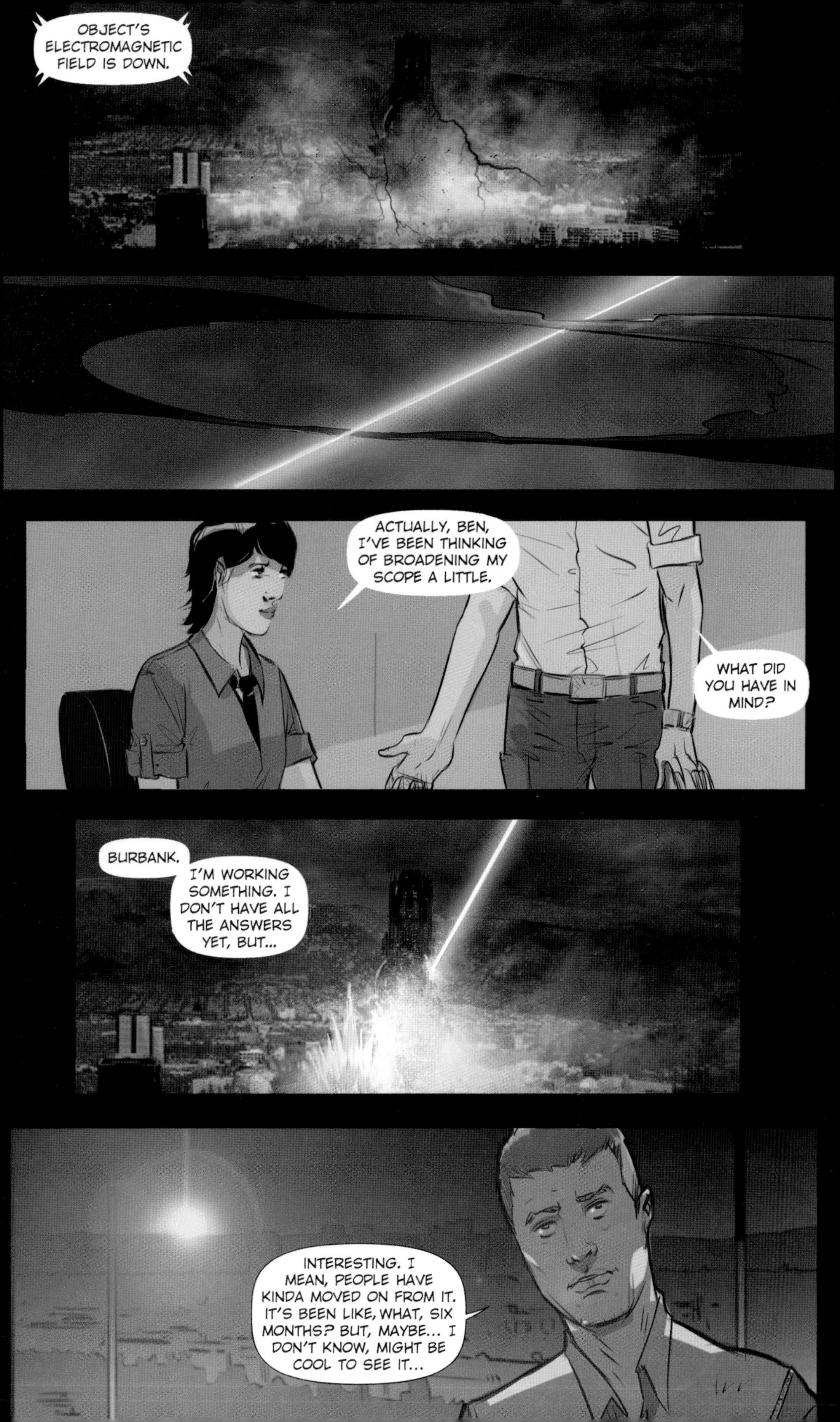
OBJECT'S ELECTROMAGNETIC FIELD IS DOWN.
ACTUALLY, BEN, I'VE BEEN THINKING OF BROADENING MY SCOPE A LITTLE.
WHAT DID YOU HAVE IN MIND?
BURBANK.
I'M WORKING SOMETHING. I DON'T HAVE ALL THE ANSWERS YET, BUT...
INTERESTING. I MEAN, PEOPLE HAVE KINDA MOVED ON FROM IT. IT'S BEEN LIKE, WHAT, SIX MONTHS? BUT, MAYBE... I DON'T KNOW, MIGHT BE COOL TO SEE IT...

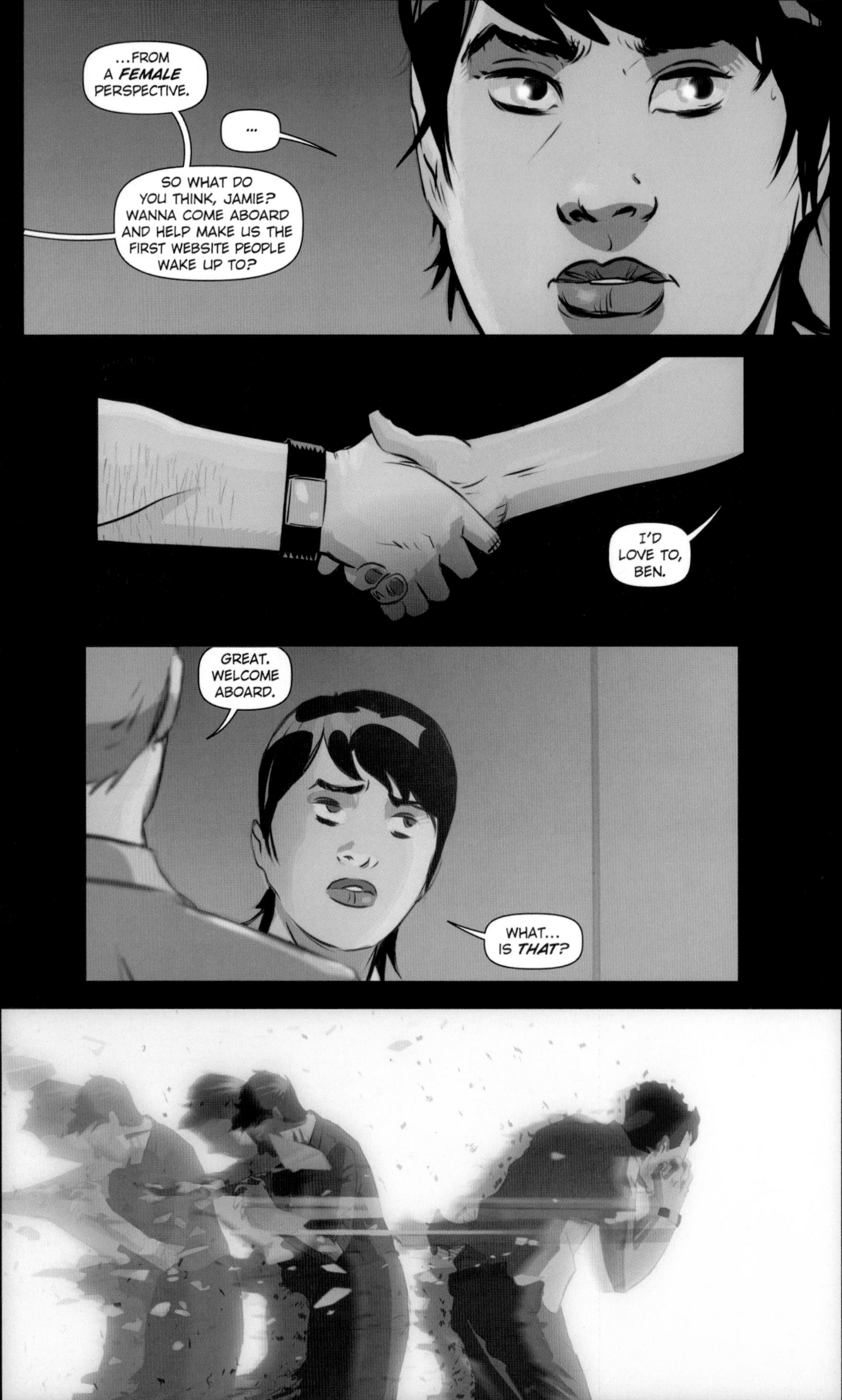
...FROM A *FEMALE* PERSPECTIVE.
...
SO WHAT DO YOU THINK, JAMIE? WANNA COME ABOARD AND HELP MAKE US THE FIRST WEBSITE PEOPLE WAKE UP TO?
I'D LOVE TO, BEN.
GREAT. WELCOME ABOARD.
WHAT... IS *THAT*?

BURBANK, CA
POST
HOWITZER ORBITAL
ATTACK

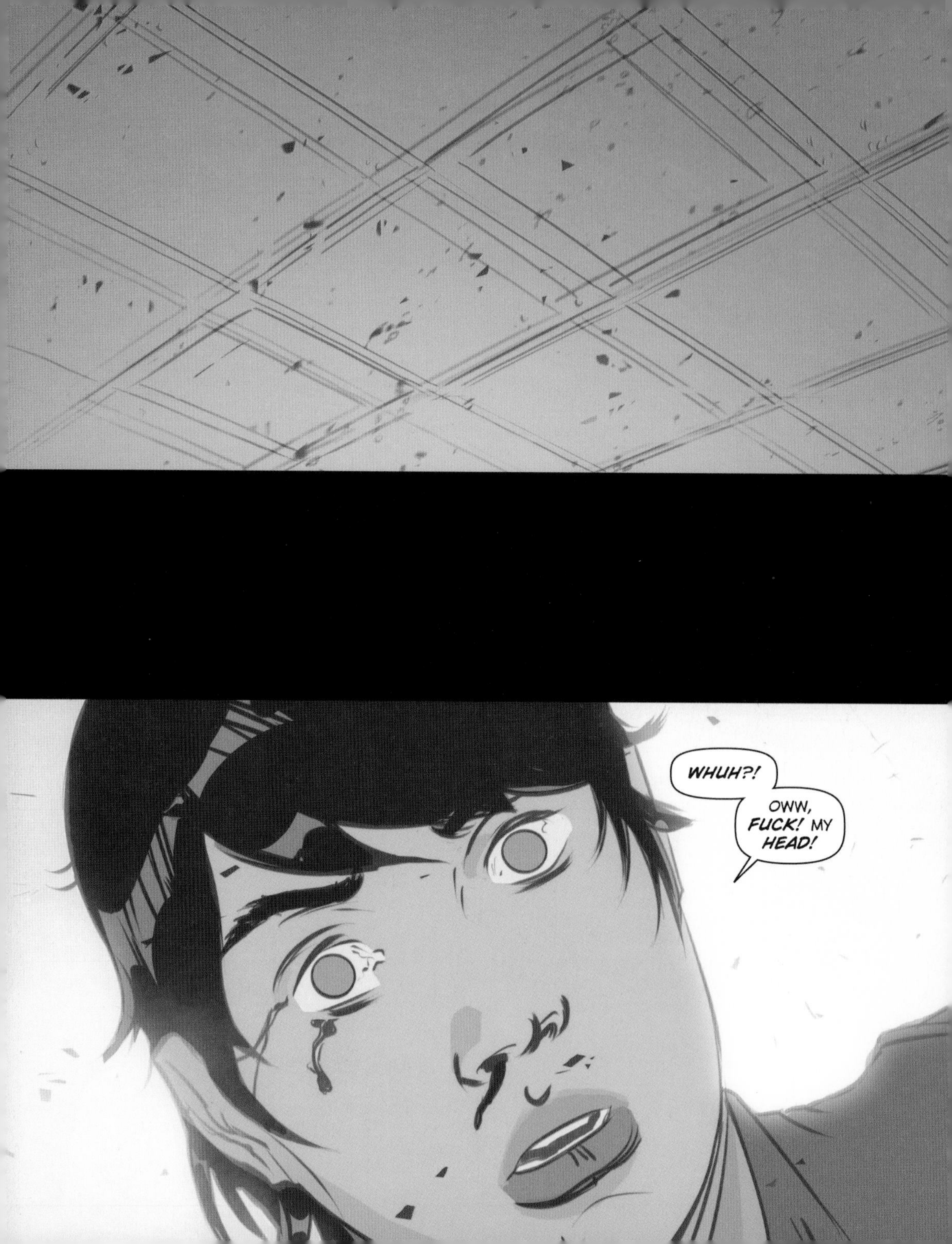
WHUH?!
OWW, FUCK! MY HEAD!

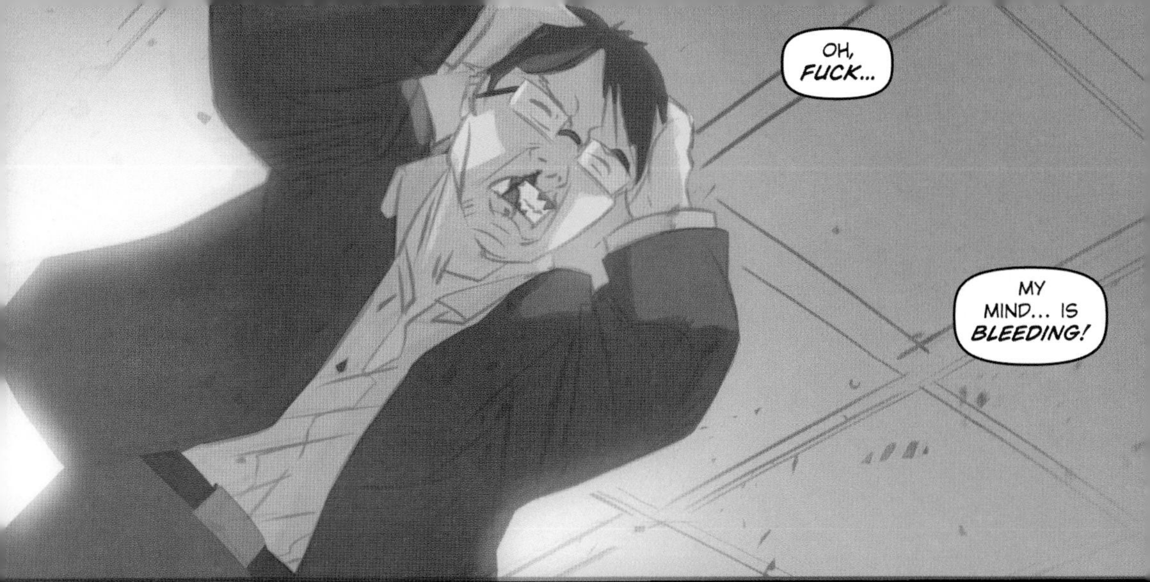
OH, *FUCK...*
MY MIND... IS *BLEEDING!*

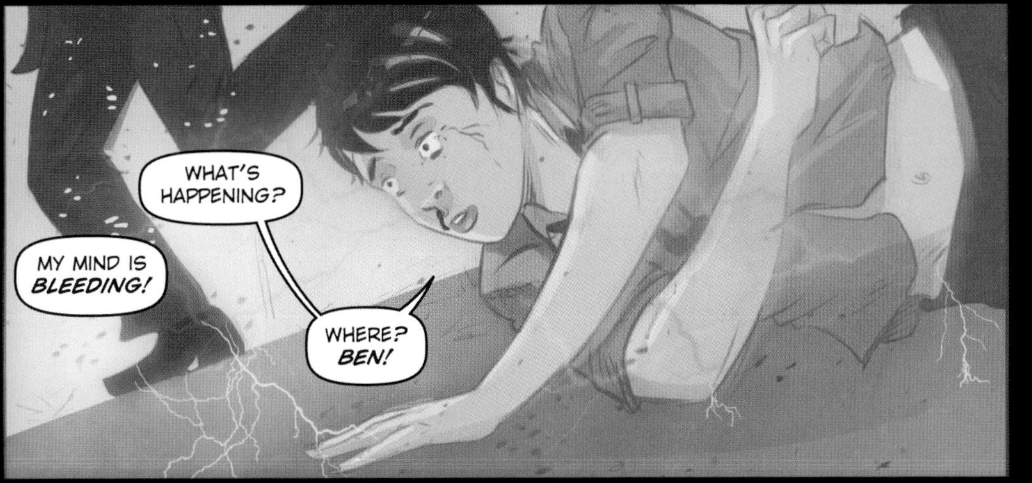
WHAT'S HAPPENING?
MY MIND IS *BLEEDING!*
WHERE? *BEN!*

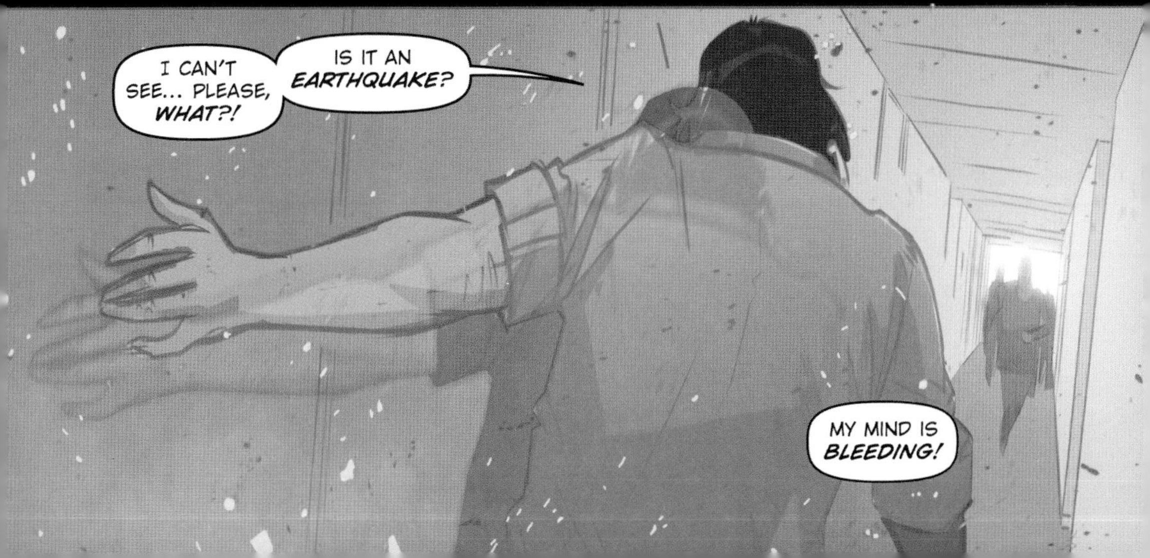
I CAN'T SEE... PLEASE, *WHAT?!*
IS IT AN *EARTHQUAKE?*
MY MIND IS *BLEEDING!*

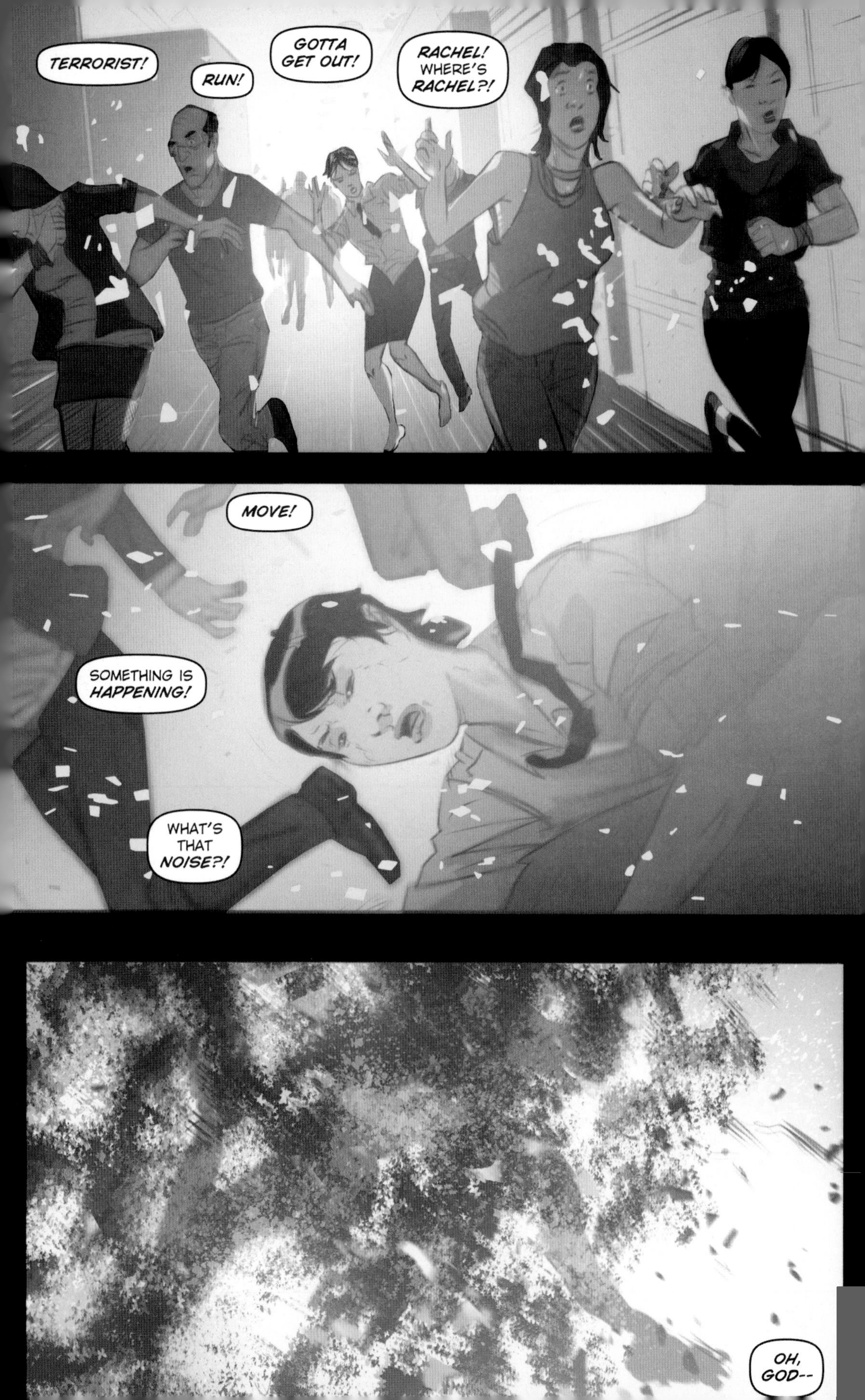
TERRORIST!
RUN!
GOTTA GET OUT!
RACHEL! WHERE'S RACHEL?!
MOVE!
SOMETHING IS HAPPENING!
WHAT'S THAT NOISE?!
OH, GOD--

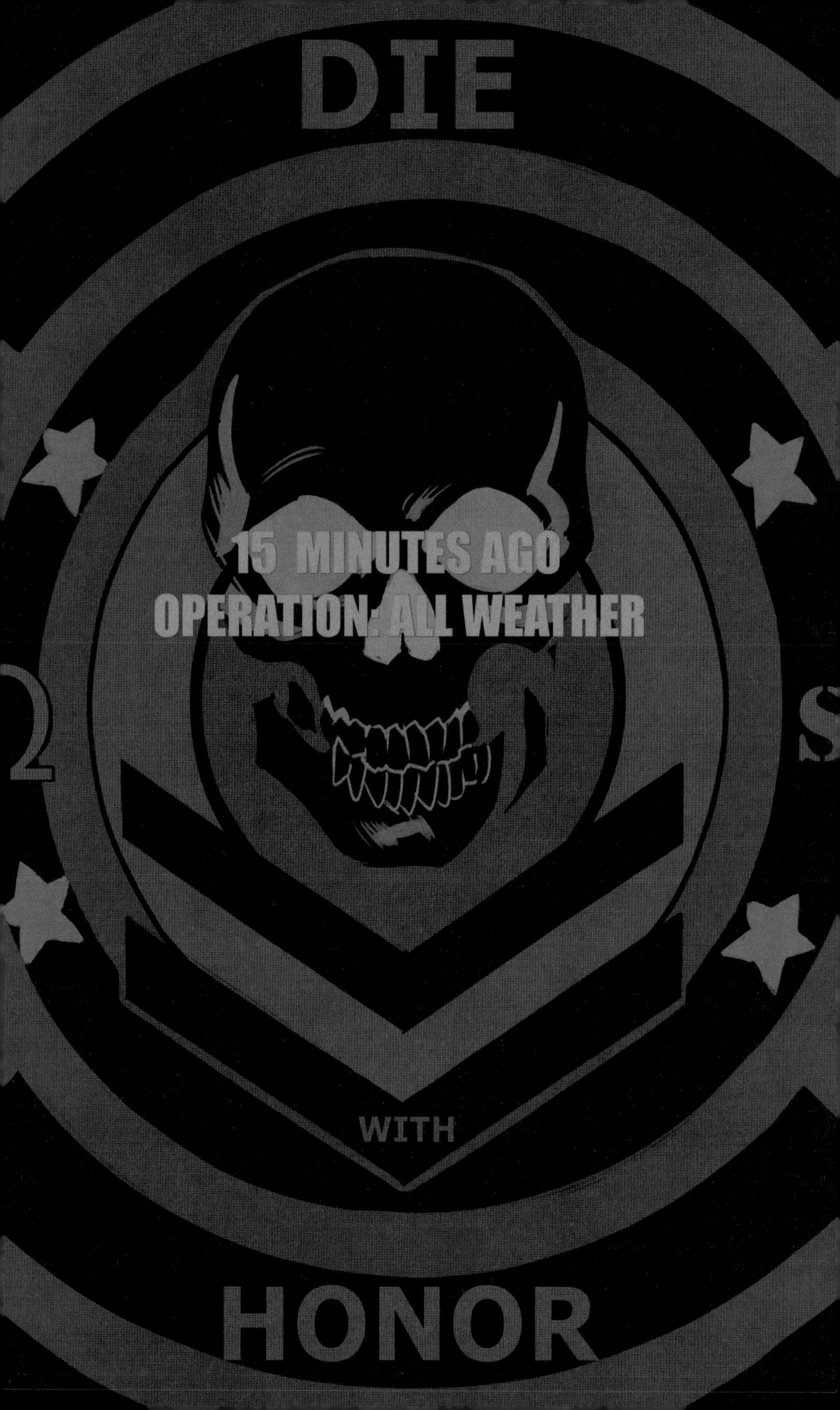
DIE
15 MINUTES AGO
OPERATION: ALL WEATHER
WITH
HONOR

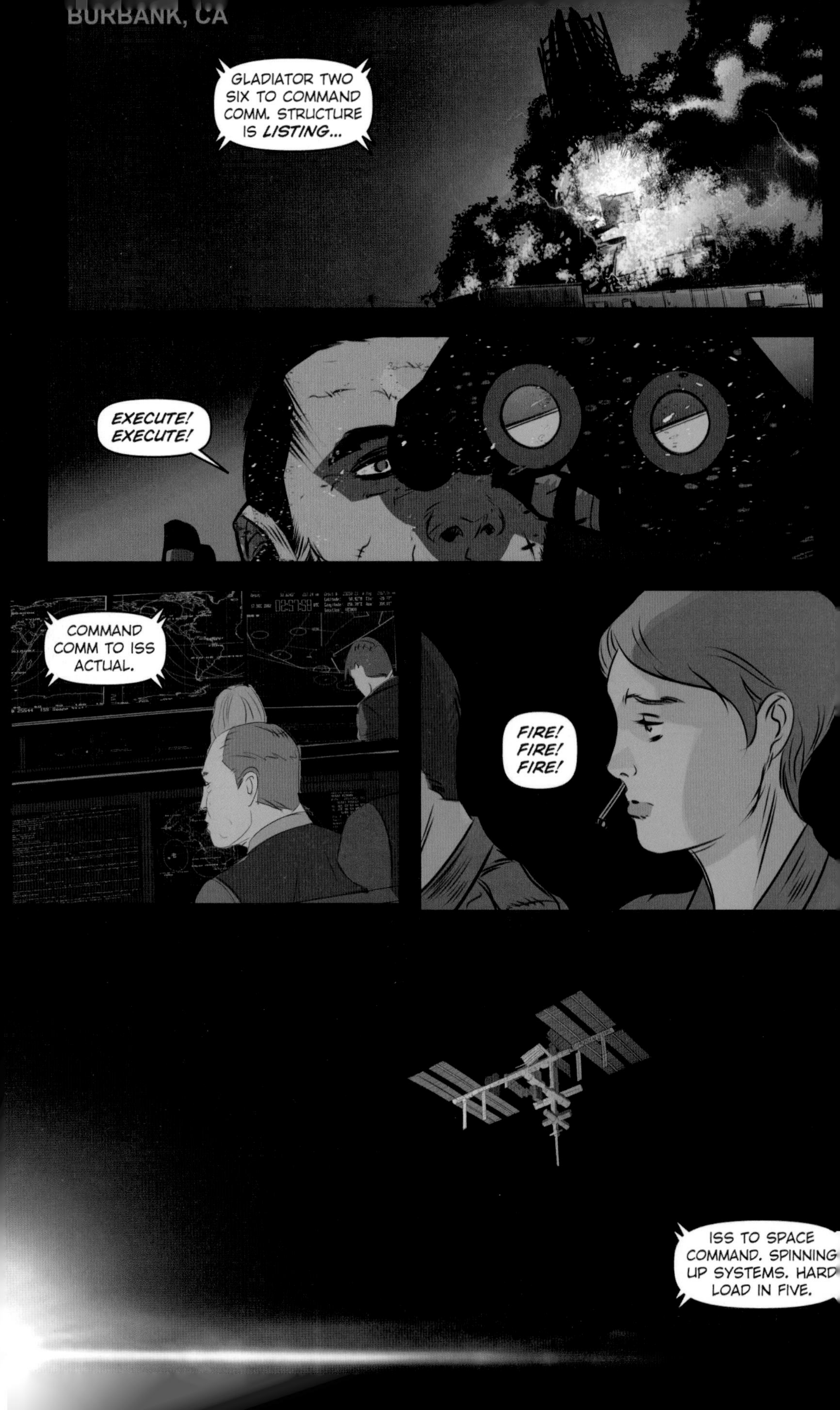
BURBANK, CA
GLADIATOR TWO SIX TO COMMAND COMM. STRUCTURE IS LISTING...
EXECUTE! EXECUTE!
COMMAND COMM TO ISS ACTUAL.
FIRE! FIRE! FIRE!
ISS TO SPACE COMMAND. SPINNING UP SYSTEMS. HARD LOAD IN FIVE.

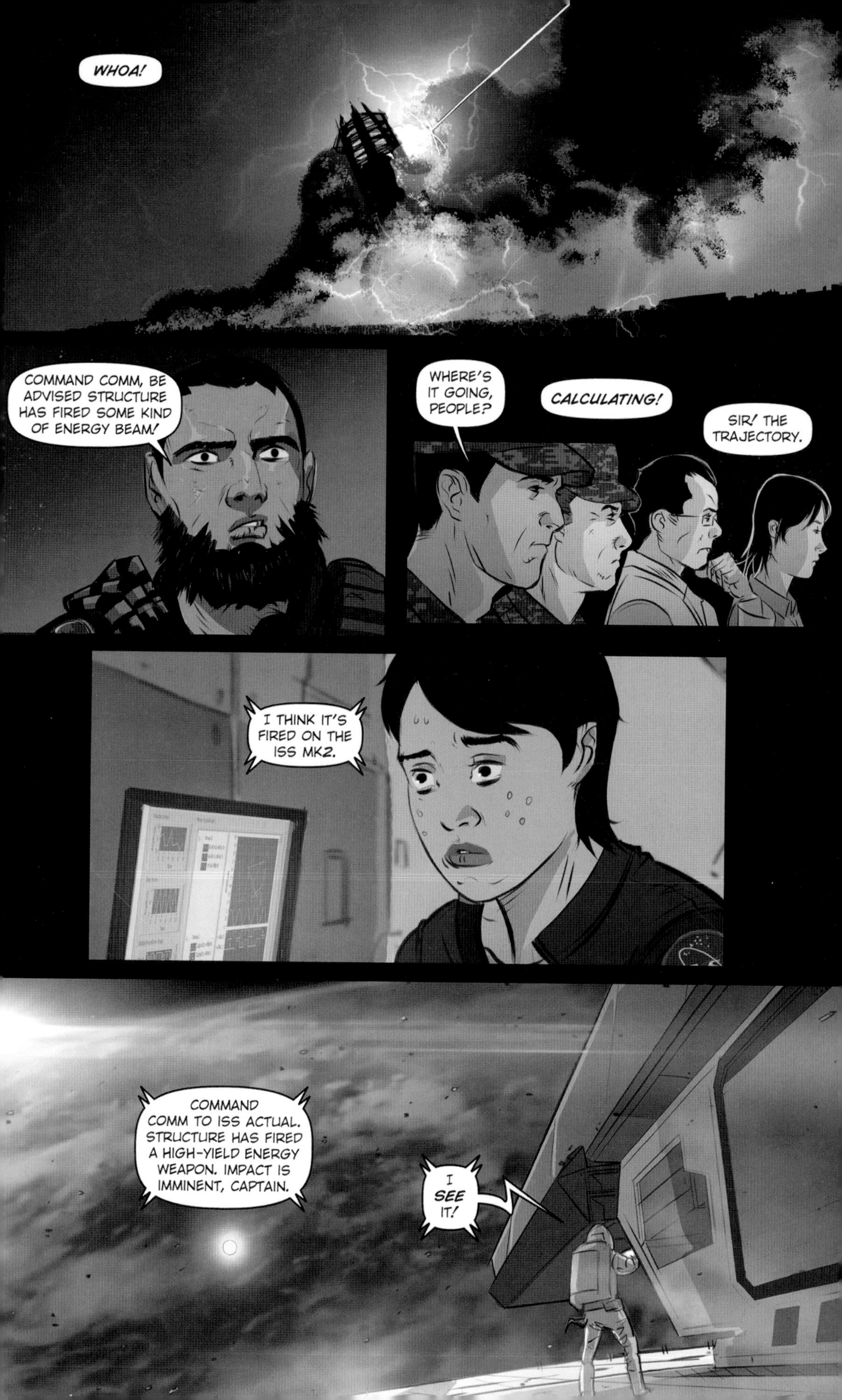
WHOA!
COMMAND COMM, BE ADVISED STRUCTURE HAS FIRED SOME KIND OF ENERGY BEAM!
WHERE'S IT GOING, PEOPLE?
CALCULATING!
SIR! THE TRAJECTORY.
I THINK IT'S FIRED ON THE ISS MK2.
COMMAND COMM TO ISS ACTUAL. STRUCTURE HAS FIRED A HIGH-YIELD ENERGY WEAPON. IMPACT IS IMMINENT, CAPTAIN.
I SEE IT!

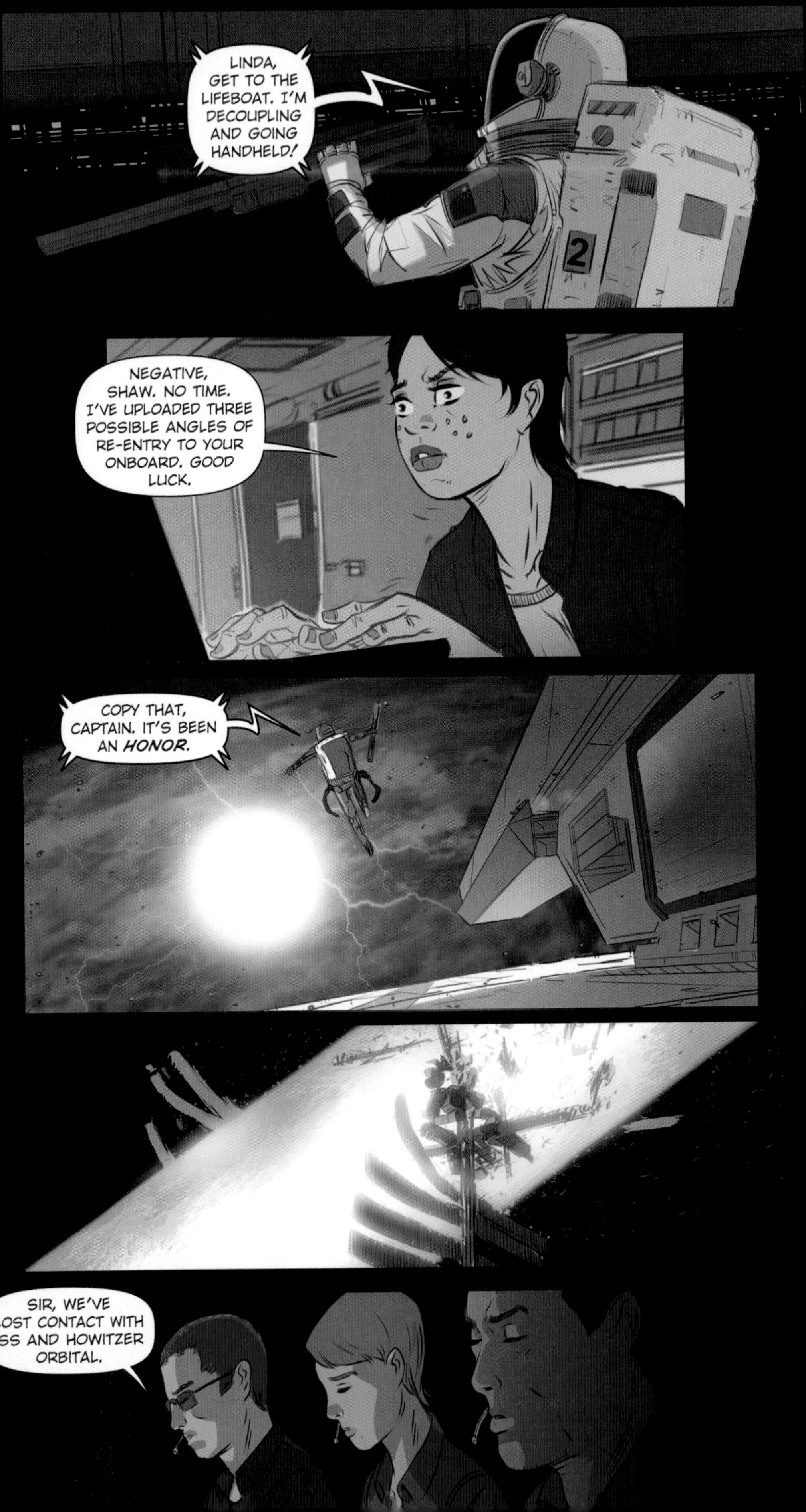
LINDA, GET TO THE LIFEBOAT. I'M DECOUPLING AND GOING HANDHELD!
NEGATIVE, SHAW. NO TIME. I'VE UPLOADED THREE POSSIBLE ANGLES OF RE-ENTRY TO YOUR ONBOARD. GOOD LUCK.
COPY THAT, CAPTAIN. IT'S BEEN AN *HONOR*.
SIR, WE'VE LOST CONTACT WITH ISS AND HOWITZER ORBITAL.

GLADIATOR TWO SIX TO COMMAND COMM...

STRUCTURE HAS LAUNCHED THREE OBJECTS!

CHRIST, WE ONLY GOT ONE SHOT OFF.

ESCAPE CRAFT, DR. ZAYVIAN?

YES, LT. FOX. PROBABLY.

WE SHOULD HAVE EVACUATED ALL OF LOS ANGELES FOR THIS.

GET ME THE PRESIDENT. WE'RE ABOUT TO BLOW HIS MILITARY BUDGET FOR THE NEXT *160* YEARS. OUR *AO* HAS JUST TRIPLED.

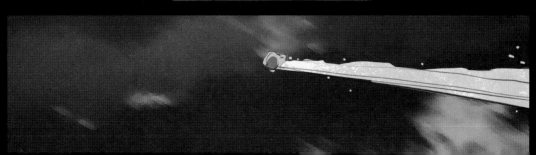

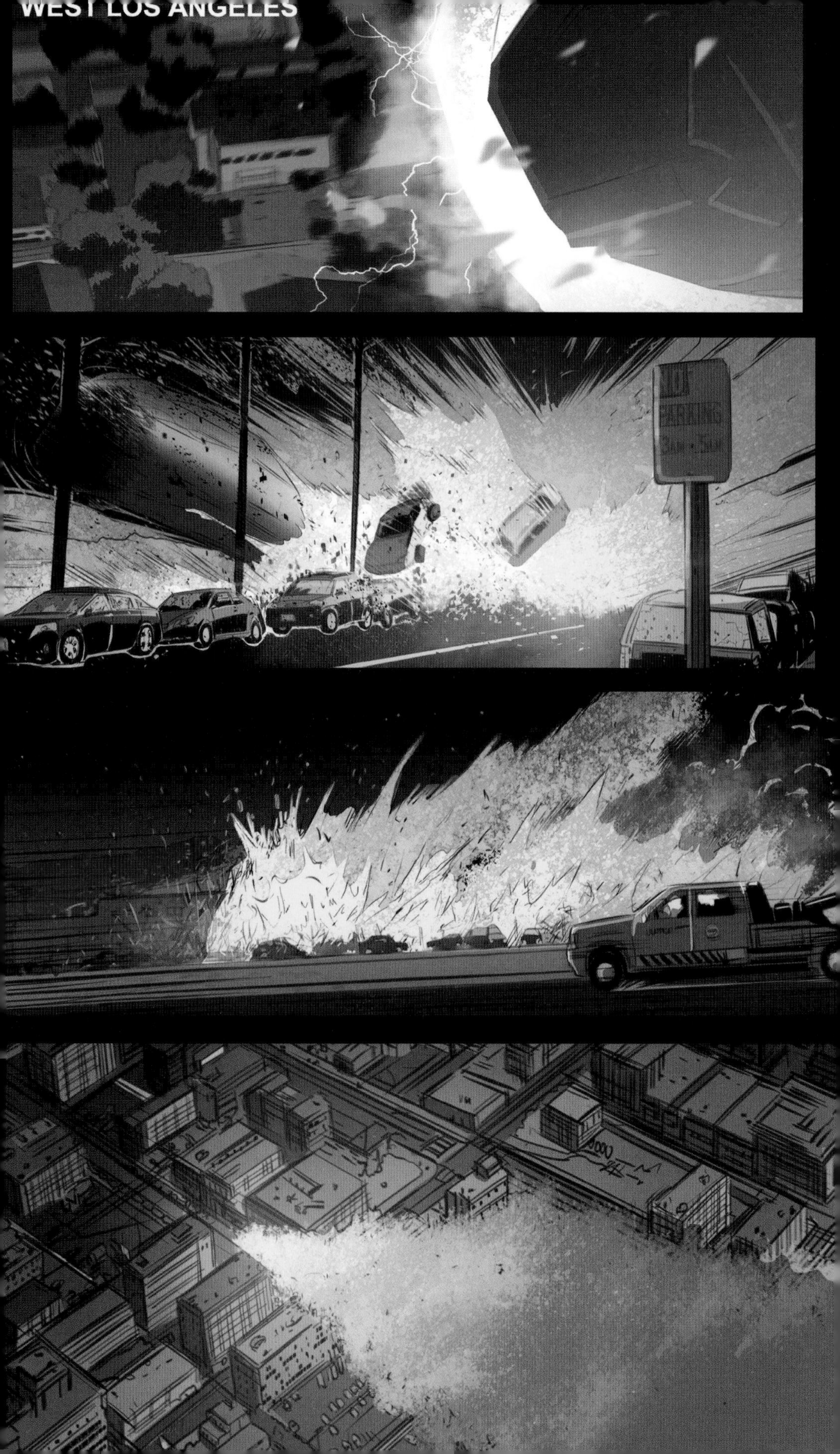
WEST LOS ANGELES

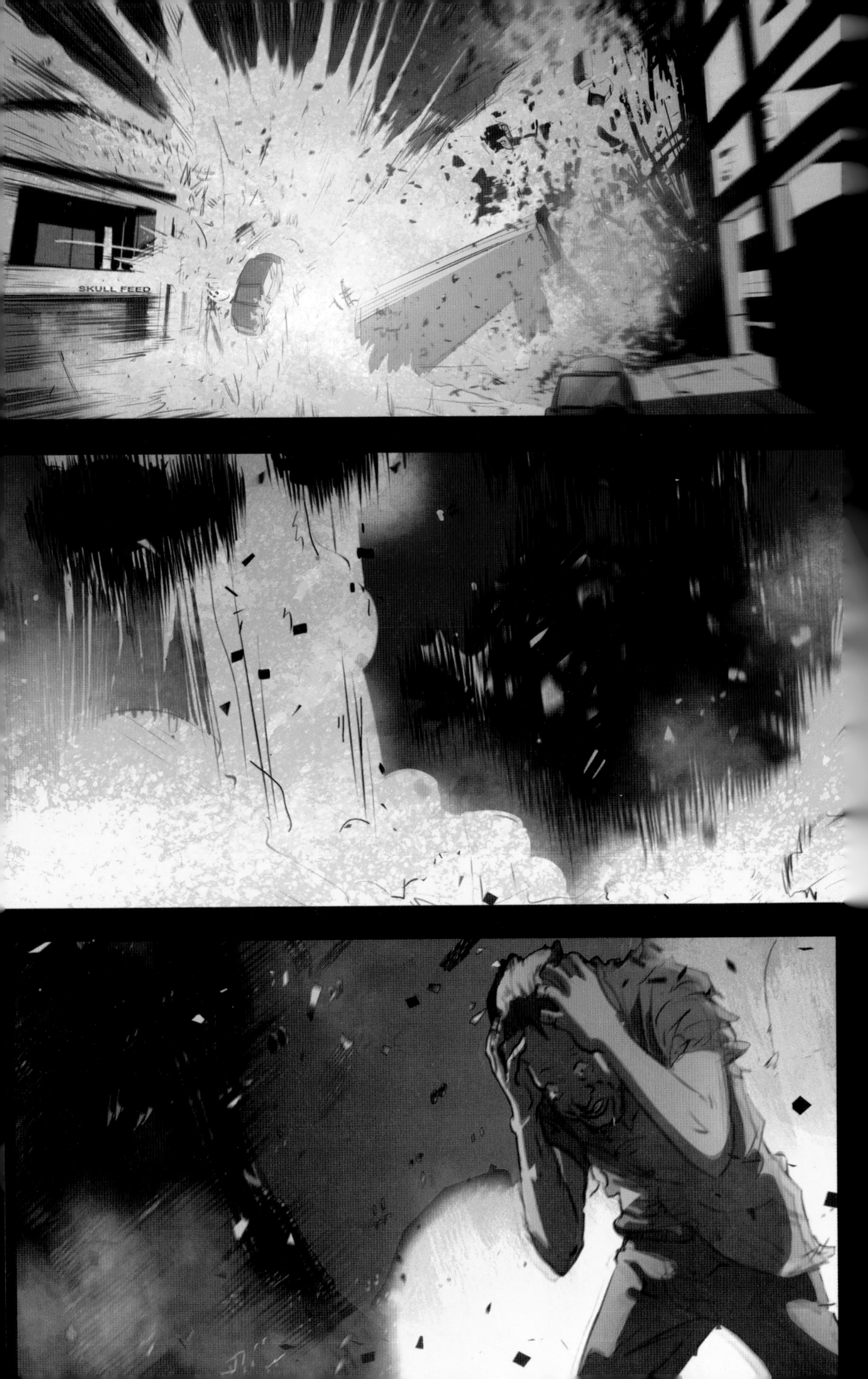
SKULL FEED

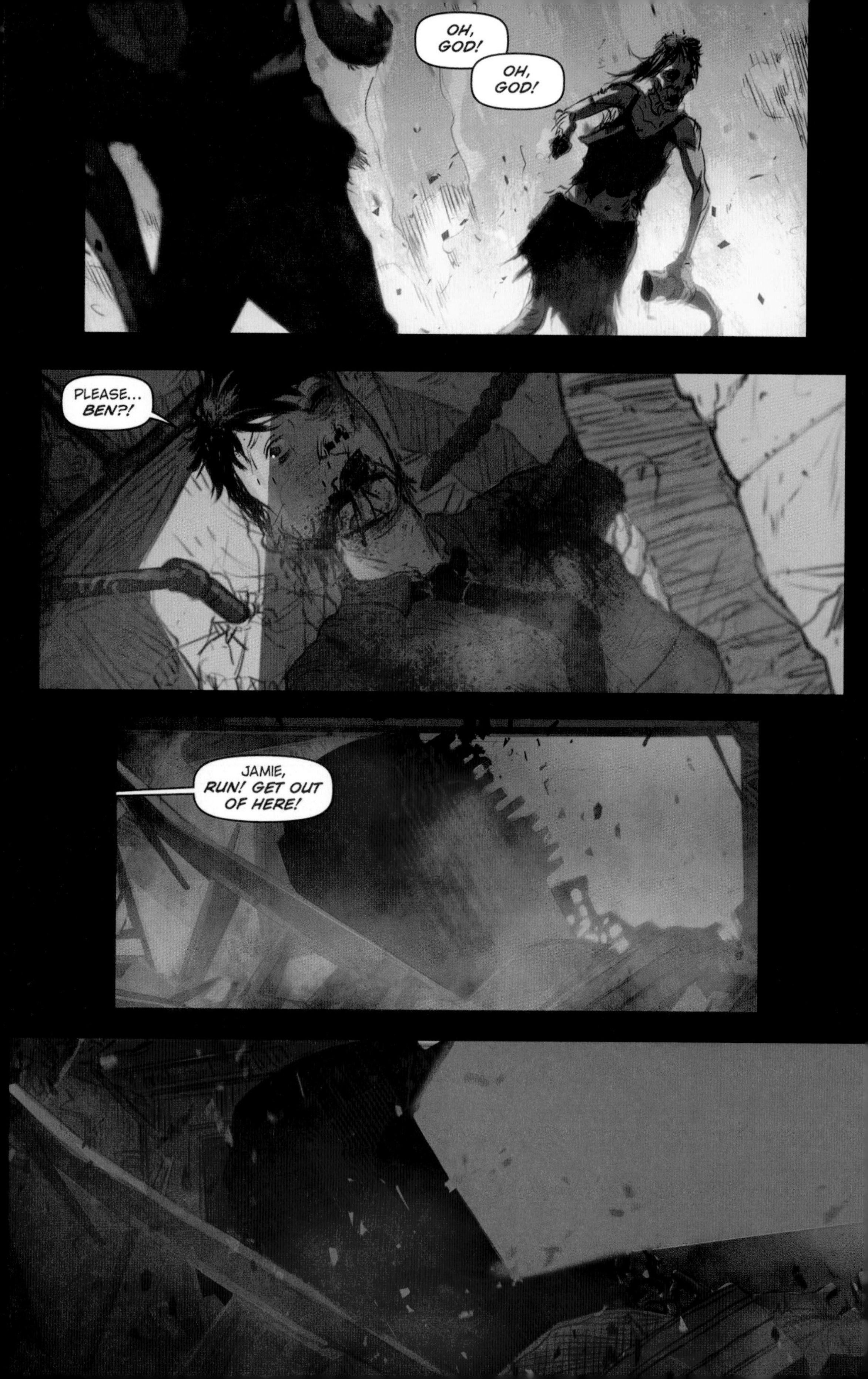

OH, GOD!
OH, GOD!
PLEASE... BEN?!
JAMIE, RUN! GET OUT OF HERE!

PLEASE, SOMEBODY...

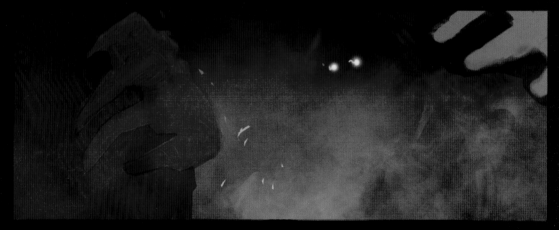

PLEASE, SOMEBODY...

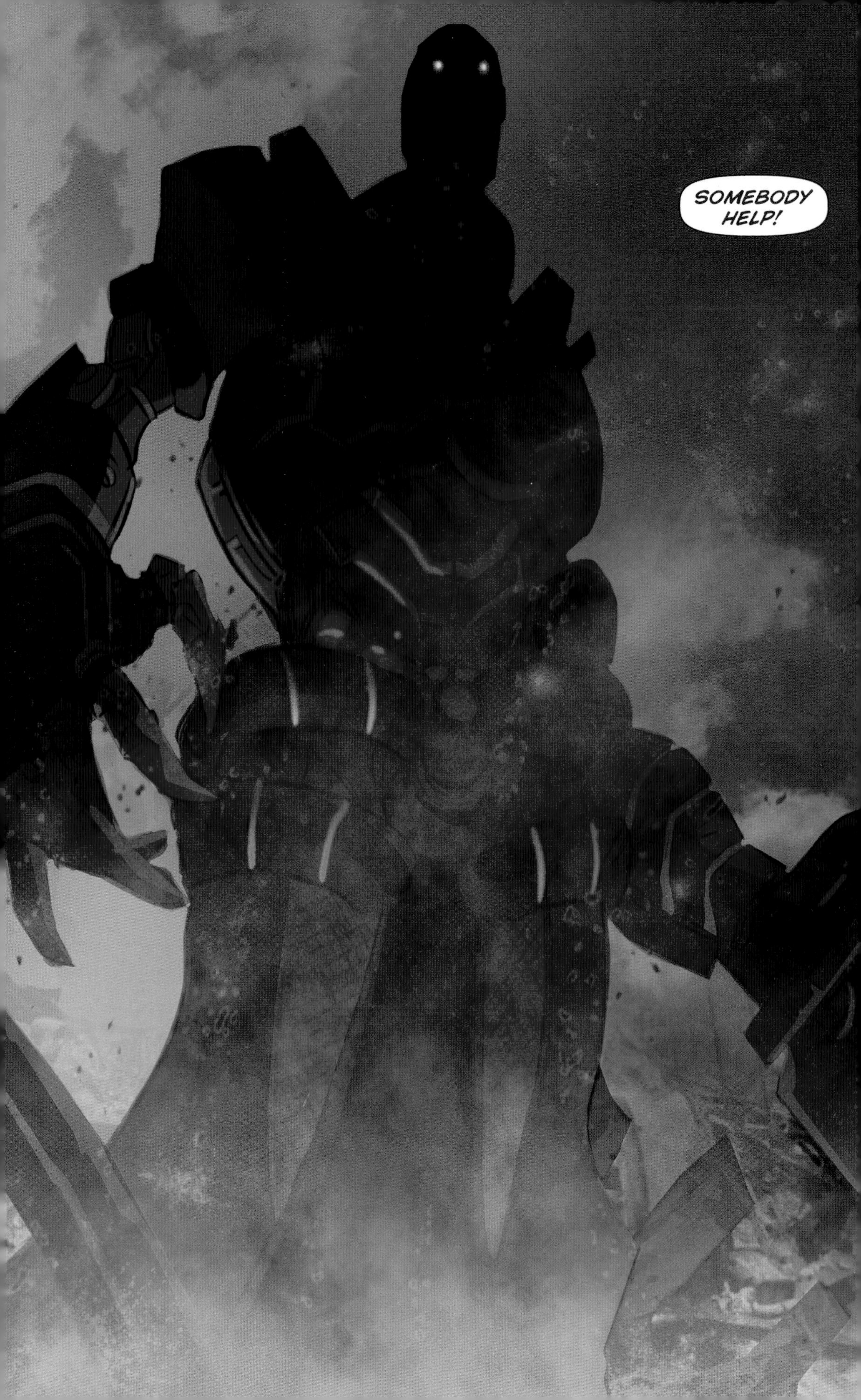
SOMEBODY HELP!

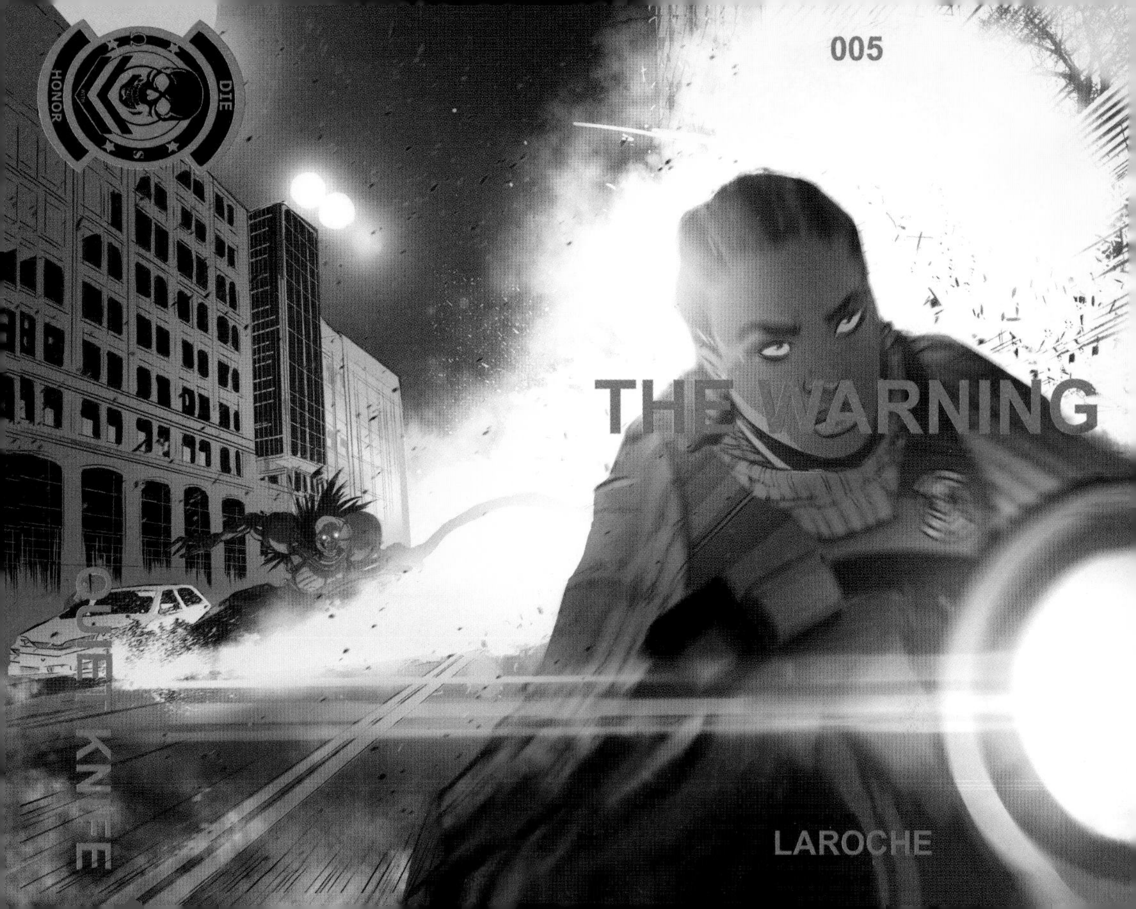
HONOR
DIE
005
THE WARNING
QUIET KNIFE
LAROCHE

QUIET KNIFE

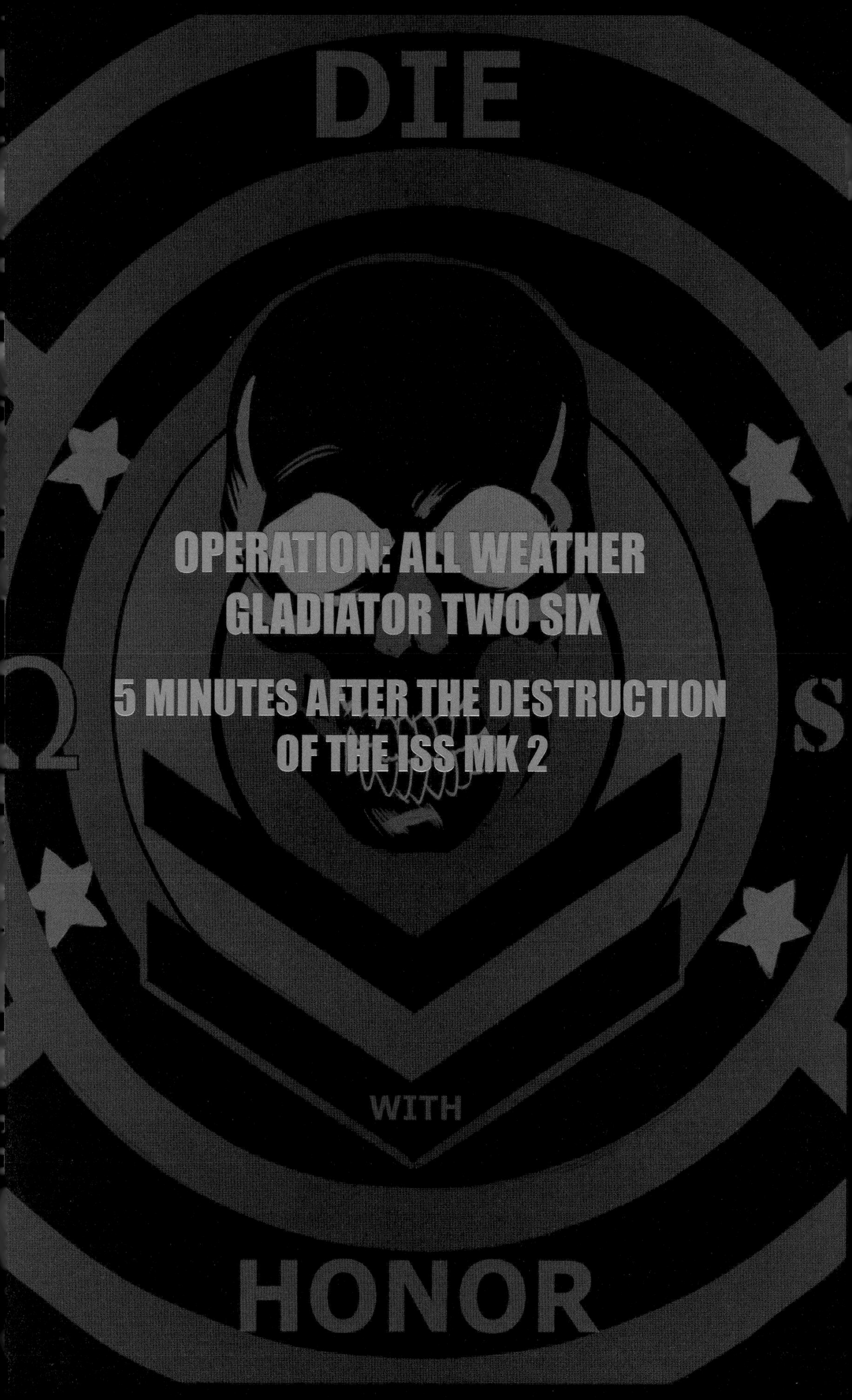

OPERATION: ALL WEATHER
GLADIATOR TWO SIX

5 MINUTES AFTER THE DESTRUCTION
OF THE ISS MK 2

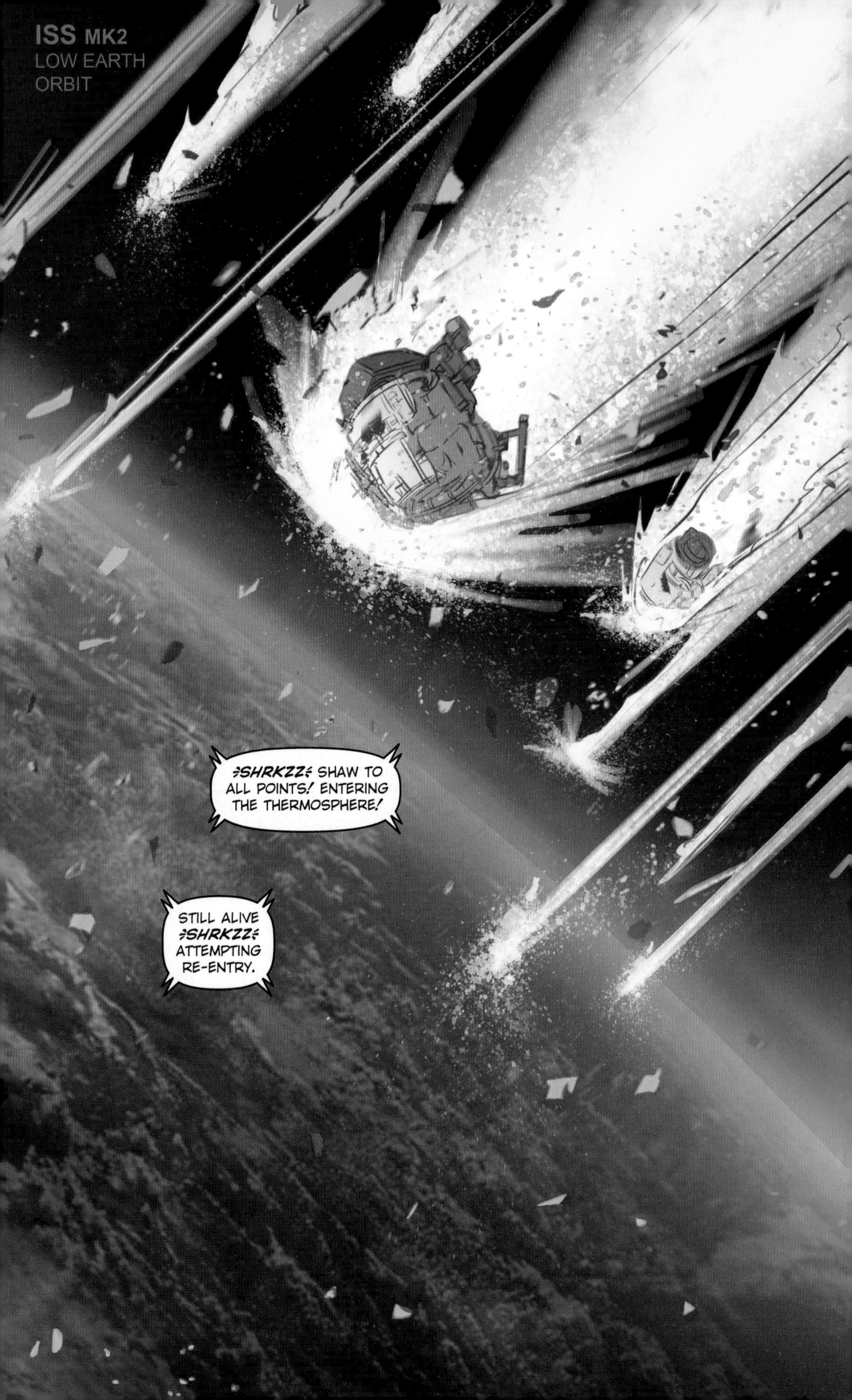
ISS MK2
LOW EARTH ORBIT
SHRKZZ SHAW TO ALL POINTS! ENTERING THE THERMOSPHERE!
STILL ALIVE SHRKZZ ATTEMPTING RE-ENTRY.

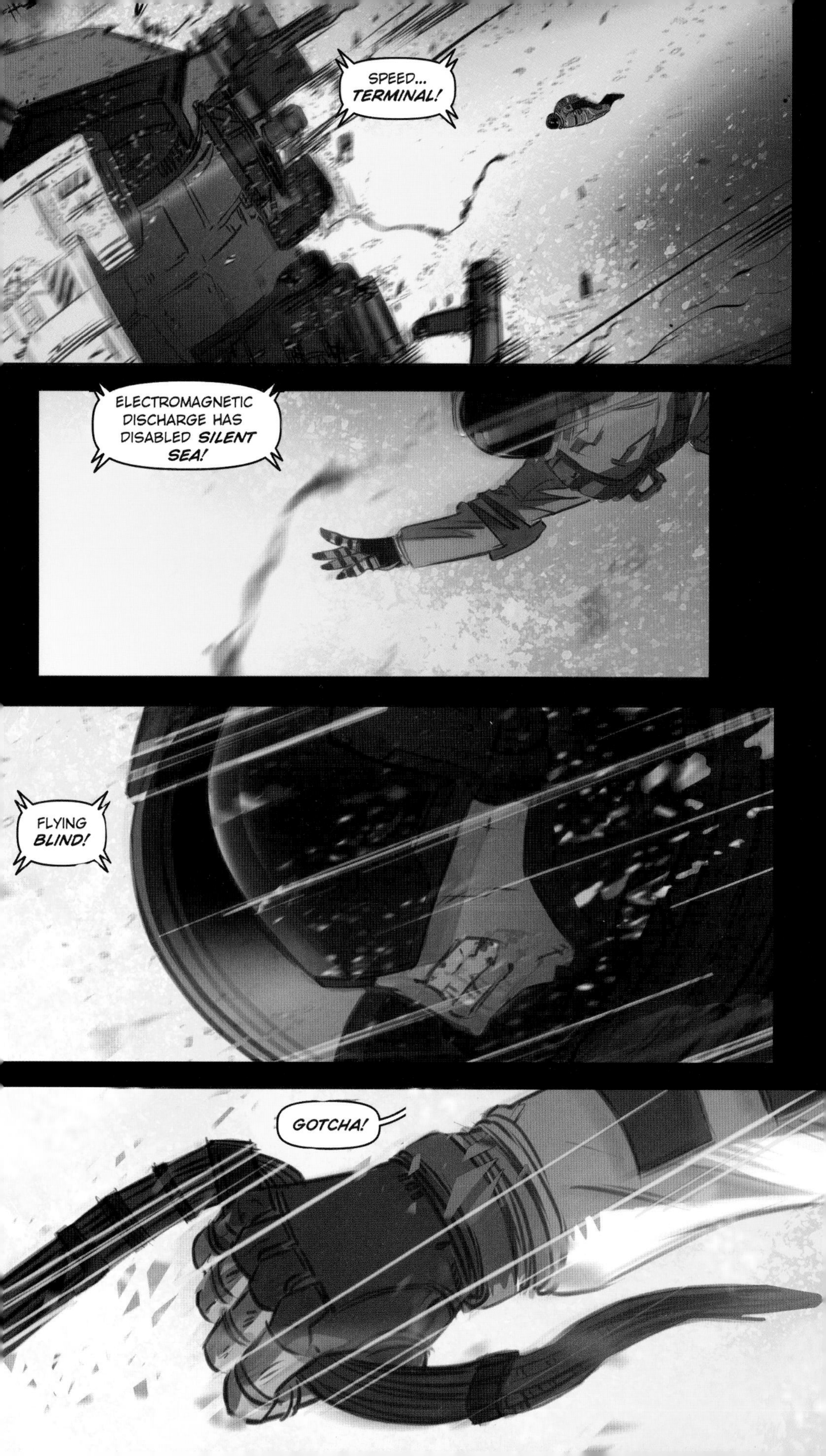
SPEED... TERMINAL!
ELECTROMAGNETIC DISCHARGE HAS DISABLED SILENT SEA!
FLYING BLIND!
GOTCHA!

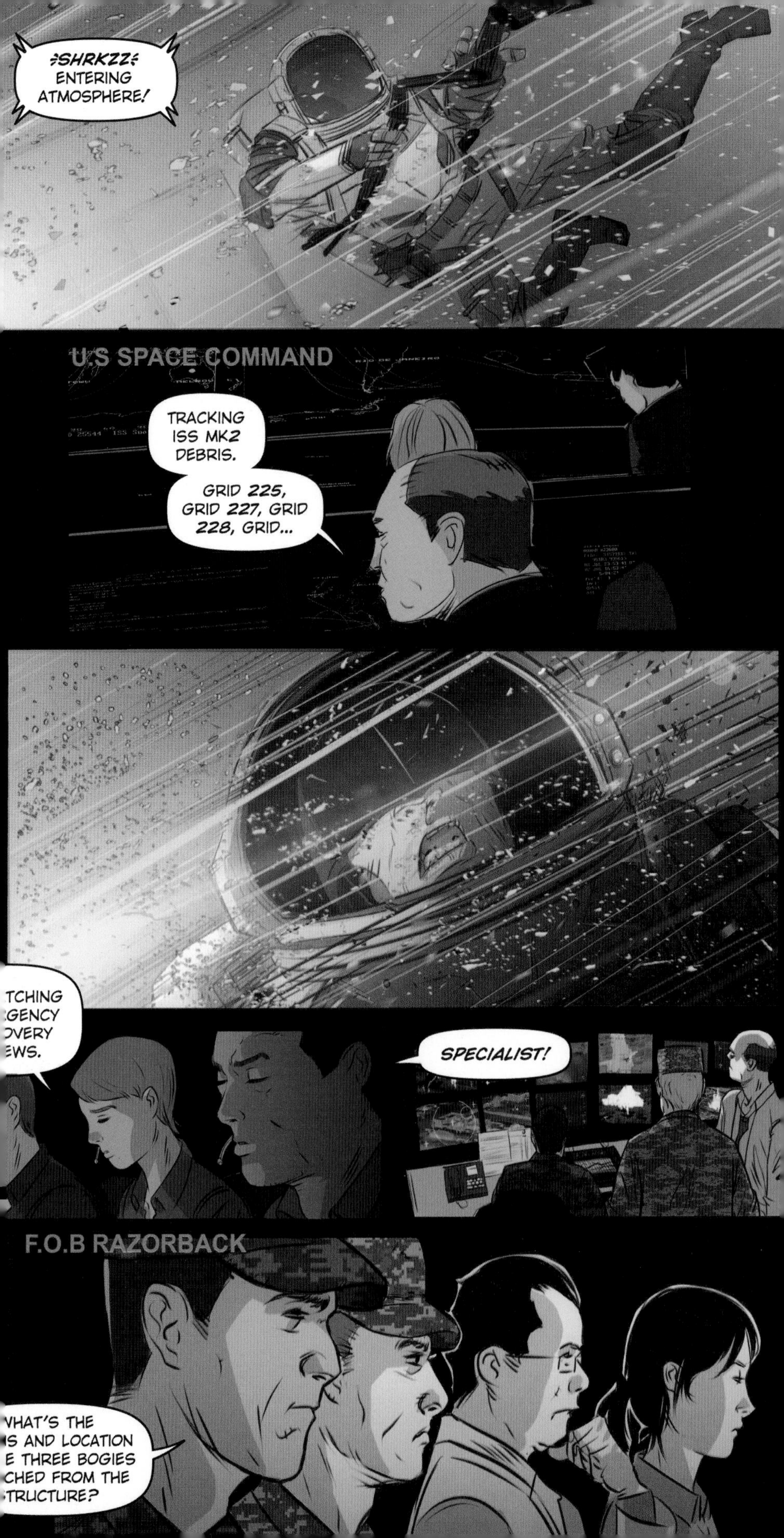

SHRKZZ ENTERING ATMOSPHERE!
U.S SPACE COMMAND
TRACKING ISS MK2 DEBRIS.
GRID 225, GRID 227, GRID 228, GRID...
TCHING GENCY OVERY EWS.
SPECIALIST!
F.O.B RAZORBACK
WHAT'S THE S AND LOCATION E THREE BOGIES CHED FROM THE STRUCTURE?

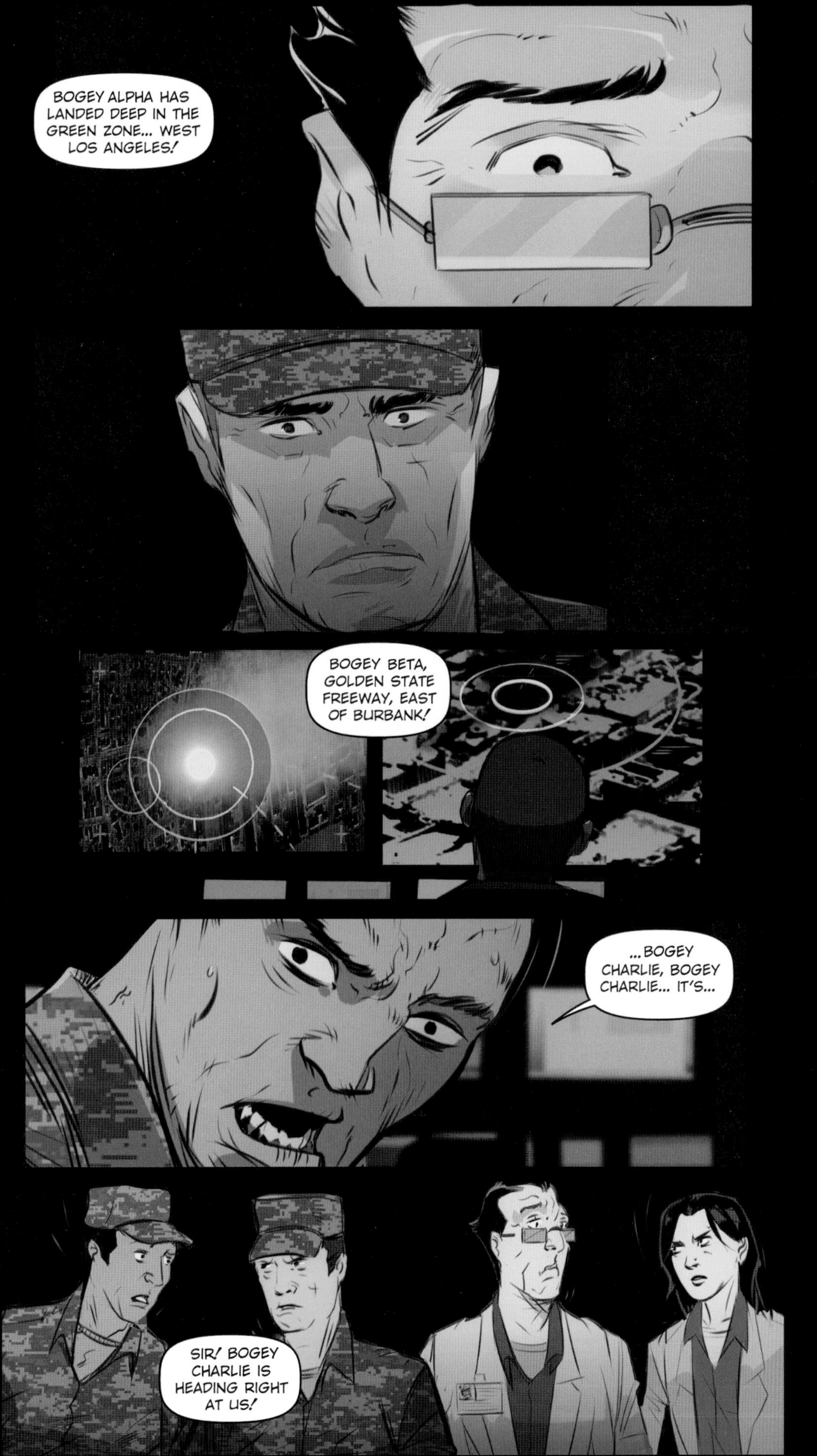
BOGEY ALPHA HAS LANDED DEEP IN THE GREEN ZONE... WEST LOS ANGELES!
BOGEY BETA, GOLDEN STATE FREEWAY, EAST OF BURBANK!
...BOGEY CHARLIE, BOGEY CHARLIE... IT'S...
SIR! BOGEY CHARLIE IS HEADING RIGHT AT US!

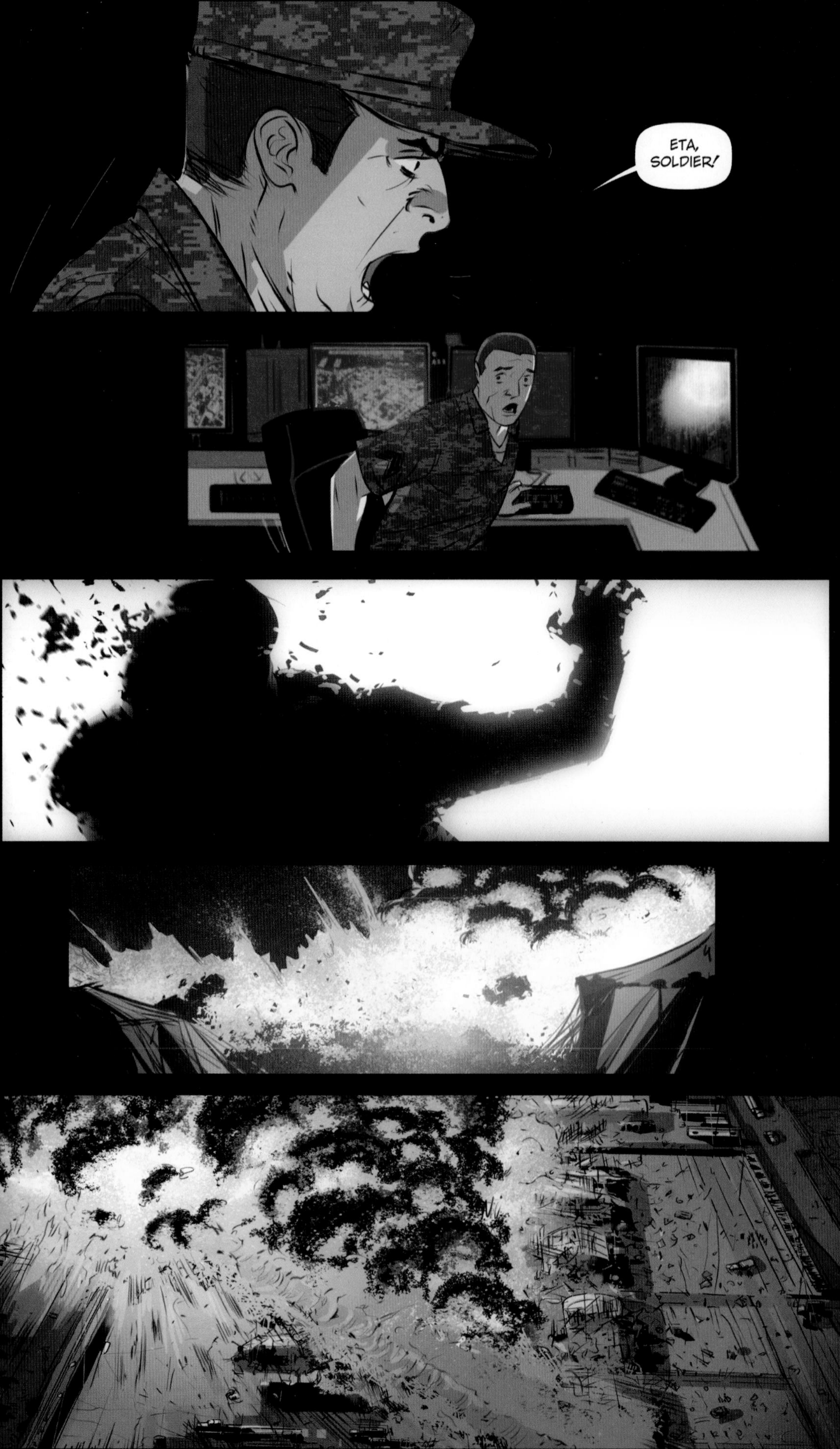
ETA, SOLDIER!

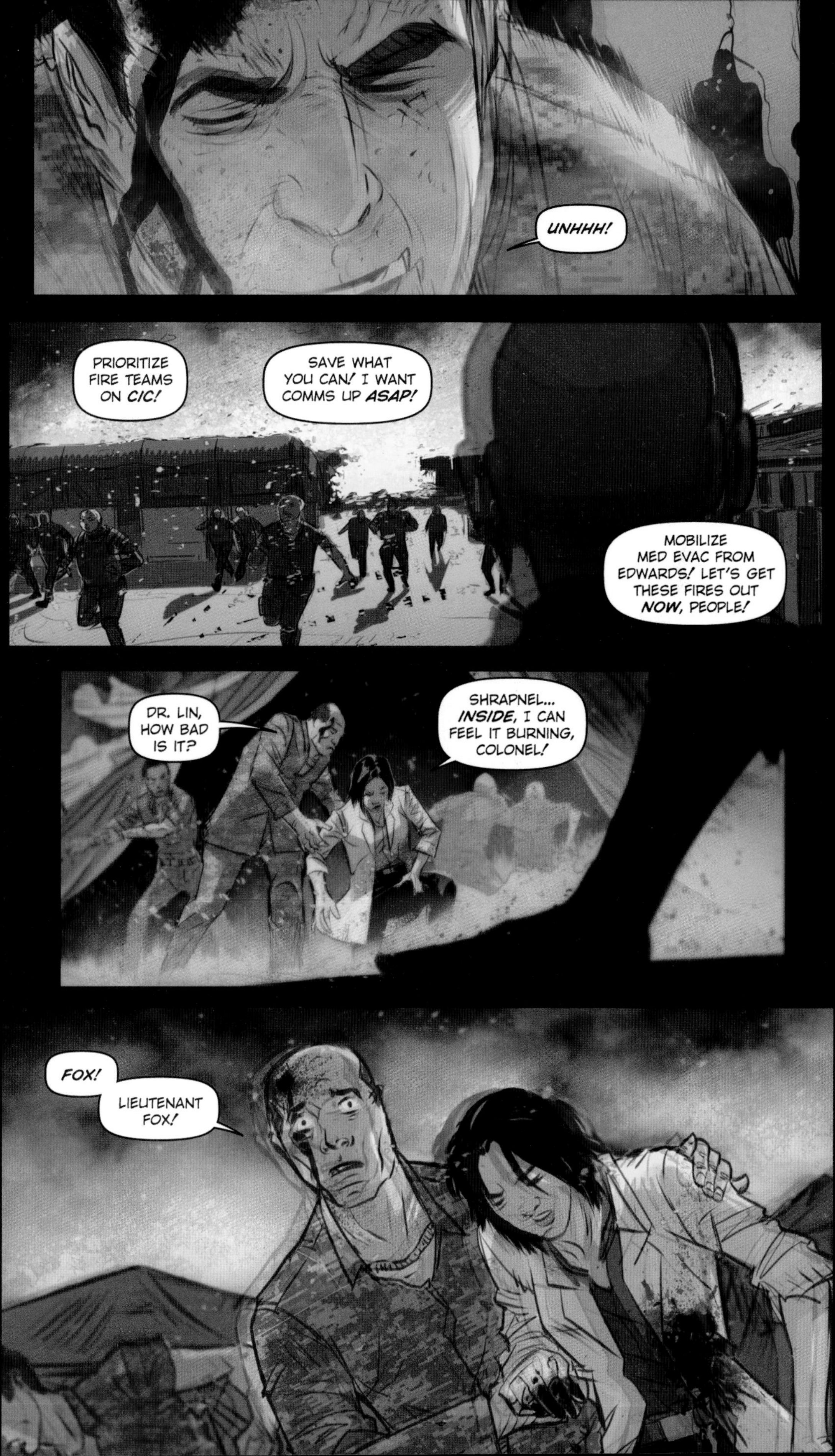
UNHHH!
PRIORITIZE FIRE TEAMS ON CIC!
SAVE WHAT YOU CAN! I WANT COMMS UP ASAP!
MOBILIZE MED EVAC FROM EDWARDS! LET'S GET THESE FIRES OUT NOW, PEOPLE!
DR. LIN, HOW BAD IS IT?
SHRAPNEL... INSIDE, I CAN FEEL IT BURNING, COLONEL!
FOX!
LIEUTENANT FOX!

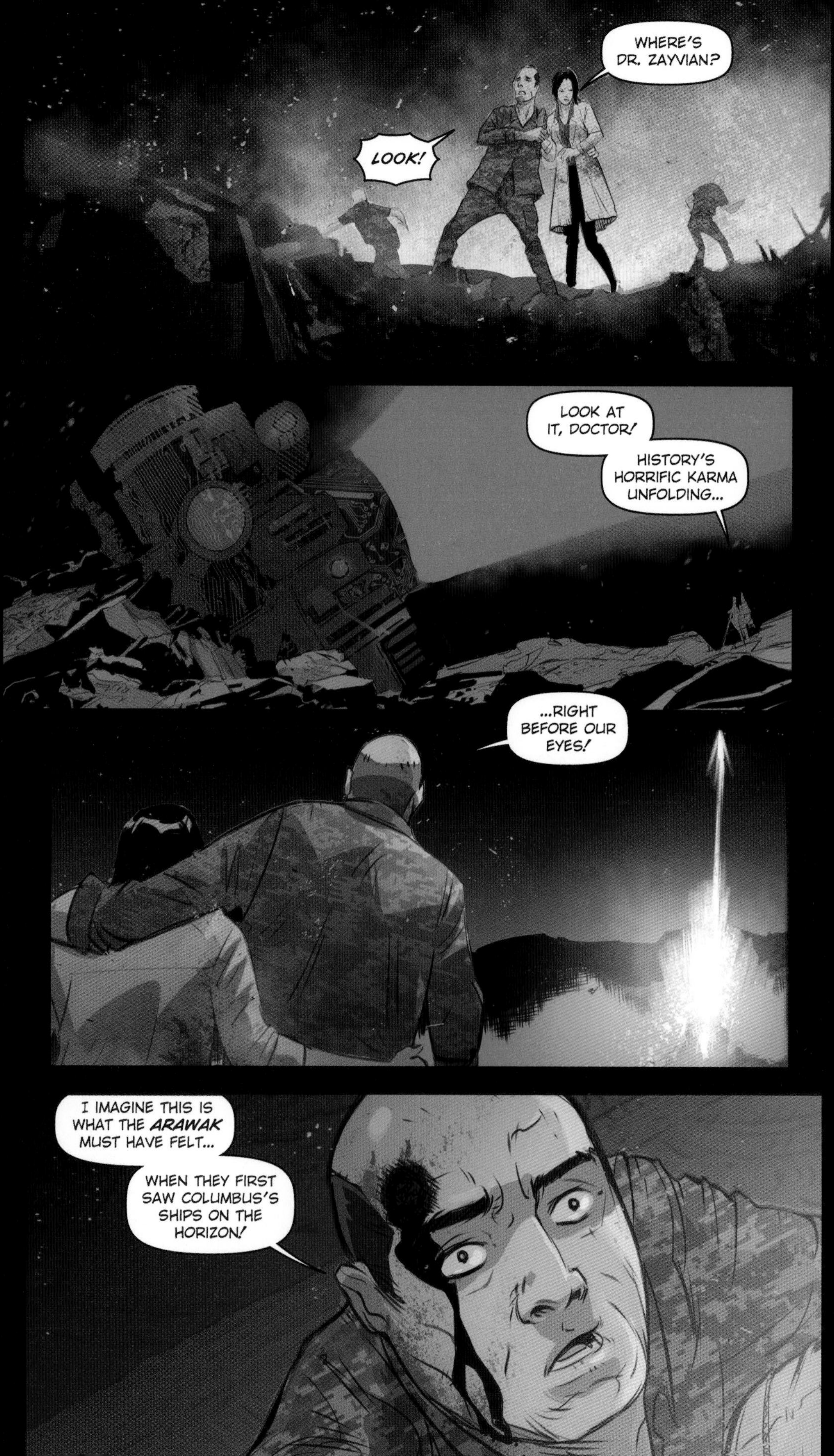
WHERE'S DR. ZAYVIAN?
LOOK!
LOOK AT IT, DOCTOR!
HISTORY'S HORRIFIC KARMA UNFOLDING...
...RIGHT BEFORE OUR EYES!
I IMAGINE THIS IS WHAT THE ARAWAK MUST HAVE FELT...
WHEN THEY FIRST SAW COLUMBUS'S SHIPS ON THE HORIZON!

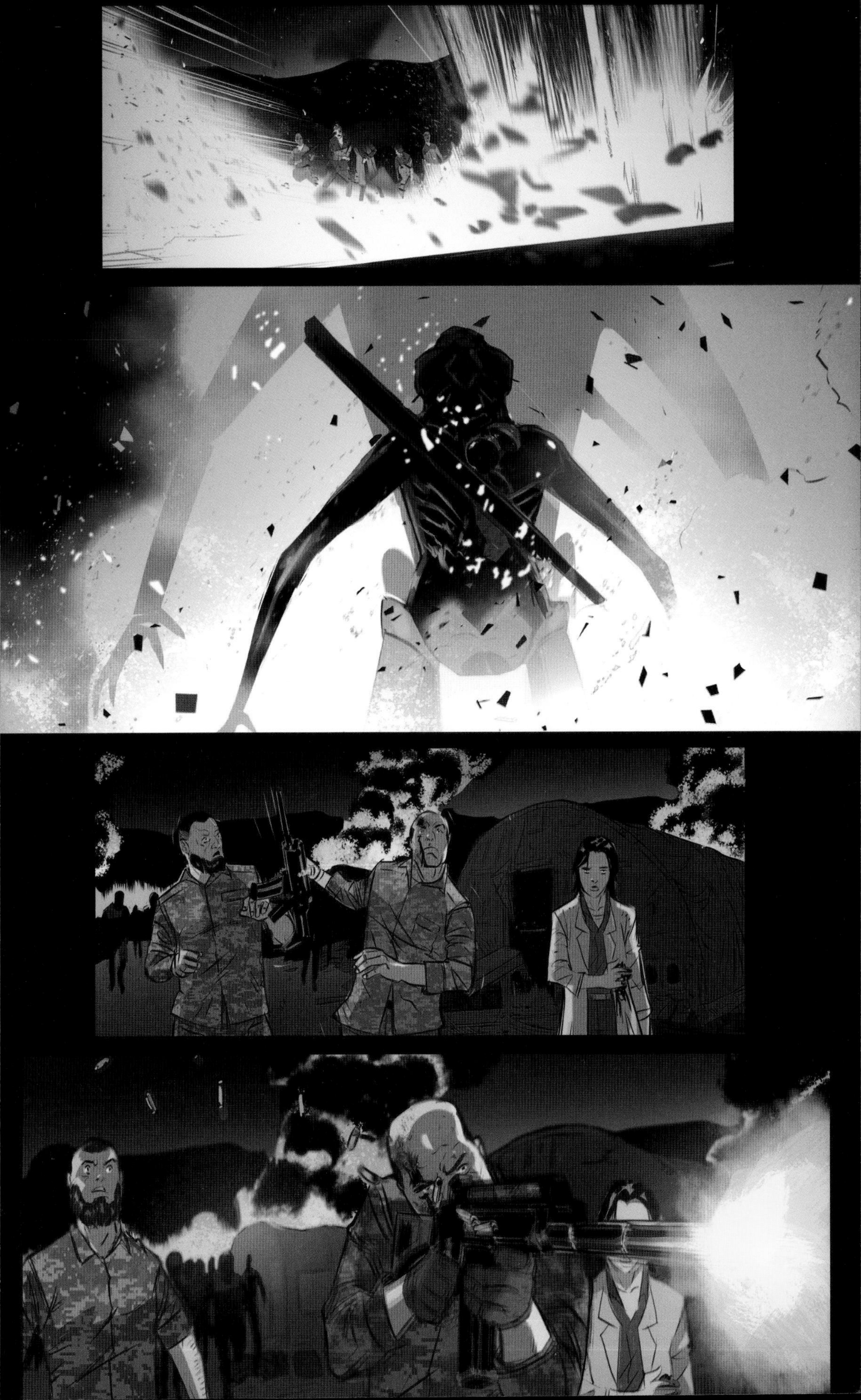

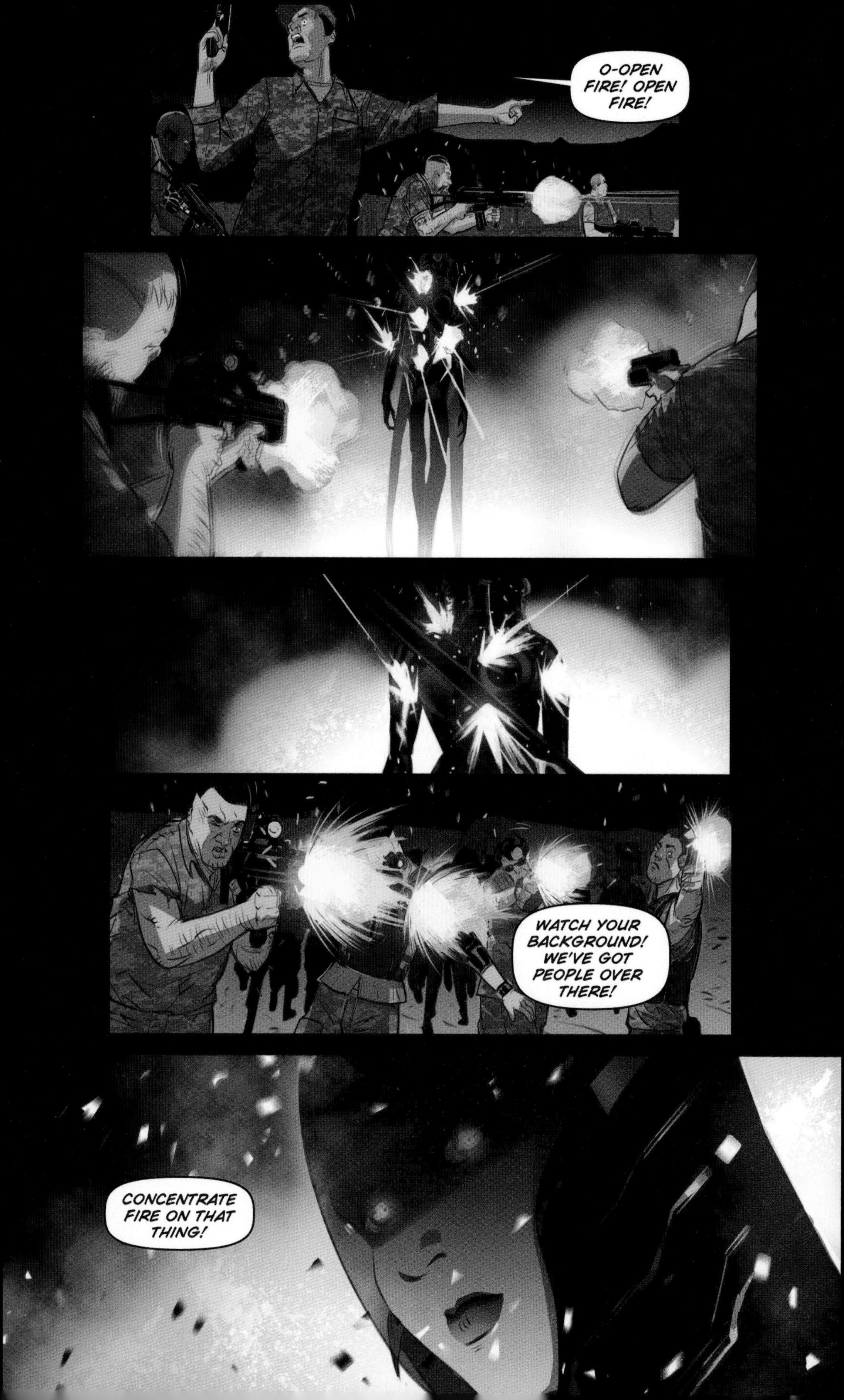
O-OPEN FIRE! OPEN FIRE!
WATCH YOUR BACKGROUND! WE'VE GOT PEOPLE OVER THERE!
CONCENTRATE FIRE ON THAT THING!

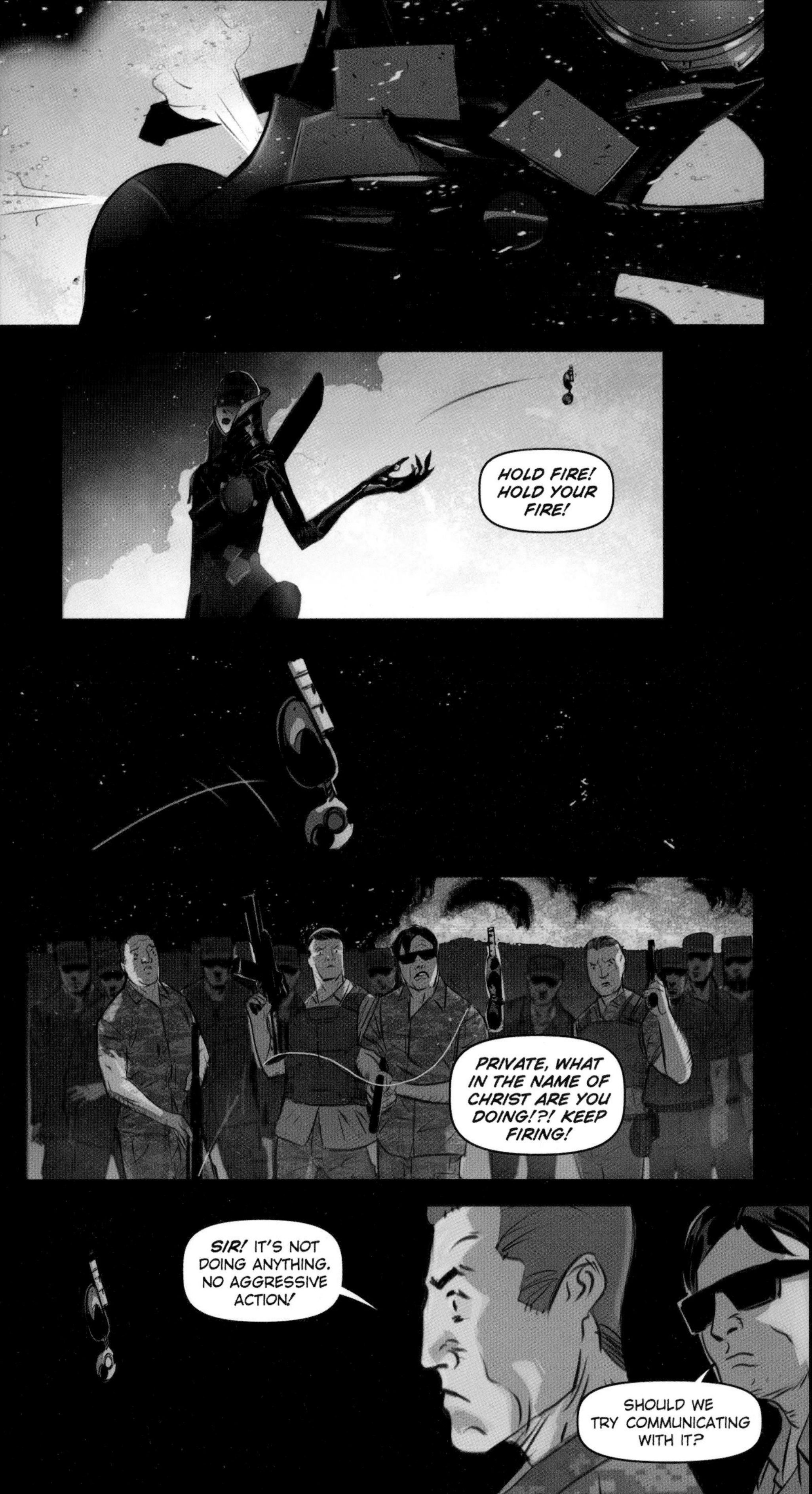
HOLD FIRE! HOLD YOUR FIRE!
PRIVATE, WHAT IN THE NAME OF CHRIST ARE YOU DOING!?! KEEP FIRING!
SIR! IT'S NOT DOING ANYTHING. NO AGGRESSIVE ACTION!
SHOULD WE TRY COMMUNICATING WITH IT?

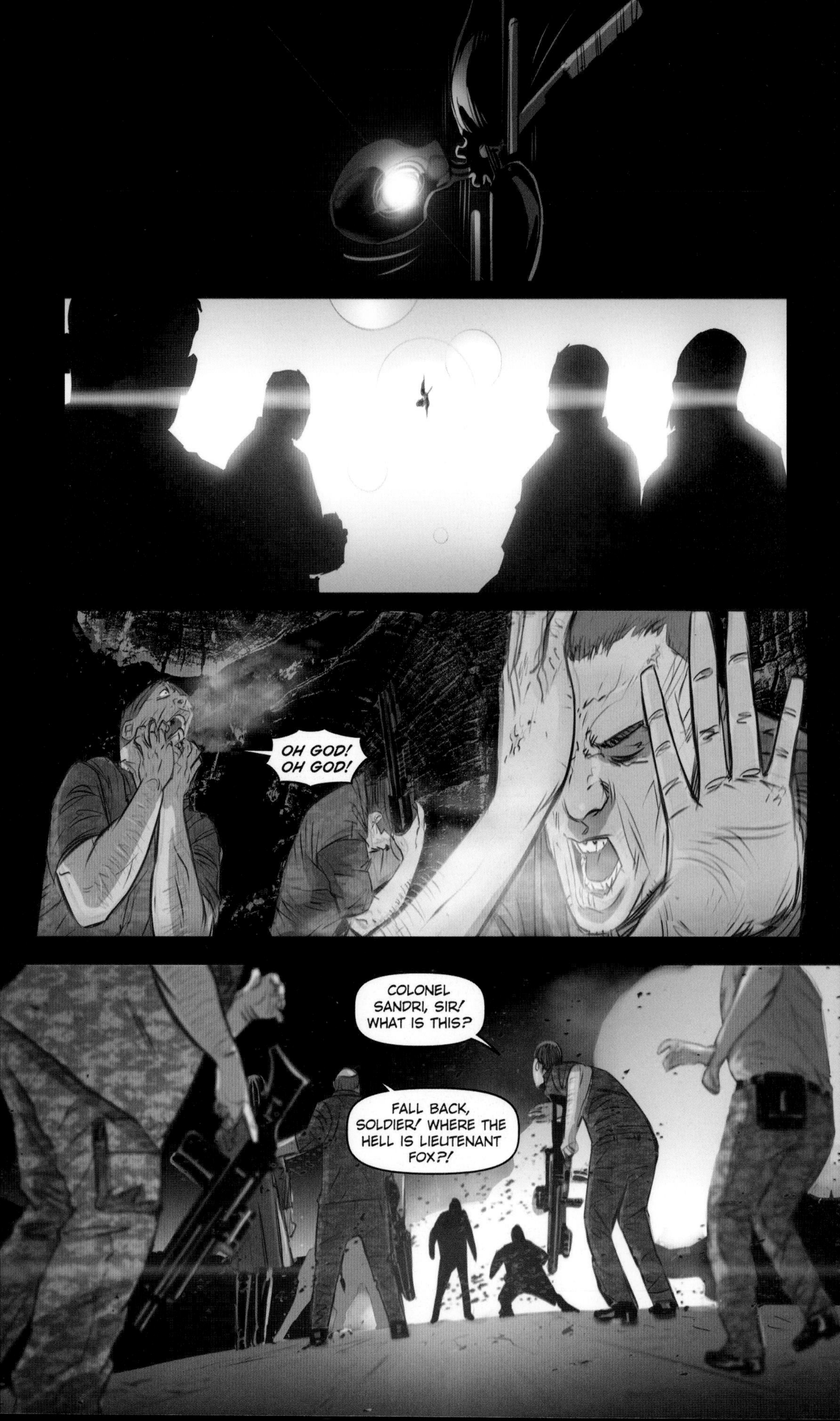
OH GOD!
OH GOD!
COLONEL SANDRI, SIR! WHAT IS THIS?
FALL BACK, SOLDIER! WHERE THE HELL IS LIEUTENANT FOX?!

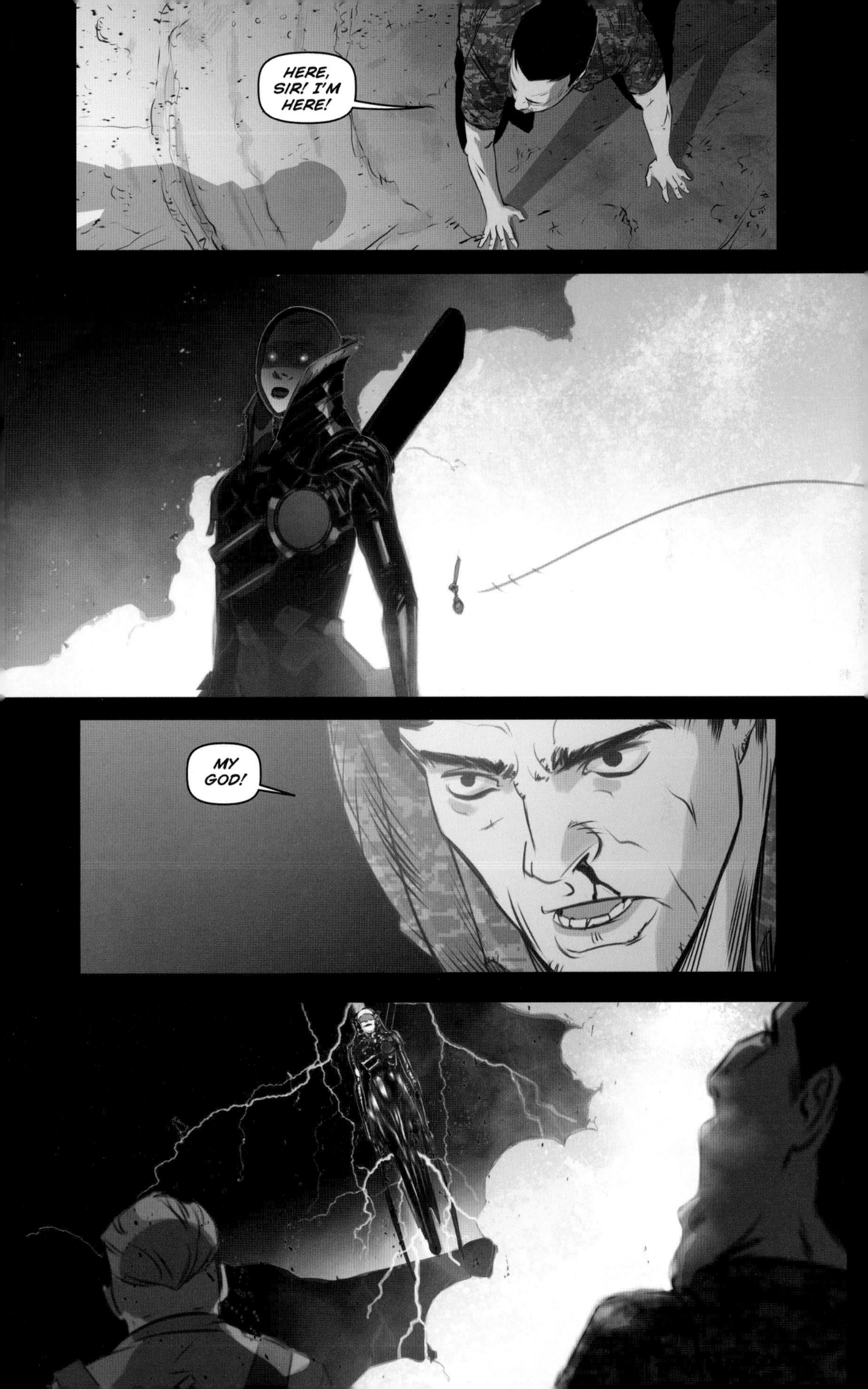
HERE, SIR! I'M HERE!
MY GOD!

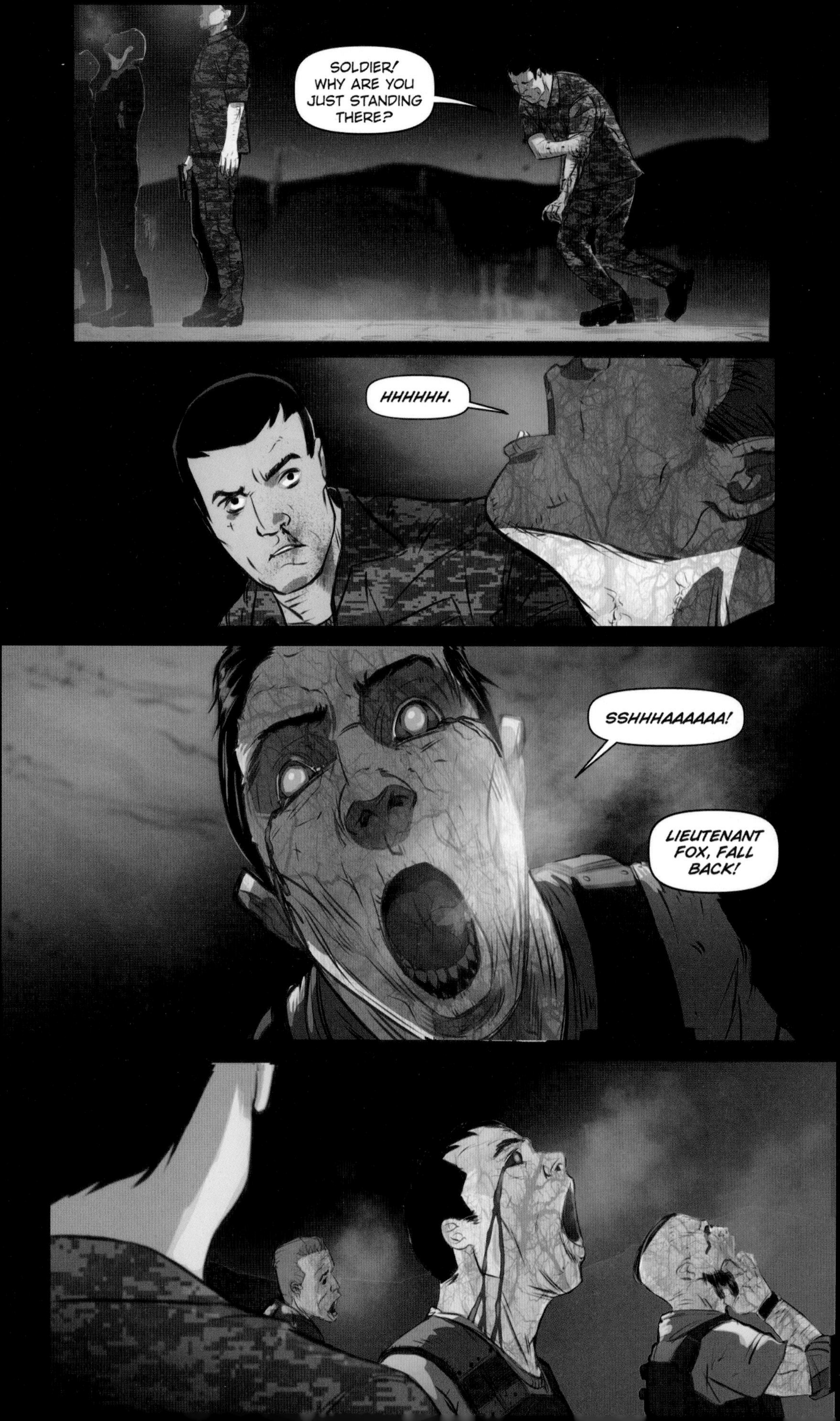
SOLDIER! WHY ARE YOU JUST STANDING THERE?
HHHHHH.
SSHHHAAAAAA!
LIEUTENANT FOX, FALL BACK!

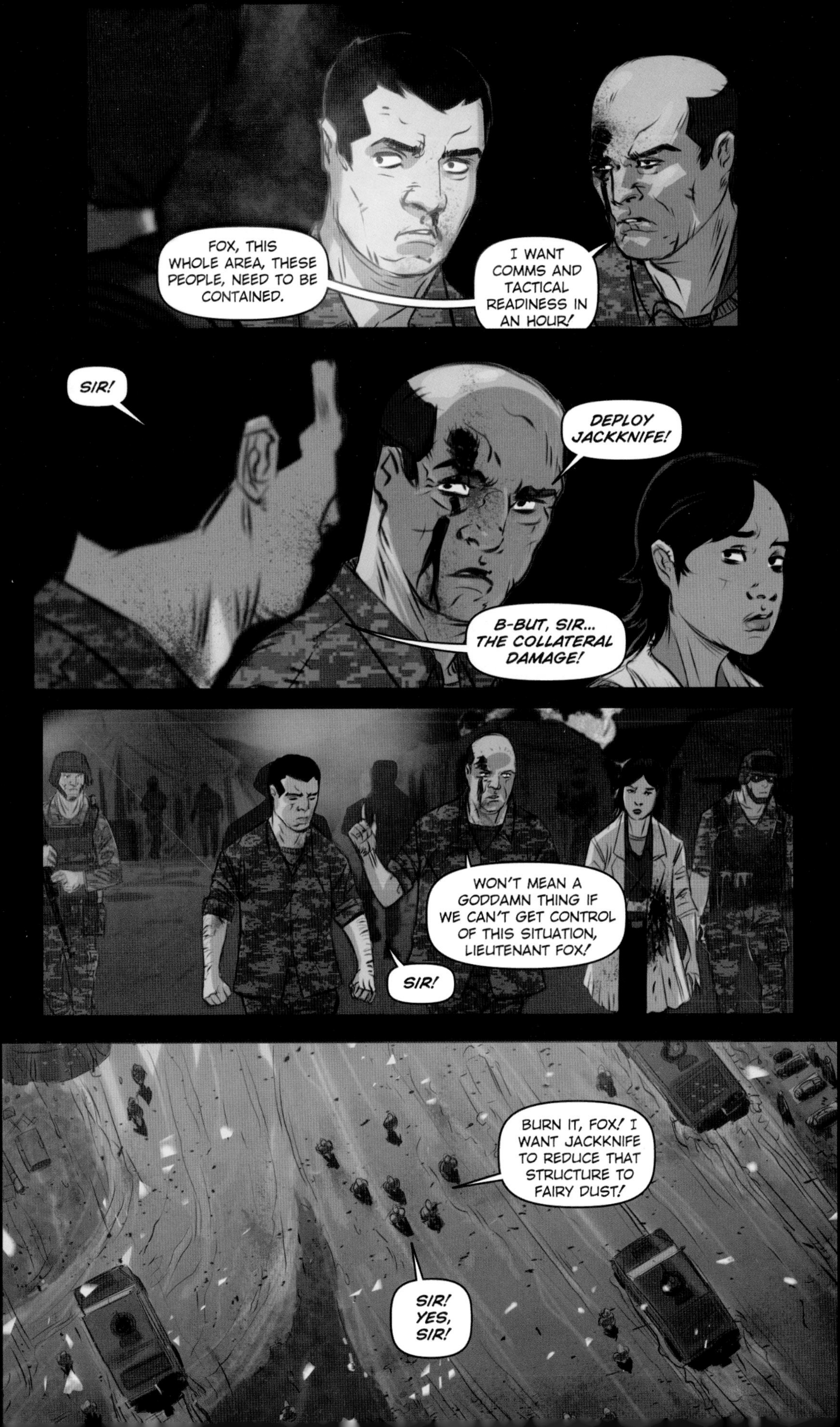
FOX, THIS WHOLE AREA, THESE PEOPLE, NEED TO BE CONTAINED.
I WANT COMMS AND TACTICAL READINESS IN AN HOUR!
SIR!
DEPLOY JACKKNIFE!
B-BUT, SIR... THE COLLATERAL DAMAGE!
WON'T MEAN A GODDAMN THING IF WE CAN'T GET CONTROL OF THIS SITUATION, LIEUTENANT FOX!
SIR!
BURN IT, FOX! I WANT JACKKNIFE TO REDUCE THAT STRUCTURE TO FAIRY DUST!
SIR! YES, SIR!

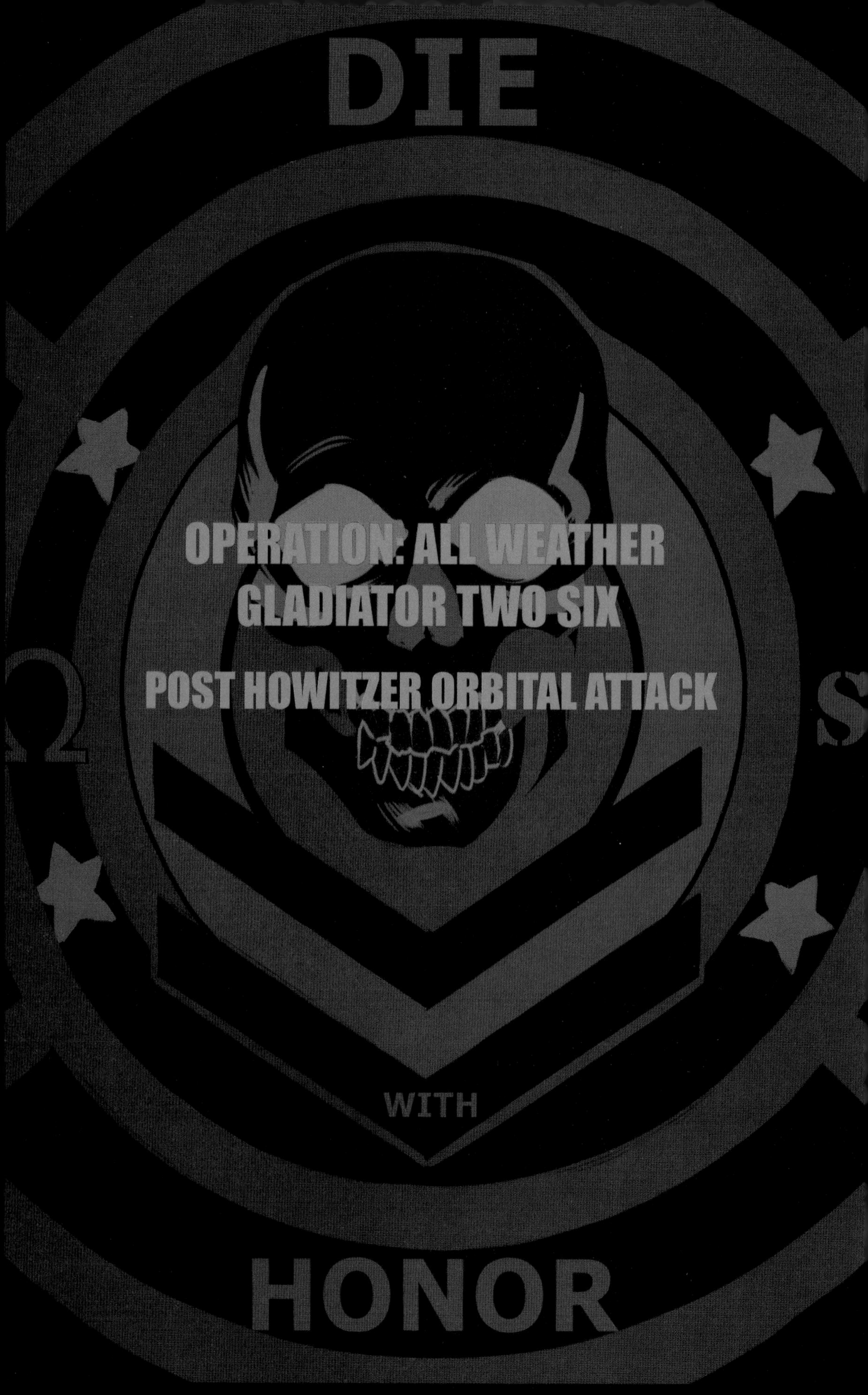
DIE
OPERATION: ALL WEATHER
GLADIATOR TWO SIX
POST HOWITZER ORBITAL ATTACK
Ω
S
WITH
HONOR

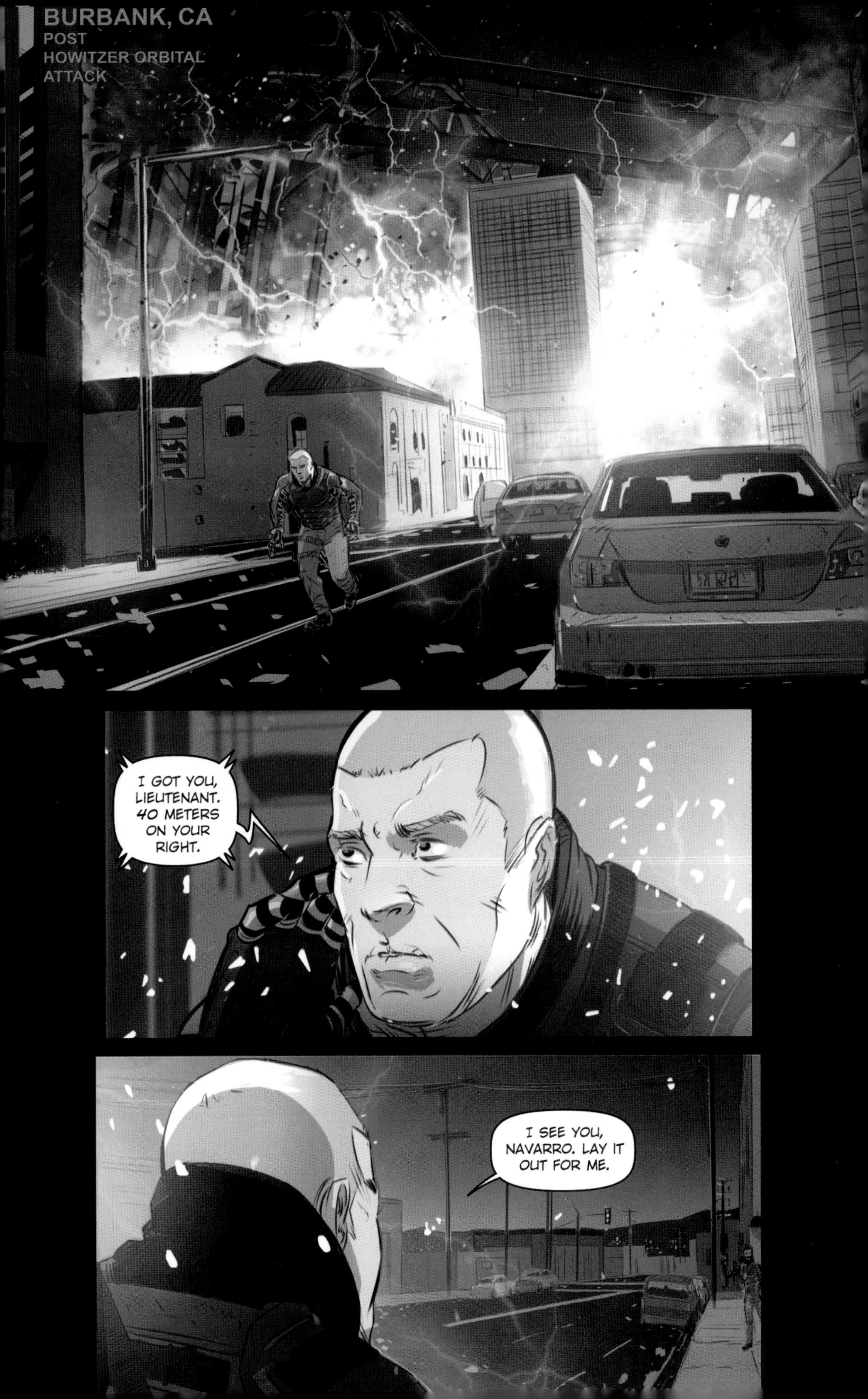
BURBANK, CA
POST
HOWITZER ORBITAL
ATTACK
I GOT YOU, LIEUTENANT. 40 METERS ON YOUR RIGHT.
I SEE YOU, NAVARRO. LAY IT OUT FOR ME.

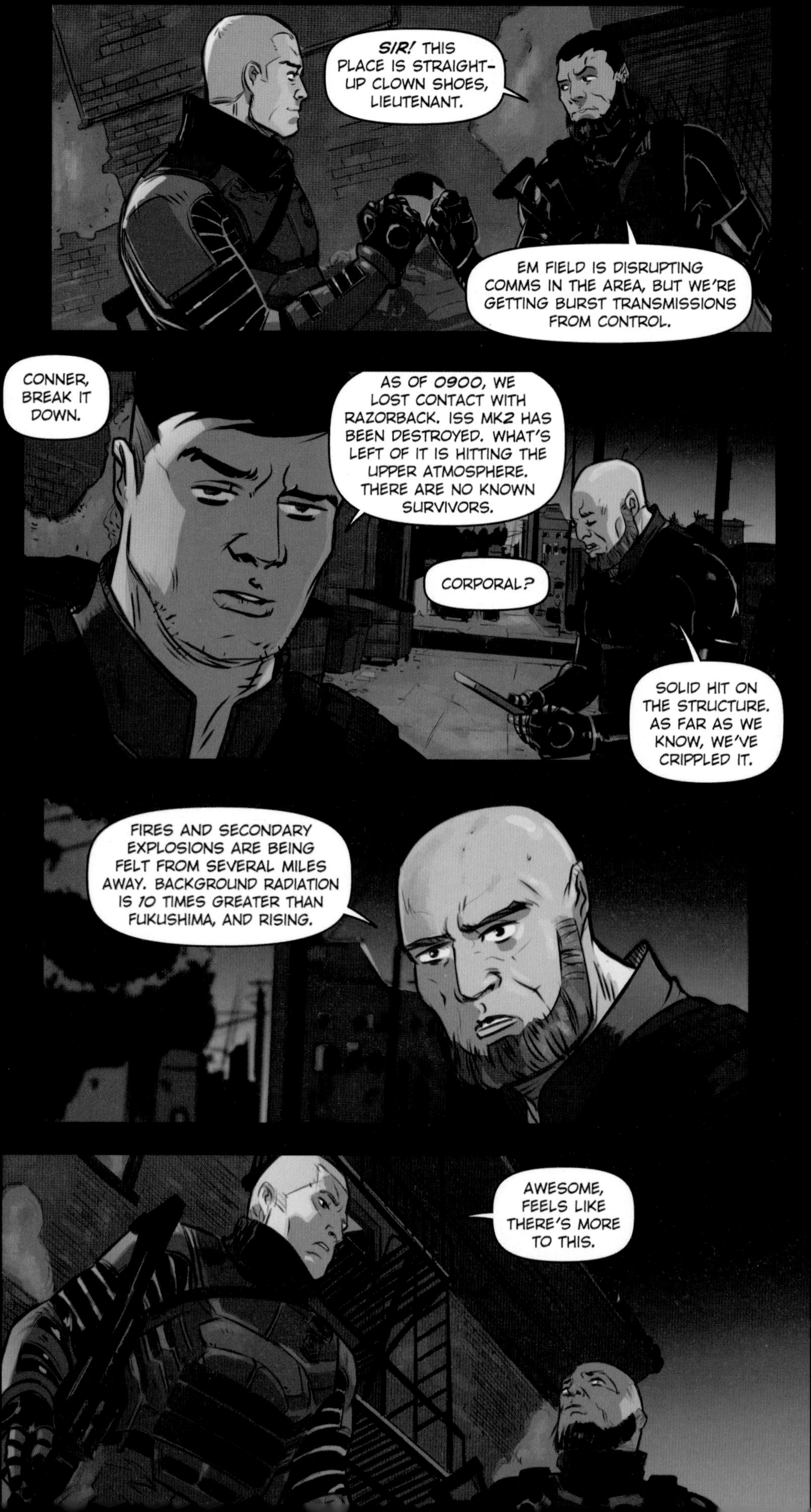
SIR! THIS PLACE IS STRAIGHT-UP CLOWN SHOES, LIEUTENANT.
EM FIELD IS DISRUPTING COMMS IN THE AREA, BUT WE'RE GETTING BURST TRANSMISSIONS FROM CONTROL.
CONNER, BREAK IT DOWN.
AS OF 0900, WE LOST CONTACT WITH RAZORBACK. ISS MK2 HAS BEEN DESTROYED. WHAT'S LEFT OF IT IS HITTING THE UPPER ATMOSPHERE. THERE ARE NO KNOWN SURVIVORS.
CORPORAL?
SOLID HIT ON THE STRUCTURE. AS FAR AS WE KNOW, WE'VE CRIPPLED IT.
FIRES AND SECONDARY EXPLOSIONS ARE BEING FELT FROM SEVERAL MILES AWAY. BACKGROUND RADIATION IS 10 TIMES GREATER THAN FUKUSHIMA, AND RISING.
AWESOME, FEELS LIKE THERE'S MORE TO THIS.

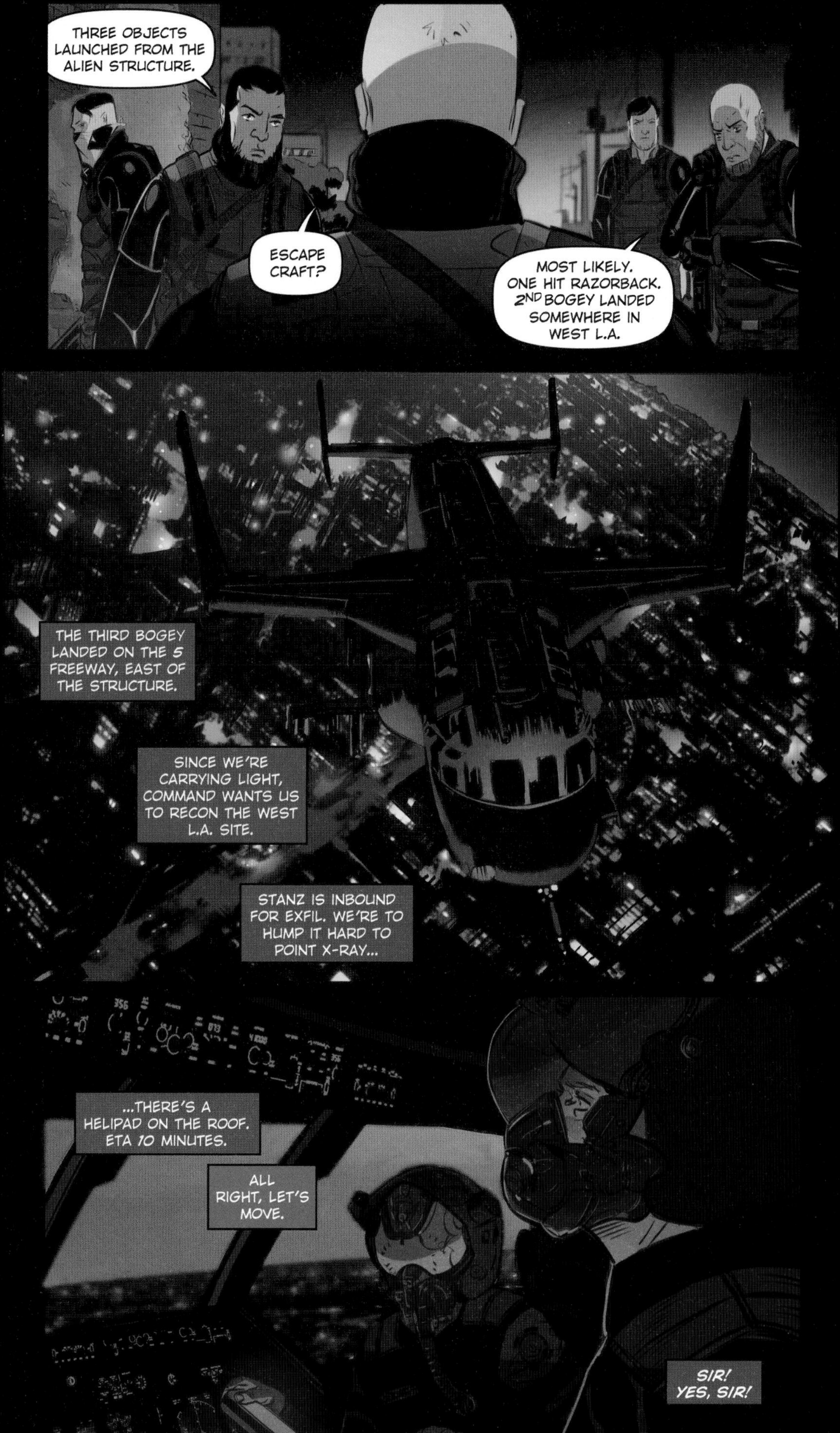
THREE OBJECTS LAUNCHED FROM THE ALIEN STRUCTURE.
ESCAPE CRAFT?
MOST LIKELY. ONE HIT RAZORBACK. 2ND BOGEY LANDED SOMEWHERE IN WEST L.A.
THE THIRD BOGEY LANDED ON THE 5 FREEWAY, EAST OF THE STRUCTURE.
SINCE WE'RE CARRYING LIGHT, COMMAND WANTS US TO RECON THE WEST L.A. SITE.
STANZ IS INBOUND FOR EXFIL. WE'RE TO HUMP IT HARD TO POINT X-RAY...
...THERE'S A HELIPAD ON THE ROOF. ETA 10 MINUTES.
ALL RIGHT, LET'S MOVE.
SIR! YES, SIR!

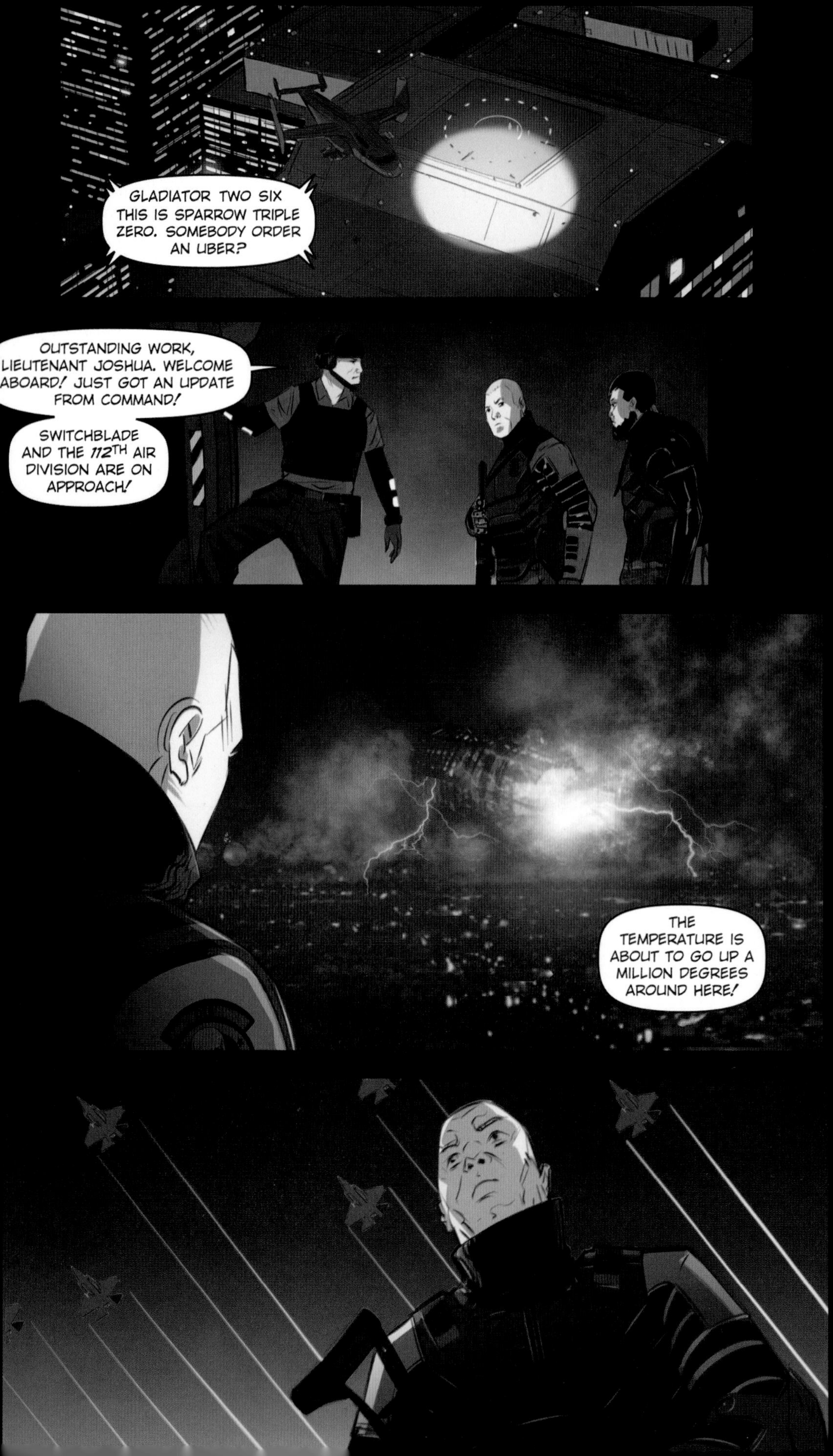
GLADIATOR TWO SIX THIS IS SPARROW TRIPLE ZERO. SOMEBODY ORDER AN UBER?
OUTSTANDING WORK, LIEUTENANT JOSHUA. WELCOME ABOARD! JUST GOT AN UPDATE FROM COMMAND!
SWITCHBLADE AND THE 112TH AIR DIVISION ARE ON APPROACH!
THE TEMPERATURE IS ABOUT TO GO UP A MILLION DEGREES AROUND HERE!

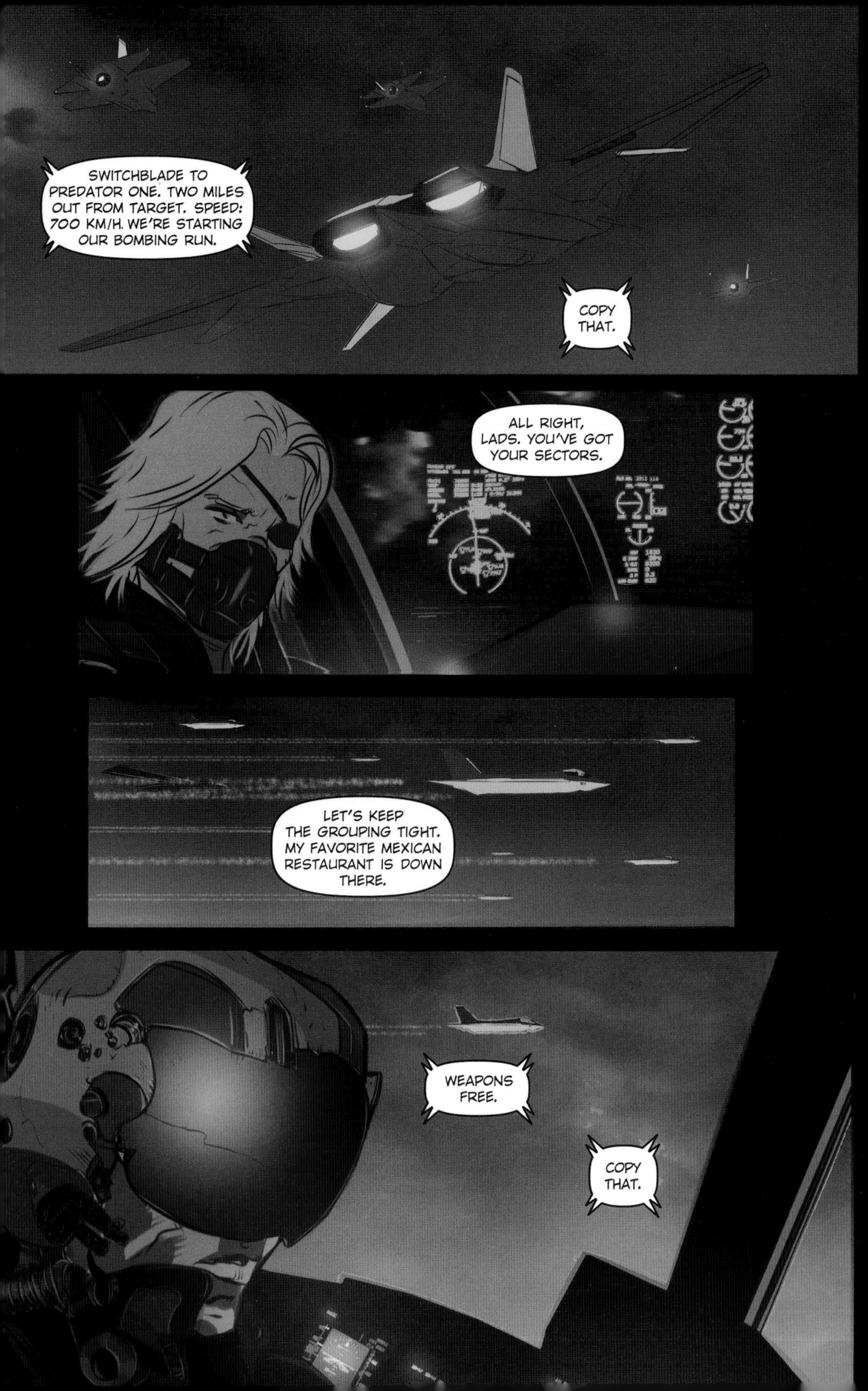
SWITCHBLADE TO PREDATOR ONE. TWO MILES OUT FROM TARGET. SPEED: 700 KM/H. WE'RE STARTING OUR BOMBING RUN.
COPY THAT.
ALL RIGHT, LADS. YOU'VE GOT YOUR SECTORS.
LET'S KEEP THE GROUPING TIGHT. MY FAVORITE MEXICAN RESTAURANT IS DOWN THERE.
WEAPONS FREE.
COPY THAT.

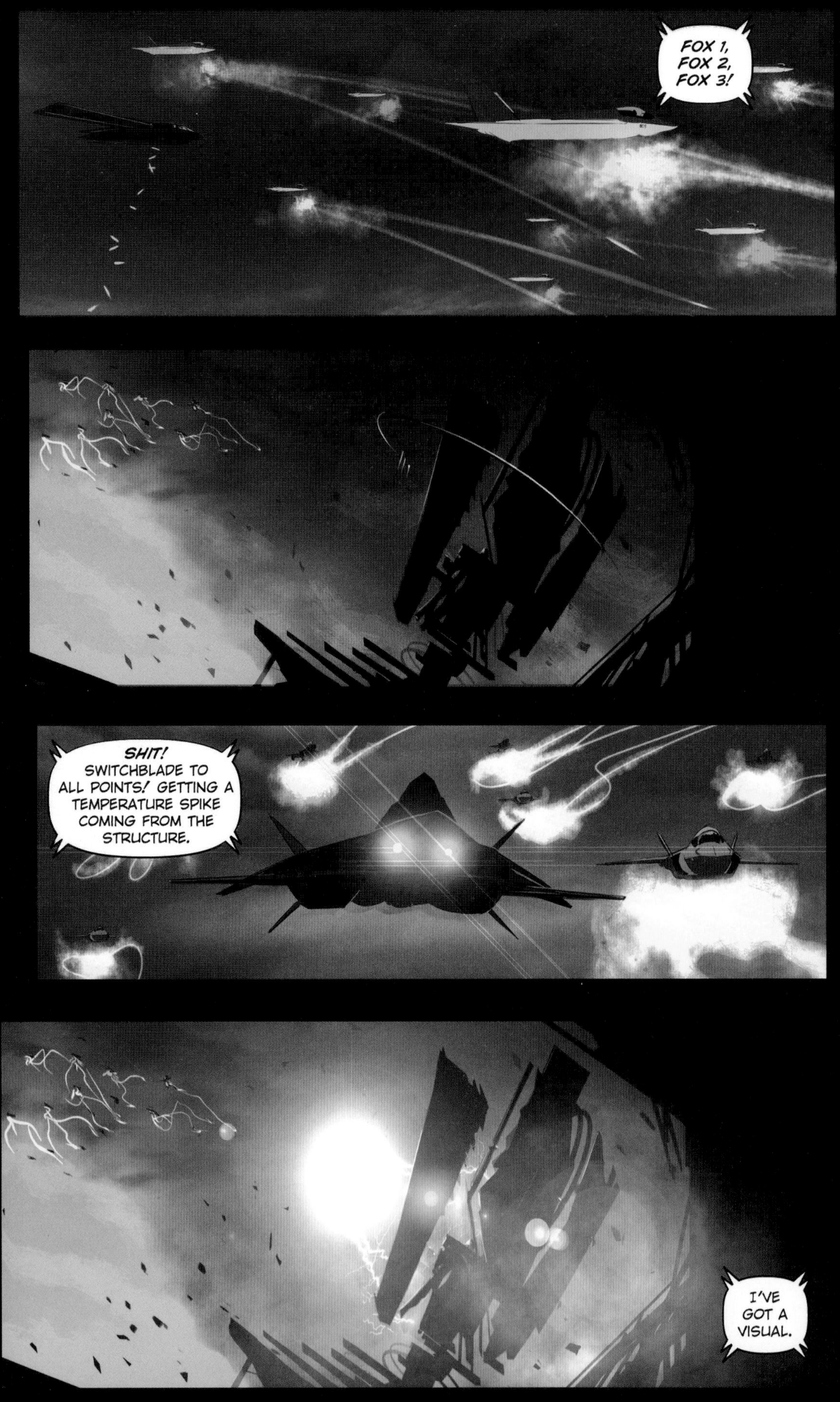
FOX 1,
FOX 2,
FOX 3!
SHIT! SWITCHBLADE TO ALL POINTS! GETTING A TEMPERATURE SPIKE COMING FROM THE STRUCTURE.
I'VE GOT A VISUAL.

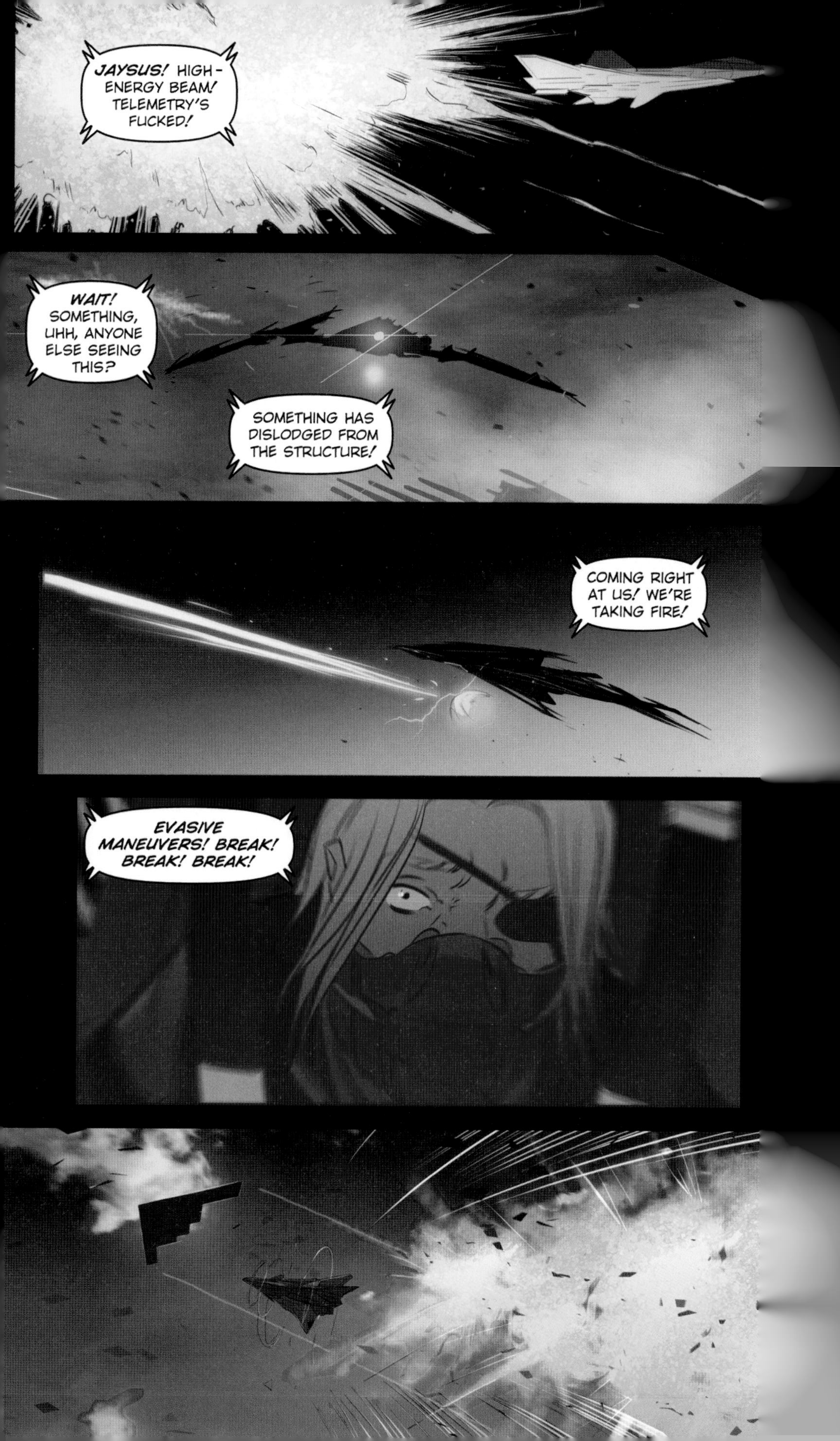
JAYSUS! HIGH-ENERGY BEAM! TELEMETRY'S FUCKED!
WAIT! SOMETHING, UHH, ANYONE ELSE SEEING THIS?
SOMETHING HAS DISLODGED FROM THE STRUCTURE!
COMING RIGHT AT US! WE'RE TAKING FIRE!
EVASIVE MANEUVERS! BREAK! BREAK! BREAK!

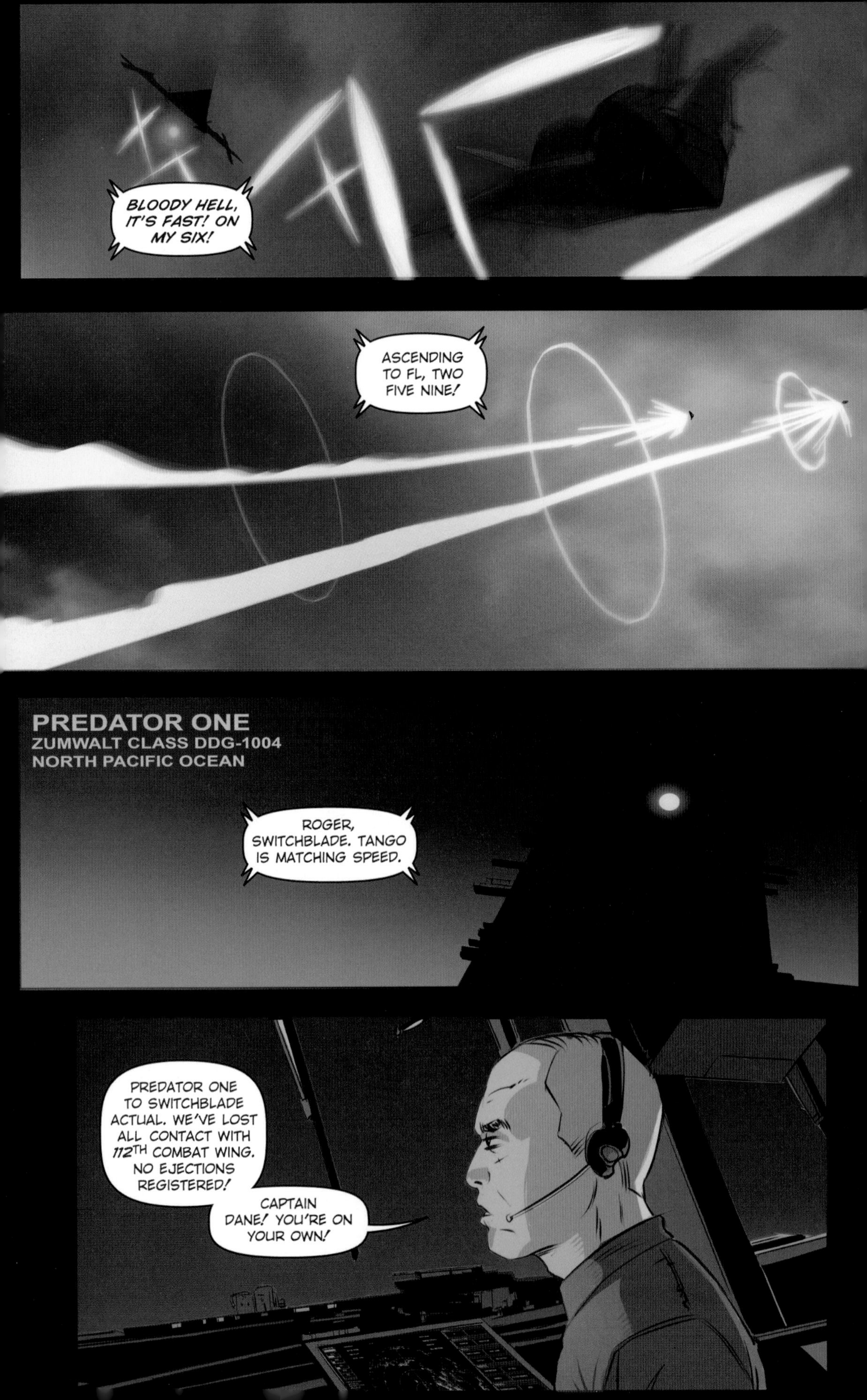
BLOODY HELL, IT'S FAST! ON MY SIX!
ASCENDING TO FL, TWO FIVE NINE!
PREDATOR ONE
ZUMWALT CLASS DDG-1004
NORTH PACIFIC OCEAN
ROGER, SWITCHBLADE. TANGO IS MATCHING SPEED.
PREDATOR ONE TO SWITCHBLADE ACTUAL. WE'VE LOST ALL CONTACT WITH 112TH COMBAT WING. NO EJECTIONS REGISTERED!
CAPTAIN DANE! YOU'RE ON YOUR OWN!

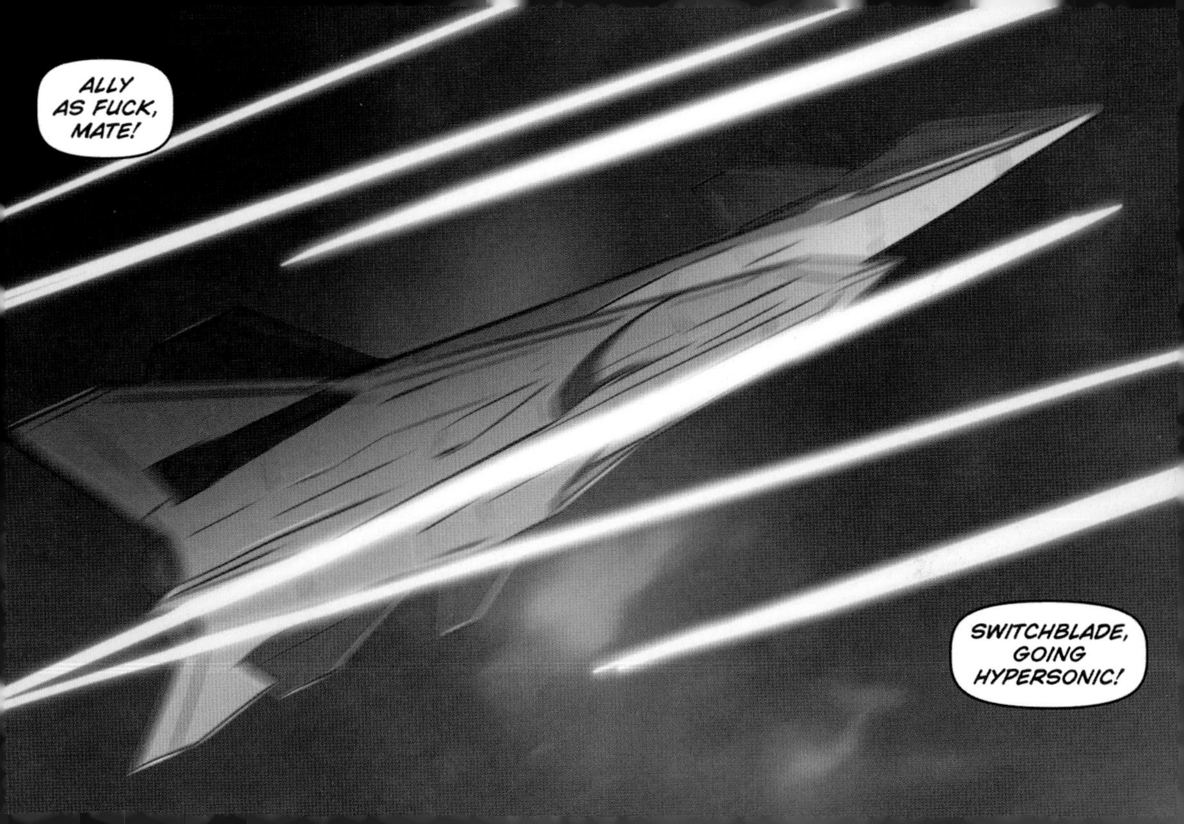
ALLY AS FUCK, MATE!
SWITCHBLADE, GOING HYPERSONIC!

THE WARNING

NATURE IN CONFLICT

SKETCH
DESIGN

LAROCHE

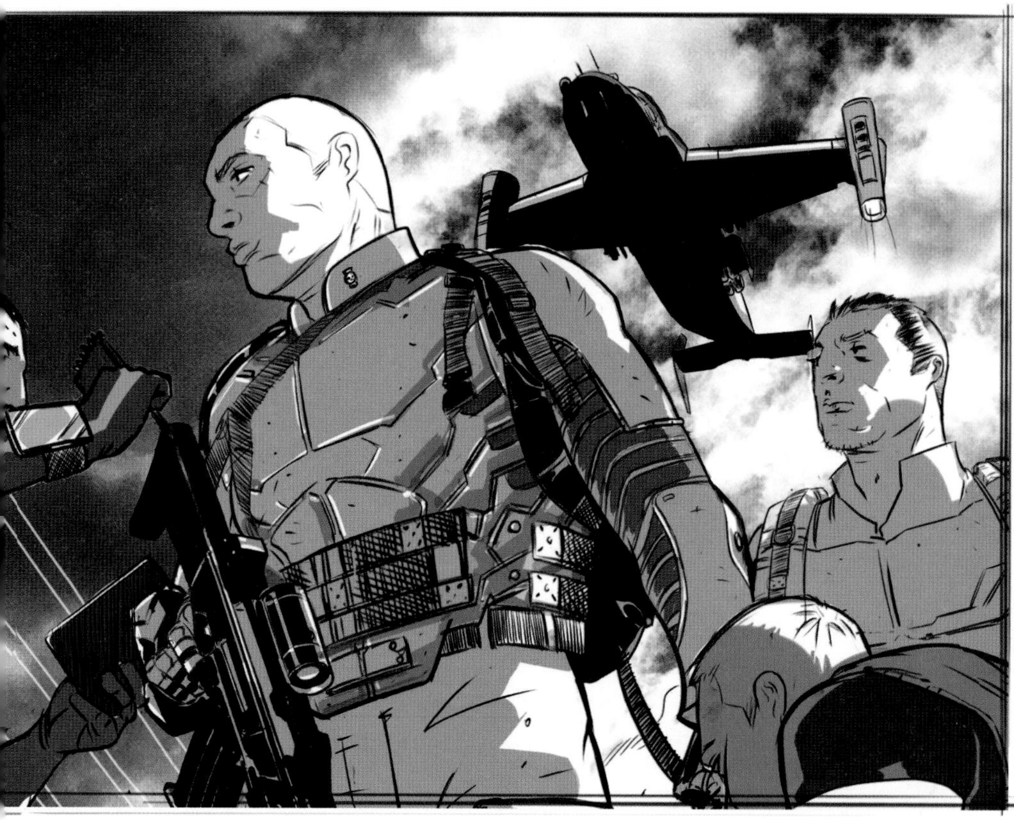

JOSHUA

SMOKE GUILLOTINE

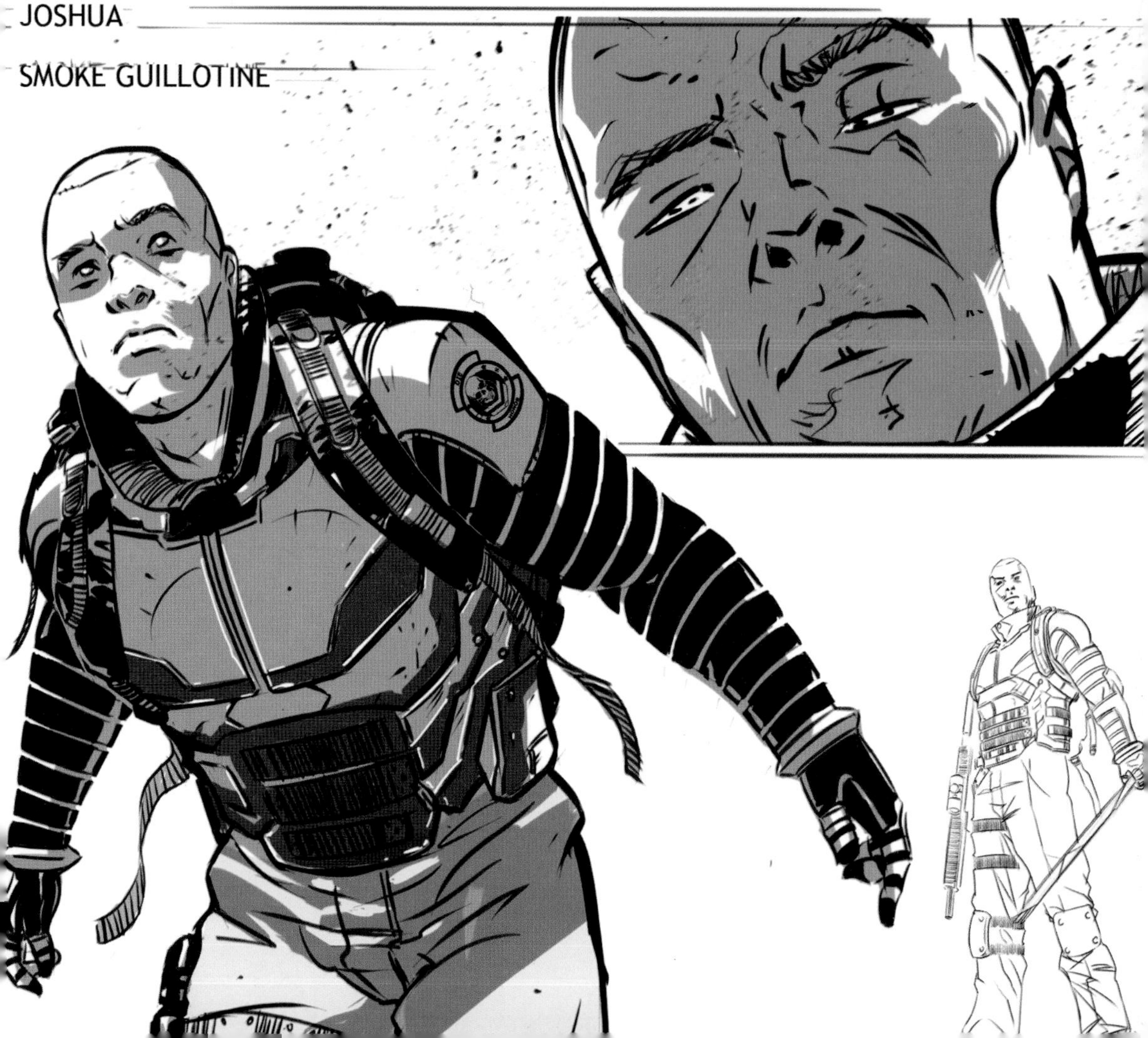

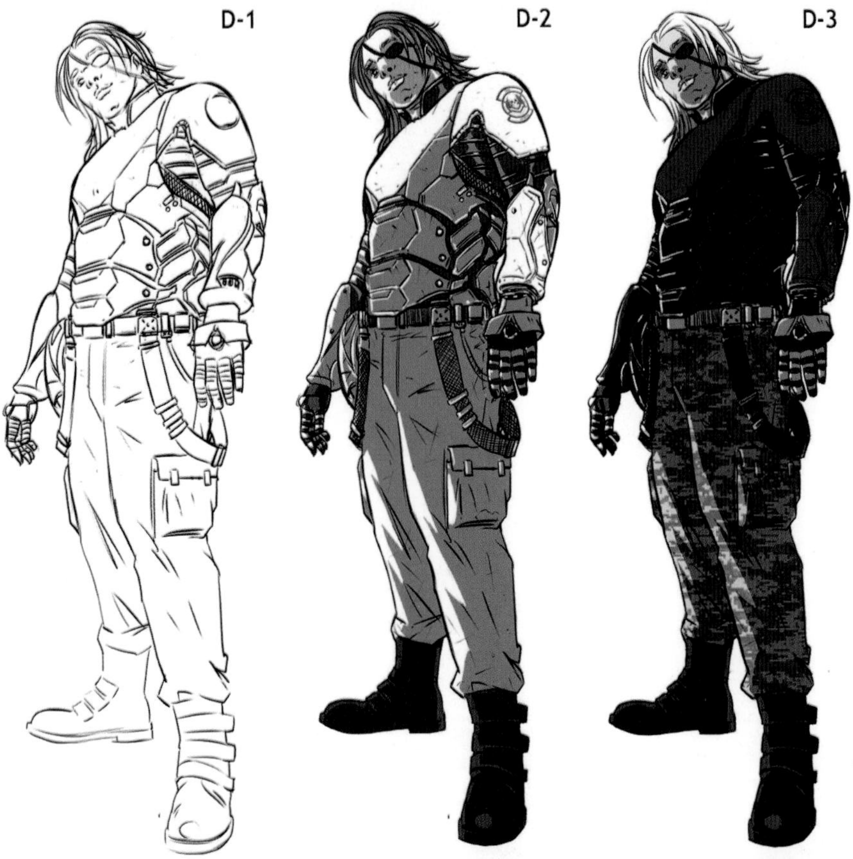
D-1
D-2
D-3

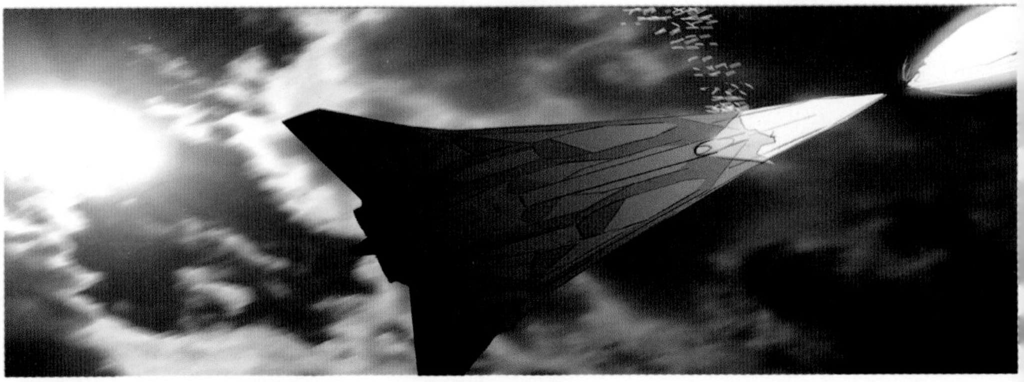

SWITCHBLADE

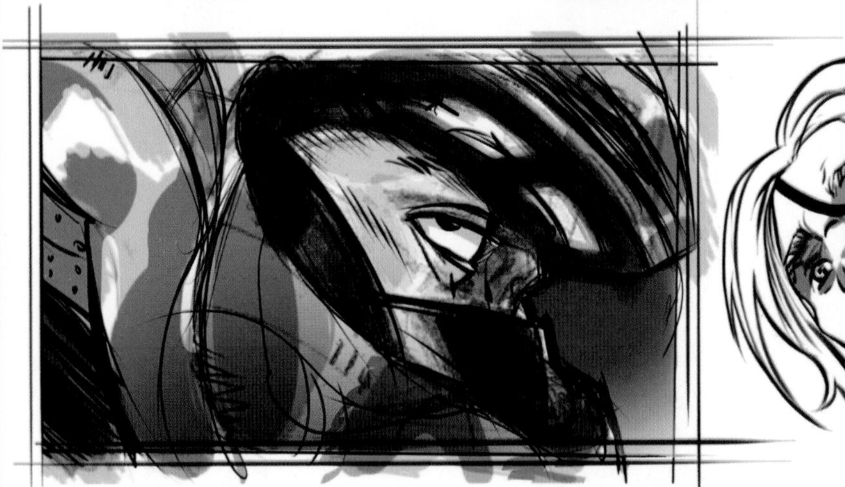

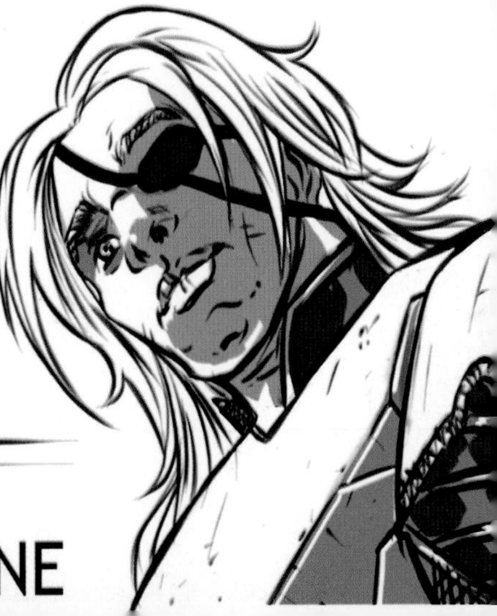

DANE

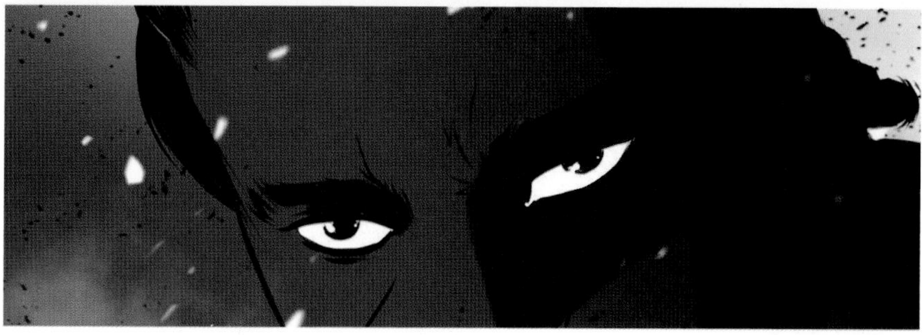

TERESA

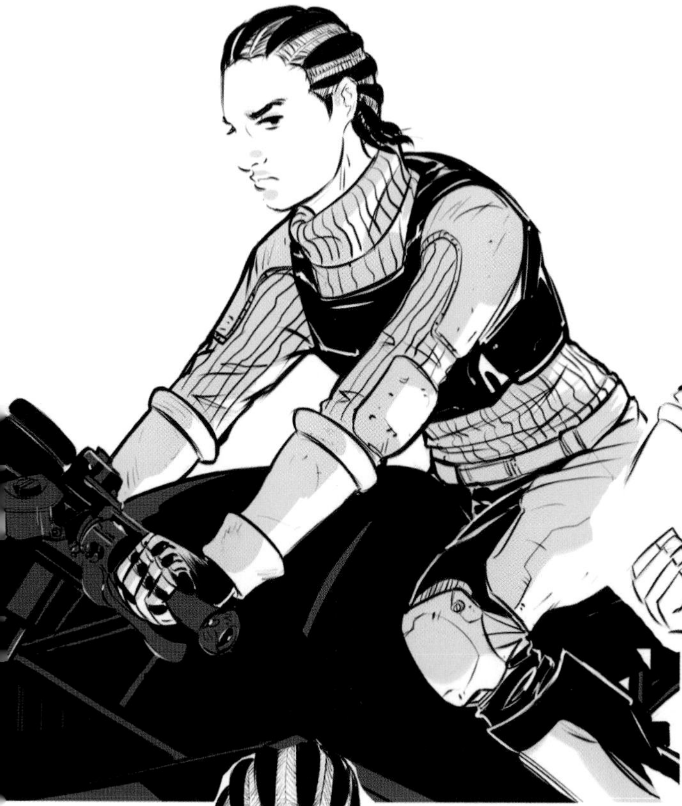

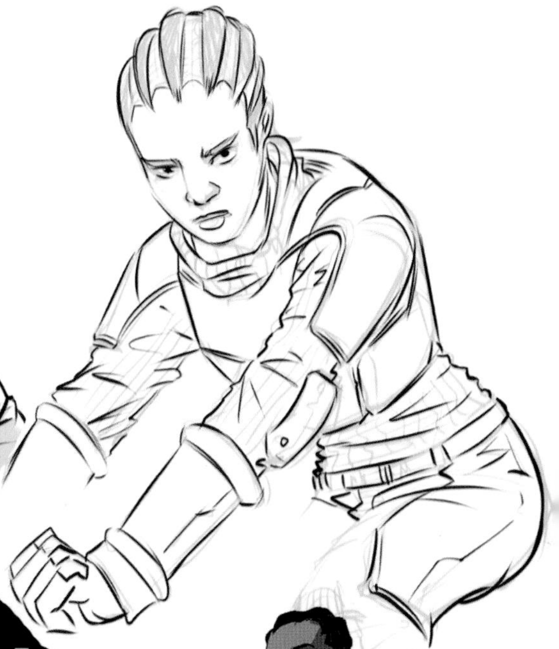

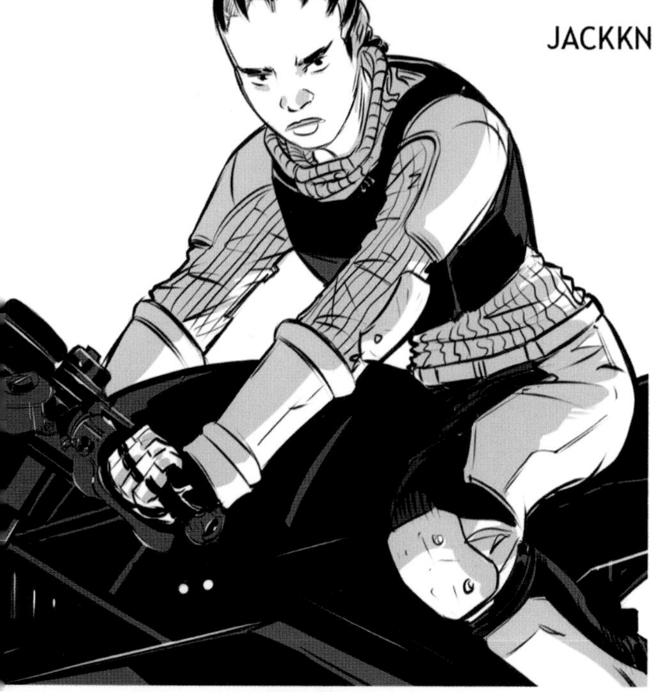

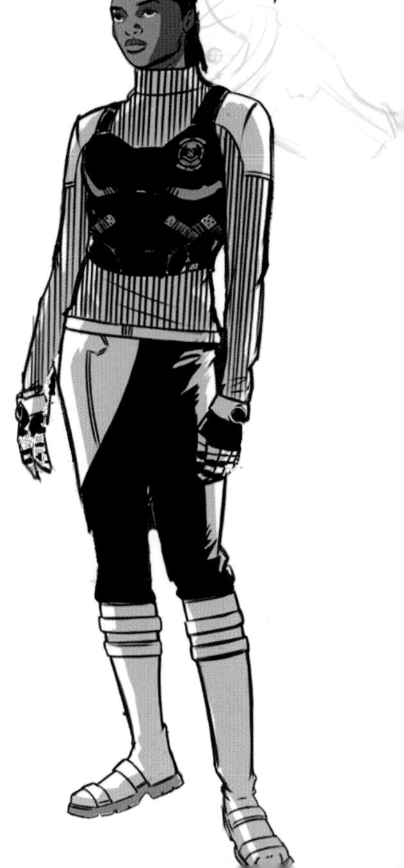

JACKKNIFE

THE RED MACHINE

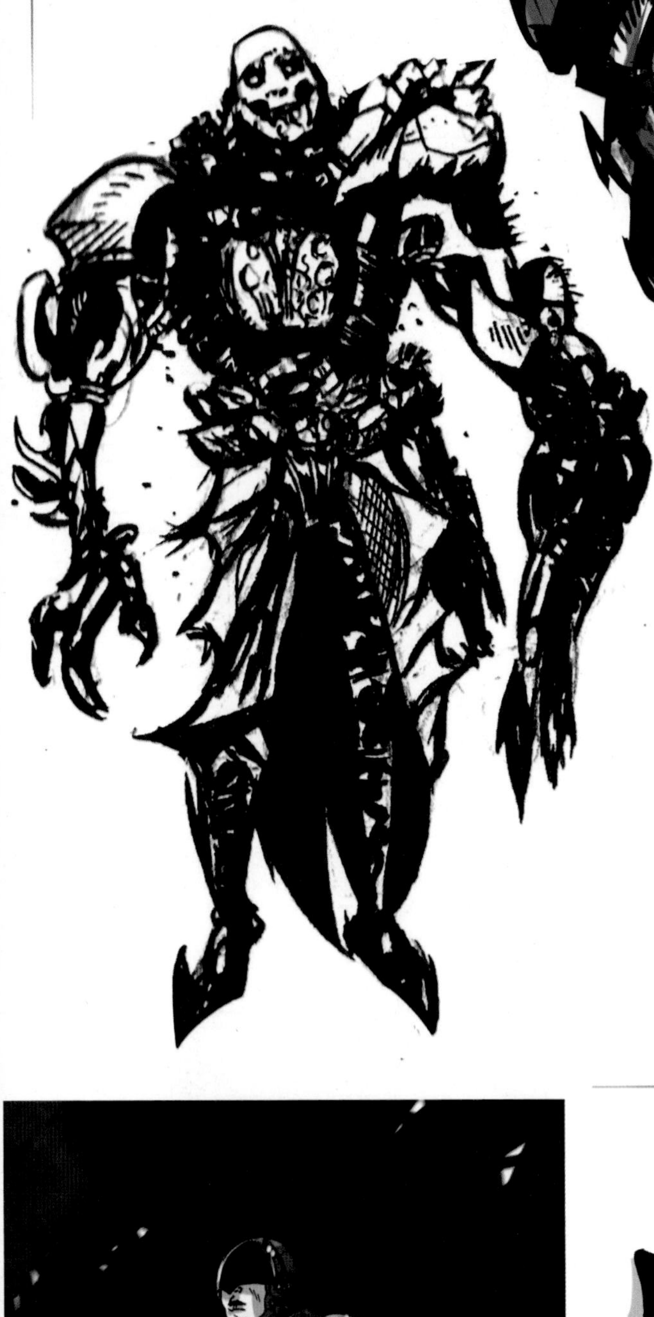

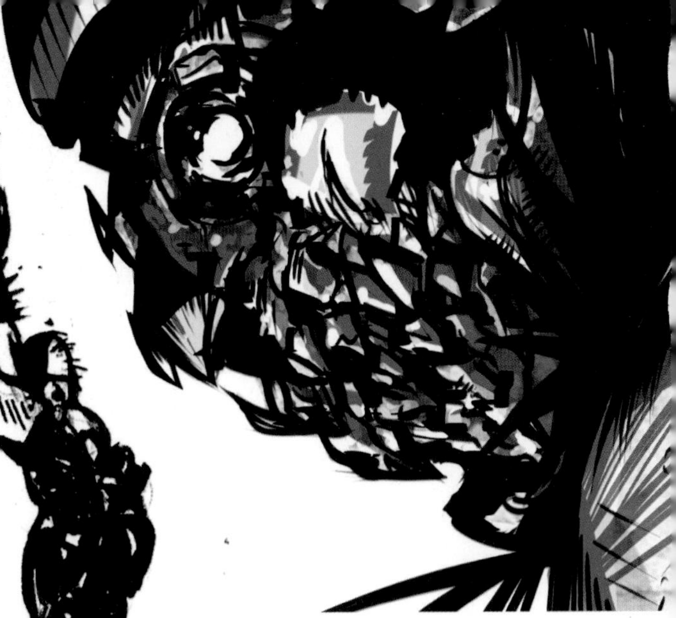

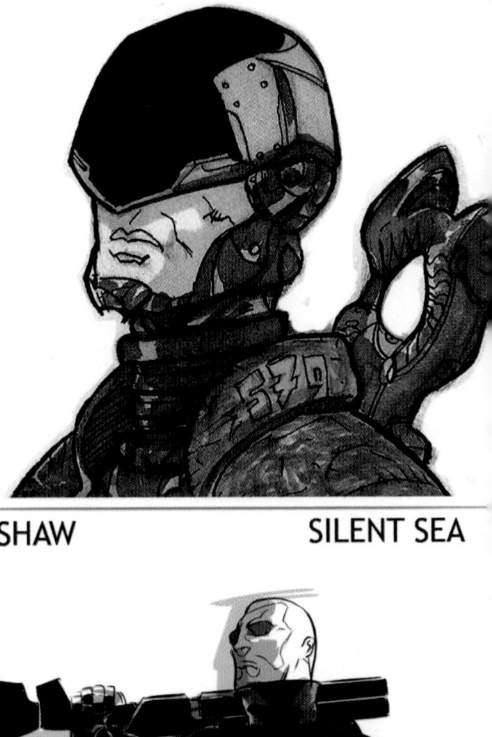

SHAW

SILENT SEA

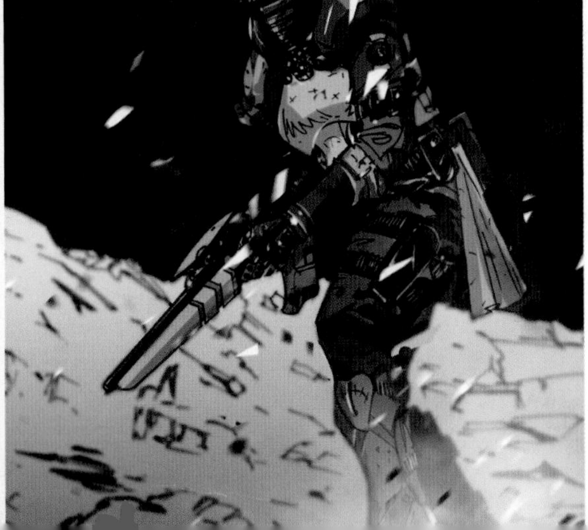

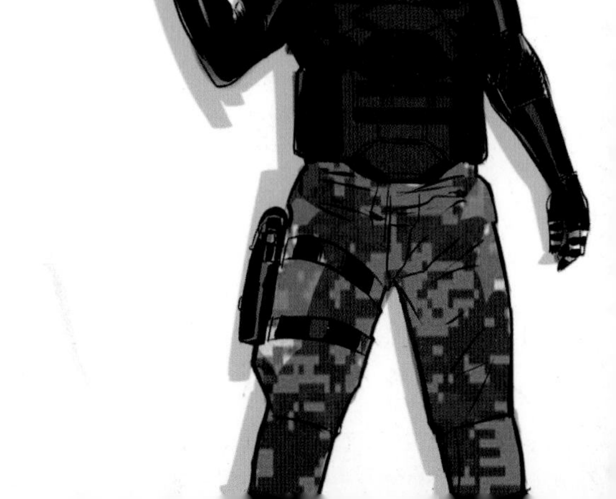